Mary Russell Mitford, Alfred Guy L'Estrange

The Life of Mary Russell Mitford

Vol. 2

Mary Russell Mitford, Alfred Guy L'Estrange

The Life of Mary Russell Mitford
Vol. 2

ISBN/EAN: 9783337416225

Printed in Europe, USA, Canada, Australia, Japan

Cover: Foto ©Raphael Reischuk / pixelio.de

More available books at **www.hansebooks.com**

THE LIFE

OF

MARY RUSSELL MITFORD,

AUTHORESS OF "OUR VILLAGE," ETC.

RELATED IN A SELECTION FROM HER LETTERS
TO HER FRIENDS.

EDITED

BY THE REV. A. G. L'ESTRANGE.

IN THREE VOLUMES.

VOL. II.

LONDON:

RICHARD BENTLEY, NEW BURLINGTON STREET,

Publisher in Ordinary to Her Majesty.

1870.

CONTENTS OF THE SECOND VOLUME.

CHAPTER I.

CHAPTER II.

CHAPTER III.

CHAPTER IV.

CONTENTS

CHAPTER V.

CHAPTER VI.

CHAPTER VII.

CHAPTER VIII.

CHAPTER IX.

CHAPTER X.

CHAPTER XI.

LIFE AND LETTERS

OF

MARY RUSSELL MITFORD.

CHAPTER I.

LETTERS FOR 1817.

To SIR WILLIAM ELFORD, *Bath.*

Bertram House, March 19, 1817.

MY DEAR FRIEND,

After having told you so positively that papa had secured the picture you wished for—after believing it as certainly yours as Bickham itself—only think how vexed and provoked and mortified I am to be obliged to announce to you that it is no more yours than Holme Lacy, and that nothing less than shooting Mr. Tagg seems likely to procure it. All this happens because the aforesaid Tagg will get half tipsy.

What do you think of Cobbett's running away? Were you surprised at it? I was not. We at one time knew a great deal of this most extraordinary man. Some dispute, relative, I believe, to an agreement with another gentleman, during which papa happened to be present and was appealed to by both parties, sepa-

rated the .families; but we had been very intimate,
and I have always regretted the great and dangerous
violence to which he has latterly abandoned himself;
whilst I was sure from his whole conduct during his
past trial, at which time we saw him every day, that he
would never expose himself to a second imprisonment.
He has courage, but he has no fortitude. He would
fight, I dare say, but he does not know how to suffer.
He was a sad tyrant, too, as my friends the Democrats
sometimes are. Servants and labourers fled before him.
And yet, with all his faults, he was a man one could
not help liking, when one had fairly gotten over the
shock of his drill-sergeant *abord.* The coarseness and
violence of his political writings and conversations
almost entirely disappeared in his family circle, and
were replaced by a kindness, a good-humour, and an
enjoyment in seeing and promoting the happiness of
others which was infinitely attractive in itself, and appeared perhaps to even greater advantage from the
contrast it exhibited with his sterner mood. He had
too, occasionally, uncommon powers of unintentional
description. Living constantly in the country, and a
very beautiful part of the country, and going out daily
into the fields or woods, he could not always divest
himself of those picturesque associations to which the
distinctness of his conceptions, and his clear and direct
language were so well calculated to do justice: and in
pointing out where a spaniel sprung a pheasant, or a
greyhound killed a hare, he would sometimes strike out
a landscape so distinct, so glowing, so vivid, that the
dullest imagination could see the very spot. This was
his forte.

I have often wondered that this strong, though probably unconscious, power did not burst through the

dreary desert of his political writings; but he always affected to despise—perhaps did despise—the graces of composition and fancy, cried down Shakespeare, and thought Butler a greater poet than Milton! Latterly, too, so much of bitterness and bile has mingled with his thoughts, that the sweet pictures of Nature were probably banished from them. He was always what Dr. Johnson would have called a very pretty hater; but since his release from Newgate he has been hatred itself—a very abstract and personification of misanthropy, which, for the more grace, he has christened Patriotism. Milder thoughts attend him! He has my good wishes, and so have his family, who were, and I dare say are, very amiable—particularly his very plain, but very clever and very charming eldest daughter.

Rather than send the envelope blank, I will fill it with the translation of a pretty allegory of M. Arnault's, the author of 'Germanicus.' You must not read it, if you have read the French, because it does not come near its sweet simplicity. If you have not read the French you may read the English. Be upon honour.

TRANSLATION OF M. ARNAULT'S LINES ON HIS OWN EXILE.

Torn rudely from thy parent bough,
Poor withered leaf, where roamest thou?
I know not where! A tempest broke
My only prop, the stately oak;
And ever since, in wearying change,
With each capricious wind I range;
From wood to plain, from hill to dale,
Borne sweeping on as sweeps the gale.
Without a struggle or a cry,
I go where all must go as I;
I go where goes the self-same hour
A laurel leaf or rose's flower!

To Sir William Elford, *Cheltenham.*

Bertram House, May 23, 1817.

Your valuable packet,* my dear friend, was waiting
for me here on my return from London. We are all
delighted with its contents—Mossy included, who by
no means deserves to be called irrational—and only
wish the Legislature may be wise enough to adopt your
suggestions.

My visit to town was very gay and very pleasant—
pleasanter, perhaps, in recollection than in reality; for
the immediate impression is nothing but bustle. Visiting London is going shopping for ideas, and it is not till
one has put the gay trifles in proper form that one
knows exactly the worth of one's bargain. There is
a great deal worth hearing this year, and still more
worth seeing; 'Don Giovanni,' which forced even my
unmusical soul to admire, and what is more, to listen;
Kemble, whom all the world is content to praise now
that he is going to bid the world Good night. The
new melodrame, by the aid of Miss Kelly and a sea-
scene, takes nightily. By-the-way, this ' Innkeeper's
Daughter' I only *saw*. I have a horror of gunpowder
and guns, loaded or not, from cannons down to squibs;
and there happens to be in this piece a fierce personage of a smuggler, never off the stage, who strides
about with a belt full of pistols, shooting everybody or
threatening to shoot, and at last, as the climax of his
offences, getting shot himself in the concluding scene.
So that, in spite of all scolding, I was in one perpetual
course of ducking and ear-stopping from first to last.
I never heard one word, and I don't think I had any
great loss.

* Pamphlet on the Game Laws, written by Sir William Elford.

Then there is the beautiful cast from the Monte
Cavallo group in the King's Mews, which gave me
a higher and more expansive feeling of the genius of
Phidias than I had gained even from the Elgin marbles. The exhibitions, too, are very good, in spite of a
prodigious overflow of stupid faces, royal and other—to
say nothing of two portentous whole lengths of the
Duke of Sussex as large as life! Canova's 'Hebe' is
really divine, and there is a monument by Chantry (of
which the idea is taken from Northcote's picture of the
princes sleeping in the Tower) which gives one the delightful feeling that there is at least one English sculptor whose works are worthy to stand in the same room
with Canova's. Then we have Wilkie's 'Comfortable
Breakfast,' and Harlowe's 'Trial of Queen Catherine,'
in which he has embalmed the whole Kemble family.
This picture was originally painted for Mr. T. Welch,
who had offered Mr. Harlow *twenty guineas* for a portrait of Mrs. Siddons. When Mrs. T—— and Mr.
Harlow met, this idea of painting the Kemble family in
a group was started and acted on ; and Mr. Welch was
astonished to receive this beautiful combination of portrait and history, instead of the single likeness he expected.* "I cannot take this for twenty guineas," said
Mr. Welch ; "you must allow me to make it a hundred."
"I will take only twenty," said Mr. Harlow, and they
parted. A short time afterwards Mr. Harlow called on
Mr. Welch :—"I will now take your hundred guineas, my
good friend. Lord Darnley has seen the picture and has
offered me five hundred ; so that you shall sell him the
picture, give me a hundred, and put the other four hundred in your own pocket." "I will do no such thing,"

---

* The picture was finished before Mrs. Siddons ever saw it; and
both she and John Kemble were painted from memory.

replied Mr. Welch; " I am delighted that you permit me
to relieve my conscience by giving you the hundred ; but
no Lord Darnley shall have the picture. I have no house
fit to receive it, and shall therefore present it to the
Green Room at Covent Garden Theatre." And so the
matter stands.

But the charm of this exhibition is a chalk drawing by Mr. Haydon, taken, *as he told me,* from a
mother who had lost her only child. It is the very
triumph of expression. People stood silent before
it. I have not yet lost the impression which it made
upon my heart and my senses. Of course it vented
itself in a sonnet, which I have taken the liberty of
sending to the artist, who will probably forgive the bad
poetry for the sake of the subject. Captain Harness,
the son of a very old friend of papa's, is intimate with
Mr. Haydon, and had his permission to bring friends to
see his picture.* He took me and another lady, and
we had the additional good fortune to see the painter.
I was very much pleased with everything; his room
full of casts and drawings and the best books in the
best languages ; his picture, which is indeed a wonderful and most magnificent performance, though he has
still six months' labour to bestow on it; and himself,
with his *bonhommie,* his *naïveté,* and his enthusiasm. It
is a thousand pities he should be such a fright! I could
not resist the vanity of mentioning your name, and there
was the very soul of gratitude in his answer. I did
not, as you may imagine, like him the worse for this.

I had, too, the great pleasure of seeing and con-
versing with a very interesting person, the Pole, Pion-
towski, who followed Napoleon to St. Helena, and has
since been sent away by the governor for an imputed

* Christ's entrance into Jerusalem,

plot. He does not at all deserve the stigma Warden passes on him of belonging to the inferior classes. On the contrary, he is a man of very accomplished manners, speaking perfectly good English, and of a most gentlemanlike appearance. We had a great deal of conversation. He is quite as much of an enthusiast as ever, and seemed to enjoy, like all enthusiastic talkers, meeting with a listener equally enthusiastic. Buonaparte is certainly writing, or rather dictating, his memoirs. He walks backwards and forwards with his hands behind him, and dictates so fast that two or three of his suite are obliged to be in attendance, that the one may take down one-half of a sentence, and another the rest; they then literally compare notes, and put the disjointed legs and wings and heads of periods together. This is writing a book as he fought a battle. It will be a most interesting work, Pioutowski says; "*tout y est motivé;*" he gives his own reasons and everybody else's. Papa and mamma join in kindest remembrances, and I am ever,

Most sincerely and affectionately yours,
MARY RUSSELL MITFORD.

[We have no information as to the nature of the claim to which reference is made in the following letter.]

To DR. MITFORD, *York Hotel, St. James' Street.*

Bertram House, July 1, 1817.

I think Mr. Ryley's letter * (which, by-the-by, I

---

* Letter to which the above refers:

"*Mitford v. Elliott.*

"SIR.—The term is now again over, and nothing done in this business. I cannot now submit to remain a tame and tacit person, and must proceed to take possession of the estate. What can be the occasion of it? I have many times had an issue tried in two terms after

see from the date you might have got yesterday) is
rather consoling, my own darling; first of all, as it
proves that they knew nothing of the termination of
the affair; and, secondly, as it does not appear they
intend to take possession of anything besides the estate.
It did not occur to me, but would it not have been a
good thing to have made over the furniture, either for
our use or to pay the debts as occasion would offer, to
some friend ?   I dare say we might have got the money
from Jacob Newberry on such a security; but everything will depend on the meeting to-day and your success with Dr. Harness.*   At all events, my own dear
love, take care of yourself in every way, and keep up
your spirits.   All will go well, I am sure, and you know
I have always been a true prophet.   If you should come
back here this week, I am sure my arm would be well
enough to meet you at Wokingham.   I dare say, if my
parcel went to Eliza yesterday, that we shall hear to-
morrow; and would not Mr. Webb be the best friend
and adviser you could have ?   But I am sure that all
will go well, and I desire you will believe it as firmly
as I do.   But see, my own dear pet, and take care of
yourself; that is the first thing necessary.

The dear pets are quite well—Mossy more amiable
than ever.   We got some nice strawberries last night, and

---

the order; it is now four.   Let me hear from you or your agent a
correct statement of the cause of delay.

            "I am, Sir,

                    "Yours truly,

                            "GEORGE RYLEY.

"Hungerford, June 29, 1817."

* Dr. Harness was trustee for the three thousand pounds, which was
settled by Mrs. Mitford's grandfather, Mr. Dickers, on his daughter and
her children.   Application was continually made to him for the release
of this money, but he never would resign the trust.

very much wanted you to help eat them. To-day there is no getting out. Walking down the lane last night we found almost all the foxgloves gathered and left by the side of the ditch. What a pity! God bless you!

Ever most fondly your own,

M. R. MITFORD.

To SIR WILLIAM ELFORD, *Bickham, Plymouth.*

Bertram House, July 7, 1817.

Your very touching letter, my dear friend, brought me the first intelligence of the dreadful loss you have experienced. I had not even any idea of danger, or surely, most surely, I should never have intruded on you those letters whose apparently heartless levity I am now shocked to remember. I write now, partly in pursuance of your own excellent system, to avoid, as much as may be, prolonging and renewing your sorrow, and partly to assure you of our sincere and unaffected sympathy. We had not, indeed, the happiness of a personal acquaintance with Lady Elford, but the virtues of the departed are best known in the grief of the survivors. To be so lamented is to have been most excellent. And the recollected virtue, which is now agony, will soon be consolation. God bless and comfort you all!

I hope soon to hear a better account both of yourself and your daughters; but do not think of writing out of form or etiquette. Write when you will and what you will, certain that few, very few, can be more interested in your health or happiness than your poor little friend. My father is in town, but mamma joins in kindest remembrances; and I am ever, my dear Sir,

Very gratefully and affectionately yours,

MARY RUSSELL MITFORD.

My arm is now much better, and I walk out every day. Once more, God bless you!

To SIR WILLIAM ELFORD, *Bickham, Plymouth.*

Bertram House, Sept. 13, 1817.

Yes, my dear friend, this fine weather has been quite a renewal of the feelings and beauty of the early summer; for the precious rains have preserved all the verdure, and we have now a second June, with its bright skies, its green hedgerows, its haymakings, and its woodbines. I cannot tell you how thoroughly I enjoy it. I should, however, certainly enjoy it much more were I not very honestly and conscientiously trying to like riding on horseback—a detestable recreation, which I abhor the more the more I endeavour to endure it. The exercise, which I do dearly love, is to be whirled along fast, fast, fast, by a blood horse in a gig; this, under a bright sun, with a brisk wind full in my face, is my highest notion of physical pleasure; even walking is not so exhilarating. Besides this experiment upon my bodily taste, I have been making one of the same nature on my mind—trying to learn to admire Wordsworth's poetry. I do not mean by "admire" merely to like and applaud those fine passages which all the world must like, but to admire *en masse*—all, every page, every line, every word, every comma; to admire nothing else, and to admire all day long. This is what Mr. Wordsworth expects of his admirers (I had almost said his worshippers); and, strange to say, a large proportion of the cleverest young men in London (your friend Mr. Haydon among the rest) do pay him this homage.

One of the circle, a Reading gentleman of the name of Talfourd—of whom, by the way, when he has completed

his studies for the bar, the world will one day hear a
good deal—talked to me about Mr. Wordsworth's genius
till I began to be a little ashamed of not admiring him
myself. Enthusiasm is very catching, especially when
it is very eloquent. So I set about admiring. To be
sure, there was the small difficulty of not understanding;
but that, as Mr. Talfourd said, did not signify. So I
admired. But, alas! my admiration was but a puny,
flickering flame, that wanted constant relighting at Mr.
Talfourd's enthusiasm, and constant fanning by Mr.
Talfourd's eloquence. He went to town, and out it
went for good. After all, I should never have done for
a disciple of Mr. Wordsworth. I have too much self-
will about me—too much spirit of opposition. By-the-by,
I wonder how Mr. Haydon manages. Docility is not *his*
characteristic. I suppose there is a little commerce of
flattery, though Mr. Wordsworth not only exacts an
entire relinquishment of all other tastes besides taste
for his poetry, but if an unlucky votary chances to
say, "Of all your beautiful passages I most admire so
and so," he knocks him down by saying, "Sir, I have
a thousand passages more beautiful than that. Sir,
you know nothing of the matter." One's conscience
may be pretty well absolved for not admiring this
man : he admires himself enough for all the world put
together.

The best estimate I ever met with of Wordsworth's
powers is in Coleridge's very out-of-the-way, but very
amusing 'Biographia Literaria.' It is in the highest
degree flattering, but it admits that he may have faults;
and Mr. Lamb, who knows them both well, says he is
sure Mr. Wordsworth will never speak to Mr. Coleridge
again. Have you met with the 'Biographia Literaria?'
It has, to be sure, rather more absurdities than ever were

collected together in a printed book before ; but there
are passages written with sunbeams. The pleasantry
throughout is as ungraceful as a dancing cow, and every
page gives you reason to suspect that the author had
forgotten the page that preceded it. I have lately heard
a curious anecdote of Mr. Coleridge, which, at the risk
—at the certainty—of spoiling it in the telling, I cannot
forbear sending you. He had for some time relinquished
his English mode of intoxication by brandy and water
for the Turkish fashion of intoxication by opium ; but
at length the earnest remonstrances of his friends, aided
by his own sense of right, prevailed on him to attempt
to conquer this destructive habit. He put himself under
watch and ward ; went to lodge at an apothecary's at
Highgate, whom he cautioned to lock up his opiates :
gave his money to a friend to keep ; and desired his
druggist not to trust him. For some days all went on
well. Our poet was ready to hang himself ; could not
write, could not eat, could not—incredible as it may
seem—could not talk. The stimulus was wanting, and
the apothecary contented. Suddenly, however, he began
to mend ; he wrote, he read, he talked, he harangued ;
Coleridge was himself again ! And the apothecary
began to watch within doors and without. The next
day the culprit was detected ; for the next day came a
second supply of landanum from Murray's, well wrapped
up in proof sheets of the 'Quarterly Review.'

Before leaving the subject of books, I must ask you
if you have read 'Lalla Rookh?' If I ever ventured
to recommend poetry to you, I think I should say, do
read that. But I dare not run the risk. I will, however, caution you, if you *should* take it up, against judg-
ing it by the first story, which is quite Lord Byron-ish
in plan and metre, and would have been equally detest-

able in sentiment and execution, but that the 'Spirit of Love, Spirit of bliss' would force itself through. No thanks to the author that it is not as hating and disagreeable as 'Lara' or 'Manfred.' I am quite convinced that he would have made it so if he could. The tale by which I would have you judge of Moore is the last, 'The Light of the Harem'—the sweetest, the lightest, the most elegant trifle ever written by man. Pray do read this—it is not above fifty pages.

We are likely to have the Duke of Wellington for a neighbour here at Lord Rivers's place, provided he should himself approve the situation, which I cannot but doubt. Strathfieldsaye is a pretty rural place enough, with a great deal of swampy-looking water, very little inequality of ground, and a belt of firs all round. Altogether it gives the idea and the feeling of water meadows, with a few fine trees scattered about, and on a hot day looks cool and pleasant; but there is nothing about it of the grand and commanding, nor even of the picturesque; nor do I think that the united powers of the architect and the landscape gardener could ever convert it into such a scene as ought to encircle a national palace. The great recommendation is, the value of the surrounding property and the extent of manorial rights. I shall be sorry to lose the greyhounds.*

Ever, my dear Sir William,

Your affectionate friend,

M. R. MITFORD.

I had not heard of Miss Austen's death. What a terrible loss! Are you quite sure that it is our Miss Austen?

* Those of Lord Rivers, which were very fine.

To Sir William Elford, *Bickham, Plymouth.*

Bertram House, Oct. 11, 1817.

What have you been doing, my dear friend, this beautiful autumn? Farming? Shooting? Painting? I have been hearing and seeing a good deal of pictures lately, for we have had down at Reading Mr. Hofland, an artist whom I admire very much (am I right?), and his wife, whom, as a woman and an authoress, I equally love and admire. (Pray, if you wish to 'cry quarts,' read her children's books—her 'Good Grandmother' and her 'Son of a Genius.') It was that notable fool, His Grace of Marlborough, who imported these delightful people into our Bœotian town. He—the possessor of Blenheim—is employing Mr. Hofland to take views at Whiteknights—where there are no views; and Mrs. Hofland to write a description of Whiteknights—where there is nothing to describe. I have been a great deal with them, and have helped Mrs. Hofland to one page of her imperial quarto volume (for which see the envelope); and to make myself amends for flattering the scenery in verse, I comfort myself by abusing it in prose to whoever will listen. There is a certain wood at Whiteknights, shut in with great boarded gates, which nobody is allowed to enter. It is a perfect Bluebeard's chamber; and of course all our pretty Fatimas would give their heads to get in. Well, thither have I been, and it is the very palace of False Taste—a bad French garden, with staring gravel walks, make-believe bridges, stunted vineyards, and vistas through which you see nothing. Thither did I go with Mrs. Hofland —"the two first modest ladies," as the housekeeper said, that she remembered to have been admitted there. *Notâ bene,* the Queen and Princesses had walked over it the week before. But the master was absent, and we had the comfort of laughing at it as much as we chose.

Mr. Haydon (who is, by-the-way, a great admirer of your landscapes), to make amends for the cramping of his genius in this mere job at Whiteknights, is projecting a very grand and noble picture—Jerusalem at the moment of the Crucifixion.

Mrs. Hofland is quite an enthusiast for the character of your friend Mr. Haydon (there is no jerk here—for talking of the noble and the beautiful one naturally thinks of him), whom she knows very little and admires very much—just as I do. She told me a thousand anecdotes of him, one of which I must tell you. He was engaged to spend the day at Hampstead one Sunday with some of the cleverest unbelievers of the age—Mr. Leigh Hunt, Mr. H——, and, I am afraid, Mr. T——; and being reproached with coming so late, said with his usual simplicity, " I could not come sooner—I have been to church." You may imagine the torrent of ridicule that was raised upon him. When it had subsided, " I'll tell ye what, gentlemen," said he, " I knew when I came amongst ye—and knowing this it is not, perhaps, much to my credit that I came—that I was the only Christian of the party; but I think you know that I will not bear insult; and I now tell you all that I shall look upon it as a personal affront if ever this subject be mentioned by you in my hearing; and now to literature or to what you will!" Is not this moral courage quite glorious?

I have just been reading Fletcher's ' Faithful Shepherdess.' What a terrible thief Milton was! All the very best and sweetest parts of ' Comus ' are stolen from this exquisite Pastoral, and in my mind nothing bettered by the exchange.

Most sincerely and affectionately yours,

MARY RUSSELL MITFORD.

[Enclosed in the foregoing letter.]

The Fishing Seat : Whiteknights.

There is a sweet accordant harmony
  In this fair scene—this quaintly floated bower ;
  These sloping banks, with tree and shrub and flower
Bedecked ; and these pure waters, where the sky
In its deep blueness shines so peacefully :
  Shines all unbroken ; save with sudden light
  When some proud swan, majestically bright,
Flashes her snowy beauty on the eye :
  Shines all unbroken ; save, with sudden start,
When from the delicate birch a dewy tear
  The west wind brushes. E'en the bee's blithe trade,
Or the lark's carol, sound too loudly here :
  A spot it is for far-off music made,
Stillness and rest—a smaller Windermere !

                                                    M. R. M.

To Sir William Elford, *Post Office, Exeter.*

                          Bertram House, Nov. 20, 1817.

I thank you, my dear friend, most sincerely for
your very kind and very entertaining letter, with its
sweet verses. I never had the wit to write a charade
in my life ; but I am grown very fond of them lately,
and that gem of yours will certainly not tend to diminish
my liking. Have you seen those of Professor Porson at
the end of Mr. Beloe's 'Sexagenarian ?' This is very
pretty and wicked and playful and man-like, is it not ?

> My first is the lot that is destined by Fate
> For my second to meet with in every state ;
> My third is by many philosophers reckoned
> To bring very often my first to my second.

If you have not seen the book and would like the
rest, I shall have great pleasure in sending them to
you.

So you do not think me a prophetess? Well, we
shall see. Not but your observation is full of truth
and *finesse* (*finesse*, French observe) and quite right

with regard to all possible cases—except mine! But,
in the first place, this prodigy of mine is full grown,
"come to his grand dimensions, sir," as the man says
when he shows the elephant; and in the second place,
it is eloquence that I expect Mr. Talfourd to excel in;
and, if there be one thing more than another which
cannot be assumed, it is this rare and admirable quality.
I will tell you all about him. He was brought up at
Dr. Valpy's, and began, *selon les règles,* to display his
genius by publishing a volume of most stupid poems
before he was sixteen. You are aware, I hope, that all
clever people begin by publishing bad poems. I will
not swear that my friend Dr. Valpy, who really hardly
knows Campbell from Fitzgerald, did not think them
very good. But the public told the truth; and there
was no helping the discovery, that he, whose verses
were detestable, wrote and talked the most exquisite
prose. So, after all Dr. Valpy could do for him, he was
sent to Mr. Chitty a-special-pleading: and now he has
left Mr. Chitty and is special pleading for himself—
working under the bar, as the lawyers call it, for a year
or two, when he will be called; and I hope, for the
credit of my judgment, shine forth like the sun from
behind a cloud. You should know that he has the very
great advantage of having nothing to depend on but
his own talents and industry; and those talents are, I
assure you, of the very highest order. I know nothing
so eloquent as his conversation, so powerful, so full;
passing with equal ease from the plainest detail to the
loftiest and most sustained flights of imagination;
heaping with unrivalled fluency of words and of ideas
image upon image and illustration upon illustration.
Never was conversation so dazzling, so glittering.

Listening to Mr. Talfourd is like looking at the sun ; it makes one's mind ache with excessive brilliancy.

This is not the secret of pleasant conversation, I grant you ; it is too exacting, too engrossing, too fatiguing ; but is it not the secret of eloquence ? After all, the most wonderful thing in his conversation is its continuance. To say that he harangues is nothing. All his talk is one harangue. It is impossible to slide in a word ; so that papa says he never can succeed as a counsel, for, if it should be necessary for him to examine a witness, he never will hold his tongue long enough to hear his answer. I can't think how he manages with Coleridge and Wordsworth, who are both such talkers that they, though professing to delight in each other's society, never meet, because neither will listen. There is another very singular peculiarity about Mr. Talfourd ; he can't spell. Dr. Valpy says there are commonly twenty faults in a letter of about ten lines—not faults of system or of affectation, but of pure ignorance, and in great variety. For instance, having occasion to write the word *hear* three or four times in a page, he would spell it in one place " heer," in another " here," and in a third " heir." How such a thing can happen to a man who has books always before his eyes I cannot imagine.

Most sincerely and affectionately yours,

M. R. MITFORD.

CHAPTER II.

LETTERS FOR 1818.

To Sir William Elford, *Bickham, Plymouth.*

Bertram House, Jan. 12, 1818.

I MUST tell you, who are so fond of riddles, a new amusement which Penelope Valpy, Miss James, and I fell into, quite by accident, the other evening. It would only do among three such discreet females, for fear of propagating nicknames; but I can't resist telling you. It is, then, nothing more nor less than translating the real surnames of different people, sometimes quite literally, sometimes with a little improvement, into different languages. Did you ever try it? I will give you a sample: Mr. Duckinfield, *Monsieur Canard-en-champ.* Somebody suggested that it was Dukinfield, and that the right translation was *Dux-in-campo;* but I stuck to *Canard.* Mr. Vane, *Monsieur Girouette.* Mrs. Wise, *Madame Le Sage.* Dr. Taylor, *Il Dottore Sartore.* Mr. Bully, *Monsieur Taureau-mensonge.* Mr. Madison, *Signor Pazzosono-figlio;* and a great many others which I can't recollect. Compound names do best. Some of our list were famous and marvellously suited the characters or conditions of the names.

Do you see what honours Mr. Haydon has gained? I hope he will get a little solid pudding as well as empty praise, and that these Russian compliments will terminate in Alexander's giving him a proper price for his beautiful picture. And yet England ought not to lose it. But unless he can find two other such friends as you and Mr. Trigcombe (oh! my dear friend, how inexpressibly I admire that liberality of yours!)—unless he can find such another, what can he do? There is no great chance that Government will be munificent on the occasion, and the picture is really too large for any private house. I understand that the same beautiful boy who sat for Solomon is the model from whence he has taken the head of Christ. Is not this odd?

I believe this principle of self-will, and hating to paint furniture pictures, is one of the component parts of an artist. My friend Mrs. Hofland's husband has just the same fancy. He will cover yards of canvas whether people buy them or not. After all, I cannot help admiring with all my heart and soul the manly, noble, independent spirit of Mr. Haydon. Don't you? He is quite one of the old heroes come to life again—one of Shakespeare's men—full of spirit and endurance and moral courage. Did you read his account of the cartoons in the 'Examiner?'

Adieu, my dear friend! Ever very sincerely and affectionately yours,

MARY RUSSELL MITFORD.

To SIR WILLIAM ELFORD, *Bickham, Plymouth.*

Bertram House, Jan. 19, 1818.

And so you think I see with the eyes of imagination, my dear friend, and "describe most accurately that which is not!" And you tell me so. Well, I shall punish you. I gave you only the outline of my fair original; now you shall have the whole portrait at full length, as good a likeness as I can make, and you must tell me whether the person to whom it belongs be not loveable. . . . I never say one word more than appears to me to be true. To be sure, there is an atmosphere of love—a sunshine of fancy—in which objects appear clearer and brighter; and from such I may sometimes paint; but that is not flattery prepense, is it, my dear friend? I never mean to flatter—no, never! But it is a great pleasure to me to love and admire, and it is a faculty which has survived many frosts and storms. It makes half my acquaintance think me silly, and the other half mad. Papa and Mrs. Rowden scold about it, and you and mamma laugh. And, after all, I am sure there is not one of you, talk as you will, that really and at the bottom of your heart wish it away. We may admire people for being wise, but we like them best when they are foolish.

Did I ever talk to you about Bear Wood, a spot about six miles from us, of remarkable beauty? It was, as you might imagine from the name, a beech wood, very old, and blended into the commons which every way surrounded it by old, stunted, ragged beech trees, half stripped of their branches, growing first in straggling clumps, and then scattered singly, forming the most picturesque and natural union with the bare and barren heath. When you got into the thicker part of the wood it was enchanting—large tangled masses of huge trees and thick underwood—holly, bramble, and fern, with all their accompaniments of wood flowers— broken by winding green paths, some formed naturally by the sheep, some purposely made by the hunters (for it abounded in game)—nowhere level, but in one part descending abruptly to a deep, long, narrow glen, filled with one of those forest pools of which the effect is so beautiful, where the clear water seems placed like a

mirror to catch the light, and reflect the deep-blue sky.
Nothing could be so delightful as to stand, on a sunny
autumn day, on the most level side of the water, and
look across the pool up to that amphitheatre of trees in
their regular confusion, with their shining bark and
their leaves changing from green to orange. It was
within *donkey-cart distance* of Mr. Webb's, and Mary
and I used to take books and work, and sit there for
whole mornings.

About a year ago this estate was sold, under the
Forest Inclosure Act, to Mr. Walter, one of the editors
of the 'Times' newspaper. He immediately resolved
to build there, and employed a certain Mr. Crabtree as his agent, steward, &c. The first operation
performed by Mr. Crabtree was to cut down all and
every one of the straggling old beech trees, whether
single or in clumps, rounding the wood territory as
completely and as smoothly as ever Buonaparte rounded
the territory of some favoured king; the next, to make
in two directions and across two commons a fine, level,
straight gravel road to the wood, nicely bordered by a
pretty little plantation of larches and firs. In about a
month down came Mr. Walter and a landscape gardener (name forgotten), who execrated poor Mr. Crabtree's cutting-downs; and, as it was impossible to make
the trees grow again outside the wood, contented himself with forming magnificent plans for the interior.
Accordingly he formed a plan for a lake where the pool
used to be—or, rather, for two lakes, united in the
middle by a cascade! (really it is well for the man that
his name is forgotten!)—and sixty persons were set to
work to dig and trench and level for this magnificent
design! All the spring, all the summer, all the autumn
were these people at work; and now Mr. Walter

(either by the benefit of his own lights, or by the advice of some third professor), having discovered that these lakes would spoil his place, has set all his sixty workmen to fill them up again, and intends to have, instead, a small natural rivulet winding along the glen. I dare say he will come back to the pool. How often one is reminded of that admirable and philosophical distich—

> "The King of France with twenty thousand men
> Marched up the hill, and then marched down again!"

I am very glad to hear so excellent an account of my noble namesakes. I always thought this Duke of Bedford a much finer character than his celebrated predecessor. His brother-in-law, Mr. Palmer, has just made me a very magnificent present. There is but one place in all Berkshire which has a really fine commanding prospect, and this is a turfy, almost inaccessible hill, called Finchamstead Ridges. Thither, at the risk of our necks, did Mr. Webb and I clamber last autumn by the help of a gig and a blood horse, and I was in one of my ecstacies about it when we came home to dinner. Well, this was in the Inclosure Act too, and Mr. Palmer bought it, and he has offered me six acres for a cottage * and a garden and a field for a cow.

Only think of my being a lady of landed property! Was ever poetess so rich! Now, if I could but scrape together money enough for my cottage, what an independent person I should be! How much would it take to build a real cottage? Would a hundred pounds do? . But it might just as well be a thousand; I should get the

---

* In another letter she writes: "Mr. Jolliffe promises me timber to build my cottage, so you find I shall get it finished at last. I want nothing now but somebody to find bricks, and somebody else to find workmanship, and then somebody to furnish it: only three somebodies —I have no doubt of meeting with them."

one as soon as the other. You must not think this
splendid donation of our dear May-pole of a candidate a
bribe. I am neither elector nor electress.

Was there ever such strange weather! Yesterday,
going to Wokingham, I picked four primroses full blown
in a ditch by the roadside, and papa some time last
month found a robin's nest with three eggs in it.

Ever very affectionately yours,
M. R. MITFORD.

To MRS. MITFORD, Bertram House, Reading.

Tavistock House,* Monday,
Feb. 24, 1818.

Papa would tell, my dearest, that I got to town
quite safe and in the very best possible condition, and
that he was obstinate, the dear darling, and would not
go to the Opera with us. He had a great loss, for it was
beautiful. I was quite as much pleased as I intended
to be, which is, you know, no very common thing. I
really did not think it possible that any music could have
so much passion. One is carried along by it as by a fine
tragedy. The ballet was exceedingly pretty—indeed
much the best they have had for these three years. The
house was, nevertheless, very empty. The Duke and
Duchess of Gloster were there; she looks very old and
faded. Only think of their making the parade of having
a carpet laid from the door to the carriage, lined both sides
with Guards, and two men with wax candles lighting them
up. Mr. Scarlett, the counsel, handed out the Duchess
without his hat. None of the king's sons but the Duke
of Gloster ever do this; he will always be ostentatious.

I am reading Shelley's 'Revolt of Islam,' and a book

---

* Tavistock House, in Tavistock Square, was the residence of Mr.
Perry.

by that same Shelley's wife (who was the daughter of Godwin and Mary Wollstonecraft), a most extraordinary thing called 'Frankenstein.' This Shelley is the heir of an immense fortune, or rather would have been the heir of an immense fortune, had he not cut off the entail of 28,000*l.* a year which he must have inherited at the death of his father. He will still have 8000*l.* per annum. Leigh Hunt may well praise him, for he has just raised, by *post obit*, 1500*l.* to relieve him of his embarrassments. Haydon's picture is not finished yet. I shall certainly pay him a visit. I hope, my own dearest love, that you take great care of yourself. How is poor Mossy? Did he bemoan me very much? God bless you, my own dearest, best beloved!

Ever and ever most fondly your own,

M. R. MITFORD.

To DR. MITFORD, *Bertram House.*

Tavistock House, Friday evening,
Feb. 28, 1818.

We have been to-day to see Munito the learned dog, and I was very much pleased with him, but past all description amused with a circumstance that occurred. The man, or rather the boy who translates for the man, came out as we entered, and, as we of course presented the free admittance card, he entered before us and announced with a fine loud voice, as if he had been announcing the Prince Regent—'The Morning Chronicle;' upon which the man who was beginning to show Munito left the poor dog in the midst to come and compliment the walking 'Morning Chronicle.' I thought I should have died with laughing. Annabelle did not enjoy it. She sneaked off to a seat as fast as possible; and I did the honours of that respectable paper. After this we

went to the Apollonicon. Have you heard it, my Drum?
It is a most wonderful rush of sound—like the wind, and
the waves, and the grand sounds of nature. I think it
better when played upon than when it plays itself. Then
we came home, and here we are very quiet and comfortable.

The party to-day consists of the Duke of Sussex,
Lord Erskine, and some more. Lord Erskine does not
know whether he shall be able to come or not, because
he is asked to the Duke of York's; but at all events
his son dines here, and he will join him in the evening.
I don't want to dine with them, and most sincerely hope
we shall not, for there is no one of literary note; but I
am afraid we shall not be able to get off. The Baron de
Stein, one of the proscribed '38, is to breakfast here to-
morrow. He was one of Buonaparte's aides-de-camp, and
stands up for him through thick and thin; this is much
more to my taste. Adieu, my own dear darlings! Best
love to the poor pets.

Ever and ever most fondly your own,

M. R. MITFORD.

Remember me to poor Lucy.

To Mrs. MITFORD, *Bertram House.*

Tavistock House, Sunday, March 1, 1818.

Having a leisure hour, my own dearest and best-
beloved, I avail myself of it to begin a letter to you,
which will be finished some way or other between this
and Tuesday. After writing yesterday, I went to Mrs.
Wilson's with Miss Bentley, and found the ladies at
home and very glad to see me. We then came home
to dress, for there was no getting excused, for the dinner,
and I had the honour of being handed into the dining-

room by that royal porpoise.* Nothing could have
exceeded his civility. He complained much of want of
appetite, but partook of nearly every dish on the table.
God bless you, my best beloved!

Every fondly your own,

M. R. MITFORD.

To SIR WILLIAM ELFORD, *Bickham.*

Bertram House, March 8, 1818.

I am just returned, my dear friend, from a three
weeks' visit to London and Twickenham. The first
part of it was to Tavistock House (Mr. Perry's), where
they do the honours of London to country curiosity in
great perfection. There I saw everything, and almost
everybody—the great and the big. The most portentous of this kind was the Duke of Sussex, next to whom
I sat at a dinner which I expected to be his last. Never
surely did man eat, drink, or swear so much, or talk such
bad English. He is a fine exemplification of the difference between speaking and talking; for his speeches, except that they are mouthy and wordy and common-place,
and entirely without ideas, are really not much amiss.

Then I saw, to leave all this nonsense, the Elgin
marbles in their new home, with that fine Torso of a
Cupid, which they have discovered lately—a Cupid
who is really the God of Love. And I saw West's
picture, very like Mr. Shelley's poem (by-the-by, I believe I illustrated Shelley's poem by saying it was like
West's picture; this is after the fashion of certain
dictionary-mongers who ring the changes upon two
words). Well, this picture disappointed me. It is not
my notion of Death—not shadowy enough. It is not
Milton's to a certainty, for his is a skeleton; neither is

* The Duke of Sussex.

it the Death of the Revelation. It is a very frightful monster, and that is all. And the confusion of the
whole picture is quite disagreeable: one has not
courage enough to try to understand it. Then I saw
the Gallery of the British Institution, with its dirty
'Bathsheba' (Oh, that ever Mr. Wilkie should paint a
picture one cannot like!), and Mr. Ward's sprawling
'Angel,' and Mr. Hofland's exquisite 'Jerusalem.'

Adieu, my very dear friend. Ever most gratefully
and affectionately yours,

M. R. MITFORD.

ENIGMA.

The highest gift of God to man
When all His wondrous works we scan ;
That which we often lose with sorrow,
And often are compelled to borrow ;
The lover's gift, the poet's song,—
What art makes short and nature long.

ON LEAVING MR. HOFLAND'S PICTURE OF ULLSWATER.

My little world of loveliness, farewell !
  Farewell to the clear lake ; the mountains blue ;
  The grove, whose tufted paths some eyes pursue
Delighted ; the white cottage in the dell
By yon old church : the smoke, from that small cell
  Amid the hills, slow rising ; and the hue
  Of summer air, fresh, delicate, and true,
That breathes o'er all its soul-entrancing spell :—
  Work of the poet's eye, the painter's hand,
How close to Nature art thou, yet how free
  From earthly stain ! The beautiful, the bland,
The rose, the nightingale, resemble thee :
  Thou art most like the blissful fairy-land
Of Spenser, or Mozart's fine melody !

M. R. M.

To Dr. Mitford, *York Coffee House, St. James's Street.*

Wokingham, April 21, 1818.

We got here quite safely, my own dear, without even the shadow of an alarm, though I even watered the horse in the stream at Arborfield, finding her thirsty, poor dear. She goes very quietly, but not so fast with me as with you—that is to say, she has an inveterate propensity for walking when she ought to trot, and does not mind my whipping a bit. But, altogether, she is a person of great accomplishments; and John behaved very well; and I like driving very much; and we had a delightful ride. Miss James says she was not at all afraid, being so assured of my being reserved to be hanged, that she would not mind going with me even in a balloon. This is very saucy, is it not? But there is something in the Wokingham air which makes impertinence grow. When I got to the Valpy's, after calling on Mrs. Newberry, I found them at dinner, and was obliged to eat quantities of veal and pudding on the very top of all those lamb-steaks and onions.

Have you read Mr. Milman's new poem? We have Mr. Milman himself in Reading; he has gotten one of the livings there, and reads and preaches enchantingly. I like his book, which I have only just begun, very much; but I don't recommend it to you—because, perhaps, you might happen to think it rather (how shall I find a civil word?)—rather longish.

Pray, have you heard that Miss Edgeworth has married, or is to marry, her stepmother's father, Mr. Beaufort? Mrs. Hofland, who is in habits of correspondence with her, wrote me word of it a month ago; but I have neither seen nor heard anything of it since; so perhaps she was mistaken. And can you satisfy my loyal fears as to the health of the Queen and the poor King? They have done

nothing but kill them alternately in Reading (a sad
Jacobinical town) all the week, to the great horror of all
loyal subjects who happen, like me, to hate black. Adieu,
my dear friend! The arrival of our little postboy full ten
minutes before his time, saves you at least ten lines of
nonsense.—Adieu!

    Ever most affectionately yours,
        M. R. MITFORD.

To SIR WILLIAM ELFORD, *Bickham, Plymouth.*

       Bertram House, June 14, 1818.

Pleasant sensations always remind me of you, my
ever kind friend. There are particular atmospheres
which one associates, one scarcely knows why, with
different people—the cold, and the foggy, and the
rainy, and the dry-hot; yours is, I think, the *fresh*—
the light, cool breeze which comes so pleasantly after a
warm, oppressive day. Do you like to be turned into
air? Well, I am just come from a walk, if walk it may
be called, which was merely a zig-zag kind of progress
from the rose bushes to the honeysuckles, from the
honeysuckles to the syringa tree, from the syringa to
the acacia, and from the acacia back to the roses.

I have been gathering sweets by night as the bee
gathers them by day. The luxury of that fresh, growing,
perfume, a flowering shrub in full bloom, is to me the
greatest of all enjoyments; and of all flowers the white
acacia is, I think, the most fragrant; of all white
acacias, the one which is my pet tree is the most laden
with blossoms; and of all evenings in which to stand
under it, this has been the pleasantest—a light wind
shaking down the loosely hung flowrets upon my pet
Mossy's black neck, and Mossy looking up and half-
suspecting some evil design, till another shower seemed

to explain the cause and remove his fears. My dear
Sir William, I cannot think how any one who was 'of
woman born,' who did not spring ready armed out of
the earth, like Minerva, can possibly submit himself
and all his ancestors—fathers, mothers, brothers, sisters,
wife, cousins of all degrees of kindred—to the horrible
ordeal of a contested election ! And only think how it
fares with our dear candidate, whose wife (Lady Made-
lina, the eldest daughter of the Duke of Gordon), has
the misfortune to have a pension, and whose uncle,
Fyshe Palmer, senior, had the *honour* to be transported
for sedition ! Think of that ! However, in spite of the
pension and the transportation, he will gain the victory ;
we are quite sure of it—quite. Besides, we have all
the—the—(dear me, I was going to say mob)—all the
gentlemen porters, and gentlemen chimney-sweepers,
and so forth, with us ; and the Weylandites, the moment
they come into the street, are over-crowed ; and we are
cheered and huzzaed, and drawn about and squeezed to
death, and everything that is charming and pretty.

Our candidate is vastly like a mopstick, or, rather, a
tall hop-pole, or an extremely long fishing-rod, or anything that is all length and no substance ; three or four
yards of brown thread would be as like him as anything,
if one could contrive to make it stand upright. Well,
he and papa were riding through the town together,
and one of the voters cried out, "Fish and Flesh for
ever !" Wit is privileged just now. Our little postboy
has Mr. Palmer's cockade on his donkey's head, and Mr.
Weyland's smart colours dangling at its tail. After all,
it's a very merry time, and as neither Mr. Lefevre nor
Mr. Palmer spend a sixpence, not a very tipsy one.
But it will soon be over. The election begins on
Wednesday, and will probably last three or four days ;

for our people, who are quite clear of bribery, mean to promote perjury as much as possible, by swearing separately all Mr. Weyland's voters. Papa is going to stay in Reading the whole election, and mamma is going to take care of him. Very good in her, isn't it? But papa does not seem to me at all grateful for this kind resolution, and mutters—when she is quite out of hearing—something about "petticoat government." I am going to stay at home, that is, I shall go in every morning and come back every night. Am I not wonderfully quiet, prudent, and domestic?

I have been reading ' Beppo,' and very much recommend it to you. I am sure you would like it, for though by Lord Byron, it is not at all Byronish, but light and gay, and graceful and short. There's a climax for you! But I must say good-bye.

Ever sincerely and affectionately yours,

M. R. MITFORD.

[Miss Mitford, when left alone at Bertram House during the election, writes in a letter to her mother :—]

I am a famous housekeeper. I have not yet starved anybody, nor let out the fire, nor lost the keys. I have written and sent off a note to the butcher; and we have cut out my nightcaps, four nightcaps, strips and all, from that yard and a quarter! There's contrivance for you! To be sure, we were two hours about it.

To Sir William Elford, *Bickham, Plymouth.*

Bertram House, July 17, 1818.

Do you know, my dear friend, that I am just at present the object of a Methodistical experiment? A very great lady is trying to convert me. Heaven help her, poor soul! The lady is—but I must tell you all about it. Everybody who knows Bath knows old

General Donkin. This old general is a sort of a cousin of ours, as cousinship goes in Northumberland—sixty degrees removed, perhaps. Papa has known him many years. They used to correspond, and the worthy veteran took such a fancy to me, whom he had never seen, that he had a mind some years ago to match me with his son, Major-General Donkin, whom I had never seen. This *par parenthèse*:—the general junior was iniquitous enough, in contempt and affront of my unknown charms, to marry one day; and the general senior, by way of consoling himself for the loss of so inimitable a daughter-in-law, took a wife himself about a year ago, he being then little better than ninety. I understand the bride and her friends were very fearful lest the general, *père*, should not live the " twelvemonth and a day" required for the pension. He has outlived the time, and may now, I suppose, die as soon as he pleases.

In the midst of all these marriages nobody married Miss Donkin, so she turned Methodist; and being by her accomplishments and busy turn a very great acquisition to that intriguing set, she is now a lady of vast consequence among them. About two months ago she came into this neighbourhood — that is, to Maidenhead—on a visit to a " minister in Lady Huntingdon's connexion." She has been sojourning thereabout with divers godly families ever since; and retaining some of the family interest for me, she wrote a note by a friend of ours whom she happened to see, partly to introduce herself, and partly to inquire into the state of my soul. My dear Sir William, you never saw such a letter! It was a mere scrap of an extempore sermon, sealed, too, with a cross and a Methodistical motto. I think my answer must have made her stare a little. I just touched slightly on the main topic of

her letter—told her very frankly that I was not so good
as I should be—and then prattled gaily about the other
parts, just as if I had been writing to you. I dare say
she turned up her eyes, but she has not done with me
yet, to my sorrow.

Mr. Hofland is coming to dine with us to-day. If
he tells me any artistical news I'll tell you. In the
mean time I must give you a sketch of my own, being
no other than a true and faithful account of the style
in which my honoured father travelled to Reading this
week to the sessions. Errands were wanted, multi-
tudinous and weighty; so he went in the cart—the real
cart—not our apology for a gig; behind him was an
open hamper, from which rose majestically a very fine,
very ugly, very big, mock bronze bust of Lord Nelson,
that he was about to present to fill a niche in the new
billiard room; before him was an empty beer-barrel;
at his side a grand pile of baskets; between his legs a
greyhound puppy, and in his hand a long coursing-stick,
the whip being broken. But the most diverting part
of the story was his behaviour. He did not enter at all
into the ridicule of it—he was neither ashamed nor
amused; but divided between serious scolding to the
awkward whip-breaker and anxious admonition to the
no less awkward placer of Lord Nelson's bust.

Sunday.

Mr. Hofland brought me the best news concerning
his own pictures. Besides his own particular talent, he
is a man eminently accomplished and intellectual,
whose conversation is singularly rich and delightful—
who talks pictures and paints poems. If you knew
him much you would, I am sure, like him exceedingly. They are kind to me beyond all bounds of

kindness, particularly Mrs. Hofland. Haydon's great picture is at last nearly finished, and he himself continues better.

My dear friend, good-bye!

Most sincerely and affectionately yours,
MARY RUSSELL MITFORD.

To SIR WILLIAM ELFORD, *Bickham.*

Bertram House, August 26, 1818.

MY DEAR SIR WILLIAM,

I have just found out a great fault in our dearly-beloved new member, Mr. Tyshe Palmer. He has the worst fault a franker can have; he is un-come-at-able. One never knows where to catch him. I don't believe he is ever two days in a place—always jiggeting about from one great house to another. And such strides as he takes, too! I verily believe he wears seven-league boots upon those long legs of his. One might as well send a letter after a swallow in September as send one travelling after him. Oh for the good days of poor Sir John Simeon! Poor dear Sir John! He was the franker for me! Stationary as Southampton Buildings, solid as the doorpost, and legible as the letters on the brass plate! I shall never see his fellow.

Pray have you such a thing as a blade of grass in your park? If you have you are much better off than we. Never was seen such drought and dust and utter dryness. The leaves are falling from the trees as in October. But it is going to rain, clouds gathering, wind changing, glass sinking, and I—going out. That last prognostic is unfailing. There will certainly be rain soon—that is, between this and dinner-time—and I shall come back sopped, and console myself by telling you all about it. So good-bye for the present.

Wednesday evening.

Did I ever give you a sketch of that excellent but very singular personage Dr. Valpy? He is to Dr. Parr what Dr. Parr is to Dr. Johnson—the copy of a copy, the shadow of a shade; very learned, very dictatorial, very knock-me-down; vainer than a peacock, or Dr. Parr, or than both of them put together. He is indeed the abstract idea of a schoolmaster embodied; you may know his profession a mile off. Well, he is going to have a Greek play performed by the boys; the Hercules—Hercules—Hercules something—I cannot remember; but I believe it is the Greek for mad, and it is to be followed by an English play for the ladies and the country gentlemen, and this English play is, what do you think? The second part of ' Henry the Fourth,' leaving out Falstaff and Justice Shallow! My dear Sir William, is not this good man essentially mad? I fairly scolded. Flesh and blood could not bear it. Ever my dear friend,

Most affectionately yours,
M. R. MITFORD.

To SIR WILLIAM ELFORD, *Bickham.*

Bertram House, Sept. 6, 1818.

This rain, which so delights farmers and sportsmen, and ladies who wear nice gowns, and in short everybody, delights not me; in the first place, because I never do like rain and love fine weather like a butterfly; in the next, because it interrupts a favourite diversion which I had found for myself, for mamma, and for Mistress Jenny Denison—the elegant and profitable amusement of picking up fir cones. You cannot think how much we enjoyed this sport. There is a good quantity still to be gathered, I assure you, though the weather has driven us in to our indoor work—mamma managing, Lucy dusting, and I sewing gown tails, writing dull letters, and reading dull books.

I have been reading the last canto of ' Childe Harold ;' —very fine, to be sure—splendid passages, grand description of waterfalls, magnificent account of the Venus and the Apollo, sublime apostrophe to the sea ; very fine, certainly. But pray—don't tell now—pray don't you think it rather tiresome all that sublimity ? Are you not rather sick—now pray don't betray me—are you not rather sick of being one of the hundred thousand confidants of his lordship's mysterious and secret sorrows ? The last ' Edinburgh Review,' I see, starts a comparison in the way of compliment between Lord Byron and Rousseau ; and truly I think, though not in the way of compliment, that the reviewer is right. They are just as mad the one as the other ; though, to do Rousseau justice, I think Lord Byron's madness the more *farouche* and disagreeable of the two. He is more like a mad bull ; Rousseau does not get beyond a mad calf. Now, mind you keep my secret !

Did you ever read the correspondence between Warburton and Hurd ? The former, from the first letter to the last, reminded me of that sturdy democrat William Cobbett ; such as he was when I used to know him, before his temper was soured and his heart cankered by imprisonment, or his head blown up like an air-balloon by the vanity which has so completely carried him off his feet. He is now, I believe, completely topsy-turvy. I have not seen him for these seven or eight years.

The cooler weather has done a great deal for my

dear mamma. She is much better, and joins papa in kindest compliments to you. Adieu, my dear friend! Ever most affectionately yours,

M. R. MITFORD.

To Sir William Elford, Bickham.

Monday morning, Sept. 10, 1815.

After finishing my letter, I remembered that I had been terribly aggrieved yesterday morning; and I must tell you the whole story. Papa and mamma have a very old acquaintance (friend, he calls himself), a prim, pedantic, priggish little person, who is by profession not only clergyman and private tutor, but, professionally also, an author and one of the literati,—that is, being obliged to preach sermons, he prints them; and, having occasion in his other vocation to open a few books, dictionaries and others, he takes the opportunity to proclaim himself a votary of the Muses. Well, this divine, who is really a very good sort of person, was an off-and-on correspondent of papa's; and, when I began to write that stuff by courtesy called verse, he deserted papa and took to writing to me. Well; this "intellectual and literary intercourse," as the gentleman called it, lived a languishing, unhealthy, dying life, like a flower under a yew-tree, and three or four years ago happily expired.

About a month ago papa got a cover and desired me to write again. I obeyed like a dutiful daughter, wrote a very kind and civil inquiry to please papa, and being in high spirits and a letter-writing mood, went on to please myself. In short, I fairly forgot the *fabrique* of the good body's head, and sent to him four or five pages of playful nonsense, such as I have sent to you by reams. The answer arrived yesterday. He never condescends

to notice our inquiries, but makes a haughty, super-
cilious apology for his silence, his "important avocations leaving little time for frivolous amusements." And
he then proceeds to analyze (paragraph by paragraph,
line by line, word by word) my unfortunate letter!

My dear Sir William, you never saw such a figure as it
cuts, this poor butterfly broken on the wheel—this daisy
picked to pieces! For though he replies to what might
be strained into the literal meanings of the words, he
very seldom condescends to quote the words themselves;
on the contrary, he translates them into solemn phrases
of his own—transmuting the glittering foil of my painted
tin into his own uncoloured lead. You never saw such
a figure as this anatomy of my letter, this *caput mor-
tuum* exhibits; just such a figure as Master Peter's
show did after Don Quixote's battle with the puppets;
such as Punch might have cut the day after Lord
Plymouth bought it; such as your kaleidoscope with
the broken glass and the crooked pins turned out upon
the table! For the first half-page I was really provoked;
but, as I went on, I yielded to the strong sense of ridicule, and was exceedingly amused, and now I value it
almost as much as Mr. Bennett (our dear Miss Austen's
Mr. Bennett) valued the letters of Mr. Collins—a person
whom, I think, my correspondent rather resembles.

And now, my dear and most patient friend, I will
really release you. I am quite ashamed of this enor-
mous letter—but you have your remedy—you need not
read it, you know. Write soon—very soon, and believe
me ever most sincerely and affectionately yours,

M. R. MITFORD.

To Sir William Elford, *Bickham.*

Bertram House, Nov. 1, 1818.

My dear Sir,

Reading has been very gay and grand lately. We have had a fine classical entertainment—a Greek play— the 'Hercules Furens' of Euripides, followed by 'The Critic.' Dr. Valpy listened to reason, to my great regret, and did not act 'Henry the Fourth' without Falstaff, by which piece of good sense he spoilt an excellent story.

Pray, sir, do you know this famous 'Hercules?' "Why, really, madam, of course I know it, but just at this moment I don't happen to recollect." Well, I will tell you, sir. Hercules is on his travels—he is making a little tour into hell—and his family on earth are in the sort of consternation which sometimes happens when the head of a house sets out on such a journey. Moreover, they are all likely to follow him, a fine fellow of a usurper, called Lycus. having passed a general sentence on the whole set. When the curtain draws up, we find this family party—Amphitryo (I believe that's the way the gentleman spells his name), who has the goodness to tell the audience the whole story, Hercules' wife, Megara, and the children of Hercules, who are all fled for refuge to the altar of Jupiter—a handy little table in front of the street-loor. They make sundry long speeches. Mrs. H. cries—Mr. A. scolds— in comes King Lycus and out-scolds him—in comes the three-bodied thing called a Chorus and out-cries her. At last Lycus proves to them how silly they are not to be killed peaceably, and they agree, Mrs. Megara-Hercules stipulating only that she and her children should retire to their toilettes, send for mourning and milliners, and die in proper form and colour. So ends act the first.

Act the second:—They appear in their black (very handsome bombasin trimmed with crape); and, whilst they are expecting Lycus, who should put up his appearance but Monsieur Hercules, just fresh from the infernal regions! You may imagine all the starts and kisses and questions—the Ahs and the Ohs!—the rage and the revenge! Hercules and Megara go to the house to wait for Lycus. Lycus comes in and is killed. All goes on swimmingly till the end of the third act, when Iris, a very pretty, good-for-nothing lady, makes her appearance with Lyssa, the Goddess of Madness, a person very much like a crazy gipsy. Well, Iris orders Lyssa to take possession of Hercules, and make him kill his wife and children. Lyssa has some remorse about this pretty exploit (by-the-way, she is the only amiable person in the play), but Iris insists, and carries her in, and Hercules begins killing, whilst the Chorus (instead of running for constables and strait-waistcoats, hiding the children in the coal-hole, and cramming the lady up the chimney) content themselves with peeping quietly through the keyhole and telling themselves and the audience all about it.

There are two acts more, but this is the end; for in those two acts, though there is a great deal said, nothing is done whatever, except that a fresh person, Theseus, another importation from the lower regions, comes in and coaxes Hercules not to kill himself. The curtain then drops very slowly to soft music, leaving Messrs. Theseus and Hercules in the midst of a hug which assuredly no Greek poet, painter, or sculptor ever dreamt of. That hug was purely Readingtonian—conceived, born, and bred in the Forbury.

I have very particular pleasure in writing you this

full, true, and particular account; because I was forced
to write an account neither full nor true—in plain
English, a *puff*—of this very play to put in the Reading
paper.

Now good-night.

Ever most sincerely and affectionately yours,
MARY RUSSELL MITFORD.

To SIR WILLIAM ELFORD, *Post Office, Bath.*

Bertram House, Nov. 9, 1818.

Yes, my dear Sir William, your prognostics were
right; a scolding letter was actually written and sent
off two days before I received the charming packet
about which you are pleased to talk so much nonsense
in the way of apology. You must forgive the scolding,
and you will forgive it, I am sure; for you know I was
not then apprised of the grand evils of mind and body
by which you were assailed—the teeth and the rats. I
hope those enemies are in a good train to be overcome
and cured—that the teeth are multiplying and the rats
decreasing. N.B. If you want a first-rate breed of cats
we can supply you. We have a white cat, half Persian,
as deaf as a post, with one eye blue and the other yellow, who, besides being a great beauty, is the best rat-
catcher in the county. Shall we save you one of the
next litter of white kittens?

You ask me about Blackwood's 'Edinburgh Magazine:' I will tell you just what it is—a very libellous,
naughty, wicked, scandalous, story-telling, entertaining
work—a sort of chapel-of-ease to my old friend, the
'Quarterly Review;' abusing all the wits and poets
and politicians of *our* side, and praising all of *yours;*
abusing Hazlitt, abusing John Keats, abusing Leigh
Hunt, abusing (and that is really too bad) abusing Haydon, and lauding Mr. Gifford, Mr. Croker, and Mr. Can-

ning. But all this, especially the abuse, is very cleverly
done; and I think you would be amused by it. I particularly recommend to you the poetical notices to correspondents, the 'Mad Banker of Amsterdam,' and
some letters on the sagacity of the shepherd's dog, by
that delightful poet James Hogg.

Were you not heart-struck at the awful catastrophe
of Sir Samuel Romilly? The sacrifice of his own reputation, the very victim of admiration and respect! Any
other man would have been suspected—any other man
would have been guarded, watched, and saved. But in
his case, the physicians themselves forgot the ascendancy of the body over the mind. They reckoned him
invulnerable even to fever and delirium. In a word,
they overlooked the mysterious fellowship of Nature
and of Fate, which levels the strongest with the weakest.
The mistake was most fatal to his country. We have
lost all our greatest—Fox, Pitt, Nelson, Whitbread, and
the poor princess; but this loss is, in my mind, the
greatest of all. He was so pure, so perfect, so kind, so
true! Talent in him was so attractive! Eloquence
so useful! Virtue so commanding! We shall never
have another Sir Samuel Romilly. I will talk of something else.

When I was telling you some of Mr. Wordsworth's
absurdities, did I tell you that he never dined? I
have just had a letter from Mrs. Hofland, who has been
with her husband to the Lakes, and spent some days at
a Mr. Marshall's, for whom Mr. H. was painting a
picture—but Mrs. Hofland shall speak for herself:—
"On my return from Mr. M.'s to our Ullswater cottage, I encountered a friend who condoled with me on
the dullness of my visit. 'Dull! It was delightful.'
'The long *triste* dinners, the breakfasts, the suppers,

the luncheons!' 'To be sure fourteen people must eat, but these said dinners were anything but dull, I assure you. Why do you call them so?' 'Because Mr. and Mrs. Wordsworth were staying there, and were so overcome by those shocking meals, that they were forced to come away. The Wordsworths never dine, you know; they hate such doings; when they are hungry they go to the cupboard and eat.' And really," observes Mrs. Hofland, " it is much the best way. There is Mr. Wordsworth, who will live for a month on cold beef, and the next on cold bacon; and my husband will insist on a hot dinner every day. He never thinks how much trouble I have in ordering, nor what a plague my cook is!" So you see the Wordsworth regimen is likely to spread.

> Very sincerely and affectionately yours,
>
> M. R. M.

To Sir William Elford, *Bickham, Plymouth.*

Bertram House, Dec. 8, 1818.

I was not altogether astonished, my dear friend, but it is true, Mr. R. V——— is actually married to your fair neighbour Miss Phœbe R———. Did I ever tell you the curious story of their courtship? And will you be very discreet, if I tell it you now? I shall run the risk in both cases. You must know that Mr. R——— had sons at school with the good Doctor, and Miss Phœbe, who is eminently of the sort of young woman that is called *sensible*—in contradistinction, perhaps, to clever— was, like other young women, a great letter-writer; so she wrote sense and kindness to her brothers, and she wrote flattery to the Doctor—and the Doctor began to think her a very extraordinary person, and he told her so—and she thought him a very great man, and she told him so. So at last the Doctor fairly fell in love with her, not for himself, but for his sons, and invited her to Reading with the open and expressed intention of giving her the choice of them. Now, poor Miss Phœbe was in that state which is of all others most favourable to the admission of a new lover—she had just lost an old one. Mr. Philip W——, to whom she was engaged, had very fairly jilted her and married another lady. So to Reading she came, and the Doctor summoned his sons, according to promise. From London, from college, from ship-board they came ; but unluckily when they arrived the fair damsel was invisible. She had taken cold on her journey, and was in the paroxysm of a rheumatic fever. The Doctor, however, took heart. He set the first-class 'Miss R——' for a theme in English verse. Is not this a fine stroke of professional gallantry ? And he sent up the melodious produce to the fair inspirer, by his eldest and favourite son, the identical Richard who is now her husband. He did not content himself with sending up copies of verses, but tea and oranges, coffee and flummery (I myself saw a basin of the last so conveyed). People wondered a little at the Doctor's French manners ; but he knew the sex, or at least he knew the woman. I tanswered. "The heart was caught," as Miss Edgeworth says, "at the rebound ;" Miss R—— swallowed the flattery and the flummery, the love and the lemonade ; she lost her heart and her fever ; and when she left her room at the end of three weeks she was again an engaged woman.

Seriously, however, this singular courtship has mellowed into a very strong and sincere attachment—an attachment which has weathered many storms, and has at last, perhaps, precipitated them into a marriage of affection rather than of prudence. I most sincerely wish them happy.

What made you think me a Republican? Much as I adore the arts of Greece, I see nothing to admire in their governments. The eternal scuffles of those little republics must have produced a great quantity of misery and marred a great quantity of good. Rome (will you forgive me for saying so?)—Rome always seemed to me the most disagreeable subject, and the Romans the most outrageous, strutting, boasting barbarians on the face of the earth—cold, hard, empty, strong, just like one of their own aqueducts. An Englishman's worst vice is more human than a Roman's best virtue. I don't even like Shakespeare's Roman plays, because they are Roman. Venice, too, was nothing very charming—a parcel of squabbling lords, little kings, sucking tyrants, and a bestridden and enslaved people. England's trial of a republic ended in a very wise and very glorious king called Oliver; and France's bloody experiment had the same conclusion. You will hardly venture again to doubt my being a very orthodox lover of a limited monarchy—the best and the freest mode of government that ever was devised by human wisdom. Don't you think we shall meet at last? Don't I improve very much?

Very affectionately yours,

M. R. MITFORD.

To SIR WILLIAM ELFORD, *Bickham, Plymouth.*

Bertram House, Dec. 28, 1818.

MY DEAR FRIEND,

Did I ever mention to you or did you ever hear elsewhere of a Miss Nevinson,* poetess, novelist, essayist, and reviewer? I have just been writing to her in answer to a very kind letter; but writing in such alarm

---

* This is a description, and a very just one, of Mrs. Charles Gore. She was the stepdaughter of Dr. Nevinson, to whom her mother was married. But her name was Moody.

that I quivered and shook, and looked into the dictionary to see how to spell The, and asked mamma if there were two T's in Tottering. You never saw anybody in such a fright. It was like writing in chains—and now that I am writing to you, for whom I don't care a pin, it's like a galley-slave let loose from the oar.

Such is my horror of being forced to mind my P's and Q's, to look to my stops and see to my spelling, to be fine and sensible and literary—and so alarming a lady is Miss Nevinson, so sure to put one on the defensive, even when she has no intention to attack. This is no great compliment to my fair correspondent—but it is the truth. Miss Nevinson is a very extraordinary woman; her conversation (for I don't think very highly of her writings) is perhaps the most dazzling and brilliant that can be imagined.

I have just been reading Hazlitt's 'View of the Stage'—a series of critiques originally printed in the different newspapers, particularly the 'Chronicle' and the 'Examiner.' I had seen most of them before, but I could not help reading them all together; though so much of Hazlitt is rather dangerous to one's taste—rather like dining on sweetmeats and supping on pickles. So poignant is he, and so rich, everything seems insipid after him. This amusement, great as it always would have been, was very much heightened to me by recollecting so well the first publication of the best articles —those on Kean in the 'Morning Chronicle.'* I was at Tavistock House at the time, and well remember the doleful visage with which Mr. Perry used to contemplate the long column of criticism, and how he used to

---

* The belief of the time was, that Hazlitt received 1500*l.* from the management of Drury Lane for those articles. They made Kean's reputation and saved the theatre.

execrate "the d—d fellow's d—d stuff" for filling up so
much of the paper in the very height of the advertise-
ment season. I shall never forget his long face. It
was the only time of the day that I ever saw it either
long or sour. He had not the slightest suspicion that
he had a man of genius in his pay—not the most
remote perception of the merit of the writing—nor the
slightest companionship with the author. He hired
him, as you hire your footman; and turned him off
(with as little or less ceremony than you would use in
discharging the aforesaid worthy personage) for a very
masterly but damaging critique on Sir Thomas Lawrence, whom Mr. P., as one whom he visited and was
being painted by, chose to have praised. Hazlitt's
revenge was exceedingly characteristic. Last winter,
when his 'Characters of Shakspeare' and his lectures,
had brought him into fashion, Mr. Perry remembered
him as an old acquaintance and asked him to dinner,
and a large party to meet him, to hear him talk, and
to show him off as the lion of the day. The lion came
—smiled and bowed—handed Miss Bentley to the dining-
room—asked Miss Perry to take wine—said once "Yes"
and twice "No"—and never uttered another word
the whole evening. The most provoking part of this
scene was, that he was gracious and polite past all expression—a perfect pattern of mute elegance—a silent Lord
Chesterfield; and his unlucky host had the misfortune
to be very thoroughly enraged without anything to
complain of.

Most faithfully and affectionately yours,
M. R. MITFORD.

49

CHAPTER III.

LETTERS FOR 1819.

To SIR WILLIAM ELFORD, *Bickham, Plymouth.*

Bertram House, Jan. 9, 1819.

CONSIDERING my doleful prognostications, you will like to know, my dear friend, that I have outlived the ball,* so I must write. It's a thing of necessity. Yes, I am living and "lifelich," as Chaucer says. And that I did survive that dreaded night, I owe principally to that charming thing, a dandy. Don't you like dandies, the beautiful race? I am sure you must. But such a dandy as our dandy few have been fortunate enough to see. In general they are on a small scale—slim, whipper-snapper youths, fresh from college—or new mounted on a dragoon's saddle—dainty light-horse men, or trim schoolboys. Ours is of a Patagonian breed—six feet and upwards without his shoes, and broad in proportion. Unless you have seen a wasp in a solar microscope you have never seen anything like him. Perhaps a Brobdignagian hour-glass might be more like him still, only I don't think the hour-glass would be small enough in the waist.

Great as my admiration has always been of the mechanical inventions of this age, I know nothing that has given me so high an idea of the power of machinery—not the Portsmouth Blockhouses, or the new Mint—as that perfection of mechanism by which those ribs are endued in

* At Mrs. Dickinson's.

those stays. I think one or two must have been broken, to render such a compression possible. But it is unjust to dwell so exclusively on the stays, when every part of the thing was equally perfect. Trousers—coat—neck-cloth—shirt-collar—head, inside and out—all were in exact keeping. Every look, every word, every attitude belonged to those inimitable stays. Sweet dandy! I have seen nothing like him since Liston, in Lord Grizzle. He kept me awake and alive the whole evening. Dancing or sitting still, he was my "cynosure." I followed him with my eyes as a schoolboy follows the vagaries of his top or the rolling of his hoop. Much and generally as he was admired; I don't think he made so strong an impression on any one as on me. He is even indebted to me for the distinguished attention of a great wit, whose shafts I was lucky enough to direct to that impenetrable target of dandyism. All this he owes to me, and is likely to owe me still—for I am sorry to say my dandy is an ungrateful dandy. Our admiration was by no means mutual. "He had an idea," he said (a very bold assertion by-the-by)—"he had an idea that I was blue-ish." So he scoured away on being threatened with an introduction. Well, peace be to him, poor swain! and better fortune—for the poor dandy is rather unlucky. He fell into the Thames last summer on a water-party and got wet through his stays; and this autumn, having affronted a young lady, and being knocked down by her brother, a lad not nineteen, he had the misfortune to fall flat on his back, and was forced to lie till some one came to pick him up, being too strait-laced to help himself.

Adieu, my dear friend. I am always

Most affectionately yours,

M. R. MITFORD.

To R. B. HAYDON, ESQ., 22, *Lisson Grove.*

Bertram House, Jan. 12, 1819.

MY DEAR SIR,

I avail myself of the influx of members occasioned by the Quarter Sessions to thank you for all the kindness of your very feeling letter, and to express once again the strong interest we all take in your welfare. *All,* I trust, has gone well with you the last month; and most of all, I hope that your strength and your eyes have continued to improve. Firm health and strong sight are indeed almost all that your friends need ask for you. Such genius, so directed, must force its way to fame and fortune.

Your kindness will, I know, be gratified in hearing that things are looking better with us. A great point has been gained before the Master of the Rolls, and though there is no great chance of a chancery suit's making haste, we have the comfort of knowing that there is little doubt of our ultimate success within no very unreasonable period. My poor uncle, too, is likely soon to be released. It seems as if the magic of your good wishes had had a favourable influence on our destiny, for the decision of the Master of the Rolls arrived the very day after your kind and inspiriting letter. I cannot sufficiently thank you for your cheering caution against mental depression. My dear sir, it was needless.

Amongst the many blessings I enjoy—my dear father, my admirable mother, my tried and excellent friends—there is nothing for which I ought to thank God so earnestly as for the constitutional buoyancy of spirits, the aptness to hope, the will to be happy, which I inherit from my father. Yes, I agree with you in all you say. I am grateful to misfortune for having shown me how much goodness and kindness exist in the world. They who have been always prosperous may be misanthropes; they cannot know a tenth part of the excellence of their fellow-creatures.

[*The conclusion of this letter is missing.*]

To Sir William Elford, *Bickham, Plymouth.*

Bertram House, Feb. 10, 1819.

I have been reading some very amusing old writings, edited a few years back—'Letters selected from the Bodleian Library,'—Hearne's 'Visit to Reading, &c.,' —and last not least, 'Aubrey's Lives' (a little softened and purified I believe). Oh! what a delicious painter of mind and body is that worshipful Master Aubrey! Why is it that English people in this age can no more write portraits like him than the present race of Italians can paint portraits like Titian? And yet we are good colourists; we can give fancy pictures well enough, as witness Scott, Miss Austen, and novelists by the dozen. But we can't take a likeness; there is no biographer of the present day who has given anything like the graphic identity of Aubrey or Izaac Walton to his hero. Boswell, indeed, has enabled us to paint for ourselves the picture of Dr. Johnson; but Aubrey would have given him in half a page. At one stroke of the pen we should have seen the lexicographer.

I think one reason why we have no Aubreys now is, that we do not sufficiently cultivate the habit of truth— severe, scrupulous truth. We paint in praise or in caricature—in oil or in fresco—led away by love or by fancy, or by naughty wicked wit. I myself, without the excuse of wit, am sometimes conscious, though I always speak as I think and believe, that memory and imagination and fondness may sometimes give too sunshiny a character to my portraits; and that the ridiculous (my pet dandy always excepted) is not quite so ridiculous, abroad and walking, as set down upon paper.

You must write soon and long. Think how much we have been disappointed by not seeing you. Papa and mamma beg their kindest remembrances, and I am ever,
Most faithfully and affectionately yours,

M. R. MITFORD.

P.S. Are you interested in the reprinting of old poetry? We are likely to have some selections printed in great style at Reading. Mr. Milman, whose taste and genius fit him so exactly for an editor of such gems, and who has the wide range of Mr. Heber's library, has been lucky enough to find a curate ready placed, who is equally qualified for the mechanical part of printing; so they are going to procure a private press and fall to printing ding-dong.

To B. R. HAYDON, ESQ., 22, *Lisson Grove.*

Bertram House, Feb. 13, 1819.

MY DEAR SIR,

My father is going to-morrow into Hampshire to course for a few days, and tells me that he hopes to be able to send you a hare. I take the opportunity to thank you a thousand times for your kind letter and kinder promise. You must not forget it—*we* shall not, I assure you; and I trust when my father goes to London you will be able to fix a time for favouring us with your company. Not content with plaguing you with a note, I have been so encroaching as to trouble you with a book, very little worth the honour of your acceptance. It was written when extreme youth and haste might apologise for the incorrectness, the silliness, and the commonplace with which it abounds; but I am

afraid it has deficiencies which are worse than any fault.
Do not think of reading it through. If your kind indulgence should lead you to look at any part, let it be
‘ Beauty,’ ‘ Sunset,’ and ‘ The Voice of Praise.’   They
are not better—that is too vain a word—but less bad
than the rest.

I am enchanted to hear you have a favourite greyhound.   My pet is neither very good nor very handsome.   I did not choose him—he chose me.   He sought
me, followed me, loved me, would be loved, and was
loved.   There is no resisting preference and affection,
come from where they may ; so he is my pet.   He has
a rival just now, in papa’s heart, in the shape of a beautiful puppy sent to me as a present, who has associations
in her favour which are almost irresistible—having been
pupped in an outhouse belonging to the identical
butcher’s shop at Stratford-upon-Avon where Shakspeare was born.   She is moreover, exceedingly beautiful—blue, all sprinkled with little white spots ; just like
a starry night.   We call her Miranda : you know it is
the coursing etiquette that the initial of the dog’s name
should correspond with the master’s.

Your pupils have done that which I thought impossible ; they have added to your fame.   Every new
arrival from town talks of their drawings.   How very
fine drawings must be to make people talk of them !
Yes ; you will certainly found a school in this land
of fogs and liberty, and we shall live to see it.*

Adieu, my dear sir.   Papa and mamma beg their
kindest remembrances and good wishes, and I am ever

Most sincerely yours,
M. R. MITFORD.

* Here there is written in pencil, by Haydon, across the letter : “ Ah
my dear friend, not with these pupils.—B. R. H.”

To Sir William Elford, *Bickham, Plymouth.*

Bertram House, Feb. 27, 1819.

I find by a letter from Mrs. Hofland, my dear Sir William, that she, poor dear woman, has sent you the Proposals of her book.* If you should have the goodness, when you go into Plymouth, merely to leave the Proposals on the table in the reading-room, it might do good. I take the liberty to make this request because it is one that cannot give you much trouble and may do good, and, above all, because the sale of these miserable fifty copies is all poor Mr. Hofland is likely to get for the paintings— drawings—journeys—his wife's writing —and, which is worst of all, the whole of the engraving." Not an engraver in London would strike a single stroke on the Duke of Marlborough's credit ; and the Duke of Marlborough had not (to use his own elegant phrase) " a brass farthing " to repay Mr. Hofland.

I can tell you when we meet some curious anecdotes of this noble Duke. Mrs. Hofland came from White-knights here. The Duke left the house at the same time, taking away with him the contents of the larder, half a cold turkey, and three-quarters of a ham. After he had driven off, he remembered that he had left behind some scraps of a loin of mutton, and actually went back to fetch them. The servants are not on board wages, observe ; and the housekeeper, knowing they could not get even a twopenny loaf without twopence, and naturally alarmed at this clearance of eatables, ventured to ask His Grace for money. After much stuttering, he gave her ten pounds. All this time, for him and his son there were waiting three carriages with four post-horses each—one of them empty. Is

* It consisted of plates from Mr. Hofland's ' Views of White-knights.'

not this stopping one hole in a cullender? Mrs.
Hofland saw the whole transaction. You should
hear her tell the story, with the Duke's stuttering,
Lord Charles's dandyism, and the poor housekeeper's
dismal whine. She cannot help laughing in the midst
of her troubles.

Catching cold will be a very easy exploit in this
weather. It freezes, snows, hails, and rains every
day regularly; demolishes my primroses, cuts up my
violets, souses poor Miranda, and dirties the white cat.
All this tornado, too, is come after an absolute spring.
A fortnight ago papa found a pheasant's nest with four
eggs in Lord Braybrooke's park; grass was springing,
flowers were blooming, and the elder leaves coming
out: now we have winter in its worst and dreariest
form — a white world every morning, a black one
every night—nothing will be easier than to catch
cold.

Did you never remark how superior old gaiety is
to new? There is a critical and comparative spirit
about us moderns, which dulls the sunshine. They
laughed where we sneer. We cannot fire a *feu de joie*
without loading it with ball cartridges. Well, I will
not talk any more of books, lest you should say, like a
friend of mine, " My dear Miss Mitford, you read so
much that you will finish by knowing nothing." This
pretty speech was made five years ago; what would he
say now? But reading is my favourite mode of idleness. I like it better than any of my play-works—
better than fir-coning—better than violeting—better
than working gowntails — better than playing with
Miranda—better than feeding the white kitten—better
than riding in a gig—better than anything except that
other pet idleness, talking (that is to say *writing*) to

you. Adieu, my dear friend. Papa and mamma desire their kindest regards. Write, and, above all, come.

Ever most affectionately yours,

MARY RUSSELL MITFORD.

To SIR WILLIAM ELFORD, *Bickham, Plymouth.*

Bertram House, March 13, 1819.

Do you know, my dear friend, that I am holding the responsible office of Critic to a volume of Translations which Mr. Dickinson is about to print at his private press as soon as ever they have undergone *my* last revisal! There's for you! translations from Dante—Tasso—Ariosto—Petrarch—Ovid, and Virgil. Very fine translations too, combining in a most extraordinary degree fidelity to the words and the spirit of the author, with the most flowing versification and the purest style. The Ugolino and Isabella stories are superb. These Italian people are my old acquaintance. I was not quite so intimate with the Latin gentlemen. I had read Dryden's Virgil, to be sure—but then it was a long time ago; and of Mr. Ovid I knew nothing at all. I have now had the honour of an introduction to his Tale of Phaëton, and I think him a very fine fellow indeed. I don't know anybody who talks so much magnificent nonsense. He goes far beyond Mr. Southey—' Kehama ' is " pale pink compared to the flaming scarlet " of the ' Metamorphoses.' The fourth Æneid, too, surprised me with its matchless beauties, and its—in my mind—intolerable faults. How Virgil could make his pious hero such a cold, heartless, abominable rascal, and his tender heroine such an incomparable fool, passes my comprehension. In the critical readings which passed between Mr. and Mrs. Dickinson and myself, we of

course did not fail to compare Mr. D.'s translations with
those of others—Pitt's, Dryden's, and Beresford's—
which last has, without intending it, all the merit of a
travestie. In the finest part of Dido's passion, where
she talks of sacrificing her faithful lover, immolating
his son, and so forth, Mr. Beresford very quietly makes
her say, "Why should not I kill Ascanius and *dish him*
to his father?" This Mr. Beresford was no other than
the author of the 'Miseries,' &c., and this doughty translation is subscribed for by all Oxford and half Cambridge. I think they ought to have known better
—don't you?

To Sir William Elford, *Bickham, Plymouth.*

Bertram House, April 8, 1819.

No, I have not fixed any time for going to town.
I don't think I shall be there before the middle of
May. It depends on half a hundred trifling contingen-
cies—or rather, I believe the country is so lovely in this
cowslip-tide—one has such pleasure in *doddering* along
the hedgerows, gathering violets and wood sorrel, listening to the woodlark, watching for the nightingale—
such enjoyment in the mere consciousness of existence
in this sunny springy atmosphere, with all its sweet
scents and sounds—that there is no making up one's
mind to leave it for smoky, dusty London. So I make
excuses to myself and my friends, and invent apologies
for staying at home, which everybody believes—even
myself. From all this you will find, my dear Sir William, that you must *come* and fetch the white kitten—
will you? You must come; the nightingales will never
fail us in such beautiful weather.

To Sir William Elford, 176, *Piccadilly.*

Bertram House, May 14, 1819.

So, my dear friend, you cannot make out my writing! And my honoured father cannot help you! Really this is too affronting! The two persons in all the world who have had the most of my letters cannot read them! Well; there is the secret of your liking them so much. Obscurity is sometimes a great charm. You just make out my meaning, and fill it up by the force of your own imagination. The outline is mine; the colouring your own. So much the better for me. There are. however, persons who write a worse hand than I. Here is my friend Mr. Dickinson; if you saw his writing! He can't read it himself. And if you heard him admire mine! *Parmi les aveugles les borgnes sont rois.* He thinks me the greatest (what is the fine grand word for a person who writes a good hand?)—the greatest calligrapher that ever trode the earth. The word that puzzled you is Undine. Can you read it now?

I have heard, in two letters from town from people who love painting, of the fine landscape which papa tells me is to be a landscape royal—O rare! He tells me, too, of the flowers which are not in the Exhibition, but which will be, I hope, next year. I always thought the anemone one of the loveliest of all flowers—the one which is fittest for painting, because it has no scent to lose, and all its charms can be given by that lovely art. Some of the purple and red single anemones preserve the rich, lost tints of the old stained glass. You are lucky, that a friend is just come to interrupt me, and save you a platitude about Nature's never losing a beauty or a secret, &c., &c.

Good-bye, my dear Sir William.

Ever most affectionately yours,

M. R. Mitford.

To Sir William Elford, *Bickham, Plymouth.*

Bertram House, May 30, 1819.

Papa having made Mr. Dundas promise and re-promise not to transmogrify you into a lady (as once before happened, you know, my dear friend), I avail myself of his obliging offer to transmit to you " these presents." How charming is the new volume of Horace Walpole's letters! He was, beyond doubt, the best letter-writer of his day—better than Gray—better than Cowper. You and I thought so always. I do not think very highly of Madame D'Arblay's books. The style is so strutting. She does so stalk about on Dr. Johnson's old stilts. What she says wants so much translating into common English, and when translated would seem so commonplace, that I have always felt strongly tempted to read all the serious parts with my fingers' ends.

Lady Pitt's death has added a thousand a year to the Duke of Wellington's new estate. This great captain of ours is a prodigiously lucky man. Besides the property, he gets a very pretty place, finely situated.

Ever most affectionately yours,

M. R. Mitford.

To Sir William Elford, *Bickham, Plymouth.*

Bertram House, June 8, 1819.

Next to reading with an undivided and enthusiastic admiration (such as I feel for the ' Faerie Queen,' you for 'Tom Jones,' and both of us for 'Pride and Prejudice ')—next to that absorbing delight, the greatest pleasure in reading is to be critical and fastidious, and laugh at and pull to pieces. Whether this be wise or not, I cannot tell; both the child and the botanist are amused in picking off the leaves of the flowers, to come at the internal structure; and perhaps the younger

philosopher, who performs this operation from the mere
instinct of mischief, is as happy—that is, as wise—as
the graver and elder demolisher. I am no scientific
puller to pieces, at all events; though lately I have
almost wished myself a reviewer, to vent my grievances
at a quantity of maudlin travels that I have been
reading—'Walks in Switzerland,' 'Autumns near the
Rhine,' 'Picturesque Tours,' ' Visits to La Trappe,' and
countless others, names forgotten. Don't you think
there ought to be a high duty on such an importation
of nonsense in these times of financial difficulty?
though very likely a tax of this sort would not catch
them. These travels are perhaps all written at home.
But to me there is a real grievance in having the bloom
brushed from the grape—in disenchanting the Dulcineas
of one's imagination—in cutting asunder the fine links
by which great names are united to local objects—in
turning that which should be a vision and a dream
into dull and flat reality; making Meillerie as common
as Old Brentford, and laying Vaucluse as open as
Hounslow Heath. I have a good mind not to read
another book of travels till Dr. Clarke's next volume.

Before I have done with books, I must ask if you have
seen an imitation of your particular favourite, Mr.
Wordsworth, called 'Peter Bell?' He, the real Mr.
Wordsworth, had announced a ditty so called; and
some wicked wit, much of your mind with regard to
that great poet, came out a week before him with this
parody by anticipation. I only saw it the other day for
five minutes; but I thought it extremely clever, particularly an epitaph on Mr. Wordsworth, which I don't
quite recollect, but which was to this effect :—

"Here Lyeth W. W.
Who never more will trouble you, trouble you."

You will agree with me that these lines are not to
be forgotten.

Adieu, once more.

Bertram House, June 29, 1819.

A novel should be as like life as a painting, but not
as like life as a piece of waxwork. Madame D'Arblay
has much talent, but no taste. She degrades her
heroines in every possible way, bodily and mental. All
her heroines—nothing can exceed her impartiality in
this respect—Cecilia, Evelina, Camilla, and Juliette,
all go into cowhouses and keep bad company. She has
no touch of Cæsar's nicety about her. Another fault,
which I think I have mentioned before, is the sameness
of her characters; they all say one thing twenty times
over. In some Russian travels—I don't remember
whether Dr. Clarke's or Sir H. K. Porter's—there is an
account of a concert of wind instruments performed by
an almost countless number of vassals of some great
lord, each of whose instruments has but one single
note, so that the living machines form themselves the
entire musical scale. Now Madame D'Arblay's characters are like these vassals. They have but one
note.

I had the other day a letter from Mrs. Hofland,
who, in the midst of a long critique on the pictures in
the Exhibition, speaks thus of a certain landscape of
your acquaintance: "Sir W. E.'s picture is a very
beautiful natural scene, most beautifully and honestly
painted—not slipped over like a whitewasher, as Mr.
Turner does things, and as your favourite, Mr. Wordsworth, writes poems" (by-the-by, Mrs. Hofland is mistaken there—Wordsworth is the highest finisher of any

poet going); "but done as if the thing was worth doing —as I take it everything should be, if done at all."

Most affectionately yours,

M. R. MITFORD.

I can't let even this little "way-bit" go unscrolled, so I must tell you that during my week of solitude I (to use Lucy's new-fangled word) "*haymaked*" with great vigour and success. The weather had not then taken its present desperate crying fit, the sun was good-humoured, 'the haymakers dexterous, their mistress both lucky and wise. In short, we got it all in without a drop of rain, untouched by either element, fire or water. There's for you! I wish you may do the same. Good-bye.

To SIR WILLIAM ELFORD, *Bickham, Plymouth.*

July 28, 1819.

"Why, wizard, thus disturb my dormant life
And raise me through the water's misty strife?
Oh, cease! your high behests with speed disclose;
With speed dismiss me to my dread repose!"

It is not from laziness, believe me, my dear friend, that I have sent you your four lines unaltered. I have been altering them all the morning, turning and twisting them twenty different ways; and, on an impartial survey of the several readings, am convinced that your version is much the best. Mine all look *patched*. Indeed, I write verses so seldom now that I have lost the little power I once possessed. The reason of my not sending you any of my attempts is, that I fear your modesty or your politeness might tempt you to prefer my bad lines to your good ones, and I would not put such a risk in your way.

Did I tell you in my last, for really I don't remember (deuce take Professor Brown's great book), that I have got a new pet? All this warm weather I sit out of doors in the plantations; just on one side of my seat is a filbert tree, the branches of which spread quite across my feet, and on these branches every day comes a young redbreast. First of all he appeared at a distance, then he came nearer, then he came close home, and now, the moment I call "Bobby," he comes. Mossy himself is not more tame or more fond; he comes on my feet and my gown, feeds almost on my hand (not quite), and has by example tamed his papa and one or two of his brothers and sisters, who come like him and feed from a board on the tree, quite close to me; but they do not, like my own Bobby, come when they are called. Is this usual in the summer? I know they are tame in the winter; but this is quite a young bird—has never known cold or hunger. He had not a red feather in his breast a fortnight ago. He likes very much to be talked to, in a soft, monotonous, caressing tone—"Bobby! Bobby! Bobby!"—and turns his little head in the prettiest attitudes of listening that you can imagine, and generally finishes by taking two or three flights across me, so close as almost to touch my face. I shall be sorry to leave him. I think I shall try to get it put in the deeds that Mr. Elliott must feed Bobby!

How very good you were to transcribe for me Mr. Cranstoun's account of young Napoleon; though perhaps one had rather that he were more like a boy. One does not imagine his father to have been so sedate a person at his age. But princes, poor things, never can be children. Their luckless station will not let them; and that, I suppose, is one reason why so few of them turn out great men. Did you ever hear that a

damsel of his own rank and age—a little princess of
the Netherlands—is desperately in love with this young
Buonaparte ? She vows she will never marry any one
else. She will have him. She is as violently in love
with him as most heroines of her years are with a doll
or a dumpling. I understand the young lady is a very
promising subject—a charming, naughty, refractory
child, full of self-will and attraction. Adieu.

Ever most affectionately yours,

M. R. M.

[The following paper, written by Miss Mitford, containing some of the dog's hair, was found in an envelope,
sealed with black.]

My own dear darling Mossy's hair, cut off after he
was dead by dear Drum, August 22nd, 1819. He was
the greatest darling that ever lived ; son of Maria and
Mr. Webb's Ruler (a famous dog given him by Lord
Rivers), and was, when he died, about seven or eigh
years old. He was a large black dog, of the largest
and strongest kind of greyhounds ; very fast, and
honest and resolute past example ; an excellent killer
of hares, and a most magnificent and noble-looking
creature. His coat was of the finest and most glossy
black, with no white, except a very little under his feet
(pretty white shoe-linings, I used to call them)—
little beautiful white spot, quite small in the very
middle of his neck, between his chin and his breast—
and a white mark on his bosom. His face was singularly beautiful ; the finest black eyes, very bright, and
yet sweet, and fond, and tender—eyes that seemed to
speak ; a beautiful, complacent mouth, which used
sometimes to show one of the long, white teeth at the
side ; a jet-black nose ; a brow which was bent and

flexible, like Mr. Fox's, and gave great sweetness and expression and a look of thought to his dear face. There never was such a dog! His temper was, beyond comparison, the sweetest ever known. Nobody ever saw him out of humour. And his sagacity was equal to his temper.

Thank God, he went off without suffering. He must have died in a moment. I thought I should have broken my heart when I came home and found what had happened. I shall miss him every moment of my life; I have missed him every instant to-day—so have Drum and Granny. He was laid out last night in the stable, and this morning we buried him in the middle plantation, on the house side of the fence, in the flowery corner, between the fence and Lord Shrewsbury's fields —that flowery corner which is so richly covered with bluebells, orchises, and pansies, and where we mean to plant primroses and cowslips. Under a fir tree, marked with his initial, he lies. We covered his dear body with flowers, every flower in the garden—cloves, carnations, jasmine, honeysuckle, sweet-william, honesty, virgin's bower, roses, and some shrubbery flowers—as well as some fine geraniums, which, as well as the rose tree, we mean to take away from here when we leave this place, for his dear sake. George and Frank Alloway buried him; and Granny, Drum, and I, Marmy, Moses, Whim, and Molly were mourners. Everybody so sorry. Everybody loved him, 'dear saint,' as I used to call him, and as I do not doubt he now is! No human being was ever so faithful, so gentle, so generous, and so fond. I shall never love anything half so well. My own beloved Mossy, Heaven bless you! Farewell! my own best beloved! I forgot to say that he was born here, at Bertram House; and that, when a little puppy of a month old,

he became so fond of me, that he would leave his
mother, Maria, to climb into my lap. He always loved
me better than all the world, my own dear Mossy; and
so I did him. God bless you, my own pet!

It will always be pleasant to me to remember that I
never teased him by petting other things, and that
everything I had he shared. He always ate half my
breakfast, and the very day before he died I fed him
all the morning with filberts. He was fond of all kinds
of fruit. His delight at seeing me when I had been out
in the gig was inexpressible. He knew the sound of
the wheels, and used to gallop to meet me, talking his
own pretty talk. He met me in this way at the white
gate on the Thursday before he died on the Saturday.
Whilst I had him I was always sure of having one who
would love me alike in riches or in poverty—who always
looked at me with looks of the fondest love—always
faithful and always kind. To think of him was a talis-
man against vexing thoughts. A thousand times I have
said "I want my Mossy," when that dear Mossy was close
by, and would put his dear black nose under my hand on
hearing his name. God bless you, my Mossy! I cried
when you died, and I can hardly help crying whenever
I think of you. All who loved me loved Mossy.

Though one of his greatest distinctions was a sweet
mildness and complacency, both of temper and of look,
yet he was most courageous and spirited and lion-like.
If any improper person came about the place he always
sent them away, and once drove off a man from the
white gate whom he thought likely to attack me.
Nobody would have ventured to insult me whilst I had
him, dear, dear darling! He was very kind to all our
other creatures, particularly poor Nell, of whom he was
very fond. All the servants loved poor dear Mossy,

especially Luce. Drum was very fond of him, so was Granny—fonder than of any other dog. We have no child of his, which is a great grief. I would give anything for one of his puppies. You understood, my Mossy, all I said, and loved to hear my voice. But you understood all that everybody said. Mamma came in one day and said, "George wants to give your dog his dinner," and Mossy got up and went to the door immediately, though she had never mentioned his name, and though he never for an instant willingly left me. God bless him! He had the most perfect confidence in me—always came to me for protection against any one who threatened him, and, thank God! always found it. I value all the things he had lately or ever touched; even the old quilt that used to be spread on my bed for him to lie on, and which we called Mossy's quilt; and the pan that he used to drink out of in the parlour, and which was called Mossy's pan, dear darling!

I forgot to say that his breath was always sweet and balmy; his coat always glossy, like satin; and he never had any disease, or anything to make him disagreeable, in his life. Many other things I have omitted; and so I should if I were to write a whole volume of his praise; for he was above all praise, sweet angel! I have enclosed some of his hair, cut off by papa after his death, and some of the hay on which he was laid out. He died Saturday, the 21st of August, 1819, at Bertram House. Heaven bless him, beloved angel!

M. R. M.

Bertram House, August 23, 1819.

His real name was Moss Trooper, only we always called him Mossy, as more affectionate.

To Sir William Elford, *Bickham.*

Bertram House, Sept. 12, 1819.

Pray have you read Evelyn's Memoirs? If not, do. Begin forthwith. The reign of the Stuarts, from Charles the First to the Revolution, has always been the part of English story that has had most attractions in my eyes. Evelyn not only gives you all the finest part of this grand fifty-years' drama, but shows the actors behind the scenes—off the stage—with their wigs thrown by and their hoops off. You meet them at dinner-parties and at plays, the Buckinghams, the Shaftesburys, the Arlingtons, the Clarendons—all the Cabal. You talk with the King and the Duke by land and by water—let houses to the Czar Peter, and show gardens to the Russells and the Sidneys—all the *dramatis personæ* of the 'Mémoires de Grammont' are before you, and half the heroes of the State Trials. Nothing can be more delightful. There are some charming letters, too, from that unlucky personage, the ex-Queen of Bohemia, whose abhorrence of the ex-Queen of Sweden is exceedingly dramatic and entertaining; and a correspondence between Lord Clarendon, when only Sir Edward Hyde, and Mr. Richard Browne, His Majesty's President at Paris, which puts the poverty of that ambulating Court in the strongest point of view possible. Only think of the Chancellor's sending the President a pistole to pay the postage of his letters, and begging the President, who had been lucky enough to light upon some wine, to pay the carriage, or he should not be able to take it in! Nothing, as I said before, can be more delightful. Pray read it.

Then I have been reading about the same people in a fine lordly book—Lord John Russell's 'Life of Lord Russell.' DON'T READ THAT. It's prodigiously heavy

indeed; it does nothing but stand still—it quarrels—it
turns up its nose—it says, How good I am to tell you
all this! You can never forget that it's by a lord and
about a lord all the way through;—that I must say,
though he's my cousin. Now Bishop Burnet tells the
same story, and he makes it interesting; but between
Bishop Burnet's book and Lord John's there is much
the same difference as between old Lord Russell alive
with his head on, and the said Lord Russell dead with
his head off.

It's a great mercy that Lord John, when he was
about it, did not take Algernon Sidney in hand. That
would have overset my patience entirely. Instead of
the cousinly and civil manner in which I have spoken
of him above, I should, I am afraid, have said something disrespectful and saucy; for Algernon Sidney is
my hero of heroes—the only rival of Napoleon in my
heart—and millions of miles above Lord Russell, whom
(to confess the truth—as a great secret—and quite in a
corner) I cannot help thinking a good deal over-rated.
He was a very good man, to be sure; too good by fifty
times, though abundantly heavy and preachy and prosy;
and, but for his excellent luck in being beheaded in
such a cause, might have lived and died without the
slightest risk of hitching in any rhyme but a dedication
or an epitaph. And (as a still greater secret—in a
still lower voice—and closer squeezed into the corner)
my opinion of his wife is pretty much the same. She
was a very good wife, to be sure, and a good mother;
though rather addicted to match-making and bishop-
making; and putting me in mind perpetually of Buck-
ingham's presentation of Richard to the mayor and
alderman: "See where his Grace stands, 'twixt two
clergymen." But to talk of her as such a miracle of

talent and character—to place her on the same line
with the Mrs. Hutchinsons, the Lady Fairfaxes, and the
Madame Rolands, is an injustice of praise for which I
can only account by the violent prejudices of party
historians, who will have angels and devils for their
personages instead of men and women. Pray don't tell.

Mr. Hofland is just now setting out on a tourification
along the banks of the Seine with no less a person than
Mr. Thelwall, the orator and democrat. One is to write
and the other to sketch; and they have bound themselves down to talk no politics. Mrs. Hofland is not a
little astonished at this conjunction; her spouse being
a Tory, not at all given to holding his tongue, and the
other a Patriot and talker by profession. She expects
nothing less than a battle royal. I expect no such thing.
. . . Strathfieldsaye remains pretty much in *statu quo*—
we hear nothing of a new house. His Grace comes to
look at it sometimes, and whirls back the same day.
He is a terrible horse-killer. Everybody regrets Lord
Rivers and the greyhounds—especially the greyhounds;
though since the loss of Mossy, I don't like the sight of
one.

Adieu, my dear friend. I shall not send this till
Wednesday, when, owing to a grand music meeting at
Reading, there will be a great influx of lords and M.P.s.

Most sincerely and affectionately yours,

M. R. MITFORD.

To SIR WILLIAM ELFORD, *Bickham, Plymouth.*

Bertram House (this pen won't write),
Sept. 26, 1819.

Our letters always cross, my dear Sir William, that
is certain. Within half an hour after Mr. Maitland had
taken *my* packet to frank, *yours* came to hand.

First of all, to answer your kind questions. I can't tell where we go, nor when. There is no more chancery suit, that is certain; but the writings are not drawn, money not paid, and so forth; and till then we shall remain here. The *where* is even more uncertain than the *when*. I have not, however, any notion that we shall migrate far from this neighbourhood; and, to tell you the truth, am desperately afraid of the famous and patriotic borough of Reading, which papa likes, for its newspaper and its justice-rooms and its elections; and which I dislike for various negative reasons.

A town of negations that Reading is—no trees—no flowers—no green fields—no wit—no literature—no elegance! Neither the society of London nor the freedom of the country. We never say a word about it, for or against—never mention the illustrious dull town; but I expect that some fine morning papa will come back and have taken a house there. And my only comfort is, that (as I foreknow), after a little grumbling and pining at the transplantation (dear me! I was just going to write "transportation"—I beg Botany Bay's pardon)—after a little shrivelling and writhing just at first—I shall settle in the new earth, put out fresh leaves, and be as sound at heart as a transplanted cabbage, or any other housewifely vegetable. The middle course, and that to which I believe my dear mamma inclines, is a cottage within a walk of Reading. This, if such a thing could be procured, I should like exceedingly. It would suit us all. Wherever we go, you shall hear all about it—never, I hope, out of your way, my dear Sir William. It would be too much to lose at once our friends and our nightingales; and at or near Reading we shall be more in your road than ever.

I have not seen the 'Welsh Mountaineers,' but your

account of the book is exactly to my taste. I care
nothing for story, and all for character. Is it not by
Catherine Hutton?

Apropos to Mr. Jeffrey and Mr. Wordsworth, I want
you to read one fair specimen of the great Laker;
and I think his best chance is, to be put in the shape
of a long parenthesis (a thing which you and I both
like, you know) into my letter. I have chosen the
'Yew Trees,' because I think it exceedingly opposite to
your notion of Mr. Wordsworth's writing, and likewise
(to be perfectly fair on my side) because I think the
lines the finest he ever wrote; but in the whole range
of English poetry it would be difficult to find any finer.

FROM MR. WORDSWORTH'S POEM ON 'THE YEW TREES.'

"But worthier still of note
Are those fraternal four of Borrowdale,
Join'd in one solemn and capacious grove;
Huge trunks! and each particular trunk a growth
Of intertwisted fibres serpentine
Up-coiling and inveterately convolved,—
Nor uninform'd with phantasy, and looks
That threaten the profane; a pillar'd shade,
Upon whose grassless floor of red-brown hue,
By sheddings from the pinal umbrage tinged
Perennially—beneath whose sable roof
Of boughs, as if for festal purpose, decked
With unrejoicing berries, ghostly shapes
May meet at noontide—Fear and trembling Hope,
Silence and Foresight—Death, the skeleton,
And Time, the shadow,—there to celebrate,
As in a natural temple scatter'd o'er
With altars undisturb'd of mossy stone,
United worship; or in mute repose
To lie, and listen to the mountain flood
Murm'ring from Glaramara's inmost caves."

The long words will remind you of Milton, as well
as the structure of the verse; but (pray don't tell) I

have sometimes thought Milton's long crabbed words were put for the sake of their length and their out-of-the-wayness. Now, Wordsworth's could not be supplied by any other. It is a perfect picture, and no other colours could have given the effect.

My dear, dear friend, I must make up my mind to finish and seal up my letter. It grows like a snowball; and if I do not fling it forthwith at your unlucky pate, it will turn into an avalanche, and crush you with its weight.

Ever most affectionately yours,
M. R. MITFORD.

To SIR WILLIAM ELFORD.

Bertram House, Nov. 9, 1819.

MY DEAR FRIEND,

Our great Berkshire Bibliomaniac (he of the Boccaccio and the Bedford missal—in other words, the Duke of Marlborough) has had all the contents of Whiteknights sold a fortnight ago, very much against his will, poor man! The *rariss:* books were all gone before—all sold at Evans's, with the sole exception of the aforesaid missal, which the Duke, by an admirable trick of legerdemain, contrived to extract from the locked case that contained it, leaving the said case for the solace of the sheriff's officers. Nothing in sleight of hand has been heard of to equal this abstraction—or rather this abduction—since the escape of the man from the quart bottle. Except the Bedford missal, the poor Duke saved nothing. Everything was sold—plants, pictures, bridges, garden seats, novels and all.

I was never before so thoroughly aware of the capricious manner in which things go at an auction where there is no reserve—no power of buying in. For in-

stance, some blue cloth curtains, which a London up-
holsterer offered to put up new at fifty guineas, fetched
a hundred and thirty! A table of the most beautiful
pollard oak, inlaid with brass and exquisite woods,
which cost two hundred and fifty guineas, fetched
twenty-three! Now, the curtains were faded, common
things, scarcely in fashion; the table was quite new, in
the very finest condition, and of a beauty which has set
everybody to the buying of pollard oaks. A sideboard
of equal splendour went equally cheap, and some trumpery chandeliers equally dear.

The pictures were very good and very bad. Many of
them had been taken in discounting bills, in the manner
explained in one of Foote's farces; so had one hundred
pair of shoes, two hundred pair of leather breeches, and
some other articles. This being known threw a suspicion over the really original paintings, which (added to
their being wretchedly hung amongst all manner of
cross-lights, the highly-finished small pictures high up,
and the large ones close to the eye—together with the
auctioneer coming from Reading who was as ignorant as
all people are who live in, or within five miles of, that
town) reduced the value from the 10,000*l.* that was expected to under 2000*l.* You may imagine what wood
the man of the hammer is made of when I tell you that,
in selling a very fine head of Christ, by Guido—an undoubted and ascertained original,—he never said one
word of the picture or the master, but talked grandly
and eloquently of the frame. I am very glad of this
incredible ignorance, since it let poor Edmund Havill
(a Reading artist) into an excellent bargain, and Mr.
Hofland, I hope, into something still better. He has
bought several pictures, particularly an exceedingly
beautiful L. Caracci.

Now, good-night, my dear friend. I dare say I shall find something more to say by Monday.

Nov. 12.

I am just fresh from Farley Hill, where I have been spending part of two days. Thank you, Mrs. Dickinson is going on very well, and sends compliments to you. Mr. Dickinson was just fresh arrived from Slough— Dr. Herschel's. Do you know anything of the worthy astronomer? I was interested by Mr. Dickinson's account of him and his goings on. He has at last been obliged to dismount his telescope, and relinquish his observations; but, till within the last year, he and his sister sat up every night, he observing, and she writing as he dictated. The brother is eighty-two and the sister seventy, and they have pursued this course these twenty, thirty, forty years. Is not this a fine instance of female devotion—of the complete absorption of mind and body in the pursuits of the brother and friend whom she loved so well? I know as little of the stars as any other superficial woman, who looks on them with the eyes of fancy rather than science, and I have no great wish to know more, but I cannot help almost envying Miss Herschel's beautiful self-devotion. It is the true glory of woman, and in an old woman still more interesting than in a young one. Poor Herschel himself lost an eye some time ago; four or five glasses snapped, one after another, as he was making an observation on the sun, and a ray fell directly on his eye. That divine luminary does not choose to be pryed into.

I must tell you a little story of Haydon, at which I could not help laughing. Leigh Hunt (not the notorious Mr. Henry Hunt, but the fop, poet, and politician of the 'Examiner') is a great keeper of birthdays. He was celebrating that of Haydn, the great composer—giving a dinner, crowning his bust with laurels, berhyming the poor dead German, and conducting an apotheosis in full form. Somebody told Mr. Haydon that they were celebrating *his* birthday. So off he trotted to Hampstead, and bolted in to the company—made a very fine animated speech—thanked them most sincerely for the honour they had done him and the arts in his person. But they had made a little mistake in the day. His birthday, &c., &c., &c.

Now, this *bonhommie* is a little ridiculous, but a thousand times preferable to the wicked wit of which the poor artist was the dupe. Did you ever hear this story? It was told me by a great admirer of Mr. Haydon's and friend of Leigh Hunt's. He is rather a dangerous friend, I think. He chooses his favourites to laugh at —a very good reason for his being so gracious to me! Good-night, once more, my dear friend. You know I always write to you at the go-to-bed time, just as fires and candles are going out. Good-night!

Ever most affectionately yours,
M. R. MITFORD.

To Sir William Elford, *Bickham, Plymouth.*

Bertram House, Dec. 4, 1819.

I thought you would laugh at the Haydon story.

I am pretty sure that the painting will be finished this spring, because the grand difficulty, the head of Christ, is at length overcome. The present head is the seventh he has painted! One of them was taken from himself! which seems to me quite as good a trait as the birthday; for, though his countenance is very intellectual and full of spirit and ardency, it is, I think, one of the very last human faces that anybody but the owner would think of copying for Jesus Christ. Pray don't tell this story of the head, which Mr. Hofland told me, and which might set our two fiery artists in a flame. You, whose poetical faith is, I believe, rather Pope-ish, would have liked to see a portrait of Pope which Mrs. Hofland says they have just had in the house—" taken very young—an undoubted original, by Jarvis; a sweeter expression, a more intelligent countenance, cannot be conceived; no unholy or selfish feeling had yet ruffled the soft serenity of the brow, which even Dr. Morris, of Aberystwith, would allow to be wide enough and high enough for a poet." Should not you have discovered this not to be my writing, even if I had omitted the inverted commas, by the continuity of the style—the absence of that perpetual hopping motion which distinguishes mine?

Most affectionately yours,
M. R. MITFORD.

To Sir WILLIAM ELFORD, *Bickham, Plymouth.*

Bertram House, Dec. 28, 1819.

Your kind and delightful letter, my dear friend, was quite a treat. Only think of my never having before seen Clarkson's ' History of the Abolition of the Slave Trade '—that most interesting book on the most interesting subject; where I met with your name mentioned in a manner even to raise my opinion of my kind correspondent, and feel prouder than ever of being called his friend. I never knew before that you had taken an active part in the abolition, still less did I imagine that the admirable idea of the section of a slave ship had originated with you. You must have seen Clarkson's book. Setting all the interest of the subject aside, is not the work powerfully written? There are none of the outward marks of fine writing, but there must be the spirit. It laid hold of my mind like a romance; I could not put it down—could not get it out of my thoughts and my memory.

By-the-way, I never hear you talk of Hazlitt. Did you never read any of his works? Never read 'The Round Table'? the 'Characters of Shakespeare's Plays?' the 'Lectures on English Poetry'? or the 'Lectures on the English Comic Writers'? The Quarterly Reviewers give him a bad character, but that merely regards politics, and politics ought not to weigh in works of general literature. I am sure you would like them; they are so exquisitely entertaining, so original, so free from every sort of critical shackle; the style is so delightfully *piquant*, so sparkling, so glittering, so tasteful, so condensed; the images and illustrations come in such rich and graceful profusion that one seems like Aladdin in the magic garden, where the leaves were emeralds, the flowers sapphires, and the fruit topazes and rubies. Do read some of the lectures. You will not agree with half Mr. Hazlitt's opinions, neither do I, but you will be very much entertained. Every now and then two or three pages together are really like a series of epigrams, particularly in the 'Lectures on the Living Poets.' There is a character of your friend Mr. Wordsworth which will enchant you.

Mamma is come back from Winchester, and joins papa in kindest regards.

Most affectionately yours,
M. R. MITFORD.

CHAPTER IV.

CONTAINING LETTERS TO MARCH, 1820, THE LAST WHICH WERE
WRITTEN FROM BERTRAM HOUSE.

To SIR WILLIAM ELFORD, *Bickham, Plymouth.*

Bertram House, Jan. 24, 1820.

IT hails and rains, and blows and thaws, so that I
cannot walk. It is so dark that I cannot see to work. I
got tipsy with green tea last night, and could not sleep,
so that I have a headache, and am stupid, and can't
understand what I read. All these are valid reasons
for writing to you, my dear friend, more especially
when reinforced with the fear of not hearing till I have
written; are they not? So write I shall, and plunge
at once into my letter as one does into a cold bath.
Here goes.

Have you read 'Ivanhoe?' Do you like it? What
a silly question! What two silly questions! You must
have read, and you must have liked that most gorgeous
and magnificent tale of chivalry. I know nothing so
rich, so splendid, so profuse, so like old painted glass or
a gothic chapel full of shrines and banners and knightly
monuments. The soul, too, which is sometimes wanting, is there in its full glory of passion and tenderness.
Rebecca is such a woman as Fletcher used to draw—an
Aspasia, a Bellario. There are faults, to be sure, in
plenty, if one had a mind to hunt after them; that

horrible old woman (an old crone is a necessity to Mr. Scott—he is literally hag-ridden)—that vapid heroine (the only comfort is that he leaves his readers with a consoling assurance that the hero likes the sweet Jewess best)—the melodramatic air, by which one feels almost as if the book were written for the accommodation of the artists of the Coburg and Surrey theatres, with a tournament in act the first, a burning castle in act the second, a trial by combat in act the third—nothing for a dramatist to do but to cut out the speeches, and there is a grand spectacle ready made. Then neither Richard nor Robin Hood quite comes up to one's notions of the lion-hearted king whose name the Saracen women used to still their screaming children, or the bold outlaw whom the fine ballads in Percy's 'Reliques' and Ben Jonson's still finer pastoral (did you ever read that beautiful unfinished drama 'The Lord Shepherd'?) have made one of the chartered denizens of one's fancy. But there is no finding fault with a book which puts one so much in mind of Froissart. 'Ivanhoe' is more like him than anything which has been written these three centuries.

I have just finished Mr. Hallam's 'View of Europe during the Middle Ages'; a very masterly work in its way, which confirms exactly Mr. Scott's view of manners, particularly the terrible vices of the higher orders and clergy, and puts one in mind of Froissart in a different way from 'Ivanhoe,' by making one long every moment for his picturesque minuteness instead of the large views and sweeping generalities of the author. I don't like philosophical historians who make wise remarks and write fine dissertations; do you? Live for ever the Burnets and Clarendons! Delightful tellers of what they saw! One page of such narrative is worth

whole volumes of disquisition. I am now reading
' Petrarque et Laure'—the last of Madame de Genlis'
last words; I believe she has already taken leave of the
public three times in form. I don't like Madame de
Genlis; I don't like Petrarch, whose *concetti* do not
appear to me redeemed by any truth of feeling, either
in love or poetry; and I don't believe in—'spite of all
the prosers and poetisers, L'Abbé de Sade and Lord
Woodhouselee included, who rave about Laura—I don't
believe in her. I have no notion that there ever was
such a person. I hold her to be, not a mistress, but a
muse. With all these mislikings to my author and
her hero and heroine, I still read on, seduced by Madame
de Genlis' enchanting style—her " perfect mastery of her
weapon, which is language."

Have you tried this lithography ? My friend Mr.
Hofland is working away at it with great zeal, and has
produced some very beautiful specimens. A nice invention, is it not? So direct and easy a medium of
multiplying the ideas of a great artist, without their
being chilled and spoilt by passing through other
hands. Better, because less difficult, than the dry
needle. And yet what glorious things fine etchings
are ! I have been looking at Mr. Dickinson's collection half last week. Glorious things they are, to be
sure; it was a temptation. Vandyke's, who darts the
needle with such fury into the copper; Rembrandt's,
so full of life and meaning; Daniel de Boussieu's, that
brother amateur of yours, whom few artists can match ;
Ruysdael's, which breathe the very soul of landscape ;
Waterloo's, whose wood scenes are such real forests, as
sylvan as ' As You Like It ;' and my favourite of all,
the delicate airy tasteful Weirotter. If I had been
inclined to thieving, I certainly should have taken one

of those tiny Weirotter's; his etchings seem made in fairyland.

Pray is the Duke of Kent dead yet? I want to know very much. Now, don't fancy it's only on account of crape and bombazin and broad-hemmed frills; though, to be sure, it will add very much to my grief to be obliged to buy a new gown, and I can't do without one. But really, one has a respect for the Duke of Kent. There is something of his old and venerable father about him. His talents, too, were certainly considerable—a fine public speaker—a charitable man. In short, between my loyal feelings and my desire not to be obliged to buy a new gown, I am very anxious for his recovery.

Now, my dear Sir William, I am afraid of not getting a frank, so you shall be let off with a single letter—a piece of good fortune which very seldom befalls you. Adieu! Pray write soon.

Most sincerely and affectionately yours,
M. R. MITFORD.

To SIR WILLIAM ELFORD, *Bickham, Plymouth.*
Bertram House, Jan. 30, 1820.

I have just heard that the King is dead. Poor venerable old man! It is fortunate for you that my paper is nearly filled and the servant waiting to take my letter into Reading, or I should have vented to you some of that fulness of thought and feeling which such an event forces into every mind.

Jan. 31.

I wish in good earnest that you would set about writing a novel. Do try. I began a novel myself once, and got on very prosperously for about a hundred pages of character and description. You would have liked it,

I think, for it was very light and airy, and laughed,
with some success, at my hero and heroine, and myself,
and my readers. I came to a dead stop for want of
invention. A lack of incident killed the poor thing. It
went out like a candle. In all those hundred pages not
one person had said a single word or done a single thing
but my heroine: and she—guess what she has done!
Turned the lock of a drawing-room door! After this it
was time to give up novel writing.

Did you, my dear friend, ever happen to read Mr.
Thomas Hope's book about furniture? Or do you
happen to recollect (which will do just as well) the
famous quizzing the said book met with in the 'Edinburgh Review?' The book itself seemed to me, when
I saw it in a fine presentation copy, all scarlet and gold,
to be a grand piece of furniture itself, and one as little
made to be read as a chair or a table. Well, this Mr.
Thomas Hope has, they say, written 'Anastasius.' The
'New Monthly Magazine' says so; but that's rather an
argument against the fact, inasmuch as the 'New
Monthly Magazine' does certainly, assertion for assertion, tell more lies than truths; but Lady Madalina
Palmer says so on good authority; so that this incredible fact must be believed. Perhaps I am talking
Greek to you all this time, and you have not read
'Anastasius.' Well, then, it's a book which, but for
this testimony, I should from internal evidence have
attributed at once to that prince of wickedness and
poetry, Lord Byron. It's altogether Grecian; is not
that like Lord Byron? It's exceedingly sceptical; is
not that like Lord Byron? It complains of a jealous
wife; is not that like Lord Byron? It is full of fine
and gloomy poetry (in prose), which is of the very same
style with Lord Byron's. It is still fuller of the light

derisive mockery—the tossing about of all good feeling, so gibing and so Voltaire-ish, which no one could or would do but Lord Byron. It is a most uncomfortable book—is not that like Lord Byron? And lastly, it is all full of the sneering misanthropic wretched author; is not that Lord Byron? If not written by him, it is certainly in his character; and a very powerful work it is for good and for evil—a sort of Eastern 'Gil Blas'— only bloodier, longer, less attractive. I shall remember it all my days; but I shall never think of reading it again.

Have you in your neighbourhood any infant prodigies? I have had the honour to be introduced to one lately—a little miss of seven years old, who is in training for a blue stocking, and is indeed, as far as pedantry and self-conceit and ignorance go, quite worthy of the title already. I have heard of this poor little girl off and on any time these two years. They told me she knew by heart all 'Richard,' all 'Macbeth,' all 'Twelfth Night,' all Virgil's 'Æneid,' and Tressan's 'Mythology'— a pretty selection for a child, is it not? On examination, the perilous part of the knowledge flew off. She had by rote about six lines of the witches—three of Richard's first soliloquy—none at all of 'Twelfth Night;' had never heard of Dido, and called Juno a man. But then the poor little thing was as unnatural and artificial as if she were really a second edition of the Admirable Crichton; played at no sport but the intellectual games of chess and dumb crambo; was pert and pale, and peaked and priggish—a perfect 'old woman cut shorter,' and the very reverse of the romping roly-poly thing, as round and blooming as a rose, and almost as silly, which is my *beau-idéal* of a child of that age. How much I abhor anything out of season! And how much I pitied this poor little girl! She is the only child of a very clever and ambitious mother, delighting in distinction of all sorts; and there has been the child's misfortune. I hope to see Mrs. Dickinson's little girl a perfect pattern of childish beauty, simplicity, silliness, mischief, idleness, and ignorance; these being, in my opinion, the very best foundations for a clever woman.

Ever most affectionately yours,
M. R. MITFORD.

To SIR WILLIAM ELFORD, *Bickham, Plymouth.*

Bertram House, Feb. 1820.

We saw yesterday a gentleman from Brighton, who received from Sir Matthew Tierney, a few days ago, an account of the King's health so exceedingly favourable that no man of character could have given it had his Majesty been in so precarious a state as has been imagined. He said the King was as well as ever he had been in his life. Now, Sir Matthew could not have said this of a man in whom the water was rising, and whose legs were cased every morning in sheet lead, as has been the constant report hereabouts for the last fortnight. Did you ever happen to hear how boldly and wisely Sir Matthew saved the King's life? He was dying—gasping. Sir Henry Halford was walking about the room with his head lost. Put that into French, if you don't understand it in English. His Majesty had been bled till to bleed seemed to kill, when Sir Matthew exclaimed, 'He will probably die in the bleeding, but he must die without it; so I'll bleed him.' He did so, keeping his hand on the pulse, and saved him.

The foregoing extract is from the last letter in our possession which Miss Mitford wrote from Bertram House. The impoverishment into which the family had been gradually sinking deeper and deeper had now at length reached its lowest point, and the last days of March, 1820, were employed in removing from the home which they had occupied for nearly twenty years, at first in affluence and comfort, but latterly with a severe economy, and a constant struggle against encroaching ruin. Every visit of the Doctor to London was followed by some fresh privation to his wife and daughter. Within six years of the completion of Bertram House—so early as 1808—great reductions had been required in the establishment. The servant out of livery had been dispensed with. There had ceased to be any lady's maid. The footman had degenerated into an awkward lad, who was not only expected to wait at table and go out with the carriage, but to make himself useful in the stable or the garden. The carriage horses were employed on the work of the farm, and it was not every day in the week on which Mrs. and Miss Mitford could command the use of them. In a year or two the chariot disappeared. It was out of repair and wanted painting, so it was parted with, and its place was never supplied. Afterwards the pictures were sent up to town in a hurry and sold by auction at Robins's.* By-and-by Mrs. Mitford is harassed by difficulties in obtaining remittances for the moderate expenses of her diminished household. She thanks her husband for sending her ten pounds, and tells him, with a grateful sense of relief, how she will go to Reading and pay the butcher and baker on the morrow. Taxes fall into arrears, and are only extorted by threatening notices from the collector. Tradesmen refuse to serve the

* A letter of Mr. St. Quintin (dated April 10, 1820, Paris, referring to long past money transactions) says, " When you were in durance vile, I got you some money on your paintings to get you out immediately."

house with the common requirements of the family till previous accounts are settled. On several occasions they are at a loss whence to procure food for the greyhounds, and once Mrs. Mitford writes imploringly to the Doctor, with the greatest earnestness, but without the slightest intimation of reproach, requesting him to send her *a one pound note* by return of post, as they are actually in want of bread. The extremity of the ruin may be conceived, not from any complaint of the wife or daughter, as may be seen from the correspondence which is in the hands of our readers, but from a letter of Mr. St. Quintin's. It is written in answer to a supplication for relief from the Doctor, and dated Paris, February 29, 1820, and says: "Your heartrending letter has overwhelmed myself and my wife with dismay. What is to be done? I really know not. You harrow up my very soul with the account of your distress."

And who was the author of this distress? The father alone. The wife, by the most careful management and self-denial; the daughter, by her literary industry; were doing everything in their power to lighten its pressure and ward off its fall. It was the sole work of the husband. The cause of all this misery was the Doctor's love of play, and its concomitant dabbling in gambling speculations. He appears to have been ready to listen and give credit to any plausible adventurer who tempted him with the prospect of becoming suddenly rich. For instance, he engaged with a brother of Mr. St. Quintin's in an extensive coal speculation. He supplied the capital, and was led to expect, according to the promise of the figures laid before him, a return of some 1500*l.* a year, but the return was never realised, and the capital, with the exception of about 300*l.*,

was lost. He was tempted by a M. le Marquis de Chabanne to advance 5000*l.* for the purpose of carrying out
some marvellous invention for lighting and heating
houses. But the money was spent, the scheme was not
approved by the public, M. de Chabanne returned disappointed to France, and Dr. Mitford, deluded and impoverished, was for several years afterwards harassing
himself by vain attempts to recover some portion of his
debt by suing the marquis in the French courts. Of these
two transactions we find intimations in a few letters of
distant dates which have chanced not to be destroyed,
and there were doubtless other speculations of an equally
impoverishing description of which every memorial has
perished. But the main, continuous, exhausting source
of the ruin was—the Doctor's love of play. He considered
himself, and was said to have been, an excellent whist
player. If that was the case, the cards must have been,
beyond all calculation of chances, continually against
him, for he seems to have been invariably a loser.
He sometimes imagined himself cheated. At least, such
a suspicion is the only clue that I can conceive to the
sense of a passage in one of his daughter's letters which
advises him " to withdraw from inferior clubs, and confine himself to Graham's, for there at least he would
play with gentlemen."

But, according to his own representations and the
belief of his wife and daughter, Dr. Mitford always was
cheated and ill-used, wronged and overreached. He had
pecuniary transactions with his brother, which always
seem to result in injurious conduct towards himself. He
bought land of Lord Shrewsbury through the agency of
the steward, and both the agent and the owner are accused of having taken him in. He lends some money
to Lord Charles Annesley, and is indignant at the delay

of its repayment.   He is compelled to sell his pictures,
but does not obtain the price at which he had valued
them, and is outrageous at the sacrifice which the auctioneer has made of his property.   He is at last compelled to sell his house and land, and here again, from
some unexplained misconduct which he attributes to
the purchaser, he becomes involved in a chancery suit,
and finds the ruin, that his strange improvidence and
reckless extravagance had so long been preparing the
way for, eventually completed.

As far as it is possible at this distance of time to ascertain his circumstances, Dr. Mitford, when he left Bertram House at the end of March, 1820, must have been
all but penniless.   Except a field large enough to save
his franchise for the county, there remained nothing
but the 3000*l.* in the funds, which the prudence of Mrs.
Mitford's maternal grandfather had secured to his
daughter's descendants, and of which the trustees,
though often solicited, would not relax their hold.   But
the interest of that money was pledged to his creditors,
and unavailable for the expenses of the family.   In short,
there was nothing between the father and mother and
hopeless destitution, but the genius and industry of the
daughter.

The family removed to a cottage at Three Mile Cross,
of which the next letter to Sir William Elford gives a
most favourable description.

CHAPTER V.

To SIR WILLIAM ELFORD, *Bickham, Plymouth.*

Three Mile Cross, Reading,
April 8, 1820.

YOUR delightful letter, my dear Sir William, arrived at the very moment when kindness was most needed and most welcome—just as we were leaving our dear old home to come to this new one. Without being in general very violently addicted to sentimentality, I was, as you may imagine, a little grieved to leave the spot where I had passed so many happy years. The trees, and fields, and sunny hedgerows, however little distinguished by picturesque beauty, were to me as old friends. Women have more of this natural feeling than the stronger sex ; they are creatures of home and habit, and ill brook transplanting. We, however, are not quite transplanted yet—rather, as the gardeners say, ' laid by the heels.' We have only moved a mile nearer Reading—to a little village street situate on the turnpike road, between Basingstoke and the aforesaid illustrious and quarrelsome borough. Our residence is a cottage —no, not a cottage—it does not deserve the name—a messuage or tenement, such as a little farmer who had made twelve or fourteen hundred pounds might retire to when he left off business to live on his means.

It consists of a series of closets, the largest of which
may be about eight feet square, which they call parlours
and kitchens and pantries; some of them minus a
corner, which has been unnaturally filched for a chimney; others deficient in half a side, which has been
truncated by the shelving roof. Behind is a garden
about the size of a good drawing-room, with an arbour
which is a complete sentry box of privet. On one side
a public-house, on the other a village shop, and right
opposite a cobbler's stall.

Notwithstanding all this, " the cabin," as Bobadil says,
" is convenient." It is within reach of my dear old walks;
the banks where I find my violets; the meadows full of
cowslips; and the woods where the wood-sorrel blows.
We are all beginning to get settled and comfortable,
and resuming our usual habits. Papa has already had
the satisfaction of setting the neighbourhood to rights
by committing a disorderly person, who was the pest of
the Cross, to Bridewell. Mamma has furbished up an
old dairy and made it into a not incommodious store
room. I have lost my only key, and stuffed the garden
with flowers. My little dog Molly, after a good deal
of staring and squeaking and running about (she seemed
conscious of some degradation from the change), has at
last pitched upon a chair to lie on when I turn her out
of my lap; and the great white cat, who was likewise
very eloquent and out of his wits, has given this very
evening most satisfactory proofs of finding himself at
home, by resuming his ancient predatory habits and
stealing all the milk for our tea. (N.B. We were forced
to go without). Moreover, it is an excellent lesson of
condensation—one which we all wanted. Great as our
merits might be in some points, we none of us excelled
in compression. Mamma's tidiness was almost as diffuse

as her daughter's litter. Papa could never tell a short
story—nor could papa's daughter (as you well know)
ever write a short letter. I expect we shall be much
benefited by this squeeze; though at present it sits
upon us as uneasily as tight stays and is just as awkward
looking. Indeed, my great objection to a small room
always was, its extreme unbecomingness to one of my
enormity. I really seem to fill it—the parlour looks
all me. Nevertheless, "the cabin is convenient," as I
said before. Its negative merits are very great.

The Cross is not a borough, thank Heaven! either
rotten or independent. The inhabitants are quiet,
peaceable people, who would not think of visiting us,
even if we had a knocker to knock at. We are a mile
nearer to dear Mrs. Dickinson; and, though I have no
conveyance at present, yet I have in perspective a bright
vision of a donkey cart. Last, and best of all, we are
three good miles from Reading. You will easily understand, my dear friend, that I have been terribly afraid
of being planted in that illustrious town, and am quite
enchanted at my escape. Not that I have any quarrel
with the town, which, as Gray said of Cambridge, " would
be well enough if it were not for the people ;" but those
people — their gossiping — their mistiness—the dense
fogs that hang about them! Oh! you can imagine
nothing so bad. They are as rusty as old iron and as
jagged as flint stones. There are exceptions, of course ;
such as prove the rule. Oh! my dear Three Mile Cross,
how much I prefer you! I am not quite rid of my
Reading-phobia yet; for this place is considered as a
mere *pied à terre*, just to wait till something shall offer
within a stone's throw of Reading, which shall be at
once pretty, commodious, and cheap—a most essential
requisite to people who have been half-ruined by an

eight years' chancery suit. In the mean time, my dear
friend, we shall certainly be here both as you go to
town and as you come back. We shall have both house-
room and heart-room for you, and I depend on seeing
you. Do pray come—you must come and help laugh
at our strange shifts and the curious pieces of finery
which our landlord has left for the adornment of his
mansion. Did you ever see a corner cupboard ? Do
come. We shall be most happy to see the gentleman
to whom I enclose this letter, and whose handwriting
you, in the proud consciousness of your own copper-
plate, think proper to scandalise. Papa had before told
me that Mr. Elford was returned for Westbury ; I did
not know it myself, because a branch of our system of
reform and retrenchment is the discontinuance of my
beloved 'Morning Chronicle.' Your opinion of Sir
Thomas Acland ought to be put up among the archives
of his family, as a title to fame, quite as valuable to
your Devonshire friend as the 'Edinburgh' review of
the Scotch novels can be to Sir Walter Scott. Sir
T. Acland must be an extraordinary man to have
awakened such enthusiasm in so excellent and calm
a judge. I wished for his success very sincerely, I
assure you.

What a curious circumstance is the discovery of
Queen Elizabeth's hair ! How extraordinary that it
should have remained undiscovered ! that at Wilton,
among her own descendants, 'the Countess of Pembroke's Arcadia' should have continued unread for so
long a period ! I suppose the lock was fairly ensconced
between some of Sir Philip's* English sapphics or dac-
tylics—which are, to be sure, the most unreadable and
skippable things ever written ; but still it is nothing

---

* Sir Philip Sydney.

less than miraculous. Do tell me anything that you hear further on this subject.

Good-bye, my dear friend. Good-night, and God bless you! Pray come and see us or you will break my heart—and let me know when you are coming.

Ever, my dear friend,

Most affectionately yours,

M. R. MITFORD.

Pray excuse my blots and interlineations. They have been occasioned by my attention being distracted by a nightingale in full song, who is pouring her world of music through my window, and really will not let me write. Good-night.

To B. R. HAYDON, Esq.

Three Mile Cross, May 1, 1820.

I know not how sufficiently to thank you, my dear sir, for your inestimable present, which I shall always value as my most precious possession. I am almost ashamed to take a thing of so much consequence;* but you are a very proud man and are determined to pay me in this magnificent manner for pleasing myself with the fancy of being in a slight degree useful to you. Well, I am quite content to be the obliged person.

So you are beginning to feel *l'embarras des richesses!* I am heartily glad of it, and malicious enough to wish you a yearly increase of the trouble of gain. Would not two or three thousand a year from the public—that best of all patrons—be almost as good as five hundred a year from Government? This Government is not deserving of the credit which would be reflected on it from such patronage. If we had a reform, indeed—but

---

* Haydon's study for the head of St. Peter.

I will not talk politics on May-day—this day of fairs
and flowers. I am going to Reading Fair myself by-
and-by, in a real market-cart, which will be delightful
—and I have already been cowsliping. Are you fond
of field flowers? They are my passion—even more, I
think, than greyhounds or books. This country is
eminently flowery. Besides all the variously-tinted
primroses and violets in singular profusion, we have all
sorts of orchises and arums; the delicate wood anemone;
the still more delicate wood sorrel, with its lovely
purple veins meandering over the white drooping flower;
the field tulip, with its rich chequer-work of lilac and
crimson, and the sun shining through the leaves as
through old painted glass; the ghostly field star of
Bethlehem (did you ever see that rare and ghost-like
flower? Dr. Clarke mentions having found it on a
tumulus, which he took for the tomb of Ajax, in the
Troad); wild lilies of the valley; and the other day
I found a field completely surrounded by wild periwinkles. They ran along the hedge for nearly a quarter
of a mile; to say nothing of the sculptural beauty of the
white water lily and the golden clusters of the golden
ranunculus. Yes, this is really a country of flowers, and
so beautiful just now, that there is no making up one's
mind to leave it; though, by dint of staying in it, one's
" wits get as mossy as the pales in an old orchard "—as
somebody said of somebody—Old Aubrey of Hobbes of
Malmesbury, I believe.

Adieu, my dear sir. I am just going to set off on
my expedition to the fair, to buy ribands and see the
wild beasts. Adieu.

Ever most sincerely and gratefully yours,

M. R. MITFORD.

To Sir William Elford.

Three Mile Cross, June 21, 1820.

This is the first warm day we have had since the beginning of May. The cherries ripen and the roses blow, without any sweetness either of scent or taste, from the mere force of habit. And what is worse still, our pump is dry—dry in all this rain—from the very same cause. The spring has been accustomed to fail in other summers, and so thinks fit to go dry in this, showing, besides this circumstance, a very terrible one to such consumers of water as I and my flowers; a strong instance of the force of habit. I have grown exceedingly fond of this little place. Did I ever tell you I disliked it? I love it of all things—have taken root completely—could be content to live and die here. To be sure the rooms are of the smallest. I, in our little parlour, look something like a blackbird in a goldfinch's cage—but it is so snug and comfortable, and out of Reading, and in Mrs. Dickinson's way—I never saw her half so often. She is rather a romantic lady, and has something of a fancy to be a cottager herself: so, as she can't compass that interesting character in her own person, she contents herself with achieving it by proxy in mine. Her baby is a lovely little thing, fat and rosy, with such eyes! so purely, so lucidly blue! Nothing but the summer sky in a calm lake can compare with them. Mr. Dickinson's name is not William but Charles. He is not the author of the book on justicing; his authorship is in another line. He shall translate good poetry, and write bad, with any man in England. It's the oddest thing in the world that a man who has taste to distinguish, and power of language to render most admirably, the very finest passages in the great Latin and Italian poets, should, when he comes to original composition, write such unreadable stuff and fancy it good.

Have you read the life of Mr. Edgeworth? You would like it. His part of the work is very amusing indeed, and his daughter's is very amiable. She over-rates him a good deal; but the mistake is so creditable to her affection, that it is impossible not to admire her the more for her error. She makes much of his speeches in Parliament; but he was no great orator. I once heard him make a speech, the most ridiculous that ever was made by man. He was a clever man notwith-standing; and, in spite of a little irregularity in his marryings and fallings in love, seems to have been an excellent moral character.

Miss Edgeworth is travelling at present with her brother, his wife and her two younger sisters. A friend of mine now in Paris wrote me word that she had met her frequently at Baron Denon's; and that she was of all the women she had ever seen the most animated and agreeable. I have not myself the honour to be acquainted with Miss Edgeworth. I only saw her at the aforesaid meeting, and know nothing more of her than that she is one of the smallest women I ever saw. She was presented at Paris, on account of her relation-ship to the Abbé Edgeworth.

You are very good in expressing so kind an interest in my occupations and amusements. They are much as usual. My method of doing nothing seldom varies. *Imprimis,* I take long walks and get wet through. *Item,* I nurse my flowers—sometimes pull up a few, taking them for weeds, and *vice versâ* leave the weeds, taking them for flowers. *Item,* I do short jobs of needlework. *Item,* I write long letters. *Item,* I read all sorts of books, long and short, new and old. Have you a mind for a list of the most recent? Buckhardt's 'Travels in Nubia,' Bowdich's 'Mission to Ashantee,' Dubois' 'Account of India,' Morier's 'Second Journey in Persia.' All these are quartos of various degrees of heaviness. There is another of the same class, La Touche's 'Life of Sir P. Sidney' (you set me to reading that by your anecdote of Queen Elizabeth's hair). Southey's 'Life of Wesley,'— very good. Hogg's 'Winter Evening Tales,'—very good, indeed (I have a great affection for the Ettrick Shepherd, have not you?). 'Diary of an Invalid'—the best account of Italy which I have met with since Forsythe —much in his manner—I think you would like it. Odellben's 'Saxon Campaign'—interesting, inasmuch as it concerns Napoleon, otherwise so-so. 'The Sketch Book,' by Geoffrey Crayon,—quite a curiosity—an American book which is worth reading. Mr. Milman's 'Fall of Jerusalem'—a fine poem, though not exactly so fine as the 'Quarterly' makes out. I thought it much finer when I first read it than I do now, for it set me to reading 'Josephus,' which I had never had the grace to open before; and the historian is, in the striking passages, much grander than the poet, particularly in the account of the portents and prodigies before the Fall; in the scene of the prophet who cries, "Woe, woe to Jerusalem!" and in that terrible incident of the mother eating her child, which is the most sublime piece of horror I ever read: the 'Fall of Jerusalem' is an admirable poem nevertheless. These books, together with a few Italian things—especially the 'Lettere di Ortis'—will pretty well account for my time since I wrote last, and convince you of the perfect solitude, which gives me time to indulge so much in the delightful idleness of reading. The 'Lettere di Ortis' is the only modern Italian novel. What a strange anomaly in

literature, that this imaginative people, from whom
almost all our old stories were borrowed, should have
no original novels now; for these letters of Ortis are
little other than an imitation of 'Werther.' By-the-by,
the author, Ugo Foscolo, is in London now, and writing
for the 'Quarterly Review.'

You do not tell me how you liked Haydon's picture.
Did the head of Christ please you? I want very much
to know. The success in a pecuniary point of view is
very great indeed. Forty thousand persons have been
to see it; and he expects to sell it for the new church
at Chelsea for three thousand guineas. Does not he well
deserve this success for his perseverance, his ardour, his
devotion to his art? But still, I want to know what
you think of the head of Christ. Is it too large?

My father is in London. Mamma joins me in kindest
remembrances. Adieu, my ever dear and kind friend.
Write very soon, and believe me ever,

Most affectionately yours,

M. R. MITFORD.

To SIR WILLIAM ELFORD.

Three Mile Cross, July 5, 1820.

Your most kind and delightful letter, my dear Sir
William, met me on my return from an unexpected and
very pleasant excursion. I came home yesterday from
passing three days in London and at Richmond; going
up in the atmosphere of Calcutta and coming back in
that of Greenland—but equally well, and enjoying
myself as much in the one as in the other. This is a
vaunt of the very first magnitude; but really I am
proud of my health, because, when my size is considered,
I think it a curiosity.

All this time was spent in seeing sights, and among others, Haydon's picture. Seriously, do you like the head of Christ? This is the question that everybody asks—for about composition, expression, colouring, there seems no doubt; but do you like the head of Christ? I did not at first, but it gained upon me; though I still think it rather too large and too pale, and with too much glory about it, and too little of mere mortal beauty. Still, the conception, the abstractedness, the looking forward and inward—all this is very grand—very grand indeed. He is now painting another great picture, the 'Resurrection of Lazarus,' different from any of the many paintings on this subject. All the other pictures represent Lazarus as rising from a horizontal position. Mr. Haydon, following the custom of Jerusalem, where all the tombs were excavations in the rock, and the bodies placed upright, represents him as walking from the hollow in which he had been enclosed, and throwing off the grave-clothes at the command of Christ, "Lazarus, come forth!" Nothing can be finer than the sketch, which I have seen. It contains about twenty figures, and will occupy, I suppose, nearly two years. Mr. Haydon himself spent a day with the friends at whose house I was staying at Richmond. I never saw any one in such health and spirits—enjoying most honestly his well-earned success. These, with some lesser sights, shopping, calling and driving about to look at streets and parks, pretty well filled up my London days.

Three sights I missed: Lord Grosvenor's 'Fathers of the Church' by Rubens (which I lost by going to Richmond the day before they were shown); Queen Caroline; and Mrs. Opie, that excellent and ridiculous person, who is now placed in Bond Street (where she can't even hear herself talk) with a blue hat and feathers on her

head, a low gown without a tucker, and ringlets hanging down on each shoulder. These sights I lost; but
the first and the last I hope to see again; and the
second I don't care if I never see at all; for be it known
to you, my dear friend, that I am no Queen's woman,
whatever my party may be. I have no toleration for
an indecorous woman, and am exceedingly scandalized
at the quantity of nonsense which has been talked in
her defence. The less that is said on the subject the
better. It is no small part of her guilt, or her folly,
that her arrival has turned conversation into a channel
of scandal and detraction on either side, which, if it
continue, threatens to injure the taste, the purity, the
moral character of the nation. Don't you agree with me?

For my part, I had rather talk about Richmond.
Do you know much of that fairy land, which has so little
to do with the work-a-day world, and seems made for a
holiday spot for ladies and gentlemen—a sort of realiza-
tion of Watteau's pictures! The Hill is grown rather
too leafy—too much like Glover's pictures—too green;
it wants crags, as Canova says; and really looked better
when I saw it last in the winter. But the water and
the banks are beyond all praise. The house where I
was staying had a beautiful garden down to the river;
and there, or on the water, I quite lived. We went to
see Pope's Grotto, which is unchanged except in the
addition of some china plates stuck about the wall;
Strawberry Hill, which is likewise a sad china-shop, but
where I walked about amongst the finery in a very
pleasant reverie, thinking of Horace Walpole and his
correspondents; Hampton Court, which I wonder to see
so deserted. What a beautiful place! what a real
palace! How can anybody leave Hampton Court and
live in the Pavilion? My enjoyment there was very

perfect. The cartoons, which I had never seen together before, though every one knows them by heart, by copies and drawings and prints, and seeing them by twos at the British Gallery—the cartoons, and Titian's portrait of himself, formed my great delight. Kew Palace—I was much gratified there, too; though in a very different way. The simplicity, the homeliness, the shabbiness even, of that royal dwelling, where there is nothing good but books and pictures, formed a pleasing contrast to the common notion of Courts. I am sure there is scarcely a country gentleman of my acquaintance who would be content with such furniture. The most astonishing things in the palace are a bust of the present Queen, which one wonders not to see removed, and Vandyke's portrait of himself, which I prefer even to the Titian.

What a glorious race of beings those great painters were! what spirit! what grace! what intellectual beauty! Where shall we find three such men as Titian, Vandyke, and Raphael? You will think me picture-mad—and really I do love pictures better than anything else in the world, except flowers and books and greyhounds, and fresh air and old friends. I will only tell you two things more of paintings, and have done ; one, that Mr. Hofland is about a landscape, a gala-day at Richmond, which promises to be his best, combining that beautiful scenery with the out-of-door gaiety which is so rare in our climate and still rarer in our art ; the other that at an old house at Richmond they have lately rummaged out three pictures which had lain unsuspected in a garret for I don't know how many years—George the Second between his queen and Lady Suffolk. You have no idea of the interest they excited—not on their own account, for they are bad ; nor on the account Royal ; but solely and

purely because they recalled the idea of Jeanie Deans.
What I admired most at Richmond was Lord Dysart's
place. Did you see it ever? It is of the style of
Charles the First or the Commonwealth—a bad style—
but so preserved—so perfect—the keeping is so complete! There is the grand, heavy, stately, quiet house,
far from the water, screened by trees, which keep off
the light and glare—the ha-ha, which parts the court
from the lawn—the grated iron gate, through which
one can almost fancy Lovelace slipping a letter to
Clarissa—the busts, the balconies, the terraces, the
fountains, the old-fashioned flower-garden full of old-
fashioned flowers, trim pinks and solid cabbage roses—
no new-fangled flaunting azalias or China roses—
nothing that can counteract the gloom and the silence
and the perfect repose. I know nothing at all of Lord
Dysart, but I honour him and his progenitors for resisting the temptation to alter, and preserving so fine a
specimen of the residence of our ancestors.

Well now, I have done. My dear Sir William, laud
the gods, that there is no danger of my going to France or
Italy. What would become of you if I were to take a
journey of that sort, when I cannot even make a trip
to Richmond without inflicting on you my seeings and
doings? I heard very little literary news. Everybody
is talking of 'Marcian Colonna,' Barry Cornwall's new
poem. Now 'Barry Cornwall' is an *alias.* The poet's real
name is Proctor, a young attorney, who feared it might
hurt his practice if he were known to follow this "idle
trade." It has, however, become very generally known,
and poor Mr. Proctor is terribly embarrassed with his
false name. He neither knows how to keep it on or
throw it up. By whatever appellation he chooses to be
called, he is a great poet. Poor John Keats is dying of

the 'Quarterly Review.' This is a sad silly thing; but it is true. A young, delicate, imaginative boy—that withering article fell upon him like an east wind. I am afraid he has no chance of recovery. Mr. Gifford's behaviour is very bad. He sent word that if he wrote again his poem should be properly reviewed, which was admitting the falsity of the first critique, and yet says that he has been Keats's best friend; because somebody sent him twenty-five pounds to console him for the injustice of the 'Quarterly.' I am very sorry for John Keats. He had a thousand faults, and a million of beauties; and he is struck to the earth by the mere effect of worldly hardness and derision upon a tender heart and a sensitive temper. I am very sorry for John Keats. Miss Porter is sick, too, of her condemned play. I have not much pity for her. Her disease is wounded vanity. An old stager, and a wholesale dealer in magnanimity, ought to know better. All my pity is for poor John Keats. Did you ever see his 'Endymion?' It is the easiest thing in the world to laugh at it, but there are passages which could hardly be equalled by any living poet. And he was so young—so likely to improve. Are you not sorry for him? Adieu, my dear friend. Write to me soon.

Ever most affectionately yours,
M. R. MITFORD.

To SIR WILLIAM ELFORD.

Three Mile Cross, August 24, 1820.

MY DEAR FRIEND,

Lady Madalina will probably call to-morrow; if not, I will wait on her on Saturday. You will comprehend, my dear friend, that your opinion has excited this desire of an acquaintance which, to confess the truth, I have hitherto rather shunned. I don't know why; but in spite of my age and my rotundity and rubicundity, which seem to take away my right to such feelings, I am by fits and starts desperately shy, and have a particular aversion to seeing people who have a desire to see one, as they would desire to see Punch; which I rather understood to be the case with the lady in question. Another thing was, that her particular friend and favourite in this neighbourhood is a person whom I do not like—a single woman of eight-and-thirty, with manners too light, too bold, too young for eighteen; rouge on her cheeks and a leer in her eyes; a rattle without an idea; full of the outward and visible signs of cheerfulness, but with none of the inward and spiritual grace; a person whose hoity-toityness is depressing beyond conception.

This was the favourite and the chosen of one whose station and talents gave her the power to choose. And this it was that gave me the impression which you must have seen, and which you have so completely counteracted. But have not you yourself sometimes judged of people by their associates? Don't you like to meet with good company in the hearts of your friends, as well as at their tables? Now that we shall have you to talk about we shall get on excellently; and except that she will be furiously disappointed, and that I shall be shy and ashamed whenever I think of my letters—those letters which are just like so many bottles of ginger-beer, bouncing and frothy and flying in everybody's face—with these trifling drawbacks, we shall admire one another as much as is proper and possible.

So you have actually altered that pretty landscape! Really I had not a notion of making a criticism when I remarked to you the effect of those sunny fields; I meant merely to admire your success in painting a view

from a hill. I have no doubt, however, but the common is
equally beautiful. I have a passion for commons. Those
pretty irregular green patches, with cottages round them,
and dipping ponds glancing so brightly, and crossing foot-
paths among the scattered trees ; seem to me the charac-
teristics of English scenery. Ah ! they are passing away !
We shall soon see nothing but straight hedgerows and
gravelled lanes. I sigh over every Enclosure Bill, and
am always delighted when some glorious obstinate
bumpkin of the true John Bull breed takes it into his
head to quarrel with the lord of the manor and oppose
one, as is luckily the case in this parish of Shenfield.

By-the-way, I heard a curious anecdote of Lord
Byron yesterday, from a very truth-telling person. A
gentleman was with him on a visit to an old house in
the country which had the reputation of being haunted.
They had been telling ghost stories all the evening ;
and in the middle of the night he was awakened by
Lord B., with his hair on end and his teeth chattering, who declared his room was full of strange shapes
and strange sounds—that he could not return to it ; and
begged his friend to allow him to sit by the side of his
bed till daylight, which he did. I have always thought
he would end by being a Methodist.

Did I mention to you the second volume of the
American book, which is so incredibly good, 'The
Sketch Book ?' It is a little sentimental—too sentimental, certainly—but the comic part is excellent, particularly the account of Little Britain. I should think
the Americans must crow over Mr. Washington Irving,
like a hen with one chick. (Do hens crow ? I suspect
here is a little confusion of metaphor.) Adieu, my very
dear friend.

Most affectionately yours,

M. R. M.

I have as yet only seen some extracts from Mr. Keats's new poems. Those extracts seem to me finer than anything that has been written these two hundred years—finer than Wordsworth even—more Dantesque, a compound of Chaucer and the old Florentine. I hope and trust he will live to answer his barbarous critics by many such works.

To B. R. HAYDON, ESQ.

Three Mile Cross, Sept. 1, 1820.

MY DEAR MR. HAYDON,

Your letter went to my very heart. It does one harm to think of those cold, proud, selfish " patrons," as they call themselves. It lessens one's faith in human nature. But the picture will sell—it must. The same heartless vanity which prevents their co-operating in your liberal, delicate, and unostentatious plan, will induce one of them to possess himself of this glorious work of art. I am persuaded of this. But it is heartbreaking to think that you, in the meantime, should be exposed to these petty cares and harassed by doubt and vexation. You ought to be lifted above all worldly care and to live among the delightful creations of your own genius. The only consolation is your elastic and buoyant spirit, which will bear you through all these trials to the prosperity you so well deserve. Fame you have already—a better and a purer fame than any living artist; and competence will follow, I am sure of it. Riches you do not want; with such reputation they are not wanted. In the mean time, my dear sir, be careful of your invaluable health, and of your eyes, your 'poor eyes' as you call them. To what complaint are they liable? No one who looked at them could fancy them subject to any. Never apologise to me for talking of yourself: it is a compliment of the highest kind. It tells me that you confide in my sympathy. Be assured you may; except my own dear family and dear Miss James, there is no one whom I regard with such admiring and respectful interest, or of whose kindness I am half so proud.

I am just now engaged in a job compared to which the water pitcherings of the Danaides were hopeful. I am persuading papa to take care of himself, and keep quiet, and go to the sea and get well. God bless you, my dear Mr. Haydon!

Ever most sincerely yours,

M. R. MITFORD.

To SIR WILLIAM ELFORD.

Three Mile Cross, Sept. 9, 1820.

I have spent a day at Coley, and extracted from Mr. Monck rather more of the royal visit* than his wife could do. The Queen really did speak to them. She said: "You do me honour; it is an excellent address." I dare say she thought so; for of all the fulsome nonsense that has been penned on her, none this surpassed! Her presence was announced by a prodigious giggling, chattering, and romping outside the door, like a parcel of boys let loose from school, which suddenly ceased, and she entered as gravely as Mr. Liston in Queen Dollalolla. Her dress we had a great deal of fun about, from the delicious ignorance of the describer. It was in the midst of the Court mourning, and Mr. Monck had put himself to charges for a black suit. But the lady herself was, it appears, in colours —"fawn colour, Mary—the colour of that cow!" How was it made? "So," buttoning up his coat. Oh! a man's coat! Pray was the rest of her apparel——

* The visit of a deputation from Reading to present an address to the Queen.

"Don't be foolish—a woman's coat—a great-coat—the thing you all wear in winter." A pelisse? "Yes, a fawn-coloured pelisse garnished with gold!"

Have you read the 'Abbot?' I have just finished it. Mary Queen of Scots is a person of whom, with all her sins, we have dreamt all our life long. There is not a creature of any imagination who has not made her romance in his own mind long before now. The Bodleian Mary, all beauty and all grace—the love of all men, the envy of all women—she who makes possible all that has been feigned of nymph or goddess—there is no writing up to what one fancies of her. Nobody has ever accomplished this feat—no one ever will. Schiller, Alfieri, the Ettrick Shepherd—three master spirits—have all failed when they wrote of Queen Mary. But I think the failure of Walter Scott the most egregious of any. He takes her down from her pedestal, makes her scold—disenchants the Lady Dulcinea del Toboso—wakens one from one's pleasant dream—brings a light before one's magic lantern, and puts out the pretty pictures. Now this is not a friend's office nor a poet's. Meanwhile, the book is pleasant reading, in spite of this fault and another, which is, that all the plot which is not Queen Mary is occupied by a twin-brother-and-sister confusion, like the Sebastian and Viola of 'Twelfth Night.' Now, it is not wise in Sir Walter Scott to remind his readers, of malice prepense, of Shakespeare's last work, and worthy to be his last work. Moreover, Catherine is as little like the delicious Viola as Henry is like the frank and generous Sebastian. Notwithstanding which, the book is a pleasant book, as you will think and say.

Ever, my dear friend,

Most sincerely and affectionately yours,

M. R. MITFORD.

To Sir William Elford.

> Three Mile Cross, Sept.—I don't know
> what—but the *last.* How many
> days has September?

Have you read or heard of 'Sir Francis Darnell,'
a new novel by Mr. Dallas? Mr. Dallas is the person
to whom Lord Byron gave the profits of the first
canto of 'Childe Harold,' he being ruined, I believe, by
an expensive wife (indeed, I have heard that she would
not dine without being serenaded by musicians); and I
cannot help thinking, though there is no visible allusion, that in the character, though not in the story,
there is an occasional hint at Lord Byron; at least that
the author means to suggest to him, and of him, that
lost fame, and lost virtue, and lost happiness may be
recovered and redeemed.

Have you seen a letter to Hannah More from an
English woman on the present crisis? It is by my
friend Mrs. Hofland—exceedingly well and even eloquently written—endeavouring to prevail on decent
ladies not to idolize the Queen and so forth; saying
herself all that she wishes Hannah to say, with more
grace and feeling, and less sternness and violence, than
Mrs. More would or could have used on the same occasion. It does her great credit. I think she should be
knighted for it—Lady Barbara Hofland! I am particularly glad that the good cause fell into her hands
instead of Mrs. More's, whom I cannot abide. She
writes just like a man in petticoats. She is a canter
and a cringer. Now, Mrs. Hof. is just the reverse of
this. She is womanly to her fingers' ends, and as truth-
telling and independent as a skylark. Good-bye.

To B. R. HAYDON, ESQ.

Coley Park, Oct. 2, 1820.

MY DEAR SIR,

These few days have brought summer back to us in all its splendour. I am writing out of doors, in our little arbour, with my attention a good deal distracted by a superb butterfly which is hovering about a large tuft of China asters close by—now fluttering round and round in the sun, and now swinging in the rich blossoms. The butterflies love China asters. So do I. They come when flowers begin to be so rare and precious; their colours are so rich, and they are so hardy. They lift up their gay heads, and *will* live, let the weather be what it may. Now good-bye for to-day. I shall not finish till I hear from you. Oh! I hope you will come! We shall be more disappointed than words can tell if you do not.

To SIR WILLIAM ELFORD.

Three Mile Cross, Nov. 11, 1820.

Dear Dr. Valpy is not very particular. He brought the other day a fair neighbour of yours into a curious scrape. Miss H—— R—— is staying at the Forbury; and they had in Reading an itinerant lecturer, a showman of the sciences, whose lectures were attended by all the house of Valpy and the upper half of the school. Well, the last lecture was on electricity. One of the boys was electrified, and the good doctor, before a hundred people, very gravely led poor Miss H—— R—— up to the youth, and desired him to kiss her, by way of completing the experiment by communicating the shock. Luckily, the boy was a lad of grace, and had too much modesty to comply. As to poor H——, she was quite enough electrified by the proposal. They say it was a curious scene. I did not see it myself, for I have a horror of those sort of things, and hate an electric apparatus as bad as a gun. I don't know why I hate either, for I have never been shot nor electrified, but I have run away pretty often from both machines. I remember when we had Mr. Walker to give us a course of lectures at school I absconded from the electricity— scudded away like a hare, and skulked under the bed till the lecturer and his apparatus were safe out of the house. And I verily believe I should do the same to-morrow rather than stay, only that now I have not sufficient moral courage to own my fear.

I don't think, my dear friend, that I quite agree with you as to the facility of imitating Scott's novels. We have had nothing like them yet, and I do not think we soon shall. Consider, with all his faults, the great and rare qualities that must be united in such a novelist; the minute and curious learning which seizes, with the certainty and ease of accurate knowledge, on all the antiquarian detail that suits his purpose; the almost magical power of placing scenes and forms before you as in a picture, and leading you through a changing country which you trace as in a map. This power of external representation is only equalled by Chaucer, Boccaccio, and, as far as scenery goes, by Spenser. And, lastly, consider his various and extraordinary delineations of character. It is quite nonsense to compare him, as the 'Edinburgh' Reviewers do, to Shakespeare in this respect. Such extravagant praise gives one the tendency to underrate him. His characters have not the exquisite freedom of Shakespeare's. There is too much identity. He is afraid to trust them out of their prescribed bounds—afraid to let them make any speech which could not instantly be assigned to the right person. The keeping is too exact to be true to our mixed and varying nature. But still the characters are finely conceived and finely drawn, and there is a noble spirit of humanity, an indulgence to human frailty, which sets a grand lesson to the world. He makes good Shakespeare's most beautiful saying, "There is some soul of goodness in things evil;" and he is, as far as I know, the only writer who has ever had candour and fairness enough to tolerate opposite bigotries. No, my dear friend, it is not the mere fixing on some peculiar piece of history to illustrate that will produce, even in powerful hands, such novels as Walter Scott's.

As to Miss Holford, I don't think she had the slightest intention to imitate him. 'Warbeck of Wolfstein' seems to me an attempt to portray, in very black and exaggerated colours, the character of Lord Byron. Did not it strike you so? Some of the anecdotes—that of the note with the orange-flowers, for instance—are stories which have been currently told of his lordship; and altogether I am afraid there can be no doubt but it was intended as a portrait. I say afraid, because Mrs. Joanna Baillie, the friend of Lady Byron, ought not to have given the sanction of her name to such a libel. He is quite bad enough, Heaven knows, without being loaded with crimes that do not belong to him.

Adieu, my dear friend, and believe me

Ever most affectionately yours,

M. R. MITFORD.

To SIR WILLIAM ELFORD, *Bickham, Plymouth.*

Three Mile Cross, Nov. 27, 1820.

Ah! my dear Sir William, we were forced to illuminate. Think of that! an illumination at Three Mile Cross! Forced to put up two dozen of candles upon pain of pelting and rioting and all manner of bad things. So we did. We were very shabby, though, compared to our neighbours. One, a retired publican, just below, had a fine transparency, composed of a pocket handkerchief with the Queen's head upon it—a very fine head in a hat and feathers cocked very knowingly on one side. I did not go to Reading; the *squibbery* there was too much to encounter; and they had only one good hit throughout the whole of that illustrious town. A poor publican had a whole-length transparency of the Duke of Wellington for the Peace illumination, and, not knowing what to get now, he, as a matter of economy, hung up the noble Duke again topsy-turvy, heels upwards—a mixture of drollery and savingness which took my fancy much. And certainly, bad as she is, the Queen has contrived to trip the heels of the ministers. But I have the honour to wish her Majesty a good-night. We shall talk of a pleasanter subject.

Have you seen Turner's 'Tour in Normandy?' An old cathedral is, in its effect on my spirits, just like Milton's poetry—absorbing, elevating, overpowering. If ever I get into one I don't know how to get out. My mother has been lately at Winchester, where they are restoring the cathedral under the directions of Dr. Nott. It will be very grand when completed; and they are making new discoveries every day. Above all, they have realised a supposition of Dr. Milner's, which, because it was in that entertaining mass of miracles and papistry, his 'History of Winchester,' nobody believed. They have discovered under the old tower a Roman foundation—real, genuine, Roman masonry, thus giving colour to the worthy bishop's notion that the church was built on the site of a Roman temple; and in clearing out the crypt, which had been filled up for years with all sorts of rubbish, several very fine mitred heads have been discovered, the most perfect specimens of monastic sculpture that have been found. They are taking casts of them. In the mean time, the chapter are vowing vengeance against Dr. Nott for spending so much money; and he, on his part—now that all has been pulled about and must be set to rights again—feels quite secure in his vocation, and has been tourifying about Normandy himself, picking up new old ideas, and setting his prebendal brethren at defiance.

The cathedral was to have been reopened this autumn with a music meeting; instead of which it is all to pieces, cannot possibly be finished for these two years, and will very probably not be completed in half a dozen. I am heartily glad of this, for these prebends are all as rich as Jews (few of them, I believe, with less than four or five thousand a year church preferment); and it's a fine thing to see that noble and almost lost art flourishing again under the auspices of the church, its ancient and munificent patroness. Don't you think so?

My friend and crony, Mr. Talfourd, has taken the 'New Monthly' in hand since last February, and his articles are exquisite, particularly his dramatic criticisms. You feel that all he says is true to the very essence. His likenesses are perfect; but he takes people at their best, and sets forth their beauties instead of their defects. I never met—not even in Walter Scott—with such lenient sympathy, such indulgence to human frailty, or such cordial delight in the beautiful and the good. With all this his writings are quite as entertaining as if he cut all he touched to mincemeat like Hazlitt. But it is the nature of the man. He has a talent for admiration and enjoyment. He is to be called to the bar next term, and I am sure of his ulti-

mate success; but I particularly wish him to make his
way soon, because he has been engaged these three
years to a sweet young woman, one quite worthy of
him, and these long engagements are sad wearing
things.

Do you ever paint game and dogs? An adventure
happened to my little pet Molly (the little spaniel with
the long curling hair, so long and white and lady-like,
that you admired so much) which would make a very
pretty picture. Molly was beating a hedgerow about a
month ago, and jumped upon a pheasant, caught hold of
its tail, and held it so fast that the bird, being a strong old
cock, and making great efforts for his life, fairly lifted
her up in the air. The struggle lasted till the feathers
gave way and the pheasant flew off, leaving the honours
of his plumage as spoil to poor Molly. Papa says that
the sight was beautiful. It happened in a very fine
spot, just under an oak pollard, with ivy and holly and
fern contrasting their leaves, and the dog and the bird
glittering like gold and silver in a bright autumnal sun.
Good-night. I shall finish in a day or two.

Tuesday evening.

I really am ashamed of this handwriting, though I
have found a delicious precedent for illegible calli-
graphy (is that fine word right?) in Fleury's 'Mémoires
de Napoleon.' He had prepared, in Elba, proclama-
tions for his landing, and gave them to his secretary
and soldiers to copy when on board the brig. They
could not read them, and returned them to him, begging
him to decipher such and such words. He could not
read a syllable of them; but, after puzzling for a
moment, threw them into the sea, and began to dictate
afresh those eloquent addresses which will last as long

as the language. What a temptation to write a bad hand, is it not? Write very soon and very long, and believe me

Ever very affectionately yours,
M. R. MITFORD.

To SIR WILLIAM ELFORD, *Bickham, Plymouth.*

Three Mile Cross, Dec. 12, 1820.

'Wallace' has two great merits; he was born before the invention of gunpowder; and he is acted by Macready —a performer, in my mind, of great versatility, taste, and enthusiasm, and with a voice so delicious that there is a pleasure in listening to it quite unconnected with the words he utters—like that of hearing fine music. He is good to look at, too, as far as picturesqueness (without beauty) goes. In one place 'Wallace,' when surprised by the treachery of his friend Monteith, drops his sword from horror and consternation, and stands senseless and motionless whilst he is seized and chained. Now it is certain that the real Wallace would have chopped Monteith's head off, together with half a score of the English soldiers', and been shocked at his friend's treachery when he had gained the victory; but that's the author's affair, and Macready manages the difficult attitude of the breathing statue with inimitable grace and beauty. He quite made one forget the absurdity till the next morning. This Mr. Macready is a very intelligent person.

I left my Mr. Talfourd in a ridiculous quandary. Colburn (the proprietor of the 'New Monthly Mag.') had engaged Campbell as editor. Campbell (after being laid up on the road and losing ten days, which in all his editorship he will never recover) was just come to town, and Colburn and Mr. Talfourd were

going to do homage to the great little man. How
Colburn could ever think of such an editor I cannot
imagine! To be sure, they are to have the lectures for
make-weights; but for anything else they could not
have engaged any one more inefficient. Do you happen
to know Mr. Campbell? I dare say not. I do. Oh!
he is such a pretty, little, delicate, ladylike, finical
gentleman! He would look so well in a mob-cap,
hemming a pocket handkerchief, or in a crape turban,
flirting a fan. He is such a doubter,—such a hummer
and hawer—such a critical Lord Eldon, so heavy and
so slow. He was full fifteen years getting up that
notable failure, the 'Specimens,' the whole of his part
of which might have been put into an eighteenpenny
pamphlet, or two sides of the 'Times' newspaper—fifteen
years was he at that! Think what will become of the
magazine, which, as Talfourd says, "is like a steam-
boat, and must come to the hour in spite of wind and
tide." Then his reputation is just of that sort (high
and tottering) which will make him afraid to praise for
fear of setting up a rival, or to blame for fear of being
thought envious. What will become of the magazine?
were the last words of Mr. Talfourd. In the meantime,
Colburn is making magnificent offers. He has proffered
twenty guineas a sheet (five more than Hazlitt gets for
the 'Table Talk' in the 'London') to Horace Smith
(one of the 'Rejected Addressers,' you know) for any
contribution, prose or verse, and he will give Talfourd
his weight in gold rather than part with him.

By way of making amends for the very great stupidity
of my letter, I shall give you a little bit of Mr. Haydon's last letter to me. It's very charming writing, I
think. Now for it:—" Edinburgh is the finest town for
situation in Europe. The two towns, Old and New, are

built on two ridges, which are joined by land bridges, like the towns of antiquity. Some streets run over the others, and afford beautiful combinations, quite surprising. Towers, arches, houses, streets, bridges, rocks, castles, craggy hills, are tunnelled together in a wilderness and profusion, a contrast and daring beauty that render the whole town like the wild dream of some great genius in architecture. I never saw such a place, and if the inhabitants proceed with taste they will make it the most beautiful thing in modern times." (Then follows the account of getting up his picture): "The effect was, thank God! decisive, the room crowded, and the public days just as great. I dined with Walter Scott. I am delighted with the unaffected simplicity of his family. Jeffrey has a singular expression — poignant, bitter, piercing—as if his countenance never lit up but at the perception of some weakness in human nature. Whatever you praise to Jeffrey he directly chuckles out some error which you did not perceive; whatever you praise to Scott he joins heartily with yourself, and directs your attention to some additional beauty. Scott throws a light on life by the beaming qualities of his soul, and so dazzles you that you have no time or perception for anything but its beauties; whilst Jeffrey seems to delight in holding up his hand before the light in order that he may spy out its deformities. The face of Scott is the expression of a man whose great pleasure has been to shake Nature by the hand; while to point at her with his finger, from the expression of his face, has certainly been the chief enjoyment of Jeffrey. I have been received by all classes with an enthusiastic hospitality. The artists met. I dined with them, and had my health drunk with three times three. Indeed, I am highly grateful, and think from the result that my Edinburgh trip will be a good move in the glorious game I am playing. Lockhart I have dined with. Wilson I think the most powerful mind I have encountered here; he is a man of great genius, and will make a distinguished figure. Mrs. Grant is very ill, though I had the pleasure to see her. My visit has confirmed my conviction of Scott's being the author of the Scotch novels; he made a complete slip the day I dined with him," &c., &c.

There is but one drawback to the honour and pleasure of receiving such letters—the dreadful necessity of answering them. I am as afraid of Mr. Haydon as a schoolboy of the rod. I don't know why, except that one's very paper blushes at the idea of encountering those tremendous eyes. And writing under fear, my letters are the most prim, correct, well-written, stupid, un-idea'd sheets of inanity that ever issued from the desk of a young lady. Ah! you would not know my pen again—for she's a goosecap, you know, and a romp, and a saucebox, and a sad idle hussey when she scampers to meet you, and never dreams of behaving prettily and holding up her head, and turning out her toes, as she does when she moves in a minuet pace and makes her curtsey to Mr. Haydon—does she? Mr. Haydon is a delightful person, notwithstanding my awe. I went to see his small picture when I was in town, ' The Agony in the Garden,' which he is painting for Mr. Philips. The figure of Christ is finished, and the head is exquisite—divine! there will be no difference of opinion about that, I am sure.

The ' Essays and Sketches of Character by a Gentleman who has left his Lodgings,' are Lord John Russell's (who, by-the-by, is much overpraised as a writer by his party—do the Whigs mean to make him editor of the

' Edinburgh Review,' I wonder? and is Jeffrey sick?).
' Advice to Julia,' is by Mr. Luttrell, another Whiggish
gentleman ; and the flaming articles about the Queen in
the ' Times' are by Captain Stirling, the author of the
' Letters of Vetus,' some years ago. I am reading the
' History of New York,' a very clever but rather long
jeu d'esprit by Diedrick Knickerbocker, *alias* Washington Irving, author of the ' Sketch Book ;' very clever—
you would like it. And now, my dear friend, good-
night. This is a pretty good dose of news and nonsense.
Write to me very soon. Ever, my dear Sir William,

Most affectionately yours,

M. R. M.

CHAPTER VI.

LETTERS FOR 1821.

To B. R. HAYDON, ESQ.

Three Mile Cross, Jan. 7, 1821.

MY DEAR SIR,

I take the advantage of a county meeting, which will make franks as " plenty as blackberries," to thank you for the London letter which was so delightful a companion to the Edinburgh one. I agree with you very thoroughly in your love for the Endless City. I am something of a Cockney in my tastes, in spite of my rustic habits. I like no other great town, but I like London and all that comes from it—books, friends, letters, gowns, are all the more welcome for bearing the London mark. The ' London Magazine ' itself is the better for its title ; and I don't think Mr. Charles Lamb would write so delightfully anywhere else.

I have been very busy—audaciously busy—writing a tragedy. We are poor, you know. When I was in town I saw an indifferent tragedy, of which the indifferent success procured for the author three or four hundred pounds. This raised my emulation, which the splendid reception of ' Virginius ' or ' Mirandola,' would never have excited ; and I began to write on the subject of ' Fiesco,' whose conspiracy against Doria is so beautifully told in Robertson's ' Charles the Fifth.' There is a German tragedy of the same name, I believe, by Schiller ; but I have neither seen nor sought for it—

probably on the same principle on which Mr. Fuseli avoids nature, for fear that Schiller should "put me out." It is finished; that is, it was finished; but as I had unluckily slid my hero off the scene like a ghost, I am advised to write the fifth act over again, which I shall do next week. It is terribly feeble and womanish, of course — wants breadth — wants passion—and has nothing to redeem its faults but a little poetry and some merit, they say, in the dialogue. I am afraid it will not be accepted and that you will never hear of it again; but I could not bear to make an attempt of the sort without confiding my many fears and my few hopes to one who will, I am sure, sympathize with both. My anxiety on this subject is not of vanity. It is not fame or praise that I want, but the power of assisting my dearest and kindest father. I am in very kind and skilful hands; 'Fiesco' is now with Mr. Talfourd, our highly gifted townsman, who gives me that which is most precious, time, and advice and criticism almost as good as yours on 'Mirandola.' I suppose it is the etiquette not to mention these things till they are actually accepted. So you will have the goodness not to speak of it.

Should you meet with any high and ample story for a tragedy, will you think of me and send it me? I wish to try some grander subject. Have you heard lately of Mr. Keats?

Ever most sincerely yours,

M. R. MITFORD.

To Sir WILLIAM ELFORD, *Bickham, Plymouth.*

Three Mile Cross, Feb. 8, 1821.

Your last letter, my dear friend, gave me more than usual pleasure. So you scold me, do you! Well, that is a greater proof of kindness than I ever expected to receive. Pray scold me again, for I like it.

Mrs. Dickinson has had great success in matchmaking lately—an amusement of which, deny it as she may, she is remarkably fond. We have a celebrated beauty hereabouts, a Miss B——, a fine, gentlemanlike, dashing, spirited girl—who, with the usual fate of beauties, attracted a good deal of admiration and very little love. On the other hand, there was a soft, ladylike, fair, delicate youth, with red whiskers and a great talent for silence, a great-grandson of three generations of Generals H——, who, well-born, well-bred, and well-estated, seemed just made to lean upon such a fine manly supporter as Bessy B——. So thought Mrs. Dickinson, and the match is made; they are already deep in settlements and wedding clothes—and the marriage will take place forthwith. How she brought him to the offer I cannot imagine. She says he did it all himself; but I don't believe her.

I must tell you of a misfortune that befel me in this case. I was dining at Farley Hill on the very day that it happened to strike Mrs. Dickinson that they would make a nice couple, and had the ill luck to sit next to Mr. H—— at table; he held his tongue in the most provoking manner possible, and, when I made him talk, talked not nonsense, but the dullest, gravest, prosiest, sense—vapid, stale, commonplace— a hundred years behind the spirit of the age—such tame moralities as the first General H—— might have discussed with one of Queen Anne's maids of honour.

Well, after dinner, as I was standing wearily before the drawing-room fire, indulging in the *ennui* engendered by Mr. H——'s silence and conversation, Mrs. Dickinson, full of her new project and wanting my

assistance to accomplish it, brought Miss B—— up to
me, and asked, in her quiet manner, " How do you
like Mr. H——'s face? What does it express?"—
"Nothing," said I, in a lazy, truth-telling tone—little
dreaming that I was giving this flattering opinion before
his future lady and love.

Notwithstanding this awkward blunder, I am really
glad of the match. They are both very worthy and
well-meaning young people; though it's a pity they
can't change sexes: and there's great chance of their
improving one another, and greater still of their being
happy together. Adieu, my dear friend. Believe me
ever most faithfully yours,   M. R. MITFORD.

To SIR WILLIAM ELFORD, *Bickham, Plymouth.*

Three Mile Cross, March 22, 1821.

Oh! my dear Sir William, I don't suppose I shall
ever have the comfort and amusement of writing a long
letter again! " First recover that and then thou shalt
hear farther." I am so busy. Since I came back from
London I have written a tragedy on the subject of
" Fiesco," the Genoese nobleman who conspired against
Doria. I am also writing for the magazines—poetry, criticism, and dramatic sketches. I work as hard as a lawyer's clerk ; and besides the natural loathing of pen and
ink which that sort of drudgery cannot fail to inspire, I
have really at present scarcely a moment to spare, even
for the violets and primroses.

You would laugh if you saw me puzzling over my
prose. You have no notion how much difficulty I find
in writing anything at all readable. One cause of this
is, my having been so egregious a letter-writer. I have
accustomed myself to a certain careless sauciness, a
fluent incorrectness, which passed very well with in-

dulgent friends, such as yourself, my dear Sir William, but will not do at all for that tremendous correspondent, the Public. So I ponder over every phrase, disjoint every sentence, and finally produce such lumps of awkwardness, that I really expect, instead of paying me for them, Mr. Colburn and Mr. Baldwin will send me back the trash. But I will improve. This is another resolution, which is as fixed as fate.

Well, I am now going to make a strange request. Will you, my dear friend, have the goodness to *lend* me those letters of mine which you have taken the trouble to keep. I am not going to publish them; of that you may be sure. But I want to write an essay on Miss Austen's novels, which are by no means valued as they deserve; and I am sure I should find better materials in my letters to you, written just after I read them, than I should be able to compound from my own recollection. Of course, I am not going to print them in the form of letters, or to have any allusions to names or persons. All that I intend is, to select any happy expressions (if I chance to find any), or any vivid descriptions—to steal from myself, as it were; and if you, my dear Sir William, will condescend to be an accessory before the fact in that petty larceny, I shall be much obliged to you. You can bring the letters with you; for I shall depend on seeing you in our smoky den, though I am rather ashamed of its dirt and dinginess.

I mean to send mamma off to Winchester—she can't bear paint—and to have it whitened and tidied up this summer; but you must let us have a sight of you, for my going to town is very uncertain. It depends on my play: and I have no hopes of its being accepted; and when I give myself a few days' holidays it will be probably later in the year, and my head-quarters will be

Richmond, Twickenham, or Kew. I have many friends in
those parts. So you must come, just to satisfy yourself
that I am fatter and rosier than ever, in spite of my
quill-driving, and as gay as a lark—my tragedies notwithstanding.

What a terrible affair this duel is! What a pity that
poor John Scott* did not at once fight Mr. Lockhart with
Horace Smith for his second ; or, which would have been
better still, say firmly that he would not fight at all in
a literary quarrel. He is now the victim of his own con-
temptible second ; a man who is a pawnbroker on Lud-
gate Hill and a dandy in St. James's Street ; and who
egged on his unhappy friend to gratify his own trumpery
desire of notoriety. I hope he will be severely dealt with.

Write and tell me where you are in town—and remember not to forget that you are to come and see us.

Most faithfully and affectionately yours,

M. R. M.

How much I shall like to see your landscape !

To Sir William Elford, *Bickham, Plymouth.*

Three Mile Cross, April 4, 1821.

My tragedy is still in Mr. Macready's hands, but I
am afraid it will be ultimately rejected. Ah ! I shall
never have the good luck to be damned ! Mr. Macready
wrote the other day to my friend and his friend who
gave him my play, and this mutual friend copied his
letter for my edification. It was, in the first place, the
prettiest letter I ever read in my life—thoroughly careless, simple, unpresuming—showing great diffidence of

* A friend of Haydon's, and editor of the ' Champion ' and ' London
magazines. He was killed in a duel with Mr. Christie, arising from a
misunderstanding with Mr. Lockhart.

his own judgment, the readiest good-nature, the kindest
and most candid desire to be pleased—quite the letter of
a scholar and a gentleman, and not the least like that of
an actor. As far as regarded my tragedy, it contained
much good criticism. Mr. Macready thinks—and he is
right—that there is too little of striking incident, and
too little fluctuation. Indeed, I have made my 'Fiesco'
as virtuous and as fortunate as Sir Charles Grandison,
and he goes about *prôné* by everybody and setting everybody to rights much in the same style with that worthy
gentleman, only that he has one wife instead of two
mistresses. Nevertheless, the dialogue, which is my
strong part, has somehow "put salt upon Mr. Macready's
tail," so that he is in a very unhappy state of doubt
about it, and cannot make up his mind one way or the
other. The only thing upon which he was decided was
that the handwriting was illegible, and that it must be
copied for presentment to the managers. This has been
done accordingly, and Mr. Macready and they will now
do exactly as they like.

I am delighted to find that you think I may succeed
as a dramatic writer. I am now occupied in dramatic
sketches for 'Baldwin's Magazine'—slight stories of
about one act, developed in fanciful dialogues of loose
blank verse. If Mr. Baldwin will accept a series of
such articles they will be not merely extremely ad-
vantageous to me in a pecuniary point of view (for
the pay is well up—they give fifteen guineas a sheet),
but excellent exercises for my tragedies. At the same
time I confess to you that nothing seems to me so
tiresome and unsatisfactory as writing poetry. Ah!
how much better I like working flounces! There,
when one had done a pattern, one was sure that one
had got on ; and had the comfort of admiring one's

work and exulting in one's industry all the time that
one was in fact indulging in the most comfortable in-
dolence.   Well! courage, Missy Mitford! (as ' Blackwood's Magazine' has the impudence to call me!)
Courage, mon amie!   If you go on dramatising at
this rate six years longer, you will get as inured to it
as to working flounces, or writing to your dear Sir
William. All your fidgettiness will disappear, Missy.
The postman is this moment waiting (I did not expect
him for this half-hour), and I have only time to say God
bless you!

M. R. MITFORD.

To SIR WILLIAM ELFORD, 54, *Piccadilly, London.*

Three Mile Cross, April 20, 1821.

I thank you very much, my ever dear and kind
friend, for your good-humoured indulgence of my im-
portunate request. And now, after having coaxed and
persuaded you to *lend* me the plaything I wanted, and
which you are afraid I shall spoil, nothing is more probable than that I may either make no use of it at all,
or that I may make the precise use which you point
out. Any way, I shall be glad to see these poor letters
again (for I do not think I have ever written any with
so little reserve—so much *con amore*), and I promise
you to keep them safely *for you*—not to spoil them, if
I can possibly help it, in any way—and to look them
over with the view to make a volume or two of them, if
I can, before I proceed to the extracting process I
threatened.

By-the-way I must tell you a remarkable circumstance which has just happened to Mrs. Hofland. They
have been for many years engaged in a chancery suit,
on the expected success of which they have placed great

reliance. It has been given in their favour, but, as the costs are to be paid out of the property, not a farthing will come to them! At first, however, they knew nothing of this, for their solicitor having neglected to write, they heard only from a neighbour that the Chancellor's decree was in their favour, and Mrs. Holland immediately set off for London to learn the particulars. She was quite overcome by what she heard, and was about to mount the outside of the Twickenham coach to return, 'all amort,' as you may suppose, when, recollecting she should save sixpence in going by the Richmond stage, and such a one being at hand, she withdrew her foot; although a most respectable woman, with her husband at her side, offered to make room for her. Home she came by the Richmond coach and saved her sixpence—and her life. The Twickenham coach was overturned an hour after, and that decent woman, in whose place she would have sat, killed on the spot. The husband had his collar-bone and a rib broken. This most striking event gave a new and just turn to her thoughts.

My other calamity need not annoy me in the least, but it does, nevertheless. You shall hear it. The Duke of Wellington's sons are at home for the Eton holidays, and they come every day to a little alehouse next door, to take lessons in French of a Jew, who is lodging there purposely to teach them. "The poor little lads, ma'am," said my neighbour, the landlord, "are kept very strict; they never look up but their tutor corrects them; and there they sit in my parlour from eleven o'clock till half-past four and never have a glass of anything." Without sympathising very deeply in the last grievance enumerated by my friend of the tap-room, I am quite indignant at the poor little boys being cheated out of their holidays. Learning French, poor souls, when they

ought to be playing cricket, or stealing birds' nests, or
doing mischief, or doing nothing! Beating Napoleon
was a joke to this wickedness. The only thing which
even looks like the holidays is their mode of conveyance, which is generally five in a gig, rain or shine.
Once they came on horseback, and then they had a
humpbacked boy on a donkey galloping after them by
way of footman to carry their books. Adieu, my dear
friend.

Most gratefully and affectionately yours,

M. R. MITFORD.

To B. R. HAYDON, ESQ.

Seymour Court, near Marlow,
May 2, 1821.

Do not you see with what a shaking hand I am writing?
I must tell you how it happens. A very kind and partial old friend, Mr. Johnson, the owner of this beautiful
place, is lately dead, and his sister sent for me to assist
her in arranging and cataloguing his very curious and
valuable library. Mr. Johnson was a great politician,
an active member of the Hampden Club; and all his
political books are left to your countryman, Mr. Northmore. So we are dividing, as well as we can, the
politics from the history, and getting the rest into order
for sale. Never, I believe, had mortal such a job since
the princess in the fairy tale, who was ordered to sepa-
rate the plumage of each bird from a room full of feathers. I have got a room entirely full of books—
French, English, Italian, and Latin, all pell-mell—no
two in their proper places, and nobody to help but a
mistress partly blind, and a maid wholly stupid. Oh!
dear me! So I have been lifting about heavy books for
these three days, and making something like a catalogue

between whiles, and I am now set down to talk to you
to comfort and refresh myself. In addition to the other
difficulties of this book-sorting, I have the strongest possible desire to *crib* as much as I can from Mr. Northmore, for, Mr. Johnson having unfortunately neglected to
renew the lives, this lovely place, and the valuable estate
round it, fall immediately to the Dean and Chapter of
Bristol, and the excellent sister, who has devoted so many
years to his comfort, will return to comparative poverty.
I hope the library will sell well. Do you know anything
of the scenery round Marlow? Oh! it is so beautiful!
Especially the view from this house, which stands on the
brow of a hill, and looks down on Marlow (a town made
to be looked at a mile off—the charm vanishes when
you approach nearer)—Marlow, so intermixed with
trees, and the Thames winding like a snake, showing
himself only by glimpses, but giving the perpetual consciousness of his presence—Bisham Abbey, that oldest
and most venerable place; and the whole prospect
crowned by hanging beech woods, just in their young
shining leaves, so enchantingly varied by gleams of the
sun wandering over them, and the hills folding in so
exquisitely. Oh! it is beautiful! I wished for you
very much last night when I went out to hear the
nightingales.

I must tell you a story which comes from Germany.
The King of Naples having arrived at Laybach before
the other sovereigns, was desirous to have the amusement of bear hunting, which, of course, was to be provided for him. But there being no bears resident in
the neighbourhood, one was purchased of a Savoyard,
and placed a few miles out of town, in a thicket. The
king, attended by a train of curs and courtiers, arrived
near the place, and the bear, finding himself in the

neighbourhood of so much good company, fancied he was to perform as usual, and came out on his hind legs in a most graceful attitude. The grace of the poor creature, alas! had no effect on the hard heart of his Neapolitan majesty, who discharged his piece, and shot him dead. This story is none of my radical inventions. It came from Lord Ashburton to Sir W. Elford, and from him to me.

Ever, my dear Mr. Haydon,

Most sincerely and affectionately yours,

M. R. MITFORD.

To SIR WILLIAM ELFORD, *Bickham, Plymouth.*

Three Mile Cross, July 1, 1821.

I had the honour a week or two ago to be introduced to your friend Mr. Bowles, the poet. I must tell you the story. Going into Dr. Valpy's the back way, I met the old butler. "Are the ladies in the parlour, Newman?" "Yes, ma'am—and ma'am, there's Mr. Bowles, the poet," quoth Newman. Well, I thought, I shall be very glad to see him, and in I walked. The Doctor met me at the door, snatched my hand, led me triumphantly up to the window where Mr. Bowles was standing, and then snatched his hand and endeavoured to join the two after the fashion of the marriage ceremony (you know how that is, my dear Sir William), introducing him as "Mr. Bowles the poet," but calling me, as I have since remembered, nothing but "Mary." Mr. Bowles, rather astounded, drew back. I, astonished in my turn at such a way of receiving the daughter of an old acquaintance (for my father has known him these thirty years), drew back too, and between us we left the dear Doctor in worse consternation than either, standing alone in the window. A minute after Miss

Valpy asked after Dr. Mitford, and all was immediately right. Mr. Bowles was very pleasant and sociable, talked a great deal of Lord Byron and the Pope question, in which we exactly agree, and in which, from not having read the prosy pamphlet in which he has so marred his own good cause, I was able to agree with him most conscientiously. Pray do you like his wife? Is not she a coarse, cold, hard woman? and rather vulgarish? All this she seemed to me. He is very unaffected and agreeable. Well, I will not trespass much longer, for with so much to do and to think of, a trespass it must be. You will write to me when you have time, and you will persuade Mrs. Waldron*— Lady Elford—into partaking of the family indulgence towards your poor little correspondent.

Most sincerely and affectionately yours,

M. R. MITFORD.

'Fiesco' has been returned on my hands as I foresaw, and I am now knee-deep in another tragedy on the subject of the Venetian Doge Foscari, who was obliged to condemn his own son.

To SIR WILLIAM ELFORD, *Bickham, Plymouth.*

Three Mile Cross, August 30, 1821.

Turn you off, my dear friend! Why, how did I know but you were tourifying and honeymooning. Turn you off! I that always begin a letter by return of post (that's an excellent new bull!), and generally send it off within three days. Turn you off! Pray, were you ever turned off in your life? And do you think me the person to begin? Eh! I have a good mind to play the affronted. But I can't write two letters for

* Whom Sir William intended to marry.

one. No, those good days of doing nothing, the history
of which used to amuse you so much, are past and gone;
I am a busy woman; I write tragedies and essays and
work my brains out. And pray, if you should be such
a flatterer as to miss my letters, and should pay me
the compliment of being a little angry, don't say, " She's
idle—naughty one!" but " Poor thing, she's busy!" I
assure you I should like nothing so well as to be able to
fling my tragedies and my articles into the fire, and read
novels for your sake, and write long, long letters about
them all the day throughout. But even now, busy as I
am, I have been reading Madame de Stäel's posthumous
works. I was curious to see what she did in the drama way;
not much to the purpose, I think, though there is some
merit in ' *Sapho*,' as that French learned lady is pleased
to spell the Lesbian muse. It is astonishing how those
French people turn every name according to the fashion
of their own barbarous tongue. There is her ' *Dix Années
d'Exil*,' too, which I detest for its abuse of Napoleon.

To tell you a secret, I had some sympathy with the
dear Emperor in his dislike of that Germanized
Frenchwoman, whose example as to conduct has done
great harm, and her example in literature has done no
good. I hate that sentimentality. However, I have
done with Madame de Stäel, and I am now stuck fast
in the mire of ' Heraline,' a novel in four mortal
volumes by our friend of the long nose, Miss Hawkins.
I never mean to finish it: and now that I read so little,
I really cannot imagine what could induce me to begin
it. Of course I don't recommend that " do-me-good "
piece of vulgarity to you.

How are you off for partridges? There are fewer
round here than were left last year. And how do your
dahlias and hollyhocks and tiger-lilies go on? I have

had some of them all, and I wish they were immortal.
The hollyhocks, especially, were the most perfect beauties I ever saw or ever imagined; garlands of rosy
blossoms a thousand times more lovely than any rose
that ever blew. Good-bye, my dear friend. My father
and mother beg their kindest remembrances. Write to
me very soon; you will, if you wish to hear—if all that
you so kindly say on that subject be not make-believe.

Most sincerely and affectionately yours,

M. R. MITFORD.

To B. R. HAYDON, ESQ.

Three Mile Cross, Oct. 31, 1821.

MY DEAR SIR,

The magnificent portion of bride-cake arrived this
morning and shall be distributed as you desire. Yes,
we will set half the pretty girls in the parish dreaming
on it. I wanted to make a bargain with one, to whom
I gave a bit just now, that she should tell me her dream.
But she says that would destroy the charm. There was no
saying a word after that, you know. By-the-by, nothing
but the sort of sacred air that breathes around bride-
cake could have preserved your munificent present and
brought it safe to us. By some accident it was sent,
not by a Reading, but a Newbury coach, and found its
way to Three Mile Cross, after being carried half way to
Newbury, through the intervention of all manner of men
and women, postboys, and chambermaids, and keepers
of turnpike gates. But everything belonging to such a
wedding and such a honeymoon as yours will turn out
right, depend on it. You see that your good luck ex-
tends even to your friends, and travels about with your
bride-cake. Oh! it will never forsake you, never! I
think that last honeymoon letter, written whilst the

fair bride was sitting, working, and smiling at your
side, was prettier even than the first. Did you read it
to her as you wrote it? Or shall I send her a copy?
It was worthy even of that charming seal. How much
you must both have felt in going into your painting-
room. Will the 'Lazarus' be finished against next
season? If anything could improve your genius, it
would be living in such a sunshine of love and beauty.

Miss James is by this time back again at Richmond.
I wished her very much to call on you last Sunday or
Monday, that she might leave with you my poor tragedy,
which I should, of all things, have liked you to read, I
have such an opinion of your judgment. But it is now
out of her hands. Only think of my shocking ill-luck
in having written on the same subject with Lord Byron.
The story of Foscari! I am so distressed at the idea of
a competition, not merely with his lordship's talents,
but with his great name; and the strange awe in which
he holds people; and the terrible scoffs and sneers in
which he indulges himself: that I have written to Mr.
Talfourd requesting him to consult another friend on
the propriety of entirely suppressing my play, which
had gone to town to be presented to the manager the
very day that the subject of Lord Byron's was announced. I rather think now that it will not be offered—
that Mr. Talfourd will suppress it; and I heartily wish
he may. If it be sent back to me unoffered, I shall immediately begin another play on some German story, and
shall take for the opening the exquisite first act of the
'Orestes' of Euripides. What astonishing people those
Greek dramatists were! I am just now reading Potter's
'Æschylus' with the intensity of admiration with which
you would look at the frescoes of Michael Angelo. Happening to express something of this enthusiasm to a

scholar of a very great name, he answered, "The 'Prometheus?' Yes, the 'Prometheus' is rather pretty— prettyish—one of the prettiest." Now what business has this man to know Greek? And what business have I to be intruding so long on you? Good-bye, my dear sir. My father and mother join me in every kind remembrance and kinder wish to you and Mrs. Haydon.

Ever most sincerely yours,

M. R. MITFORD.

To SIR WILLIAM ELFORD, *Bickham, Plymouth.*

Three Mile Cross, Nov. 23, 1821.

Your picture, my dear Sir William, must, with your fine taste and execution, be charming. I have always had a preference for close, shut-in scenes, both in a landscape and in nature, and prefer the end of a woody lane, with a rustic bridge over a little stream, or a bit of an old cottage or farmhouse, with a porch and a vine and clustered chimneys peeping out amongst trees, to any prospect that I ever saw in my life. I dare say that this taste of mine is as wrong as I confess it to be ignoble, for I never met with any one who agreed with me in my opinion. But your picture will be quite poetry. I hope you will send it to Somerset House. Talking of pictures (this is not a jerk), we were a little astonished, in common with all his friends—for he had kept it a profound secret—at Mr. Haydon's marriage. It is entirely a love match, and I hope and trust that it will make him as happy as he deserves to be all his life long. He speaks of her (for I have heard from him several times) as still more amiable than beautiful; and as it has been a long acquaintance, and not a very short courtship, there is every reason to believe that he is right. She is in Devonshire just now, to put the final

close to some matters of business, and he is gone to
Scotland to put up his picture. I had a letter from him
to-day dated Edinburgh.

Sunday.

I have got a frank for to-day, and having, unluckily,
been hindered by those gadflies, morning visitors, must
finish at the gallop. We have been very gay at Reading, with our triennial theatricals—Dr. Valpy's Greek
play. There is nothing so charming as that classical
amusement (by-the-way the Doctor always makes me
write the official *puff* account, and I have been hunting
more minutes than I ought to have spared from my
letter to find a Reading paper to show you what a
famous theatrical critic I am, but I can't find it, so you
must believe my own puff of my puffing)—nothing so
charming as the Greek play, with its beautiful accuracy
of costume, every fold copied after some antique statue,
its fine groupings, and the delicious sound of that magnificent language. The play this year was the 'Orestes'
of Euripides, of which the opening scene is perhaps
one of the finest and truest exhibitions of nature that
has ever been given by any poet in any language. The
Greek play was enchanting; but every pleasure has its
alloy; and Dr. Valpy, against all prayer and all warn-
ing, was determined to make us pay for our precious
delight by inflicting on us after the 'Orestes' the three
last acts of 'King John,' as altered from Shakespeare
by himself. Fancy the worst parts of Shakespeare's
worst play, with the most iniquitous alterations ever devised by schoolmaster, acted by a rabble of boys of all
ages and sizes!—all bad; some thick and some stunted
like pincushions; others pointed and angular and sharp-
limbed, as it were, like scissors; the Dauphin, a little
round short fellow, not taller than a thimble; and King

Philip, a shot-up limber lad, tall, and bent in the middle like a broken thread paper! Oh, that King John! I shan't recover it for two years. Ever since the Greek play I have been trying as well as I can, in French and English and Italian translations, to get at the Greek dramatists, and am so in love with Æschylus and Sophocles (Euripides, though very fine, is rather in a lower style—more pathetic than sublime) that I can really hardly think or talk of anything else, Sophocles in particular; and, of all Sophocles, 'Philoctetes' exceeds all that I have ever seen before. There never was, and never will be, anything like the Greek dramatists. The moulds are broken. The English romantic drama is not more different from them in form than the French in spirit. The English translations of Sophocles are abominable. I find that I get at him best from a literal version in French prose, and I have half a mind to *do* the 'Philoctetes' into English from that source, declaring, of course, in the Preface that I know nothing at all of Greek.

God bless you, my dear friend! I hope to hear a better account of both your invalids. Kindest regards from all.

Ever yours,

M. R. M.

CHAPTER VII.

To SIR WILLIAM ELFORD, *Bickham, Plymouth.*

Three Mile Cross, Jan. 3, 1822.

THIS is the first real absolute letter (notes that are dated "Tuesday morning" and "Wednesday evening," and so forth, don't count in this case)—the first genuine letter that I have sat down to write in 1822, and it shall be addressed to one of the kindest and best of my correspondents. Your very long and delightful letter gives the best possible proof of health and spirits, and I assure you, my dear Sir William, it is quite a consolation to think of a dear friend who is well and happy.

Have you read the 'Pirate?' And do you like it? I think you will say "No" to both questions. You have not probably yet had time to read it, and you have heard enough of the story to be pretty sure that you shall not like it. I don't at all. There is a great deal too much about Zetland superstitions and Zetland manners and Zetland revelry, and there is an old witch who would of herself be enough to spoil the finest thing that ever was written. What a fancy the Great Unknown has for a witch! I verily believe this Norma is the ninth or tenth of that species which he has produced, and of all of them she is the worst—by far the worst. He has given her a poem in prose to recite, after the fashion of

Ossian, Chateaubriand, and those sort of people. And
there is such a quantity of her too! Altogether the
'Pirate' is perhaps nearly on a par with the later
works, for there has been nothing very great since
'Ivanhoe' (notwithstanding the beauty of one or two
scenes in the 'Monastery')—nothing like 'The Antiquary,' and 'Waverley,' and 'Guy Mannering,' and 'Old
Mortality;' the 'Antiquary' being, to my taste, the one
and unrivalled of them all. I thoroughly agree with
you, for your reasons and others, as to the certainty of
the books being written by Sir W. Scott.

Yes, the second volume of the 'Sketch Book' is certainly a little heavy, a little mawkish, and a little un-
faithful in the English details. Mr. Washington Irving
is excellent in humour, and in old Dutch colonists and
other American diversities, but he must not meddle
with us proud English. I wish he would give an
American novel, with all the peculiarities of that ridiculous country. We have a fine specimen of New York
manners close by. A rich friend of ours was taken in
by Mr. Birkbeck's fine plausible lies (there's a fine illustration of my system for you; that book of Birkbeck's
seemed as true as 'Robinson Crusoe!'), and, intending
to embark some 20,000*l.* or 30,000*l.* in Illinois, sent
out a son of seventeen to reconnoitre. Mr. Fearon's
fine 'Antidote' and other accounts soon determined
him to keep his money in England; but the son stayed
on, not in Illinois—that disagreed with him—but in
New York, and is only lately returned—a very good
sort of young man, I believe, but the most complete
Transatlantic coxcomb that ever eyes beheld. He is
solemn, smooth, and smirking—smiling like Malvolio,
though not, like him, cross-gartered—superficial as a
newspaper or a review—talking in a strange, outlandish

jargon, half of it too fine for common wear, and half too
coarse—a mixture of tissue and sackcloth—gallant to a
distressing degree; he never sees you seated but he
cants an ottoman under your feet, or standing or walking but he claps a chair down behind you, so that the
singer at a piano sometimes finds herself blockaded by
a double row of seats. His cloakings and shawlings are
worse than any cold, and he walks in a dancing step.

Jan. 9.

I have just been reading Lord Byron's plays. The
'Two Foscari' was, of course, the first object with me.
But he has taken up the business just where I left it
off, so that his play does not at all clash with mine.
The Doge is well executed, I think; but young Foscari,
notwithstanding good speeches, is utterly imbecile—an
ultra-sentimentalist, who clings, no one knows why or
wherefore, with a love-like dotage, to the country, which
has disgraced and exiled and tortured, and finishes by
killing him; and his wife, Marina, is a mere scold.
Both that and 'Sardanapalus' are miserably wire-drawn
and spun out. One is really quite tired in reading
them. 'Cain' is of a higher strain, and yet, though
there is nothing in it bolder than Milton has put into
the mouth of his Satan, one is somehow shocked at
Lucifer's speeches in 'Cain,' which never happens in
'Paradise Lost.' The impression is different. I don't
know why, but it is so. Altogether, it seems to me that
Lord Byron must be by this time pretty well convinced that the drama is not his forte. He has no spirit
of dialogue—no beauty in his groupings—none of that
fine mixture of the probable with the unexpected which
constitutes stage effect, in the best sense of the
word. And a long series of laboured speeches and set

antitheses will very ill compensate for the want of that excellence which we find in Sophocles and in Shakespeare, and which you will call Nature, and I shall call Art.

Pray, do you ever paint animals? We have a greyhound, called May Flower, of excelling grace and symmetry—just of the colour of the May blossom—like marble with the sun upon it; and she kills every hare she sees—takes them up in the middle of the back, brings them in her mouth to my father, and lays them down at his feet. I assure you she is quite a study while bringing the hares—the fine contrast of colour—her beautiful position, head and tail up, and her long neck arched like that of a swan—with the shade shifting upon her beautiful limbs, and her black eyes really emitting light! I wish you could see May Flower. Farewell, my dear friend. I have only room to say how much

I am always yours,

M. R. MITFORD.

To Sir WILLIAM ELFORD, *Bickham, Plymouth.*

Three Mile Cross, Jan. 9, 1822.

I met with a great curiosity about a month ago —a lady who had never read, scarcely heard of, the Scotch novels. She was called by all Reading "a remarkably clever, sensible, accomplished woman" (you know that, ninety-nine times out of a hundred, ladies of this character are eminently foolish), educated her daughters, talked Italian, read Latin, and understood thorough bass. She came into a friend's house where I was calling, and, finding the 'Pirate' on the table, poured out at once this ostentatious ignorance. You never saw anybody so proud of not knowing what all

the world knows—never! She actually looked down
upon us, till I thought my friend was going to be
ashamed, and make apologies for having read these
glorious books. She took heart, however (my friend),
and the lady visitor began to inquire what the Scotch
novels were—"'Waverley?'" She had heard of 'Waverley.' "'The Scottish Chiefs?'" "Oh, no! certainly
not the 'Scottish Chiefs'"—and why we praised them;
and at last, hearing that there was nothing very con-
taminating for her daughters, and that, at all events, as
they would infallibly catch the disorder some day or
other, they might as well be inoculated under her
own eye, she consented to borrow this 'Waverley,' of
which she had heard, and which we, moreover, assured
her was historical. She returned it in a day or two
with a short critique, intimating that there was much
trash in the book, but that some parts were tolerable.
I think of cultivating her acquaintance; besides, I want
to see the Misses (they are grown up). I wonder what
form vanity takes in them, and what they say about
'Waverley!'

I do not know the author of 'Valerius.' Report
gives it to Mr. Lockhart, the son-in-law of Sir W. Scott,
author of 'Peter's Letters,' and reputed editor of Blackwood's very amusing and naughty magazine. I think it
is his by the style, which is like that of 'Peter's Letters.'

I hope you are all well.

I am ever most affectionately yours,

M. R. M.

To Sir William Elford, *Bickham, Plymouth.*

Three Mile Cross, March 2, 1822.

In all the variety of letters and modes of letters which
we have at different times sent to one another, pray did

we ever try that fine classical thing a fragment? If not, I have the pleasure of beginning the practice most Pindarically in the middle of a subject. "Ruin seize thee, ruthless king" is not a finer instance of abruptness. I was talking, I believe, of Mr. Milman's new poem, the 'Martyr of Antioch.' I know that you don't read much of things printed in uneven lines, and I fancy that nine-tenths of Mr. Milman's readers care as little for poetry as you do; only that very few have the honesty to say so. They read him for fashion, for the honour and glory of reading a poem, and the soberer credit of reading a good book. It's a sort of union of sermon and romance—a Sunday evening amusement which mammas tolerate and papas smile upon. So, the book sells; and it ought to sell, for it is full of splendid passages, with only one *faux pas.* All the heathen persons, odes, and descriptions are worth a million of the Christian hymns and people. Indeed, Mr. Milman has a fine sense of classical beauty. He would make a glorious thing of some old Grecian story!

By-the-by (coming back to our eternal theme, the author of 'Waverley'), I heard a day or two back from the young American traveller of whom I have, I think, elsewhere made honourable mention, that Captain Scott is much suspected, by those who are most with him in Canada, of having at least some share in the novels. He is certainly eternally writing; and if that be not the subject, no one can guess what it is. Adieu, my dear friend.

Ever most affectionately yours,

M. R. MITFORD.

To Sir William Elford, *Bickham, Plymouth.*

Three Mile Cross, April 12, 1822.

I thank you very much, my dear Sir William, for your very kind and entertaining letter. The story of the housemaid and the picture is delicious; and I enter into it the more thoroughly, from having lately rescued some blotted papers of my own from the fangs of an animal of that species. My dramatic scene looked, as she said, such a 'tatterdemalion piece of scribble,' that she clawed it up in her paw, much as a monkey would seize on an open letter, and was actually proceeding to light a fire withal, when I snatched my precious manuscript from her devouring fangs. I wish you had seen the look of contempt with which this damsel of ours—a *ci-devant* schoolmistress—looked at my composition! I dare say she would have whipped any one of her scholars that wrote only half as ill.

Now, what shall I talk about? We have got Mrs. Opie's new novel of 'Madeline' in the house, but I have not opened it yet. One knows the usual ingredients of her tales just as one knows the component parts of a plum-pudding. So much common sense (for the flour); so much vulgarity (for the suet); so much love (for the sugar); so many songs (for the plums); so much wit (for the spices); so much fine binding morality (for the eggs); and so much mere mawkishness and insipidity (for the milk and water wherewith the said pudding is mixed up). I think she has left off being pathetic—at least I have left out that quality in my enumeration. Yet she is a very clever woman, and a good-natured woman; and though my exceeding fastidiousness with respect to style and elegance and gracefulness in writing deprives me of any pleasure in her works, there are a great many very good judges who admire her writings greatly. I hope you won't tell her this by way of a compliment, though I have lately met with a misadventure which would go near to tying one's pen down to its good behaviour all one's life. A discreet correspondent of mine (female, of course) inquired my opinion of a recent publication. I wrote her a very fair character of the work (which I did not very much admire) —a fair and candid character, with just enough of sweet to flavour the sour (like sugar in mint sauce). It was not a sweeping, knock-me-down critique—but a light, airy, neatly-feathered shaft — whose censure looked almost like praise. So much the worse for me. My goose of a correspondent took it for complimentary; and, by way of recommending me to the author of the cut-up work, fairly read him the passage out of my letter, and then in her reply gravely told me what she had done! Of course she will never get any but how-d'ye-do letters from me again as long as she lives.

To confess the truth, my dear friend, I am so thoroughly out of heart about 'Foscari' that I cannot bear even to think or speak on the subject. Nevertheless the drama is my talent—my only talent—and I mean to go on and improve. I *will* improve—that is my fixed determination. Can you recommend me a good subject for an historical tragedy? I wish you would think of this, and if you have none in your own mind, ask any likely person. It should have *two* prominent male parts—and I should prefer an Italian story in the fourteenth, fifteenth, sixteenth, or seventeenth century, as affording most scope, and being less liable to blame for any deviation from truth in the plot than any well-known incident in the greater States. I once thought of our Charles the First. He and Cromwell would form two very finely-contrasted characters—but the facts are too well known. Farewell, my dear friend.

Ever most sincerely and affectionately yours,

M. R. MITFORD.

To SIR WILLIAM ELFORD, *Bickham, Plymouth.*

Three Mile Cross, April 28, 1822.

Oh! my dear friend, how very, very sorry we are to hear of your accident! And yet, since it is so happily past, and has been borne with such cheerfulness and good-humour, it seems almost as much a matter of congratulation as of condolence. Mrs. Dickinson, who is just returned from town, was here soon after your letter arrived, and took the warm interest you can so well imagine in its contents. By-the-way, as a painter, you should have seen Mrs. Dickinson herself! She was just a thing for a painter to look at—dressed in a high gown of rich black satin, made close to her beautiful shape, with a superb ruff of "Flanders lace," a magnificent plume of feathers, and a veil that really swam about her like a cloud. She looked just like the portrait of some Spanish or Venetian beauty by Velasquez or Titian. Mr. D. is better—and the little girl "the very moral" of him. What a strange thing family-likeness is! How impossible it seems that a little fair, blooming, laughing, round-about apple-blossom of a child should resemble an old weatherbeaten stern-looking man, as shrivelled and yellow as a golden pippin! I am sorry for it; I wanted the child to be like her mother.

Pray, pray, my dear Sir William, do you read 'Blackwood's Magazine,' and 'John Bull?' Or do you leave to me—a Whig—the sole enjoyment of these Tory iniquities? To be sure there is in these modest periodicals a fine, swaggering, bold-faced impudence—a perfection of lying and of carrying it off—which is delightfully amusing. One should think that it could be only one man's gift, but the endowment must be general. It will be a heavy day for me when 'John Bull' goes to the shades. I read no other newspaper. And, in my secret soul (don't tell Mr. Talfourd) though he and I both write in the 'London' along with the Procters, the Reynoldses, and the Charles Lambs, I like 'Blackwood's' better. By-the-by, do you ever see the 'London Magazine?' Charles Lamb's articles, signed 'Elia,' are incomparably the finest specimens of English prose in the language. The humour is as delicate as Addison's, and far more piquant. Oh! how you would enjoy it! Do borrow or hire *all* the numbers of Taylor and Hessey's 'London Magazine,' and read all Elia's articles, as well as the 'Table Talks,' and the 'Confessions of an English Opium Eater,' and the '*Dramatic Sketches*,' and tell me how you like Charles Lamb.

Your very affectionate friend,
M. R. M.

To B. R. HAYDON, Esq.

Three Mile Cross, June 13, 1822.

A thousand thanks, my dear sir, for your kind and delightful letter. I felt that I had not deserved it, for I must have appeared sadly inattentive and undeserving, by being three days in town without waiting on Mrs. Haydon. But you know how it happened. When the morning came I was fit for nothing but to be packed off home. In fact, a country lady who lives almost literally in the open air, in green fields or flowery gardens, is terribly out of her element in London in hot

weather. All the time that I was in Norton Street I
felt just as I suppose that patriarchal larch-tree of Scotland must have done when crammed into a garden-pot
and coddled amongst the myrtles and orange-trees of
the Duke of Athole's greenhouse. . . . I cannot tell
you, my dear Mr. Haydon, with what pleasure and interest I read your fresh and glowing account of your
mutual happiness. No wonder that you fear society;
or, rather, that you fear that fine company which does
not deserve the name of society, and which seems to me
good for nothing but to spoil the mind, the manners,
and the very beauty, of women. For my part, I think
that ladies are now-a-days all alike—all accomplished—
all literary—all artificial—with heads divided between
quadrilles and criticism. If routes and reviews had been
extant in Shakespeare's time we should not have had
the Violas and the Desdemonas.

George Whittaker has given me ' Cœur de Lion,' by
Miss Porden, to review. He let me have it before publication, so that, happening to meet the fair author that
evening at the house of a mutual friend, and mentioning
to her that I had her new poem, she was in an astonishment past telling (my friend the bookseller having told
her there was not a copy ready), and I do verily believe
takes me for the least in the world of a fibber. She's a
very pleasant young woman, rather affected at first sight
—at least people take her for affected, because she has
a Lord Burleigh-ish way of shaking her head, and uses
more action than is common in an English lady; but
her conversation is very earnest and natural. She is
ugly of course—all literary ladies are so. I never met
one in my life (except Miss Jane Porter, and she is
rather *passée*) that might not have served for a scarecrow to keep the birds from the cherries. It's a pro-

digiously strange and disagreeable peculiarity. The fair vision was here last night, not in black satin but in white silk (N.B., white silk not half so elegant as black satin), and the little apple blossom, whom her mamma does not dress by one half so well as she dresses herself. Only fancy that poor little girl this hot weather in a stiff ruffling pelisse of Waterloo-blue silk, all tied up the front with great bows of ribbons, and a bonnet to match. She really looked, as I told her mamma, like the woman in a Dutch weatherglass. Moreover, her sponse has been here to-day, and I am afraid got soused in the thunderstorm, owing to his gallantry. He came in a beautiful pony-chaise and gave me a ride in it before he went home. I do so love a drive in a pony-chaise! If my 'Foscari' were to succeed, I should be tempted to keep one myself. You know, everything that I want or wish I always say "if 'Foscari' succeeds." I said so the other day about a new straw bonnet, and then about a white geranium, and then about a pink sash, and then about a straw workbasket, and then about a pocket-book, all in the course of one street. Good-bye, my dear sir.

Ever most sincerely yours,
M. R. MITFORD.

To SIR WILLIAM ELFORD.

Three Mile Cross, July 31, 1822.

Pray, my dear friend, have you heard the strange story of Lord Byron's consignment to Mr. Murray? It may be in the newspapers, for I do not see them; but it came to me in the freshness of MS. from a literary friend, and I shall tell you the story at a venture. Lord Byron has sent to Murray's a dead child to be interred in Harrow Churchyard, in a spot particularly pointed

out, with directions to have a splendid mausoleum
erected over it; but, if that be not permitted, then a
tablet is to be placed in a part of the church, also indi-
cated, where his eye used to rest when a schoolboy,
with the inscription,

> " He shall not come to me,
> But I shall go to him."

Very appropriate, when one remembers on what occasion David spoke those words.

To SIR WILLIAM ELFORD, *Bickham, Plymouth.*

Three Mile Cross, Oct. 12, 1822.

MY DEAR FRIEND,

Since I wrote to you I have been once or twice to
London on the business of my play, which Mr. Charles
Kemble (there is another delightful person!—I am the
least in the world in love with him—don't tell Mrs.
C. K.—he is the successor to Napoleon in my imagination)—which Mr. C. Kemble (you will begin to think my
passion not quite disinterested) promises to bring out the
first of the season. Of course nothing can be fixed till
Mr. Macready returns from his Italian tourification,
which will be, I suppose, early in next month. You
shall hear in time to beat up for recruits amongst any
of your play-going London friends; if a man of your
fashion have such a thing as a play-goer amongst his
acquaintance. Nothing, I believe, is certain in a
theatre till the curtain is fairly drawn up and let down
again; but, as far as I can see, I have, from the warm
zeal and admirable character of the new manager and
his very clever and kindhearted lady, every reason to
expect a successful *début.*

During my last stay in town I had the very great

pleasure of seeing Mr. Haydon's lovely wife. She is really a charming woman—splendidly beautiful. I never saw so fine a piece of natural colouring as is formed by her dark eyes and hair, and her brilliant complexion— and with exceedingly sweet and captivating manners. I admired her so much that I could hardly take my eyes from her to look at his picture. That is very grand indeed! The effect of the living eye in the corpse-like face is miraculous! I hope and trust it will produce an immense effect.

I would not delay my news about my play even one post; and have no M.P. under hand. Wish for me and 'Foscari.' You have all my kindest and gratefulest thoughts, though a tremendous pressure of occupation will not allow me to express them so often as I used to do. God bless you, my dear friend!

Ever yours,

M. R. MITFORD.

Did you ever see a glowworm half way up a high tree? We did last night. It was a tall elm, stripped of large branches almost to the top, as the fashion is in this country, but the trunk clothed with little green twigs, upon one of which the glowworm hung like a lamp, looking so beautiful!

To SIR WILLIAM ELFORD, *Bickham, Plymouth.*

Three Mile Cross, Nov. 16, 1822.

First, my very dear friend, let me thank you heartily and sincerely for your very kind and delightful letter. Secondly, let me pray you to thank Mr. Elford and your charming daughter for two that have given me great pleasure. I do not write to them, because when I have so good a channel for conveying my thanks, it would be but troubling them. My occupation is, writing another tragedy—my amusement is, gardening. I have now in my little garden one of the most beautiful chrysanthemums ever seen—worth coming from Bickham to see, if you be a chrysanthemum fancier. It is a very large double white flower, almost as pure and splendid as the double white camellia, and has in the inside a spot larger than a shilling of the deepest, richest purple. You never saw anything more magnificent. We imagine that this extraordinary colouring must have proceeded from some of the purple plant being mixed in with the root of the white, which is in itself a very beautiful contrast; but the white, with the purple inside, is really superb. It is covered with blossoms, and excites the envy of all the gardeners and half the ladies in the neighbourhood.

Farewell. I see no company, read no books, and, as mamma says, keep all my wit for the magazines. Ever, my dear friend,

Most gratefully and affectionately yours,

M. R. MITFORD.

'Foscari' is again delayed; but Charles Kemble, my dear Charles Kemble, says—almost swears—it shall be acted this season, and with new dresses and scenery. The play that is now going to be produced was written two years ago for the new actress, Miss Kelly.* There has been a terrible commotion in consequence of C. Kemble's reluctance to delay mine. If it were not for my absolute faith in *him* I should despair. Once more, good-bye.

* A pupil, it was said, of Mr. Macready, who succeeded in Juliet, and failed in everything else.

CHAPTER VIII.

LETTERS FOR 1823.

To SIR WILLIAM ELFORD, *Bickham, Plymouth.*

Three Mile Cross, Feb. 28, 1823.

MY DEAR FRIEND,

I have no frank, but I have at last the pleasure of being able to give you good news; and I think you would rather pay postage than not hear it. After a degree of contention and torment and suspense such as I cannot describe, one of my plays—my last and favourite play—is, I do really believe, on the point of representation, with my favourite actor for the hero. He (Mr. Macready) read it in the green-room on Wednesday, and I suppose it will be out in ten days or a fortnight. Mr. Kemble behaved very fairly and honourably—has given Macready full power in getting up the play; and, with that admirable actor (certainly the best since Garrick) and this play (certainly worth a thousand of 'Foscari'), we can do very well without him. 'Julian,' or 'The Melfi' (for I really don't know which they call it), is a tragedy on a fictitious story. I am afraid to tell you what the critics say of it—but not afraid to stake on it my dramatic hopes. Mr. Macready will be supported by Mr. Bennett (the new actor), Mr. Abbott, Miss Lacy, and Miss Foote. So you must write to your play-going friends; for I am sure that ardent spirit,

Macready, will drive the matter on. It is odd enough that I and this zealous friend of mine have never met! He is just such another soul of fire as Haydon—highly educated, and a man of great literary acquirements—consorting entirely with poets and young men of talent. Indeed it is to his knowledge of my friend Mr. Talfourd that I owe the first introduction of my plays to his notice.

Forgive this short note. I have many letters to write, and have been for the last fortnight exceedingly unwell; but this news would cure me if I were dying. *I know* that I shall be quite well to-morrow.

Ever most affectionately yours,
M. R. M.

[On the second Saturday of March, 1823, 'Julian' was performed, with Mr. Macready as the principal character. It was successful. Miss Mitford went to town for a few days on a visit to Mrs. Hofland, in Newman Street, to witness its first representation and to enjoy her triumph.]

Copy of a letter to WILLIAM MACREADY, ESQ.

Three Mile Cross, April, 1823.

MY DEAR SIR,

Do not fancy yourself engaged in another "Mirandola" office, when I take the great liberty—too great, perhaps—of requesting you to read over the enclosed scheme of a play on the story of Garzia de Medici, and to tell me if you think it be worth attempting—in one word, Yes or No! The subject first struck me in the 'Life of Benvenuto Cellini;' and on re-perusing whilst in town the intense but terrible tragedy of 'Alfieri,' I was still more caught by the contrast of character which it offers, and the dreadful truth of the catastrophe. I have somewhat injured the collision of various characters in one family, which is so striking in his play. I have omitted one of the brothers, which seemed necessary to disencumber the plot; but he could be restored, if necessary. Altogether, I do not like the subject so well as not to be very ready to abandon it if I could find a better. Procida *is* a better, but then—would that be quite right? Well, you will tell me what their 'Procida' is; and perhaps we may find out the real author.* If it be by a woman—really a woman, and writing for money—heaven forbid that I should jostle with her! If it be Mr. Milman, I should not mind taking the field—Francesca da Rimini—beginning with the scene of Phædra from Euripides, and making the brother—I forget his name, Paolo—quite unconscious of his love till it bursts on him suddenly in reading with her the old romance. That would be very fine, if we had a great actress—but Miss Lacy! Oh! Rienzi? I don't think you like Rienzi; and perhaps Gibbon has done too much for the story, and it might be censured as too political. The temptation is, that there exists, or that I have fancied, some slight resemblance of character and history between him and Napoleon. Both were of obscure birth—both governing by force of mind—both driven headlong to ruin by an indomitable self-will—rising by liberty and falling by ambition. Surely there is enough resemblance to justify an attempt to portray the man who, with all his faults, has possessed my imagination all my life long! But I am afraid of the attempt. It would be an over-excitement—I should get nervous and fail. Massaniello, the fisherman of Naples—is he promising? Am I likely to find any-

* Mrs. Hemans. It was produced under the name of 'The Sicilian Vespers.'

thing to the purpose in Froissart? I have not seen
that delightful book for many years, but I remember
a romantic story of the Count of Orthes and his son; I
don't, however, think it would do for tragedy, though
the old chronicler is full of high and chivalrous incident.
I must read him for that. I am half afraid of attacking
Greek or Roman story; because women, from mere
want of learning, from the absence of real depth, are
always pedantic, and spread their thin gold leaf over an
immense quantity of surface. And yet history is best
for a thousand reasons. Well, if I were wise I should
form a strong resolution to conquer my besetting sin
of idleness—to renounce " *le délicieux far niente,*" as
Rousseau calls it, and work hard this summer, so as to
produce two or three tragedies from which you might
choose, if any were worthy of your choice, and throw
the others into the fire.

My father, who *would* go to town, tells me, as your
dear sister does, that ' Julian ' went splendidly on Wednesday, and not amiss, considering the wet night, on
Friday, and that you think it rising. But you must
not perform that fatiguing part again when you are not
well—no, not for all the Julians in the world. I have
implored your sister not to let you. Are you amenable
to this sort of management? By-the-way, if the play
do reach the ninth night, it will be a very complete
refutation of Mr. Kemble's axiom that no single performer can fill the theatre; for, except our pretty
Alphonso,[*] there is in ' Julian ' one, and only one. Let
him imagine how deeply we feel his exertions and his
kindness! Have you seen the attack upon *us* in the
' London?' Can you guess the author? It is evidently
one who does not understand, who has never felt, the

* Miss Foote.

pleasure of gratitude—the delight of being thankful; but I hope that it is not—that it cannot be—no, I will not suspect that a man of genius could write that sneering and heartless article. To make amends, Mr. Haydon writes me word that Mr. Hazlitt has applied to Mr. Jeffrey for his sanction to review ' Julian ' in the ' Edinburgh.' This is a great compliment, and will be, if the request be granted, a great advantage ; he will do it so well. Of course this is quite in confidence.

I am frightened to look at the length of this letter. I may say, with Anacreon's dove, " I have chattered like a jay." Pray forgive it, and believe me always, my dear sir,

Most sincerely yours,
M. R. MITFORD.

To Sir William Elford, *Bickham, Plymouth.*

Three Mile Cross, April 25, 1823.

My dear Friend,

I am but just returned from town, whither I have been led by one of the evil consequences of dramatic authorship—that is to say, a false report—and lose not a moment in writing to thank you for your zealous kindness.

I have no time to tell you the story of the strange mistake which led me to London, and really my soul sickens within me when I think of the turmoil and tumult which I have undergone, and am to undergo, for Charles Kemble will not suffer me to withdraw my tragedy of ' The Foscari,' and threatens me with a lawsuit if I do. In the mean time I am tossed about between him and Macready like a cricket-ball—affronting both parties and suspected by both, because I will not come to a deadly rupture with either. Only imagine what a state this is, for one who values peace and quietness beyond every other blessing of life! In the mean time, they have stopped 'Julian' at the end of the eighth night, though it was going brilliantly to brilliant houses, and (but this is quite between ourselves) have not paid me for the third and sixth nights.* To be sure, I have Charles Kemble's personal word, and I believe him to be an honest man; but to undergo all this misery, and not get my money, would be terrible indeed! To crown all, Mr. Hamilton, of the 'Lady's Magazine,' has absconded above forty pounds in my debt. Oh! who would be an authoress! The only comfort is, that the Magazine can't go on without me; and that the very fuss they make in quarrelling over me at the theatre proves my importance there; so that, if I survive these vexations, I may in time make something of my poor, poor brains. But I would rather serve in a shop—rather scour floors —rather nurse children, than undergo these tremendous and interminable disputes, and this unwomanly publicity.

Pray forgive this sad no-letter. Alas! the free and happy hours, when I could read and think and prattle for you, are past away. Oh! will they ever return? I am now chained to a desk, eight, ten, twelve hours a day, at mere drudgery. All my thoughts of writing are for hard money. All my correspondence is on hard business. Oh! pity me, pity me! My very mind is sinking under the fatigue and the anxiety. God bless you, my dear friend! Forgive this sad letter.

Ever most faithfully yours,
M. R. MITFORD.

---

* Miss Mitford received 200*l.* for 'Julian' from Covent Garden— 100*l.* cash on the 9th of May, and 100*l.* by bill payable on the 12th of October.

Three Mile Cross, May 13, 1823.

The kind interest which you are so good as to take in me, my dear and true friend, is a great consolation. That Macready likes me I know; but I have perhaps suffered even more from his injustice and prejudice and jealousy than from the angry attacks of the Kembles. Do not misunderstand me : our connection is merely that of actor and author; but his literary jealousy, his suspicion and mistrust have really the character of passion. And yet he is a most ardent and devoted friend; and it seems ungrateful in me to say so much, even to you, with whom, I know, it will remain sacred. I intend, if Macready remains in Covent Garden (remember that this is most strictly confidential), to write a tragedy on a very grand historical subject (Rienzi, *vide* Gibbon, vol. xi. or xii.), and send it to him to bring out without a name.

Mr. Davison has taken to the ' Lady's Magazine,' and promises, if not " indemnity for the past, security for the future." I told you, I believe, that the late editor had run away upwards of forty pounds in my debt, after having, chiefly by my articles, increased the sale of the magazine from two hundred and fifty to two thousand. However, I hope Mr. Davison will go on, for he is sure pay; and that sort of drudgery is heaven when compared with Covent Garden. In the mean time there is one thing which, to so old and kind a friend, I venture to mention. My father has at last resolved—partly, I believe, instigated by the effect which the terrible feeling of responsibility and want of power has had on my health and spirits—to try if he can himself obtain any employment that may lighten the burthen. He is, as you know, active, healthy, and intelligent, and with a strong sense of duty and of right. I am sure that he would fulfil to the utmost any charge that might be confided to him; and if it were one in which my mother or I could assist, you may be assured that he would have zealous and faithful coadjutors. For the management of estates or any country affairs he is particularly well qualified; or any work of superintendence which requires integrity and attention. If you should hear of any such, either in Devonshire or elsewhere, would you mention him, or at least let me know? The addition of two or even one hundred a year to our little income, joined to what I am, in a manner, sure of gaining by mere industry, would take a load from my heart of which I can scarcely give you an idea. It would be everything to me; for it would give me what, for many months, I have not had—the full command of my own powers. Even 'Julian' was written under a pressure of anxiety which left me not a moment's rest. I am, however, at present, quite recovered from the physical effects of this tormenting affair, and have regained my flesh and colour, and almost my power of writing prose articles; and if I could but recover my old hopefulness and elasticity, should be again such as I used to be in happier days. Could I but see my dear father settled in any employment, I know I should.

Believe me ever, with the truest affection,

Very gratefully yours.

M. R. M.

P.S. The Duke of Glo'ster went once, if not twice, to see 'Julian.' You know him, I believe.

To B. R. HAYDON, ESQ.

Three Mile Cross, May 29, 1823.

MY DEAR SIR,

I have no words to say how deeply we feel your situation. Oh! it is a dishonour to the age and to the country, as well as a grief to you and to those who love you. But it cannot last—that, thank Heaven! is impossible. Parliament, or the king, or the public, must do the duty which they owe to the great artist, the excellent man, whose pure and admirable character has never given them an excuse for the neglect of his genius. Be assured that it cannot last. Have you thought of my proposal of an appeal to the king? It can do no harm; and eloquently as you write, I am sure that it would touch him. Pray think of this. It is terrible to think of you amongst these men, bearing, as you say, "the mark on their countenance." It is like an imprisoned antelope—a caged eagle. But it cannot last, thank Heaven! And you will come out a free and a happy man, with fresh cause to love your sweet wife and your noble art. Pray try the king; I have great confidence in his kindly nature. Surely Sir W. Knighton, your townsman, cannot refuse to present an appeal to him. Do try.

I am enclosing a number of notes for the twopenny post, to a friend in Parliament, and shall add this. The direction is heartbreaking,* but it cannot last, I am sure of that. Pray let me know how you are, and, above all, the moment that anything is done for your release. God bless you, my dear friend!

Most faithfully and admiringly yours,
MARY RUSSELL MITFORD.

* The direction was, " B. R. Haydon, Esq., Historical Painter. King's Bench Prison."

To Sir William Elford, *Bickham, Plymouth.*

Three Mile Cross, August 21, 1823.

I hasten, my dear and kind friend, to reply to your very welcome letter. I am quite well now, and if not as hopeful as I used to be, yet less anxious, and far less depressed than I ever expected to feel again. This is merely the influence of the scenery, the flowers, the cool yet pleasant season, and the absence of all literary society; for our prospects are not otherwise changed. My dear father, relying with a blessed sanguineness on my poor endeavours, has not, I believe, even inquired for a situation; and I do not press the matter, though I anxiously wish it, being willing to give one more trial to the theatre. If I could but get the assurance of earning for my dear father and mother a humble competence I should be the happiest creature in the world. But for these dear ties I should never write another line, but go out in some situation as other destitute women do. It seems to me, however, my duty to try a little longer; the more especially as I am sure separation would be felt by all of us to be the greatest of all evils.

My present occupation is a great secret. I will tell it to you *in strict confidence.* It is the boldest attempt ever made by woman, which I have undertaken at the vehement desire of Mr. Macready, who confesses that he has proposed the subject to every dramatic poet of his acquaintance—that it has been the wish of his life—and that he never met with any one courageous enough to attempt it before. In short, I am engaged in a grand historical tragedy on the greatest subject in English story—Charles and Cromwell. Should you ever have suspected your poor little friend of so adventurous a spirit? Mr. Macready does not mean the

author to be known, and I do not think it will be found
out, which is the reason of my requesting so earnestly
your silence on the subject.   Macready thinks that my
sex was, in great part, the occasion of the intolerable
malignity with which 'Julian' was attacked.   They, at
least, cannot call this a melodrame.   My wish is to do
strict poetical justice, in the best sense of the word, to
both the men and both their causes.   What is your
opinion of Cromwell?   Mine is, that he was a man
acting under an intense conviction of the justice of his
cause, and little scrupulous as to the means employed
in its furtherance.   His domestic character appears, in
the old memorials and letters and State papers which I
have been consulting, to have been delightful and
amiable past expression.   I shall give only the short time
of Charles's being in town before his execution, not at
all varying from history, except by bringing in the
queen and giving Cromwell a Royalist daughter.   Do
you think I shall succeed?   Macready says he is sure
of it.   But I fear, I greatly fear.   He himself will probably have no power at all next season, since I find
they have engaged Mr. Young.

Pray, my dear friend, if you should hear of any situation that would suit my dear father, do not fail to let
me know, for that would be the real comfort, to be rid
of the theatre and all its troubles.   Anything in the
medical line, provided the income, however small, were
certain, he would be well qualified to undertake.   I
hope there is no want of duty in my wishing him to
contribute his efforts with mine to our support.   God
knows, if I could, if there were any certainty, how willingly, how joyfully, I would do all; but that there is
not.   Pray forgive this long detail, and the apparent
vanity with which I have spoken of my tragedies, casting

off all the usual circumlocutions, and writing my
very thoughts; but I have learnt to know myself too
well for vanity, my weakness, my impatience, my many
faults. If I were better, more industrious, more patient,
more consistent, I do think I should succeed; and I
will try to be so. I promise you I will, and to make
the best use of my poor talents. Pray forgive this
egotism; it is a relief and a comfort to me to pour forth
my feelings to so dear and so respected a friend; and
they are not now so desolate, not quite so desolate, as
they have been. God grant me to deserve success!

Ever, my dearest and kindest friend,

Most gratefully and affectionately yours,

M. R. MITFORD.

Pray forgive the sad stupidity of this letter. Since
I have become a professed authoress, woe is me! A
washerwoman hath a better trade. I am but a shabby
correspondent. Pray forgive it, and continue to think
of me with your old invaluable kindness.

To B. R. HAYDON, ESQ., *Paddington Green.*

Three Mile Cross, August 24, 1823.

Pray are you a cricketer? We are very great
ones—I mean our parish, of which we, the feminine
members, act audience, and "though we do not play,
o'erlook" the balls. When I wrote to you last I was
just going to see a grand match in a fine old park
near us, Bramshill, between Hampshire, with Mr. Budd,
and All England. I anticipated great pleasure from
so grand an exhibition, and thought, like a simpleton,
the better the play the more the enjoyment. Oh, what
a mistake! There they were—a set of ugly old men,
whiteheaded and baldheaded (for half of Lord's was

engaged in the combat, players and gentlemen, Mr.
Ward and Lord Frederick, the veterans of the green)
dressed in tight white jackets (the Apollo Belvidere
could not bear the hideous disguise of a cricketing
jacket), with neckcloths primly tied round their throats,
fine japanned shoes, silk stockings, and gloves, instead
of our fine village lads, with their unbuttoned collars,
their loose waistcoats, and the large shirt-sleeves which
give an air so picturesque and Italian to their glowing,
bounding youthfulness: there they stood, railed in by
themselves, silent, solemn, slow—playing for money,
making a business of the thing, grave as judges, taciturn
as chess players—a sort of dancers without music, instead
of the glee, the fun, the shouts, the laughter, the
glorious confusion of the country game. And there
were we, the lookers-on, in tents and marquees, fine and
freezing, dull as the players, cold as this hard summer
weather, shivering and yawning and trying to seem
pleased, the curse of gentility on all our doings, as
stupid as we could have been in a ball-room. I never
was so much disappointed in my life. But everything
is spoilt when money puts its ugly nose in. To think
of playing cricket for hard cash! Money and gentility
would ruin any pastime under the sun. Much to my
comfort (for the degrading my favourite sport into a
" science," as they were pleased to call it, had made me
quite spiteful) the game ended unsatisfactorily to all
parties, winners and losers. Old Lord Frederick, on some
real or imaginary affront, took himself off in the middle
of the second innings, so that the two last were played
without him, by which means his side lost, and the
other could hardly be said to win. So be it always
when men make the noble game of cricket an affair of
bettings and hedgings, and, may be, of cheatings.

And now God bless you! Kindest regards and best wishes from all.

Ever yours,

M. R. MITFORD.

To B. R. HAYDON, Esq., 8, Paddington Green.

[*Fragment.*]

October, 1823.

I have a sneaking kindness for portraits. I do not mean the faces on the Royal Academy walls, but those portraits which *escaped* from the great painters, Titian, Rubens, Rembrandt; and that is the way that yours will be considered, not only by posterity, but by that near part of posterity, the next generation, the Englishmen of twenty years hence. Paint plenty of portraits and plenty of humorous pictures. It is your peculiar talent, and do tell me what this one is about. I am so stupid that I have not been able to guess.

CHAPTER IX.

To Sir William Elford, *Bickham, Plymouth.*

Three Mile Cross, Jan. 18, 1824.

My dear Friend,

I should have written to ask after you all had I not been for nearly six months very much and very painfully engrossed. My dear mother has had an attack of that terrible complaint, the spasmodic asthma, which continued for several months. The spasms came on every night at twelve or one o'clock, and continued for three or four hours with such violence that I have feared, night after night, that she would die in my arms. At last, the very great skill of a medical gentleman in this neighbourhood relieved her; though the remedies were so severe that for months she continued as weak as an infant, and the very first day that she thought herself well enough to venture to church she took cold, and the tremendous disorder reappeared, if possible with greater violence and greater obstinacy. At last, I thank God! she is again convalescent; and as we have her now fast prisoner by the fireside, and do not mean to let her peep out till the sun shines on both sides of the hedges, I humbly trust that this invaluable parent and friend may yet be spared to me. But you must imagine how much we have all suffered. My dear father's anxiety, great as it

was, did not, however, incapacitate him from being the
kindest and most excellent of nurses.   He was a thousand times more useful than I ; for the working of this
perpetual fear on my mind was really debilitating,
almost paralyzing, in its effect.   We are now happy
amidst all our cares and poverty, and feel as if a
hundredweight of lead had been taken from our heads
by her recovery.   God grant that it may be perma-
nent !   You may imagine that this has been no slight
interruption to my business.   Nevertheless, I am hoping
to get out a little volume of very playful prose (" You
will like it, I promise you," as Mr. Haydon said to me,
a week ago, about his picture of ' Silenus and Nymphs')
some time this season.   It would have been out before
now if I had been able to go to London and arrange
matters with my friend and bookseller, George Whittaker.   This young and dashing friend of mine (papa's
godson, by-the-by) is this year sheriff of London, and is,
I hear, so immersed in his official dignities as to have
his head pretty much turned topsy-turvy, or rather,
in French phraseology, to have lost that useful append-
age ; so I should not wonder now, if it did not come
out, till I am able to get to town and act for myself in
the business, and I have not yet courage to leave
mamma.   It will be called—at least, I mean it so to
be—' Our Village ;' will consist of essays and characters
and stories, chiefly of country life, in the manner of the
' Sketch Book,' but without sentimentality or pathos—
two things which I abhor—and will be published with or
without my name, as it shall please my worshipful
bibliopole.   At all events, the author has no wish to be
incognita ; so I tell it you as a secret to be told.

   I wish you had seen my friends Mr. Macready and his
sister, for she is travelling with him.   You would have

been pleased with both; and Miss M. would have had
one point of sympathy with you in her exceeding
passion for my letters. (N.B. I have not written her
a line since September.) They are very fascinating
people, of the most polished and delightful manners,
and with no fault but the jealousy and unreasonableness
which seem to me the natural growth of the green-
room. I can tell you just exactly what Mr. Macready
would have said of me and of 'Julian.' He would have
spoken of me as a meritorious and amiable person, of
the play as a first-rate performance, and of the treat-
ment as "infamous!" "scandalous!" "unheard of!"
—would have heaped every phrase of polite abuse which
the language contains on the C. G. managers; and then
would have concluded as follows:—"But it is Miss Mitford's own fault—entirely her own fault. She is, with
all her talent, the weakest and most feeble-minded
woman that ever lived. If she had put matters into
my hands—if she had withdrawn 'The Foscari'—if she
had threatened the managers with a lawsuit—if she had
published her case—if she had suffered me to manage
for her; she should have been the queen of the theatre.
Now, you will see her the slave of Charles Kemble.
She is the weakest woman that ever trode the earth."

This is exactly what he would have said; the way in
which he talks of me to every one, and most of all to
myself. "Is Mr. Macready a great actor?" you ask. I
think that I should answer, "*He might have been a* VERY
GREAT *one.*" Whether he be now I doubt. A very
clever actor he certainly is; but he has vitiated his
taste by his love of strong effects, and been spoilt in
town and country; and I don't know that I do call him
a very great actor. Kean is certainly more intense;
but I doubt very much if there be really a great actor

now alive, except Liston.   At least, I am sure I never
saw one who came up to my conception of any of
Shakespeare's characters.   I have a physical pleasure
in the sound of Mr. Macready's voice, whether talking,
reading, or acting (except when he rants).   It seems to
me very exquisite music, with something instrumental
and vibrating in the sound, like certain notes of the
violoncello.   He is grace itself; and he has a great deal
of real sensibility, mixed with some trickery.   But
having seen him in 'Virginius,' the best of his parts,
you are aware of his merits.

By-the-way, that play seems to me a very fine one
(does it to you?) though the curtain ought certainly to
have dropped at the end of the fourth act.

You are very good and kind and flattering in what
you say of publishing my letters; but, if there were no
other reason against that measure, think how freely I
have spoken of contemporary authors, and remember
that I am a writer of plays, and that the slightest
enmity may be vented on me fatally.   Besides, I would
not for the world hurt people's feelings.

When you see 'Our Village' (which, if my sheriff be
not bestraught, I hope may happen soon), you will see
that my notions of prose style are nicer than these
galloping letters would give you to understand.   No;
our correspondence must wait for half a century * (like
the hoards in Horace Walpole's box), and then be edited
by your great-grandson.   . . .   I could not help indulging myself with writing to you, though I ought to
have been otherwise busy; but I will make up for it.
God bless you, my dear friend !

Always most affectionately yours,
M. R. MITFORD.

---

* That half-century is well-nigh over.

To B. R. HAYDON, 51, *Sovereign Terrace, Connaught Place.*

Three Mile Cross, Monday night,
Feb. 9, 1824.

MY DEAR SIR,

I have to congratulate you most heartily on your
escape from two such disagreeable oddities as your late
landlord and landlady, and to wish you all prosperity in
your new abode. I do not wish you happiness, for you
have it. With such a wife and such a boy, and such a
consciousness of those blessings, I do really think you
the happiest man in the world.

I found in the 'New Monthly,' in one of Mr. Hazlitt's
delightful Table Talks, the terrible story of Mr. Wordsworth's letter to you, which spoils his poetry to me;
for there was about his poetry something personal. We
clung to him as to Cowper; and now—it will not bear
talking of. The article on 'Jeremy Bentham' is also, I
think, by Mr. Hazlitt. I wonder if he ever heard a
story told to me by your countryman Mr. Northmore,
a great Devonshire reformer, one of the bad epic poets
and very pleasant men in which that county abounds.
He said that Jeremy Bentham being on a visit at a
show house in those parts, at a time when he was little
known, except as a jurist, through the translations of
M. Dumont—certainly before the publication of the
Church of England-ism, or any such enormities—Mrs.
Hannah More, being at a watering-place in the neighbourhood, was minded to see him, and availed herself
of the house being one which was shown on stated
days, to pay a visit to the philosopher.

He was in the library when the news arrived; and,
the lady being already in the antechamber and no
possible mode of escape presenting itself, he sent one
servant to detain her a few minutes, and employed

another to build him up with books in a corner of the room. When the folios and quartos rose above his head, the curious lady was admitted. Must it not have been a droll scene? The philosopher playing at bo-peep in his entrenchment, and the pious maiden, who had previously ascertained that he was in the room, peering after him in all the agony of baffled curiosity!

Your Frank must be a charming little fellow. Give my love to him and his dear mother. How well I can fancy you darting about in your half-furnished house, doing half everybody's work with your own rapid hands! No wonder that when the bustle was over you should feel a little languid, like a young lady after a ball. All happiness be with you and yours!

Ever very sincerely,
M. R. MITFORD.

To SIR WILLIAM ELFORD.
Three Mile Cross, March 5, 1824.

MY DEAR FRIEND,

In spite of your prognostics, I think you will like 'Our Village.' It will be out in three weeks or a month; and it will be an obligation if you will cause it to be asked for at circulating libraries, &c. It is not one connected story, but a series of sketches of country manners, scenery, and character, with some story inter-mixed, and connected by unity of locality and of pur-pose. It is exceedingly playful and lively, and I think you will like it. Charles Lamb (the matchless 'Elia' of the 'London Magazine') says that nothing so fresh and characteristic has appeared for a long while. It is not over modest to say this; but who would not be proud of the praise of such a *proser?* And as you, in common with all sensible people, like light reading, I say again that you will like it.

Pray have you read the American novels? I mean the series by Mr. Cooper—'The Spy,' &c. If you have not, send for them, and let me hear the result. In my mind they are as good as anything Sir Walter Scott ever wrote. He has opened fresh ground, too (if one may say so of the sea). No one but Smollett has ever attempted to delineate the naval character; and then he is so coarse and hard. Now this has the same truth and power, with a deep, grand feeling. I must not overpraise it, for fear of producing the reaction which such injudicious enthusiasm is calculated to induce; but I must request you to read it. Only read it. Imagine the author's boldness in taking Paul Jones for a hero, and his power in making one care for him! I envy the Americans their Mr. Cooper. Tell me how you like 'The Pilot.' There is a certain Long Tom who appears to me the finest thing since Parson Adams. God bless you, my dear friend!

Ever very sincerely yours,
M. R. MITFORD.

One cannot help regretting the destruction of Lord Byron's Memoirs; though, from what the 'Examiner' says of his feelings (and on this point the 'Examiner' is. I suppose, good authority), it might not perhaps have been quite proper to publish them at present without great omissions. My friend, Mrs. Franklin (I mean Miss Porden "that was," as Richardson would say), the epic poetess, and wife of the man of the North Pole—my friend Mrs. Franklin, who lives in an atmosphere of Albemarle Street gossip, wrote me an account of these Memoirs which I will transcribe for you *verbatim*. "On inspection they were found so disgraceful in every way that they could not be published, either on his account or that of his readers. A friend of mine, who was at Naples when he gave them to Moore (a whole sackful of detached papers), and who read them in the carriage as they afterwards travelled through Italy together, told me at the time that if ever they met the public eye it must be with such changes and curtailments as would almost destroy their authenticity. No one whom he ever met, if but once and in the most casual manner, seems to have escaped vituperation in his black journal; and his pen was always dipped in the deepest gall when writing of those who at the moment were his greatest intimates—Hobhouse, for instance!"

Now, if this be at all true (and Mrs. Franklin is undoubtedly a person of veracity), it is certainly a very good reason for not publishing what would give so much pain to many unoffending individuals. But there must be parts that are harmless; why not publish them? And why utterly destroy the last relics of so remarkable a man? But that little man-milliner of a poet seems to me to have a sort of design of turning good as he grows old: witness his attack on Rousseau. Shall I confess to you, that except his *jeux d'esprit*, which are capital, I am no admirer of that dandy song-writer. And—I am half afraid to say it—but I was no very ardent enthusiast for Lord Byron. I admit his stupendous powers—his exquisite *morceaux;* but he was too melancholy—too morbid—too sneering. He attacked Napoleon; he failed in the drama, and did not find out that he had failed. And the want of purity! God forbid that I should be a canter; but the want of purity—the harm that both he and Mr. Moore have done to the young men and women of the day—must not be overlooked, though I trust it is forgiven. After all, it is a great

light that is quenched *—a most powerful instrument
for good and for evil ; and the evil will pass away, and
the good will remain.   Peace to his spirit!

Adieu, my dear friend.   I trust that you are going on
well with your sitters.   They who come to you now are
persons of taste.   In a very short time it will be the
fashion to come, and therefore no criterion.

Always most sincerely yours,

M. R. MITFORD.

[Sir William Elford, in answering this letter, expressed his opinion that the sketches of rural life given
in ' Our Village ' would have been better written in the
form of letters.]

To SIR WILLIAM ELFORD, *Bickham, Plymouth.*

Three Mile Cross, June 23, 1824.

MY DEAR FRIEND,

I am quite delighted that you like my book.   Your
notion of letters pleases me much, as I see plainly that
it is the result of the old prepossessions and partiali-
ties, which do me so much honour and give me so
much pleasure.   But it would never have done.   The
sketches are too long, and necessarily too much connected, for *real* correspondence ; and as to anything
make-believe, it has been my business to keep that out
of sight as much as possible.   Besides which, we are
free and easy in these days, and talk to the public as a
friend.   Read ' Elia,' or the ' Sketch Book,' or Hazlitt's
' Table Talk,' or any popular book of the new school,
and you will find that we have turned over the John-
sonian periods and the Blair-ian formality to keep company with the wigs and hoops, the stiff curtseys and low

---

* Lord Byron had died in the preceding April.

bows of our ancestors. In short, my dear friend, letters
are now-a-days more the vehicles of kindness, and less
of wit than they used to be. It was very convenient,
when people who wrote books were forced to put stiff
stays on them, to have a sort of dishabille for the mind
as well as for the body, and to write a letter as they
put on a *robe de chambre*. But now the periodical press
takes charge of those bursts of gaiety and criticism
which the post was wont to receive; and the public—
the reading public—is, as I said before, the correspondent and confidant of everybody.

Having thus made the best defence I can against
your criticism, I proceed to answer your question, " Are
the characters and descriptions true ?" Yes! yes! yes!
As true as is well possible. You, as a great landscape
painter, know that in painting a favourite scene you do
a little embellish, and can't help it ; you avail yourself
of happy accidents of atmosphere, and if anything be
ugly, you strike it out, or if anything be wanting, you
put it in. But still the picture is a likeness ; and that
this is a very faithful one, you will judge when I tell
you that a worthy neighbour of ours, a post captain,
who has been in every quarter of the globe, and is
equally distinguished for the sharp look-out and the
bonhomie of his profession, accused me most seriously
of carelessness in putting " The Rose " for " The Swan,'
as the sign of our next-door neighbour ; and was no less
disconcerted at the *misprint* (as he called it) of B for
R in the name of our next town. *A cela près*, he declares the picture to be exact. Nevertheless, I do not
expect to be poisoned. Why should I ? I have said
no harm of my neighbours, have I ? The great danger
would be that my dear friend Joel might be spoilt ; but
I take care to keep the book out of our pretty Harriette's

way; and so I hope that that prime ornament of our village will escape the snare for his vanity which the seeing so exact a portrait of himself in a printed book might occasion.

By-the-way, the names of the villagers are true—of the higher sketches they are feigned, of course. But I will give my dear Miss Elford, who seems interested in knowing the exact state of the case, a key. Her note is charming. I never saw a more beautiful simplicity; and when she speaks of her sister, it is quite enchanting to see how the love breaks out. Yes! I shall give her the key, and will only thank you, in the first place, for promoting the sale; and tell you, in the second, that it sells well, and has been received by the literary world, and reviewed in all the literary papers, &c., better than I, for modesty, dare to say.* God bless you, my dear friend!

Always most sincerely and affectionately yours,

M. R. MITFORD.

To Miss Jephson, at the Rev. G. Smith's, Castle Martyr, Ireland.

Three Mile Cross, July 10, 1824.

We have a pretty little pony-chaise and pony (oh! how I should like to drive you in it!), and my dear father and mother have been out in it three or four times, to my great delight; I am sure it will do them both so much good. My great amusement is in my garden. I am so glad you have a little demesne of your own too; it is a pretty thing to be queen over roses and lilies, is it not? My nook of ground is very

---

* Mrs. Hall writes: "My 'Sketches of Irish Character,' my first dear book, was inspired by a desire to describe my native place, as Miss Mitford had done in ' Our Village;' and this made me an author."

beautiful this year, rosy as one of the poems in 'Lalla Rookh,' crammed with all sorts of flowers, and parted from, or joined to, the long open shed where we sit, and which Harriette and mamma call the arcade, by a double row of rich geraniums. I look at them now without any tender fears, because Mrs. Reeve has promised to house them for me during the winter—a very precious piece of hospitality. By-the-way, Mrs. Reeve, besides bringing her charming self to Whitley (the only thing that could have consoled me for the loss of our dear friends), has also imported a most valuable and faithful female servant—a warmhearted Irishwoman, who loves everybody that her mistress loves; so that, with old faithful Rainer at the gate with his face of welcome, hers at the door, and her mistress's in the parlour, Whitley is quite itself again. Nevertheless, I never go to it without wishing for our dear friends.

Being a good deal unhinged by the anxiety I suffered during my dear father's illness, and therefore unfit for writing (though not at all ill, and now getting the better even of that nervousness), I have been reading an immense number of books, old and new, good and indifferent. Will you have a specimen of the brief one-, two-, or three-word character with which I put them down in a catalogue which I keep of works as I read them?

Captain Hall's 'South America' (the Loo-Choo man excellent).

Landor's 'Imaginary Conversations' (very, very good —very, very bad).

'Captain Rock' (witty and tiresome—is it true?).

Charles Lamb's Works (for the third time—and that is saying enough).

'Redgauntlet' (for the first, and I fear the last).

'The Inheritance' (clever—too clever—but not genial —not amiable—written by one who sees faults too plainly by half).

'Wilhelm Meister's Apprenticeship' (Mignon a gem —the setting rather German).

'Letters to and from Lady Suffolk' (very particularly naughty—especially the maids of honour).

'Travels,' I forget where—by, I forget whom—just exactly nothing at all.

Are you not glad that I am come to an end of my list and my letter?—come to the thousand loves and good wishes that attend you from all here? Adieu!

M. R. MITFORD.

To B. R. HAYDON, ESQ., 8, *Paddington Green.*

Three Mile Cross, July 11, 1824.

MY DEAR FRIEND,

I like to hear of your painting ex-mayors (corporate bodies are generally generous), and eating corporation dinners. I shall have a respect for the aldermen of Norwich as long as I live for their choice of a painter. Is it possible that the Exhibition has closed and 'Silenus' not been sold?

You will be glad to hear that my dear father continues to recover, although he has not yet got up his strength. My mother is better too. Some little hay was got in in a magical sort of way between the showers. The Northumberland people have an idiom of " *saving* hay " for " making hay "—which is exceedingly proper for this year, when all hay not spoilt by the wet may literally be said to be saved. I tell you all these little pieces of good fortune, because, as I generally trouble you with my bad news, it seems but fair to give you a glimpse of the sun when it does peep out for a minute between the showers.   I should not omit, when reckoning up my felicities just now, to tell you that my little garden is a perfect rosary—the greenest and most blossomy nook that ever the sun shone upon.   It is almost shut in by buildings; one a long open shed, very pretty, a sort of rural arcade, where we sit.   On the other side is an old granary, to which we mount by outside wooden steps, also very pretty.   Then, there is an opening to a little court, also backed by buildings, but with room enough to let in the sunshine, the north-west sunshine, that comes aslant in summer evenings, through and under a large elder tree.   One end is closed by our pretty irregular cottage, which, as well as the granary, is covered by cherry trees, vines, roses, jessamine, honeysuckle, and grand spires of hollyhocks. The other is comparatively open, showing over high pales the blue sky and a range of woody hills.   All and every part is untrimmed, antique, weather-stained, and homely as can be imagined—gratifying the eye by its exceeding picturesqueness, and the mind by the certainty that no pictorial effect was intended—that it owes all its charms to " rare accident."   My father laughs at my passionate love for my little garden—and perhaps you will laugh too; but I assure you it's a " bonny bit " of earth as ever was crammed full of lilies and roses, to say nothing of a flourishing " green——.

[The rest is wanting.]

To the Rev. WILLIAM HARNESS, *Hampstead.*

Three Mile Cross, July 29, 1824.

MY DEAR FRIEND,

Do you think you have interest enough with Mr. Campbell * to get an engagement for a sort of series— 'Letters from the Country,' or something of that sort— altogether different, of course, from 'Our Village' in the scenery and the *dramatis personæ,* but still something that might admit of description and character, and occasional story, without the formality of a fresh introduction to every article. If you liked my little volume well enough to recommend me conscientiously, and are enough in that prescient editor's good graces to secure such an admission, I should like the thing exceedingly.

Mr. Talfourd urges me to write a novel. Do you think I could? I beg a thousand pardons for tormenting you with my poor concerns; but I have an entire reliance on your kindness, and to get money, if I can, is so much my duty, that that consciousness takes away at once all the mock modesty of authorship, for the display of which the rich have leisure. I write merely for remuneration; and I would rather scrub floors, if I could get as much by that healthier, more respectable, and more feminine employment.

Give my very best love to your sister—our very best love—and accept my father's and mother's best regards.

Ever, my dear friend,

Your obliged and affectionate

M. R. MITFORD.

* Thomas Campbell, author of 'The Pleasures of Hope,' and at that time editor of the 'New Monthly Magazine.'

What you say of Haydon's picture grieves me much. Some parts of his other pictures (I have not seen this) always seemed to me very, very fine—the head of Lazarus, for instance; and he himself—oh! how you would like him!—is a creature of air and fire; the frankest, truest man breathing; absolutely free from pretence or trickery. There are three moderate wishes that I should like to see realized: you—a bishop (how should you like the wig?); Mr. Talfourd—Attorney-General; and Mr. Haydon—President of the Royal Academy. The middle wish, if not to the letter, will yet, I think, come true in the spirit; for he is getting on incredibly, and will be the Mr. Scarlett of twenty years hence; the other two will, I hope, follow in order. Once again, good-bye. My postscript threatens to be longer than my letter—but you know by experience that a woman's pen, like a woman's tongue, is a difficult thing to stop. Have we any chance of seeing you in Berkshire?

For the last time, good-bye!

To Miss Jephson, *Castle Martyr, Ireland.*

Three Mile Cross, August 28, 1824.

My dear Emily,

I thank you most heartily for your very welcome letter.

My dear mother continues better, and is, of course, not so close a prisoner as in the winter; but she has not yet ventured so far as Silchester, and, indeed, I am half afraid to propose so long an excursion. She has only once been in Reading, and generally speaking, goes nowhere but to Whitley, and then only for an hour, on some fine morning, when there is neither sun, nor wind, nor dust. It is impossible to be more delicate than she

is. My dear father, too, I am sorry to say, continues
poorly. He cannot bear exercise or exertion of any
kind; and yet the activity of his mind continuing un-
diminished, there is all the difficulty on earth to keep
him quiet. They both send their most affectionate love
to you, and talk of you and think of you very often
indeed.

You are very good in inquiring into my plans. I
write as usual for magazines, and (but this is quite
between ourselves—a matter strictly confidential), I
have a tragedy, which will, I may say certainly—as certainly as one can speak of anything connected with the
theatre—be performed at Drury Lane next season. It
is on the story of Rienzi, the friend of Petrarch; the
man who restored for a short time, and in so remarkable a manner, the old republican government of Rome.
If you do not remember the story you will find it very
beautifully told in the last volume of Gibbon, and still
more graphically related in L'Abbé de Sade's ' Mémoires pour la Vie de Petrarque.' We do not speak of
it, because Mr. Macready talks of bringing it out as
written by a man, to avoid the great annoyance of newspapers, &c., so unpleasant to a female writer. This is
my first sheet anchor, of course; but I am also pressed
to try a novel, by almost every one who has read my
little volume—more especially by Mr. Milman, who (by-
the-way) has just married and brought home a very
beautiful wife. But I am half afraid of a novel, and
more inclined to try a second volume of ' Our Village,'
for which there are plenty of materials close at hand.
What do you advise? There is great danger of falling
off always in continuations; but I am so afraid of a
novel. After all, I suppose the bookseller is, in this
respect, the best counsellor.

I have been much occupied lately by a friend who has resided for the last six years in Paris, and cannot help telling you a story illustrative of the state of society there.

A lady of her intimate acquaintance was about to open her house for company—that is to say, to give *soirées*, once a week. On this being known, she was waited upon by an agent of the police, who requested to see a list of the persons invited, as it was necessary that some friend of Government should be amongst them.

" Really, sir," said the lady, " I would rather relinquish the thing altogether than introduce a spy amongst my guests."

" Just let me see the list, Madame," retorted the policeman ; and having looked at it, continued, " You need not trouble yourself—neither need I ; for there are four or five of us invited already !"

Better be at Three Mile Cross, my dear Emily, or in your wilder and more beautiful country, than in that polished prison—that Ear of Dionysius.

What weather for the seaside ! How you must enjoy it ! We almost see the corn ripen before our eyes.

God bless you, my dear friend ! Do not fail to write to me, and to talk to me of all that interests you ; it will all interest and gratify me, especially all that tends to make you happy.

Ever most sincerely yours.

M. R. M.

To B. R. HAYDON, ESQ., *Paddington Green.*

Three Mile Cross, Sept. 23, 1824.

MY DEAR FRIEND,

Your last charming letter was delivered to me by my friend Mr. Monck, at a large dinner-party, where he knew he should meet me. I put it in my little bag till I could steal away to read it after dinner.

Before that opportunity arrived, a friend of mine, who resides in Paris, but has been on a visit in this neighbourhood, asked me if I could furnish her with any autographs of celebrated persons, for the widow of Bernardin St. Pierre.

" I want more than the signature," continued my unconscionable friend ; " the mere handwriting will not do —something characteristic."

When I went to her room to read your letter after dinner, imagine how I was struck with the glorious conclusion—the three last lines :—" For my part, I love my country, and would lay my head on the block to insure her advancement in art.—B. R. HAYDON." They seemed to me the very motto to your character— the very inscription to put under a picture or a bust of you. So, as my friend assured me that the name and sentiment would be prized as they ought to be, I even cut them off for Madame St. Pierre.

What are you about? Portraits? I ought to be very busy, for my bookseller has sent to me for two volumes more of ' Our Village ;' and then a novel ! Oh ! dear me !

God bless you, my dear friend ! Love to dear Mrs. Haydon.

Ever most sincerely yours,
M. R. MITFORD.

To Miss JEPHSON, *Castle Martyr, Ireland.*

Three Mile Cross, Friday, Oct. 22, 1824.

MY VERY DEAR EMILY,

We are just recovering from a dramatic crisis in Reading. Dr. Valpy's triennial Greek play has been represented, last week and this, with splendid success. It was the ' Alcestis' of Euripides, a drama which has, you know, great extrinsic interest; embodying a lovely trait of female devotedness; alluded to by Milton in that sonnet of which I remember our talking together in this very room; mentioned still more finely by Wordsworth in the ' Laodamia;' and, finally, being that identical play which Charles Fox was found reading when he had lost his whole fortune at a gaming table, and his friends were fearful of his committing suicide. In spite of all this, the play is not so fine as I thought it when it was acted here fifteen years ago, and the world of the Greek drama were fifteen years younger with me. I should have been quite out of humour at the destruction of the illusion which I had entertained respecting it in my own mind had not the admirable acting of one boy given me a delight such as I never thought to feel from anything theatrical again. It was the mean, selfish, odious part of Admetus, which he made exquisitely noble by an exhibition of passion the most natural and consummate that I ever beheld. He is about sixteen, short and fair, the son of a dancing master of the name of Richardson. They talk of bringing him up to the bar, but I want him for the stage. His talent is altogether dramatic—peculiar, distinctive, nothing but dramatic. And the stage is fame and fortune—the bar is starvation and obscurity.

Little Richardson is quite a Macready in embryo. I said to him one evening, behind the scenes, " Well, you have the principal part." " I don't know," answered he; " there is a great deal to say, and that is all you can say for it. Alcestis is the heroine, and, if there be a hero, it is Hercules. He is the only one who does anything but talk." " At all events, you have a mag-

nificent dress." "Dress!" rejoined my grumbler, pointing
to the splendid god of the silver bow—"dress! Look at
Apollo!" These plays would have annoyed me exceedingly on these accounts but for the interest I took in
this boy.

I had a letter from Mr. Haydon yesterday, containing
an anecdote of Sir Walter Scott, which I will transcribe
for you in the very words of our great painter. " A
friend of mine has been spending some time with Sir W.
Scott. He (Sir Walter) is liable to perpetual intrusion of
every kind. A stupid chattering fellow got at him by
a letter and stayed a week. He was a sad bore, and my
friend and another young dog were obliged to retire to
a window to avoid laughing. Sir Walter hobbled up to
them and said, ' Come, come, young gentlemen, I assure
you it requires no small talent to be a *decided bore.* Be
more respectful!' I like this ; there is the geniality of
the Unknown in it." I like it too, and so I hope will
you, although it has hardly left me room to say that my
father and mother are both better, and both send their
kindest remembrances. Adieu, my very dear friend.

>Believe me always,
>>Most affectionately yours,
>>>M. R. MITFORD.

Fragment of a letter to R. B. HAYDON, ESQ., 8, *Paddington Green.*
>>>Three Mile Cross, Oct. 28, 1824.

No! no! no! not wild about all those boys, only
about one of them. The boys generally did the thing
surprisingly well. We had a pretty Alcestis, and a very
magnificent Hercules, but it was Admetus only that
showed such extraordinary genius. The part, you know,
is odiously mean and selfish, and cowardly and com-
plaining; everything that a woman likes least. The

boy is not at all handsome—pale and short, and fair and old-looking—not at all the lad to catch a woman's eye. Nothing but genius, that life-pulse genius, could have inspired me with the enthusiasm which I did feel, and do feel, on his account. Some of the things which he did (things which, to my certain knowledge, nobody there could have taught him) were as grand and fine as anything that Kean does in Othello, perhaps finer, for they were as passionate, as intense, but more chaste. He is unspoilt by the exaggeration of a great theatre. I am sure of his being so very great, not only by the impression which he made on me and Mr. Talfourd, but by the dissimilar effect on some wiseacres of my acquaintance, whose blame is praise. It is a fine thing to have two or three fools of whose folly one is so certain that it is a standard. Say the reverse of what they say, and you must be right. I wish you had seen this boy Richardson.

I heartily agree with you in admiration of the 'Agamemnon' of Æschylus. He was perhaps the most wonderful of the three great poets, although Sophocles seems to me the most perfect. His 'Philoctetes,' besides the fine romance of the first scene, moves one to deeper pity and livelier indignation than any play I ever read out of Shakespeare. One hates Ulysses with a heartiness that does one good, but he is a very detestable person always, even in Homer. Euripides has exquisite scenes, but only scenes—no whole play, like the 'Philoctetes,' or the 'Œdipus,' or the 'Antigone'—nothing that approaches in situation to the 'Prometheus.' Yet there are beautiful scenes, too, in 'Euripides,' especially those two of Phædra in the 'Hippolitus.'

I once thought of writing a tragedy on the story of

Francesca of Rimini, and using those two scenes, and I
still would do so if we had a great tragic actress—one
who could give an intense and fervid personification of
passionate, unhappy, but yet pure love. All this seems
very blue, but although I have no knowledge of Greek,
I have read these plays very often in translations, both
French and English. And, setting aside the immense
power of that most extraordinary language, whose *inter-
fusing* quality seems quite unapproached by any modern
tongue—setting this aside, I do not hesitate to say that
there is more in one scene of Shakespeare than in all
the Greek drama put together. And yet there is more
in the Greek drama than in the French, the Italian, the
Spanish, or (setting aside Shakespeare) the English.

To SIR WILLIAM ELFORD, *Bickham, Plymouth.*

Three Mile Cross, Nov. 9, 1829.

I begin my answer, my dear and valued friend, as
soon as I receive your welcome letter, although I may
probably not have an opportunity of sending it off for
some days. My father and mother, to commence with
that which, as most interesting to me will be most ac-
ceptable to you, are better than they have been. *He* is
much older for his terrible illness, but otherwise quite
recovered, and my dear mother has had a cold, but has
not suffered another attack of her dreadful complaint.
This has set me a little free from the nervousness which
used to beset me whenever a breath of air blew upon
her, to her great annoyance. I am most grateful for
these blessings, as you may well believe.

First, let me tell you that I am very much gratified
by your kind friend Mr. Cranstoun's approbation, and
that I will take heed, if I write another volume—if I
Our-Village-it again—I will try to profit by his criticism.

By-the-way, you will be glad to hear that our dear friend Mr. Haydon has now made up his mind to portrait painting, has plenty of employment, and is going on well. He has sold his 'Silenus,' and, in short, will prosper now I trust in God! He is a most delightful person, and, above all, a capital correspondent, writing me two or three letters for one tiny note.

We have a dispute respecting Lord Byron and Wordsworth which is of great use in these communications. Nothing like a good standing quarrel to which people may fall ding-dong. These two poets are cut and come again, like a goose pie at Christmas. You will guess, of course, that he is all for Byron, I all for Wordsworth. And truly this last book ('The Conversations of Lord Byron,' as collected by Captain Medwin) gives me no small cause to crow. His infamous libertinism, his intolerable effeminate vanity, his utter want of taste— Wordsworth, Milton, Shakespeare cried down — Dr. Johnson's criticisms, Moore's songs, and his own plays (about the three worst things of their sort in the language) cried up! Truly my dear and very clever adversary is put to his trumps, and forced to say that " I am a woman, and therefore ——." I have never had any respect for Lord Byron's talents since he failed so egregiously in the drama, and did not find it out. Scott failed in the drama too, but then he made the discovery and drew back, and, accordingly, nobody remembers 'Halidon Hill,' and everybody adores the novels.

Friday (I don't know the day of the month, but the last Friday in November).

Since writing the enclosed I have been to town; and am, and have been, hard at work altering a play which

I hope to get out within a month at Drury Lane. It is on the subject of Rienzi. Macready is with me heart and soul. His new wife is a pretty, little, gentle, creature—very young and very timid. Kindest regards from all. Say everything for me to dear Miss Elford.

Always most affectionately yours,

M. R. MITFORD.

To B. R. HAYDON, ESQ., 58, *Connaught Terrace, Portman Square.*

Castle Street, Saturday evening,
Dec. 20, 1824.

MY DEAR FRIEND,

I am commissioned by Mr. Talfourd to tell you, with his very best compliments, that next Tuesday is fixed for Miss Foote's trial; and that, if you will come here at eight o'clock precisely on that morning in a coach, he will equip you in a spare wig and gown of his own, and take you with him to the court. You had better come in an *old* black coat and waistcoat,—old, observe, because the powder of the wig will spoil them. Mr. Talfourd could supply you with these articles also, if you think you could get into them. I don't—he being a delicate, womanly man, and you a sort of lesser Hercules. If you dislike the masquerade, which I think will be capital fun, he will do all he can to get you in *in propriâ personâ.* But the court is so small and expected to be so crowded with barristers, that, as the greatest painter in Europe and nothing else, you are likely to be turned out; whereas, as a mere trumpery lawyer whom no one knows, you are safe. At all events you must be here precisely at eight. I am so sorry that I shall not see this famous frolic, being engaged on Monday to dine and sleep at Hampstead; but you must come back in your legal costume, that I may see you. It would be too bad to be in a position in which I should at once lose the personal participation of the fun, and the almost equal gratification of your account of it, which, if I were actually in the country, you would infallibly send me.

Ever yours,
M. R. M.

CHAPTER X.

To B. R. HAYDON, ESQ., *Connaught Terrace.*

Three Mile Cross, Feb. 3, 1825.

MY DEAR FRIEND,

If you see Mr. Young, do say how much I am flattered at his ready acceptance of the part, and that it was not withdrawn owing to any disrespect towards him. You may send letters to me through Mr. Monck always. He talks of taking the liberty to call and look at my picture. I am sure you will, if you see him, be pleased with his frankness and originality. He is a great Grecian and a great political economist—a sort of Andrew Marvel in Parliament; living in a lodging close to the House, with an old woman, who cooks him alternately a beefsteak, a mutton chop, or a veal cutlet: he does not indulge in a lamb chop till after Easter. He votes sometimes with one party and sometimes with another, as he likes their measures; respected by all, notwithstanding his independence; and idolized here in the country for his liberality, his cheerfulness, his good-humour, and his unfailing kindness.

God bless you all, my dear friend! Say everything for me to your loveliest wife, and believe me always

Most faithfully yours,

M. R. MITFORD.

To Sir William Elford, *Bickham, Plymouth.*

Three Mile Cross, Feb. 19, 1825.

My very dear Friend,

I believe that if I could conquer my own predilection for the drama I should do wisely to adhere to the booksellers; for the little prose volume has certainly done its work, and made an opening for a longer effort. You would be diverted at some of the instances I could tell you of its popularity. Columbines and children have been named after Mayflower; stage coachmen and postboys point out the localities; schoolboys deny the possibility of any woman's having written the cricket match without schoolboy help; and such men as Lord Stowell (Sir William Scott—the last relique, I believe, of the Literary Club) send to me for a key. I mean to try three volumes of tales *next* spring—having given over the intention of a second volume, in which there is always danger of falling off. Heaven knows how I shall succeed!

If you can think of a pretty story, do send it me; for that is my want. Of course I shall copy as closely as I can Nature and Miss Austen—keeping, like her, to genteel country life; or rather going a little lower, perhaps; and, I am afraid, with more of sentiment and less of humour. I do not *intend* to commit these delinquencies, mind. I *mean* to keep as playful as I can; but I am afraid of their happening in spite of me. Pray, talking of tales, have you seen Mrs. Opie's 'Lying?' She is all over Quakerized, as you of course know—to the great improvement, as I hear (for I have not seen her) of her appearance. It is certainly a pretty dress. She *thee's* and *thou's* people; calls Mr. Haydon "friend Benjamin;" and directs to the Rev. William Harness after the same fashion, "William Harness, Hampstead." With all this, she is just as kind and good-humoured as ever; and Mr. Haydon told me that, in about a quarter of an hour's chat, she forgot her *thee's* and *thou's*, and became altogether as merry as she used to be. She has really sacrificed upwards of a thousand pounds copy-money for a novel, which she had contracted for; and yet I believe there are difficulties still as to her admission to the sisterhood. You also may have heard say that a certain Mr. Gurney is in some sort the cause of this conversion, and that there are difficulties there also; but of this *I* say nothing.

Whilst in town, I put myself in the way of a conversion of another sort, by going to hear Mr. Irving. Did you ever hear him? If not, do; he is really worth a little trouble. I had read a hundred descriptions of him, and seen half a score prints, which I took for caricatures, till I saw him; and then he seemed to me a caricature of his portraits—more tall, more squinting, more long black-haired, more cadaverous, more like Frankenstein. His sermon, too, was even odder than I expected, in matter and manner; the *latter* seems to me as good as possible, the *former* sometimes good, but full of pretension and affectation of every sort. I have no doubt whatever but that the Rev. Edward Irving is the vainest person that lives at this moment; and I that say so have got the honour of being acquainted with divers actors and sundry poets. I could not have conceived so much quackery possible in the pulpit. A small adventure befel me which I cannot help telling you. I went with an old lady, who, at the end of two hours and a half, was really ill with the heat and crowd, and asked me to go out with her. Of course I complied. When we got to the door we found a gentleman with his back planted against it, who point blank refused to let us out. Heard ever any one of being shut into a

chapel ! Mr. Milman says an action would lie for false
imprisonment; and, being in a barrister's house, I might
have had law cheap. My poor old friend, however, was
suffering; and I was not quite young enough in the
world to be taken in. I therefore turned to the
loiterers in the aisles, and picking out my man—a fine
spirited looking person, the most anti-puritanical that
you can imagine—I said to him, " Sir, this lady is
indisposed, and that gentleman—" " G— d—n me,
madam," exclaimed my hopeful ally, "this is some
d—d whim of Dawkins's—I'll let you out." And forthwith he and another young man of his sort sprang at
once on the luckless Dawkins (an elder of the congregation)—displaced him *par voie du fait*, and gave us
free egress from the Caledonian Church, under the very
nose of the pastor.

On telling this story the next day to Charles Lamb,
he told me that a friend of his, having sat through
two hours of sermon, walked off in the same way;
but, just as she was leaving the church, Mr. Irving
himself addressed her in a most violent manner from the
pulpit, whereupon she turned round, smiled, nodded,
curtsied, and then walked off. I certainly could not
have done that, nor was it right, although Mr. Irving
himself has turned a house of worship into a mere public
place—a Sunday theatre—where he delivers orations
half made up of criticism and abuse, and preaches for
five hours a day such sermons as never were called
sermons before. If you have not heard him you will
accuse me of levity; but I assure you the most scrupulous people speak of him as I do—everybody, indeed,
except the select few who compose his exclusive admirers—and even they praise him just as they praise an
orator, and cry up his discourses just as they cry up a

clever article in a magazine. I am sorry for this; for
the man, in spite of his execrable taste, has power—
great power. He fixes the attention, provokes you very
much by the most inconceivable bombast, but never
wearies you. He certainly has power, and if he should
have the good luck to go so completely out of fashion
as neither to be followed, praised, nor blamed, which is
likely enough to happen in a year or two, I should not
wonder to find him become a great orator.

Adieu, my very dear friend. This is something like
my old budget of sauciness—in length at least—and I
am afraid in carelessness and illegibility; but I am
quite sure of your indulgence, and of that of your kind
family. Say everything for me to them all, especially
to Miss Elford.

Ever most gratefully yours,

M. R. M.

To B. R. HAYDON, Esq., *Connaught Terrace, Portman Square.*

Three Mile Cross, March 3, 1825.

MY DEAR FRIEND,

Pray should you like to be an M.P.? Did the
thing ever take your fancy? I cannot understand the
charm at all; but a charm there must be, notwithstanding, and a very strong one. What a prodigious sensation you would make in the House! Good Lord, how
they would stare! Our friend Mr. Talfourd will be
there some day or other, beyond a doubt—and he will
make a sensation too. He has just made a most splendid
display at the Berkshire Assizes; I wish you had heard
him. I was in court one day, during which he *led* in
every cause—all of them interesting; two prosecutions
for maltreating a negro boy, and one defence for libel.
They were of the highest local importance—one of them
a special jury cause, and the court (a very large one)

was crammed to suffocation, including all the first
people in the county. He spoke in the libel case for an
hour and a half; and really I never before witnessed
such an exhibition of high and passionate eloquence;
quite different from the ordinary eloquence of the bar,
from its being far finer and purer in kind, as well as
mightier in power. No cant, no commonplace, no clap-
traps, no bitterness; appealing to the highest and loftiest
feelings, the deepest and noblest sympathies of our
nature! Such eloquence is a grand and glorious thing.
He swayed the multitude as a steed is swayed by its
rider. You might have heard a pin drop, till he ceased;
and then the irrepressible applause was so tumultuous
that it was not for a long time that the judge could get
the court quiet enough to be heard, when he threatened
to send the clappers to gaol; confessing, at the same
time, that he did not wonder at the plaudits bestowed
on the young and most eloquent pleader, only they had
chosen a wrong place. You may imagine that this was
a very proud day for Mr. Talfourd and for his friends.
We dined together at Dr. Valpy's after the court closed;
and I never remember being so much excited and
gratified in my life. He spoke of you with great enthusiasm—and has quite recanted about Kean; dis-
gusted, of course, at the quantity of cant that has been
written about him.

Have you read Dr. Antommarchi's account of the
last days of Napoleon? It appears clearly to me that
the exceeding ignorance of that Italian co-operated
with the climate and the gaoler in killing him. Only
think of never giving calomel till the two or three last
days! The effect that it had, even then, proves what
it might have done if administered sooner. My father
says that he has no doubt but the accumulation of

acrid bile in the stomach produced the ulcer. But foreign physicians are old women. Altogether it is a very painful book to read, and yet one that I could not help reading. Everything about that great man has for me a charm absolutely inexpressible. I rejoice that you do not mean to paint Mrs. Haydon in lace and velvet; they are too poor, too millinery for her. She is a creature of poetry. The only costume I could fancy for her would be Oriental—rich and splendid as her matchless beauty. Kindest love to her and the dear little ones. God bless you, my dearest friend!

Ever most faithfully yours,

M. R. MITFORD.

To the Rev. WILLIAM HARNESS, *Hampstead.*

Three Mile Cross, April 22, 1825.

MY DEAR FRIEND,

Many thanks for your kindness about Mr. Campbell. I have sent him two articles to the care of Mr. Colburn. In future, I will send them to his house, when I can get a frank or a private hand. My little book is in a third edition, which is encouragement for a novel. Do you know who wrote the critique in the 'Quarterly,' which has certainly done me so much good? Now for the plot of my novel, although I am so afraid of the undertaking, that I am quite persuaded it will never be good for anything. I mean to take a whole village—one of those islands of cultivation and habitancy which are found amidst the downs of Wiltshire, or the vale of Berkshire—that which is called in these parts the low country. There I mean to place an old and splendid, but nearly deserted residence, belonging to an impoverished nobleman, whose park, &c. are rented by a Mrs. Ellis, widow of a rich farmer—

a comely, kindly dame, with one very pretty, spoilt, romp of a daughter, about sixteen. The book shall open with a letter to Mrs. Ellis from a lawyer in London, informing her that an old stockbroker, her great uncle, whom she had never seen in her life, is dead, having left a miser's fortune between her and the descendant of some other niece then abroad. The lawyer, who is also the agent for the nobleman her landlord, informs her that the mansion and estate, part of which she rents, are to be sold, and advises her to purchase them. In the course of further communications he makes an offer, on the part of the old lord, of his only son to her only daughter. Mrs. Ellis catches eagerly at the proposal, and requests the lawyer's lady to provide a governess forthwith for her Kate. Accordingly a lady-like young woman of three or four and twenty, a Miss Clive, arrives; and, shortly afterwards, come the nobleman and his son—apparently to finish the sale, but in reality to commence the courtship. The father is much more anxious for this match than the son; and gradually it shall ooze out that there had been an old attachment between the latter and Miss Clive, the governess, whose father had been an officer in the same regiment; that it had been broken off by the remonstrances of Lord N. (I have not named him yet) with Miss Clive; and still more gradually it shall be felt, that the old love is reviving—interrupted, of course, by the proper quantity of hopes and fears, and a good deal of the usual coquetry on the part of the pretty little Kate, who, herself in love with a scapegrace nephew of Lord N.'s, takes no small pleasure in perplexing her lover and all about her. At length, things come to a crisis; Kate declares to her mother that she will not have the man selected for her, and he, on his part, affirms to his father that he will marry none but Augusta Clive. Lord N. reproaches Miss Clive with breaking her promise to him. At last it is discovered that Augusta is herself the heiress to the other half of the miser's property; and that, finding both her name and person unknown to Mrs. Ellis, she has availed herself of her sending for a governess to make, under that title, an interest in the affections of her relations, and perhaps to examine into the faith of her lover. Of course all parties marry and are happy as usual.

This is a very rough sketch; but I send it to a master, whose fancy can easily supply the lights and shades and the colouring. Is the story, do you think, sufficiently original? It is free from vice and pecuniary evil (both of which are so unpleasant in books); and the conclusion will be comfortable and satisfactory. I see that I must not make too much perplexity about nothing (that provoking fault of Madame D'Arblay's novels), and that I must get as much incident and character as I can. Do tell me anything you think might mend it. But I shall finish 'Charles' first.

Most gratefully and affectionately yours,

M. R. MITFORD.

To SIR WILLIAM ELFORD, *Bickham, Plymouth.*

Three Mile Cross, May 21, 1825.

MY DEAR FRIEND,

I thank you for remembering my request, although it is with sincere regret that I read your opinion. To me, Dr. Darling* seemed a fine portrait, both as to expression and colour. As to myself,† it seemed a strong unflattered likeness—one that certainly would

* Portrait by Haydon.　　　† Haydon's portrait of her.

not be very calculated to feed a woman's vanity, or to
cure the public of the general belief that authoresses
are and must be frights. But really I don't think it
much uglier than what I see every day in the looking-
glass; and I especially forbid you from answering this
observation by any flattery, or anything whatsoever.*

I am sorry that the portrait is not more complimentary; because it vexes my father to hear it so much
abused, as I must confess it is, by everybody except Miss
James, and the artist, who maintain that it is a capital
likeness—quite a woman of genius, and so forth. Now,
my dear friend, I entreat and implore you not to mention to any one what I say. I would not have Mr.
Haydon know it for worlds. It was a present, in the
first place, and certainly a very kind and flattering
attention; and, in the second, my personal feelings for
him would always make the picture gratifying to me
for his sake were it as ugly as Medusa. He is a most
admirable person, whose very faults spring from that
excess of brilliancy and life with which, more than any
creature that ever lived, he is gifted. I never see him
without thinking of the description of the Dauphin's
horse in 'Henry the Fifth'—all air and fire—the duller
elements have no share in his composition. You know,
I suppose, that he has a commission for an historical
picture.

Pray write again soon. God bless you, my very dear
friend!

Ever yours,

M. R. M.

---

* The fault of the portrait was, that everything was larger than life.
It represented a Brobdignagian fat woman seated in a bower of Brobdignagian honeysuckles.

To Miss Jephson, *Bath.*

Three Mile Cross, May 27, 1825.

My dear Friend,

We rejoice to hear that you are well and in England, and with friends whom you love so much. Oh! how I wish you were passing near us! I have been sitting all the morning in my little garden, with its roses and stocks of all kinds; and rich peonies and geraniums; and purple irises and periwinkles; and yellow laburnums and globe anemones; and greens vivid and beautiful even as flowers, making altogether the finest piece of colour I ever saw—and I really yearned after you—you would have liked it so much. It is provoking to show such a thing to common eyes. which go peeping about into the detail, pulling the effect to pieces as children do daisies. Besides the nightingale and the scent of lilies of the valley, my garden, on which my father rallies me so much, is my passion. But you will forgive me for over-rating it. It is, at least, a mistake on the right side, to be too fond of one's own poor home—and no mistake at all to wish you in it.

I am now busy finishing a tragedy on the story of Charles and Cromwell for Covent Garden next season; after which I shall set to work at the 'Heiress' ding-dong. One alteration I have made in the plan; Augusta shall not know that she is entitled to a share in the property. I shall give my miser an involved pedigree, and make a difficulty on all sides in tracing the descent; which will give rise to some good comic scenes, and will give to the whole work something of interest, independent of love. After all, I am really and unfeignedly afraid of my power in this line of composition.

Your story of Carlo is very pretty. May has puppies: we had seven-and-twenty applications; and, as poor May has only eight, were obliged, keeping one, to refuse twenty friends. The one kept is a little white beauty—May in miniature. It fell down the other day and hurt—almost dislocated—its hip. We picked it up, poor little thing, and rubbed it with camphorated spirits of wine, during which operation it lay in my lap quite quiet and patient, whilst May sat close by, shivering and whining and moaning at every touch, just as if it had been her limb that was hurt, and not the puppy's. The scene was really affecting.

Pray excuse this blotted scrawl—for which I have no other excuse than that of being a blotter by profession. I wish I could write tidily! My father and mother join in most affectionate remembrances—and I am ever,

My own dear Emily,

Most faithfully yours,

M. R. M.

To Sir William Elford, Bickham, Plymouth.

Three Mile Cross, June 23, 1825.

My dear Friend,

I write to you *de provision*, as Madame de Sevigné says, although I have no M.P. under hand; but I am tired to death—I have been all the morning talking, entertaining morning visitors (the deuce take 'em)—and all the afternoon gardening, planting and watering flowers (deuce—no, not deuce take them—I love them too well); and so, being fairly worn off my feet and off my tongue, it has occurred to me out of my great friendship and affection to bestow the bloom of my weariness, the first moments of yawning and grumbling, on you. Are you not exceedingly obliged to me?

My mother is so well as to be staying with a relation in Hampshire, so that my father and I are left to keep house together. *He* is housekeeper—mamma thinks him the trustier of the two—so she left those ensigns of authority, the keys, in his possession; and they are only lost fifty times in an hour. We were in great danger of going without dinner, because such a thing was not thought of till it was wanted to be eaten; but we have dressed a great bit of beef, and now we are independent. All these troubles amuse us excessively, and I can't tell you which is the most in fault of the two—only I rather think I am. Dear me, if mamma knew the disorderly life we lead, what would she say!

Good-bye, my dear Sir William, for to-night. Next time I am thoroughly done up I shall write to you by way of resting myself.

Most affectionately yours,
M. R. M.

To B. R. HAYDON, ESQ., *Connaught Terrace.*

Three Mile Cross, July 18, 1825.

MY DEAR FRIEND,

I have just received your hot-weather letter, which I could return point by point—only that the country is the country, and London is London; and that we have a long shed open to the north, which runs along one side of my little garden, where we live entirely, looking out upon that bright piece of colour, my flower beds. *Your* verses amused me exceedingly. I do think they are yours—at least they might be; for there is the very mixture of honest fun and strong humour and fine high fancy which you would put into such a subject. I have a theory, very proper and convenient for an old maid, that the world is over-peopled, and always hear with some regret of every fresh birth. I hold old maids and old bachelors—especially old maids, for an obvious reason—to be the most meritorious and patriotic class of his Majesty's subjects; and I think the opinion seems gaining ground. Three persons in this neighbourhood especially, all friends of mine, are stanch in the creed; only, unluckily, their practice does not quite accord with their principles. The first, an old maid herself, I caught last week in the act of presiding over a dozen of country-town ladies, cutting out baby linen for a charity—'The Maternal Society,' save the mark! Bounties upon babies! The second, an admiral of the last edition, called on me on Saturday with a very rueful face to announce the birth of a daughter (he has a pretty young wife and six children under eight years old)—"Well," said I, "it must be endured." "Yes," said he, "but who would have thought of its being a girl!" The third, a young married woman, was brought to bed this very morning of twins—a catastrophe which I have been predicting to her this month past. Never fear for dear Mrs. Haydon—there is a wonderful providence in such cases. Besides, there is a purity of health about her; and she is so loving and so precious that she will be taken particular care of—depend upon it.

When I last saw my portrait it seemed to me as like as what I see every day in the looking-glass; and even if it were as ugly as Medusa I should always think it the greatest honour of my life that it was painted. There is a long letter from me to you somewhere on the road. God bless you, my dear friends! Believe me always,

Most affectionately yours,
M. R. MITFORD.

To B. R. Haydon, Esq., *Connaught Terrace.*

Three Mile Cross, Aug. 11, 1825.

I congratulate you on your boy Frank not being prematurely clever! We have a precocious child here, the daughter of a dear friend, and the heiress of ten thousand a year, who frightens me for her own destiny and her mother's happiness. She is like a little old fairy; with eyes over-informed, preternatural in their expression. She really startles me. If there be one thing that I deprecate more than another, it is that precociousness. You know who says

"At Christmas I no more desire a rose
Than wish for snow in May's new-fangled shows;"

and a wiser thing even he never said.*

I have just been reading Mr. Combe's and Mr. Deville's books on phrenology. Really I half believe. The names of the organs are most absurd—most unphilosophical—most un-English. If they were altered I believe a great deal of the objection against the science would disappear. It is at all events an interesting pursuit, taken moderately. God bless you, my very dear friends!

Ever most faithfully yours,
M. R. Mitford.

To the Rev. William Harness, *Hampstead.*

Three Mile Cross, Wednesday.
Oct. 9, 1825.

My dear Friend,

Although I have no member under hand, I write without waiting the uncertain chance of meeting with one—first, to thank you for your very kind attention

* Shakespeare. The lines are in 'Love's Labour Lost,' Act i. Scene i.

about the money—secondly, to give you all the information I myself possess respecting the play. Mr. Kemble found 'Charles' on his table on his return from abroad—read it immediately—thought it "admirable though somewhat dangerous"—and sent it at once to the licenser. For three weeks we heard nothing of it. At last came a note from Mr. Colman to say "that, in consequence of the exceedingly delicate nature of the subject and incidents of ' Charles the First,' he had received instructions to send the MS. to the Lord Chamberlain, that he might himself judge, on perusal, of the safety of granting a license." Accordingly the piece is gone to the Duke of Montrose, who is in Scotland. And there we stand. Is not this very strange and unusual?

Have you read Pepys's Memoirs? I am extremely diverted by them, and prefer them to Evelyn's, all to nothing. He was too precise and too gentlemanly and too sensible by half;—wrote in full dress, with an eye, if not to the press, at least to posthumous reputation. Now this man sets down his thoughts in a most becoming dishabille—does not care twopence for posterity; and evidently thinks wisdom a very foolish thing. I don't know when any book has amused me so much. It is the very perfection of gossiping—most relishing nonsense.

How long do you stay at Hampstead? I shall tell you the fate of 'Charles' as soon as I know it. Do let me know what you think of Mr. Fitzharris. Kindest love to dear Mary.—Mamma's to all of you. Ever, my dear friend,

Most sincerely yours,

M. R. MITFORD.

To the REV. WILLIAM HARNESS, *The Deepdene, Dorking.*

Three Mile Cross, Oct. 30, 1825.

MY DEAR FRIEND,

You are the only friend whose advice agrees with my strong internal feeling respecting the drama. Everybody else says, Write novels—write prose! So that my perseverance passes for perverseness and obstinacy, which is very discouraging. There is a most splendid subject for historical tragedy which has taken great hold of my imagination:—Henry the Second— introducing, by a pardonable anachronism, the whole story of Becket, Eleanor, and Rosamond, and the rebellious sons. I should only take the best and worst of these, Henry and Geoffrey—Richard and John being too familiar to the stage; and the death of Prince Henry would supply, what in the story of so long-lived a monarch is very material, a good conclusion. This would certainly be a fine subject, and quite untouched. But the licenser! The chief temptation is of course Thomas à Becket, whom I should make as like as I could to what he was—a mixture of prelatic haughtiness and personal austerity—the haircloth peeping under the prince's robes; and the great scene would be an excommunication, not of the king, but of the ministers and the nation; certainly a fine thing to do · but the licenser! Henry, an enlightened prince, at least two centuries before his age, must have the better of the argument. But may we touch the subject? And Eleanor and Rosamond, odious as the queen was and must be—would that do?

I have a good mind to write to Mr. Colman and ask. I would, if I knew any way of getting at him. Certainly I mean no harm—nor did I in 'Charles'; and the not licensing that play will do great harm to my next, by making me timid and over careful. Let me know what you think about Henry the Second.

You cannot imagine how perplexed I am. There are points in my domestic situation too long and too painful to write about. The terrible improvidence of one dear parent—the failure of memory and decay of faculty in that other who is still dearer, cast on me a weight of care and of fear that I can hardly bear up against. Give me your advice. Heaven knows, I would write a novel, as every one tells me to do, and as, I suppose, I must do at last, if I had not the feeling of inability and of failure so strong within me that it would be scarcely possible to succeed against such a presentiment. And to fail there would be so irremediable! But it will be my lot at last.

God bless you, my dear friend! Kindest love to dear Mary. I hope we shall see you here, or at least at Reading. Pray, pray contrive it.

Ever most gratefully yours,

M. R. MITFORD.

Yes! I have read Madame de Genlis with great amusement. What a delightful mixture of cant and affectation and shrewdness and vanity she is! I had a peculiar pleasure in reading these volumes, as they completely justified the contempt I had always entertained for the authoress; a contempt chiefly grounded on her *good* characters, of which the exaggerated and morbid virtues proved so decidedly a defective moral sense.

To the Rev. William Harness, *Hampstead.*

Three Mile Cross, Dec. 1, 1825.

My dear Friend,

I followed your advice, and requested Mr. Rowland Stephenson to ask Mr. Colman if the ' Charles ' could not be altered so as to be licensable, and to-day's post brought me a packet from Miss Stephenson, enclosing the following from Mr. Colman to her brother-in-law. I transcribe it word for word :—

" *Private.*

"28th Nov. 1825. Brompton Square.

" My dear Sir,

" It is much to be regretted that Miss Mitford has employed her time unprofitably when so amiable a motive as that of assisting her family has induced her to exercise her literary talents ; but it would be idle and ungenerous to flatter her with hopes which there is no prospect of fulfilling.

" My official opinion of her tragedy is certainly unfavourable to the author's interests. I was, however, so far from wishing it to prejudice the Lord Chamberlain that the play was submitted to his perusal at my suggestion. He therefore formed his own judgment upon it and decidedly refused to license its performance.

" As to alterations—the fact is, that the subject of this play and the incidents it embraces are fatal in themselves—they are an inherent and incurable disease —the morbid matter lies in the very bones and marrow of the historical facts, and defies eradication. Indeed it would be a kind of practical bull to permit a detailed representation of Charles's unhappy story on a public stage, when his martyrdom is still observed in such solemn silence that the London theatres are actually closed and all dramatic exhibitions whatever suspended on its anniversary.

" I give Miss Mitford full credit for the harmlessness of her intentions, but mischief may be unconsciously done, as a house may be set on fire by a little innocent in the nursery.

" Believe me, my dear sir, most truly yours,
" G. COLMAN.

" Rowland Stephenson, Esq.,
        Lombard Street."

Now, is not this a precious *morceau ?* But there is no use in contending.

Poor mamma's failure of faculty is very peculiar. You might see her twenty times for twenty minutes, and yet not perceive it ; or, on the other hand, she might in one twenty minutes show it a hundred times. She mistakes one person for another—one thing for another—mis- joins facts—misreports conversations—hunts for six hours together after a pincushion which she has in her pocket, or a thimble on her finger—and is totally ab- sorbed in the smallest passing objects. *This* is, in one respect, fortunate, since it prevents her from foreseeing greater evils. But then again, it deters her from sup- porting me in any effort to mitigate them. So that, from her incapacity, and the absolute inertness of my father in such matters—an obstinacy of going on in the same way which I cannot describe—I find myself com- pelled to acquiesce in a way of living which, however inexpensive, is still more so than we can afford, for fear of disturbing, and perhaps killing her. If she were herself she would rather live on dry bread in a garret than run in debt ; and so would I, merely as a question of personal comfort.

Well, it is very wrong to worry you with these grievances, which must have their course, especially now,
that you are yourself tormented about the church.
You cannot imagine how sorry we all are for that sad
affair.

I have not yet written to Mr. Campbell, but I certainly shall. It is the best way. I am quite delighted
with your edition of Shakespeare. It must do. The
Life is like the portrait prefixed to it; the old beloved
well-known features, which we all have by heart, but
inspired with a fresh spirit. I did not think it possible
to make a scanty narrative seem so full. Only I have
a favour to beg; in the next edition leave out the
latter part of Malone's ill-natured note on Milton's
verses. I don't think that Milton did mean to speak
ill of Shakespeare ; and, at all events, there is no need
to dwell on a slight offence towards the memory of
Shakespeare in such a man as Milton—his worthiest
admirer and most exquisite eulogist. You, especially,
who have so admirably vindicated Ben Jonson from
such a charge, ought not to admit Mr. Malone's sour
observation into your pages, of which the tone is, generally speaking, so genial.

Ever most gratefully and affectionately yours,

M. R. MITFORD.

To B. R. HAYDON, ESQ., *Connaught Terrace.*

Three Mile Cross, Dec. 18, 1825.

MY DEAR FRIEND,

I heartily agree with you about Sheridan and
about Moore. *Wits* (for neither of them are in the true
sense *Poets*) are essentially of a lower order of mind.
Better have written any comedy of Shakespeare than
' The School for Scandal.' Better have written ' The

Merry Wives of Windsor' than all other comedies put together. Notwithstanding the marvellous variety of character in that delicious piece, there is a harmony which pervades it and prevents any feeling of discrepancy—all is in keeping. And 'As You Like It' and 'Much Ado About Nothing'—what exquisite things are these! The notion of anybody being jealous of Shakespeare! I have never thoroughly liked Scott since the passage in 'Kenilworth' where he is introduced as a player, with an intentional degradation. Have you seen Mr. Harness's new edition of Shakespeare? The Life is very spirited and good, and there is a delightful portrait, which one is sure is like.

How very unlucky I am! Only to think of George Whittaker's having stopped payment! It was lucky that I had not parted with the copyright of my little book; but there are the profits of my last large edition unaccounted for, and other trifling things—more than we can afford to lose. I have been so urged by friends and importuned by booksellers (amongst others by Longman's house), that I have at last actually begun a novel. Wish me success! It is a tremendous undertaking, for I write with extreme slowness, labour, and difficulty; and, whatever you may think, there is a great difference of facility in different minds. I am the slowest writer, I suppose, in England, and touch and retouch perpetually.

Adieu, my dear friend. Kindest regards from my father and mother.

Ever most truly yours,

M. R. M.

[The following is in answer to a letter from Miss Mitford, requesting Charles Kemble to produce 'Foscari.']

"Dec. 20, 1825.

" My dear Madam,

" I am fearful that I shall not be able to comply with your request. My word is already pledged to the production of so much novelty of one kind or another, that, were there no other reasons against ' Foscari's' being acted, I might almost say it is impossible. It is, I hope, unnecessary for me to say that I shall be happy of any opportunity of being useful to you, or to assure you that I am with great sincerity,

" Your faithful servant,
" Charles Kemble."

1826.

[Miss Mitford went up to town in the beginning of this year in the greatest hurry, to collect, if possible, money due to her from publishers and booksellers. She stayed at Mrs. Holland's, for some days, but seems to have received little from her debtors beyond invitations and compliments.]

To the Rev. William Harness, *Hampstead.*

Three Mile Cross, March 4, 1826.

My dear Friend,

Your kind letter has given me the greatest possible relief. To have been—however unintentionally—the cause of serious annoyance to you, would have been insupportable.

How very striking that circumstance of Mr. Deville and little N——n* is! I really think there is a great deal of

* The boy was about five years old. His father was an Englishman, his mother a Portuguese. Of this Deville was perfectly ignorant; but his words, on feeling the boy's head, were: " A wonderful development! I never found the *perceptive* organs so strong in any English head, nor the *reflective* organs so strong in any foreign head before."

truth in the system. What a pity that they have not amongst them some accurate writer, who knows the power of *words*, and would sweep away the strange jargon which has crept amongst them from the cockneyism of Deville and the Germanism of Spurzheim! Mr. Combe's book is the best on the subject. Have you seen it?

I enclose my charades, which in all but their faults might more truly be called *yours*. If you think the thing will remain intact till next year (for I am sure that my novel cannot appear before), then it would be better to suppress them, and insert one therein, more carefully written and *àpropos* to the story; but if it seems to you probable, that some will make their appearance before (and really one wonders that the idea has not been seized), then these might be sent to a magazine.* Do as you judge best. Ten guineas a sheet is very bad pay for a magazine in double columns like ' Blackwood '; I have twelve for those of which the printing is so much opener, and after the rate of twenty or thirty from the annual publications; but that I should not mind. It could not make much difference.

By-the-way, I wrote about ' Rienzi,' as it was right to do. You and I were talking of Mrs. Radcliffe's Romances. Mr. Talfourd gave me the other day a very interesting account of her posthumous works,† containing a real genuine ghost story—a *bonâ-fide* ghost— simple in its construction, but excessively powerful whenever the supernatural agency is introduced, and full of remarkable felicities of expression. The scene is at Kenilworth, in the reign of Henry the Third. But

---

* They were published with others in Blackwood. Mr. H. gave Miss Mitford the plans for the three first of the series.

† Mr. Radcliffe, after his wife's death, placed her MSS. in Mr. Talfourd's hands to be edited.

Mr. Talfourd says that by far the finest things he has seen of hers are her manuscript notes on different journeys in England—simple, graphical, without a single word to spare—and with a Cobbett-like power of putting a scene before your eyes. Some few of these will be incorporated in the Memoirs, but not nearly all. Her biographer says that the trouble of drawing up this life, under the jealous supervision of Mr. Radcliffe, exceeds anything that can be imagined; to use his own illustration, it is worse than drawing an affidavit, from the fidgetty scrupulousness he shows about things of no manner of consequence. Considering the lies we have to encounter, it is something to find that there is anybody left in the world who cares for truth, however unimportant. Mr. Radcliffe is an old gentleman, quite of the old school; who—notwithstanding he has since her decease married his housekeeper—retains the fondest affection for his more illustrious wife—calls her the dear deceased, and cries whenever she is mentioned.

Have you heard anything of Sir Walter Scott's affair lately? Mr. Haydon wrote me word, a day or two ago, that he had had a letter from him, in which he said that he had lost a large fortune, but that he should have a competence left. When does your church open? Make our kindest regards to dear Mary. God bless you, my dear and kind friend!

Ever most sincerely yours,

M. R. MITFORD.

To the REV. WILLIAM HARNESS, *Hampstead.*

Three Mile Cross, March 23, 1826.

MY DEAR FRIEND,

I write, although I have no frank, because an idea has just taken such possession of me that I cannot rest

without asking your advice and co-operation concerning
it. I want to write a grand opera on the story of
'Cupid and Psyche,' with Weber's music. It has been
done as a ballet I know, and I think there is a French
play on the subject, by Molière, but I know nothing of
the sort in English, or in great music. Do you? Just
look at the story, and see how dramatic it is—how full
of situation and variety, both for dialogue and poetry,
for music and scenery ; the response of the oracle—the
funeral procession—then the Cupid part—then the labours—the hell—the apotheosis ; and, moreover, I am
quite sure that I could give it a strong *human* interest,
by plunging myself into the beautiful story and entirely
forgetting the allegory. I wish with all my heart you
would ask Mr. Kemble whether, if I were to put all my
strength into such an opera, he could get Weber to
compose the music, and whether Weber would like the
subject. It has seized my imagination most strongly,
and there would be no fear of the licenser in this case,
I suppose. Do pray ask. I am *sure* that I could do
my part satisfactorily. Kindest love from all here.

Ever most gratefully yours,
M. R. MITFORD.

To the REV. WILLIAM HARNESS, *Hampstead.*

Three Mile Cross, April 3, 1826.

MY DEAR FRIEND,

I am quite delighted with Mr. Blackwood's approbation of the charades, and still more so, infinitely more
so, with yours. Pray write some, and send to 'Blackwood,' and let us come out together afterwards in a
joint volume. You can't think how much I shall like
to Beaumont-and-Fletcher it with you. I have sent
him two more—"Match-lock" and "Block-head." After

writing the first (which is quite a little drama of the Commonwealth days), it occurred to me to look for the word. Accordingly, I searched in one folio Johnson, and in half a dozen small dictionaries, and no such word! Was not this a most absurd difficulty? To have written a charade upon a non-existing word! However, in Todd's Johnson, at last I found it. So that trouble is happily over.

April 16.

This note has been awaiting a letter from you, and I hasten to reply to your very kind one received yesterday. I have written, but not sent, another charade on "Mess-mate." I tell you this to avoid any awkward jostling of words. I quite long to see your story. I shall like it I am sure. Let me know, as soon as you hear anything of Psyche. It might make an exquisite opera, and I do think that I could manage it.

Mrs. Trollope, who has been reading 'Rienzi,' and who is a most kind and warmhearted person, has set her heart on getting it out either with Kean or Macready. I don't know how she may succeed with the former; but I think I know enough of the latter worthy, to predict her non-success. Mr. Milman—induced, I believe, by her praises—also wished to read it, and has written me a most kind and gratifying letter respecting it, with excellent criticisms. He likes the play; and I am myself quite sure that, with a great actor, it could not fail. But I am so unlucky—am I not? I have not yet begun the Psyche, having been engaged in preparing another volume of 'Our Village,' which I think of bringing out. Does Apuleius say what oracle they consulted? And what was the mode of consulting an oracle—the ceremony? Was there a sacrifice? I wish with all my heart that Mr. Kemble may take the opera.

I think of writing another charade on "Black-wood"—a good local subject. You'll find writing charades very amusing. I like nothing else. Poor mamma has been very unwell, but is much better. Kind love from all.

Ever yours most sincerely,

M. R. M.

To the REV. WILLIAM HARNESS, *Hampstead.*

Three Mile Cross, May 2, 1826.

I thank you heartily, my dear friend, for your kind letter. My father went to London Monday morning and returned Tuesday night, having settled the business of my second volume, I think, very fairly. George Whittaker buys that and the copyright of the first volume for 150*l.*, or rather his brother-in-law buys the work for him. I might certainly have got 200*l.* elsewhere, but I think the price fair, considering the extreme depression of the trade. Don't you? Last year it would have been worth 300*l.* at least. Blackwood sent me the magazine, with a most handsome letter, requesting a continuance of my contributions, and begging me to accept of an order on Messrs. Cadell for 10*l.* 10*s.*, as a retaining fee. This is pleasant, and quite explains why his magazine is so good. Liberal men are sure to have things well done. He spoke of you most handsomely. By-the-way, I begged to reserve the copyright.

I must read the 'Martyr' as soon as possible. She is a glorious woman—a great and delicious poet; but certainly not dramatic in any of her doings. She always wanted spontaneity—vividness—presentness, if I may use such a word. It was that want which made her plays—full as they are of the noblest thoughts and the most racy diction—altogether unfit for the stage.

There must have been a want, when we have seen the majestic 'Jane de Montfort'* fail in the hands of Mrs. Siddons, who seemed born to embody that grand conception of genius. Macready used to say that it was want of passion. But there is passion—high passion, both in De Montfort and Basil. What they want is *life*.

A thousand thanks for the 'Oracle,' and best love from all.

Ever yours,

M. R. M.

To B. R. HAYDON, ESQ., *Connaught Terrace.*

Three Mile Cross, May 4, 1826.

MY DEAR FRIEND,

I am always delighted to hear from you, but never in a fuss if I do not, because I am so sure of your kindness that I only think you are busy. The 'Alexander' must be a fine thing. I quite agree with you; he is the man for my money. It is the *doers* of the world—the Alexanders and Cromwells and Napoleons—that are the materials of painting and poetry, and not the mere talkers and thinkers and writers. I shall long to see it. I hear from Hannah Rowe, who is here, that you are as well and as brilliant as ever.

Poor Sir Walter Scott! Captain Kater told me, when I was in town, that he had heard from undeniable authority, that a letter had been sent to him, signed only with a single initial, authorizing him to draw for 30,000*l.* on a particular banker. A most noble gift! But, still, Sir Walter must feel it very hard to be deposed, at his time of life, from the station which he held in the world, as well as in literature; the more especially as the great falling-off in the late works rendered it de-

* By Mrs. Joanna Baillie.

sirable for his fame that he should cease writing. But what is his reverse of fortune compared with Napoleon's! I hope your patron will soon be able to cash his bills. Most fervently I hope this on your account, and also on his. I rejoice to hear so good an account of your invalids. God bless you all!

Ever yours,
M. R. MITFORD.

To B. R. HAYDON, ESQ., *Connaught Terrace.*

Tuesday morning, 11th July, 1826.

MY DEAR FRIEND,

I should be delighted to take in your article on the rabbit, only my second volume is printed and ready for delivery—and has been for these three weeks, but is kept back by the booksellers till the election flurry subsides. But you must keep it for me; I shall have another volume probably in the spring.

It's very delightful to hear that Sir Walter's loss is only forty thousand pounds, which cannot affect his comfort or even the prospects of his children, vexatious as it must be. I confess to you, my dear friend, that with every respect for the genius of Scott, I am one of those who think that he has had his reward both in fame and money. I have been credibly informed that he received eight thousand guineas for 'Woodstock'! Now, just look at 'Woodstock,' and tell me if the author who receives eight thousand four hundred pounds for that book has any reason to complain? I do not say that so delightful a writer—so great a one as he has been, so pleasant a one as he is—is overpaid, but simply that he is well paid and can afford a few remarks from the good-natured world.

Have you read Cooper's novel, 'The Last of the

Mohicans?' I like it better than any of Scott's, except the three first and the 'Heart of Mid-Lothian;' and it interests me more even than those, as giving a true and new picture of a new and great people. How wonderfully America is rising in the scale of intellect! A friend lent me lately an essay on Milton's life and writings by Dr. Channing of Boston, compared with which Macaulay's article in the 'Edinburgh,' that was so puffed and cried up, is mere drivelling.

If you have not read the American novels, do. Depend on it that America will succeed us as Rome did Athens; and it is a comfort to think that by their speaking the same beautiful language, Shakspeare and Milton will not be buried in the dust of a scholar's library, but live and breathe in after ages as they do now to us.

This weather is dreadful. My garden, which a week ago was really like a bit of Paradise, so far as flowers and beauty go, is now so scorched and withered that it is a grief to look at it. My father has been poorly. My mother, thank Heaven! keeps tolerably well, and so am I, when I am quiet. I wish, heartily, we had any chance of seeing you. I trust you keep well. God bless you all, my dear friends!

Ever yours,
M. R. M.

To *the* REV. WILLIAM HARNESS, *Heathcote Street, London.*

Three Mile Cross, August 26, 1826.

MY DEAR FRIEND,

After my last good-for-nothing, pettish, and suspicious letter (which pray burn), I have been made quite ashamed of myself by receiving the following most kind one from Mr. Kemble :—

"Since the receipt of yours of the 28th of July, I

have been troubled with many cares, or I would have attended more promptly to the questions it contained. To your first question—'Do you think that Mrs. Radcliffe's posthumous romance would answer as a drama?' I answer that not having read it I am unable to say whether it would or not. To your second question—'Have you employed any one to dramatize it?' I answer, No. You surely must be as good a judge of the fitness of the subject for the stage as any one; and if you set about it let me warn you that it will not be a great success unless you contrive to introduce some good comic character into the story. A comedy! a comedy! still a comedy! say I, and without songs, or at most with not above two. It is in vain to write tragedies till we have an actress to give proper effect to them.

From what you say respecting the little time that would be requisite for you to arrange 'Gaston de Blondeville,' you might perhaps finish that and a comedy too. The last time I spoke with Mr. Young on the subject of 'Rienzi,' he seemed to me to have changed his opinion in some measure with regard to it. Have you read the French tragedy of that name, which was acted last winter in Paris with great success? I shall be in London in the course of a week or ten days, and am ever, dear madam, &c.,

"C. KEMBLE.

"Harrogate, 22nd of August."

Now this letter is enough to make me hate myself, when I think with how much suspicion and mistrust I had been led to regard this kind person. I don't quite know what he means about the 'Rienzi.'

How shall I excuse my pestering you with all my dramatic hopes and fears?—all my sins of thought and weaknesses of character? But you are so very, very kind. Have we any chance of seeing you here? Mr. Milman made a great display last Wednesday at the Bishop's Visitation, preaching a sermon which I was so unlucky as not to hear, but which everybody speaks of as a most splendid piece of oratory—on the Philosophy of Preaching. I hope he'll print it.

I hope you are getting a great deal of money at your church, I mean that you have the rents from the pews, so that your popularity may be profitable as well as pleasant to you. It's one of the worst results of being poor, that it makes one think of nothing but money, whether for one's self or one's friends.

God bless you, my dear friend! Kindest regards from my father and mother.

Ever most gratefully yours,
M. R. MITFORD.

To the REV. WILLIAM HARNESS, *Deepdene, Dorking.*

Three Mile Cross, Oct. 27, 1826.

MY DEAR FRIEND,

I am very troublesome to you, but it is all your own fault; be less kind, and you'll get rid of the torment. I have no frank, but I can't help answering your most welcome note; the more especially as I had before written to you a letter, which you had not received when that note was written, requesting you to forward our dividend in two half notes;* whereas I have now to request you to keep the money till my father and you meet, which will very probably be almost immediately on your arrival in town.

---

* The dividend on the small sum in the funds still remaining of Mrs. Mitford's fortune, was received by the Rev. W. Harness as executor to his father, who was Mrs. Mitford's trustee.

I suppose that I must be in town next Wednesday or
Thursday; I don't at present know where, but incline
to take a lodging near the theatre, with my father, for
a week; and perhaps if Mary be returned (I depend
on you for not hurrying her back before the time she
would otherwise come), and you are sure that I should
not occasion you any inconvenience, I may be tempted
to accept your most kind invitation for a day or two,
after that period. It would be such an indulgence!
such a holiday! But it must depend on two circumstances; the success of the play (for if that fail I shall
scud away home like a rabbit to its burrow), and my
dear mother's health. I have promised also to spend
a day, or perhaps two, in case all be favourable, with
Mrs. Trollope, of Harrow, who is so good as to make a
great point of it; so that my visit to Heathcote Street
might be made to suit your convenience, before or
after that.

Perhaps if there be really any chance of 'Gaston'
(which Mr. Kemble has not read yet), I had better
come to you then. But we shall meet, at all events,
on Saturday night; for whether in good or evil fortune, you are amongst the few whom I must see on
that eventful evening. You cannot imagine how nervous I am! So much seems to hang on it; 'Gaston;'
the American plays,* which the success of 'Foscari'
would certainly bring forward; and a volume of 'Dramatic Scenes,' which I have long intended to publish,
and which a really successful tragedy would undoubtedly
sell. By-the-way, my second volume is published at
last, and I hope waiting for you in Heathcote Street—
at least I desired it to be sent there.

* 'Rienzi' and 'Charles the First,' which had gone to America with
Macready.

'Gaston' is a mere melodrame—but, Mr. Talfourd says, a singularly good one—intended to *act* and not to *read*. I thought of nothing but effects from beginning to end. Well, I have tired you of my doings.

Kindest love from my dear mother.

Ever yours,
M. R. MITFORD.

There are no words for Mr. Kemble's kindness from the beginning of this affair to the end.

To MRS. MITFORD, *Three Mile Cross.*

London, 45, Frith Street, Nov. 2, 1826.

MY DEAR GRANNY,

I got here quite safe and well, and you will be delighted to hear that Drum * is looking extremely well, and the apartments are delightful. We all went to the play last night, Betsy and all, to see ' Clari,' the new farce, and ' Charles the Second.' Charles Kemble is very great indeed in ' Charles the Second,' and Farren in the farce, and Miss Paton in ' Clari.' I saw none of my people except Mr. Serle and Miss Henry. Miss Henry is very pretty, and Mr. Serle well-looking and pleasant-spoken. Charles Kemble is at present as hoarse as a crow, but it's to be hoped he'll get better before Saturday. I understand that they are all as sanguine as possible, and that Mr. Young is more zealous than any one. This is very pleasant. Mr Warde is also all zeal. I am expecting him every moment, as he appointed to be here this morning. Mr. St. Quintin breakfasted with us; he is looking well, but old. Mrs. St. Q. has sent you a beautiful cap of her work, which I shall bring you down. Mr. Talfourd joined us at the play; he is very sanguine, and much struck with Mr. Young's

---

* Pet name for Dr. Mitford.

acting. William Ogbourn has also been here to-day, and he is also sanguine. Betsy was prodigiously pleased. Mrs. Hofland, whom I saw yesterday, has quite lost her voice; both she and her husband are looking more deplorable than ever. My gown does capitally, and is just what they wear. We are in a great fright about the Duke of York, who is worse again. Heaven grant he may live over next week! There was a report last night that he was dead, but that is not so. He is alive this morning, but very ill.

I hope you got both dear Drum's letter and the 'Times' newspaper, which I sent by the boy, and that you have by this time received the new number of 'Blackwood,' in which I am very pleasantly mentioned in the last article, the 'Noctes Ambrosianæ.' This will do good. Drum wrote yesterday to Newberry to let you have five pounds, which I hope you have received by this time. If he does not send it to you, send Will with a note to him for it. And pray, my dearest dear, take great care of yourself, and be sure to let me hear exactly how you are; and give my love to poor dear Molly and the owl. God bless you, my very dearest! I shall leave Drum to finish.

Ever your own,
M. R. M.

To Mrs. Mitford,* *Three Mile Cross.*

45, Frith Street, Saturday night.
Nov. 5, 1826.

I cannot suffer this parcel to go to you, my dearest mother, without writing a few lines to tell you of the complete success of my play. It was received, not merely with rapturous applause, but without the slightest

* This was addressed outside, " Mrs. Mitford, *Good News.*"

symptom of disapprobation, from beginning to end. We had not a single order in the house, so that from first to last the approbation was sincere and general. William Harness and Mr. Talfourd are both quite satisfied with the whole affair, and my other friends are half crazy. Mrs. Trollope, between joy for my triumph and sympathy with the play, has cried herself half blind. I am, and have been, perfectly calm, and am merely tired with the great number of friends whom I have seen to-day. Mrs. Story has been here the greater part of the morning—kinder and warmer-hearted than any one that ever lived, except dear, dear Mrs. Trollope, who has also been with me most part of the day; Mrs. Morgan, Hannah Rowe, and my own darling Marianne, who stayed with me during the whole of the time that the play was acting, which I passed at George Robins's; and men innumerable. Marianne is going with me on Monday to the tragedy. Of course I shall now stay rather longer than I intended; having the copyright of the play and a volume of ' Dramatic Sketches ' to sell, if I can. We shall probably take these very comfortable lodgings for another week, but certainly not longer.

I quite long to hear how you, my own dearest darling, have borne the suspense and anxiety consequent on this affair—which, triumphantly as it has turned out, was certainly a very nervous business. They expect the play to run three times a week till Christmas. It was so immense a house that you might have walked over the heads in the pit; and great numbers were turned away, in spite of the wretched weather. All the actors were good; but it was a great thing for Mr. Serle and Mrs. Sloman, who made each what is called a hit. Mr. Young gave out the tragedy amidst immense applause.

God bless you, my dearest mother! Papa is quite well, and happier than you can imagine. He had really half a mind to go to you, instead of writing—so much do both of us wish to share our happiness with you. But I knew that you would be sorry that he should encounter so much fatigue. God bless you, once more, my dearest! Let dear Mrs. Fielde know how well all has gone.

Ever most fondly your own,

M. R. M.

[The agreement between the theatre and Miss Mitford for 'Foscari' was 100*l.* on the third, the ninth, the fifteenth, and the twentieth nights. The copyright, together with a volume of 'Dramatic Sketches,' was sold to Whittaker for 150*l.*]

To Sir William Elford, *Oakampton Hall, Wivilscombe, Somerset.*

Three Mile Cross, Nov. 17, 1826.

I thank you most sincerely, my dear Sir William, for your congratulations. Hitherto the success has been very brilliant. We can hardly expect it to last—since to continue to pull people so thoroughly undramatic as we English are become to a theatre in this deadest of dead seasons, to witness the representation of a quiet tragedy, would be next to a miracle. But great good has been done, if (which Heaven avert!) the tragedy stop not to-night. A real impression has been made, and a reputation of the highest order established—to say nothing of that which with me is now everything, the money. My second volume, having been out only a fortnight, has again gone to press. A strange thing to say, that little volume has done real mischief to my tragedy. You cannot have lived so long in the world without finding that people will never allow anybody the power of doing two things well; and, because it is admitted that I can write playful prose, there be many who assume that I cannot write serious verse. Let them go and cry at 'Foscari' (if 'Foscari' continue)—for I assure you that during two acts the white handkerchief is going continually, to my great astonishment.

I am just returned from passing a brilliant fortnight in London, where I saw Mr. Haydon and the picture that he is painting for Lord Egremont—'Alexander Taming Bucephalus;' and heard a great deal more literary news than I have head to remember or time to tell. For, alas! my dear Sir William, the holiday time of our correspondence is past. I am now a poor slave of the lamp, chained to the desk as the galley slave to his oar, and am at present triply engaged; for the monthly periodical publications, which I have been too much engaged to supply; to the annual books, which to my sorrow are just on, and have begun dunning me again; and to my own bookseller, who has bought a volume of 'Dramatic Scenes,' which I have still to finish.

Adieu, my dear friend. Kindest respects to all your family, especially to my dear friend and correspondent, Miss Elford.

Always most affectionately yours,

M. R. MITFORD.

I don't wonder at what you tell me about Hazlitt. If you won't quote me as an authority (for one had as soon provoke Satan as that man, being, as I am, a dramatic writer), I'll tell you a good story about him. My friend, Archdeacon Wrangham, who is a thorough-

paced bibliomaniac — a complete collector of scarce
books, and never purchases any other — bought the
Sally-Walker book (the ' Modern Pygmalion,' was not
it called ?*) on speculation—it being so exceedingly *bad*,
that he was sure it would soon become *scarce*.   I think
this an admirable piece of anticipation.

* The title of the book was ' Liber Amoris.'

CHAPTER XI.

LETTERS FOR 1827 AND 1828.

To SIR WILLIAM ELFORD, *Totnes, Devon.*

Three Mile Cross, March 5, 1827.

I THANK you very sincerely for your most kind note, my dear friend, which afforded us all the greatest pleasure, from the proof that it contained of your good health and good spirits—your unchangeable vigour of mind and of hand. Mr. Jones* is very good—very kind. There is no love lost; I was delighted with his pictures and his conversation. He is certainly out of health, and complained to me of being obliged to leave the high classical and romantic style, in which he delights, and of which he has so many splendid sketches, for the battle pieces, of which he is weary, and the old Flemish and German towns, which employ his hand rather than his imagination; but of which two kinds his commissions mainly consist. He complained also of the *number* of commissions, being overworked. But, after all, that's a very good misfortune for an artist now-a-days. He had a scheme of making drawings from Sophocles, as Flaxman has done from Homer and Æschylus, which, as he only deferred it out of compliment to that fine veteran, he will, I hope, now that he

---

* The Royal Academician.

is gone, carry into speedy effect. Sophocles deserves
to be so illustrated. I have an enthusiasm for his plays
only second to that which I entertain for Shakespeare.
Did I tell you (*à propos* of art) that William Havell,
who went out with Lord Amherst to China, and has
remained ever since in India, is now returned—much
improved as an artist, and with a most rich collection
of drawings. He writes as well as he paints; so I suppose we shall have a splendid work on Ellora, his attention having been mainly directed to that remarkable
spot, of which we know just enough to wish to know
more. What a stupendous labour those caverns must
have been! The Pyramids seem to me less wonderful.

Say everything for me to your dear daughters. My
father and mother join in kindest remembrances, and I
am always, my dear Sir William,

Most affectionately yours,

M. R. M.

To the Rev. William Harness, *Heathcote Street.*

Three Mile Cross, March 30, 1827.

My dear Friend,

Your most kind letter and my little note crossed
as usual; but my father, who gives a delightful account
of you and dear Mary and your pretty house, says that
you would like to hear my scheme for 'Inez'; so I shall
write it as carelessly as usual, trusting to your quickness
for comprehending and your indulgence for forgiving
my puzzle-headed way of telling the story. There are
two French plays, one English, and one Spanish, on
the subject, but I follow none of them; my plot is my
own, and closer to the narrative given in an old Portuguese chronicle—lent by Mrs. Maria Graham (now

Mrs. Callcott) to Miss Skerrett for my use—than any
of the other dramas. This is not of much consequence,
one way or the other, so that the play be interesting;
but if one can get effects in the history, it's as well.

The play opens with a scene of courtiers, &c., who
speak of the arrival of an ambassador from Castile at the
Court of Lisbon, to enforce the immediate union of the
Princess Constance, sister of the King of Castile, to
Don Pedro, Infant of Portugal, she having been a long
time resident there, and her brother thinking her
trifled with. The King Alphonso (Young) and Don
Manuel, his minister (Warde), enter and receive the
Ambassador. The King agrees that he is right, and
sends for Don Pedro to inform him that the marriage
shall take place forthwith. Pedro (C. Kemble) enters,
equipped for hunting; answers decidedly "No!" and
after a short skirmish with his father (sufficiently respectful and rather gay), a fiery defiance to the Ambassador, and a contemptuous scoffing at Don Manuel, goes
out. The King and his minister are left together, and
Don Manuel insinuates that the Infant's repugnance to
the marriage results from his attachment to Donna
Inez de Castro, the maid of honour who had accom-
panied the Infanta from Spain. The King disbelieves
the charge, which he places to the account of Manuel's
jealousy, who had been a rejected lover of Inez.
Manuel asks his leave to try an experiment, and they
go out. Then a short scene with Inez and Pedro; he
tells her that he has got quit of the Ambassador and
his proposal, and conjures her to renew her vow to him
not to suffer any circumstance to induce her to reveal a
secret which subsists between them. She promises,
and goes out with him, or promises to go to a certain
window to see him mount his steed, and he proceeds to

the chase. Then a scene between the King, Constance, Manuel, Inez, &c.,—the Court of the Princess. The King soothes Constance with the assurance of a speedy union, and invites the Ambassador and the whole train to a nuptial banquet that evening. Some one rushes in with an account that Pedro is killed or dangerously hurt in hunting; the Princess, deeply offended, is cold and haughty; the King, who knows the tale to be false, is almost passive, or only engaged with Manuel in watching Inez, who is in an agony of fear, urging one and another to go or send, until she hears him approaching, rushes towards him, and falls fainting with suppressed joy. (Now this will require a very fine actress, and, if well done, will be a great hit. Can Miss Jarman do it, do you think?) Inez is removed; Pedro tries to explain away her agitation; the King is stern; the Princess haughty; and Manuel throws out so many sarcastic hints that Pedro, wrought up to a pitch of passion, challenges him to fight in a wood without the town that very evening. In a scene between the King and Manuel, Manuel works up the King to propose that, as the only way to remove Inez from the Infant, she and Manuel should be married that night, taking advantage of the Prince's absence on the challenge that he had given, and Manuel consenting not to meet him. Then the banquet; and the King, Princess, and Ambassador all announce to Inez that she must immediately marry Don Manuel—a very passionate scene of entreaty and struggle on her part. Just as they are forcing her to the altar, Pedro rushes in and claims her as his wife—his wedded wife. "That is high treason on her part by the law of the land," says Manuel; "she will not say so." "I do! I do!" replies Inez; and she is borne away to prison. In the next scene she is arraigned

before the King and Council, Pedro being present, and
condemned to death. She is taken away, and a very
passionate scene ensues between the King and Pedro,
he imploring his father not to sign the sentence—which
the King at last does—and his son leaves him, re-
nouncing his father, and swearing that Inez shall not
die. In the next scene it is understood that Pedro is
rousing the troops and the people, by whom he is much
beloved, to revolt. The Princess enters, and begs
Inez's life. The King himself becomes much softened,
and sends Manuel to her with commission that, if she
will sign an act of divorce, she shall live. Then the
Prince, who has stormed and taken the palace, comes
in at the head of a body of people to demand Inez.
The King refuses to speak with him until the troops be
dismissed. They are sent off, and a tender scene of
reconciliation between the father and son takes place,
the King consenting to forgive Inez unconditionally,
and even holding out hopes of confirming their marriage. "But where is Inez?" says Pedro; "let me fly
to her!" and he goes out. Then Manuel is discovered
with Inez in her prison, trying to persuade her not
only to sign the divorce, but to fly with him, and become his wife, telling her that Pedro is in arms, that
he must be taken, and that it is the only means to save
his life. She remonstrates passionately, and Pedro is
heard approaching, when Manuel catches her in his
arms, stabs her, and delivers her dead or dying to her
husband, who loudly demands her, declaring that so, at
least, he makes her his own.

Now, if you dislike any part of this, tell me, for there
are not ten lines written. Pedro's part will be very
fine—fiery and tender. The King will be good, too;
and Manuel's villany shall, if I can contrive it, be

somewhat redeemed by sarcasm and subtlety, and excused by his violent passion for Inez, whose character ought to have a great actress. . . .

God bless you, my dear friend! Kindest love from all here to you and to dear Mary.

Ever most gratefully and affectionately yours,

M. R. MITFORD.

What fools the Whigs are not to join Canning! He's a greater man than all of them put together, and that, I suppose, is the reason they hang back.

To ——.

Sunday, June, 1827.

If my truest and most affectionate sympathy can be any consolation to you, my dear friends, be assured that you possess it. I can think of nothing else. Would to God that I had anything more available to offer, but we are as poor as poor can be—have only received one hundred pounds yet from the theatre—and are ourselves living on credit. Heaven protect and bless you all is the earnest prayer of

Your affectionate friend,

M. R. MITFORD.

To SIR WILLIAM ELFORD, *Totnes, Devonshire.*

Three Mile Cross, June 20, 1827.

Have you heard of Mr. Lough, the new sculptor? Mr. Haydon says nothing like his model of 'Milo' (eight feet high) has been seen since the Phidian age. His account of him personally is very interesting. He is the son of a small farmer in Northumberland, and two years ago was sheaving corn. A few months ago a friend of Mr. Haydon's found him in his obscure lodging

in London, tearing up his shirts for rags to keep his
clay model moist. For three months he went without
animal food, having spent all his money for materials
for his great work; and it being winter and he without a
fire in the same room with a damp clay figure, he used
(to borrow his own words) "to go to bed and shiver
asleep." That is now past, and I trust for ever. The
'Milo' is exhibiting. Five or six persons have put
down their names for eighty guineas each to have it
done in marble, and more will probably follow their
example. Mr. Brougham and Sir John Paul have each
given him a commission for five hundred pounds, and
the former left fifty pounds on his table; and the exhibition is clearing fifty pounds a week. I may as well
add, for it is to their great honour, that the present
subscribers to the 'Milo' are the Duke of Wellington,
the Duke of Northumberland, Lord Egremont, Lord
Rivers, and Mr. Sotheby. Mr. Lough is said to be a
fine creature, full of simplicity, modesty, and ardour.

[The end of this letter is lost]

To B. R. HAYDON, ESQ., *Connaught Terrace.*

Friday evening, Sept. 27, 1827.

MY DEAR FRIEND,

I was quite certain when we parted that the
'Mock Election' would be done, and more than half
converted to the belief of its being an excellent subject.
The hold that it has taken of your fancy is almost a
pledge for your success. So I have only to say *Vogue
la galère.*

I have liked my little garden the better ever since
you honoured it by your presence—you came among
the flowers quite like a sunbeam. I never can see you
without feeling assured that you are born for good

fortune—born "to leave many people in your debt," as
the gipsy woman said. How high has the subscription
mounted? If both the 'Eneles' and the 'Mock Election' sell as they ought, you will have the comfort
and blessing of money beforehand—the greatest happiness, I should think, that there is in the world.
How large is the King's Bench picture to be? Finish
very highly. Humour depends almost wholly on things
being clearly made out;—and don't care about morality
and pathos—stick to fun.

Adieu, my dear friend. Kindest love from all to all.

Ever yours,

M. R. MITFORD.

A propos of Art, we have an artist here taking views
of the village in order to bring out a series of illustrations of my book. They are to be executed in a newly-
invented sort of lithography on transfer paper which is
said to have nearly the effect of line engraving, and will,
I should think, answer well.

To the REV. WILLIAM HARNESS, *Heathcote Street, London.*

Oct. 16, 1827.

No, my dear friend, I did not write the 'Chapters on
Churchyards.' I am quite ashamed of being ten pounds
in Mr. Blackwood's debt—I mean ten pounds' worth of
articles; but I firmly mean to pay him the moment
'Inez' is put out of hand. If you write to him say so.
I have been torn to pieces by the annuals, who will have
at least twenty articles of mine amongst them. How
capital 'Reverses'* was! I don't know when I have
been so delighted with anything. The tone of fashion,
and the little air of laughing at fashion even whilst
adopting it, were admirable, and you and your books

* A tale in 'Blackwood's Magazine.'

done to the life—only you should not have thought of shooting the Newfoundland. But the conclusion makes amends for all, and is so like your own real manner, that I should have known it for yours anywhere.

Adieu, my dear friend. Kindest love to dear Mary and to yourself from all.

Ever most affectionately yours,

M. R. MITFORD.

1828.

To the REV. WILLIAM HARNESS, *Heathcote Street, London.*

Three Mile Cross, Jan. 6, 1828.

MY DEAR FRIEND,

Have you a mind to see a picture of me which is going to be engraved by Mr. Cousins—young Cousins, who did the print of young Lambton? It will be for the whole of next week at the artist's, Mr. Lucas's, lodgings (No. 3, Newland Terrace, Kensington), and if you should be going that way I really wish you would call and see it. I want your opinion. To me, and to everybody here, it seems a really fine work of art, and has an elegance which you are especially likely to value. But I know my own enthusiasm, and am so much caught by the young man's personal character, that I have a laudable distrust of my own judgment, so far as he is concerned. He is only twenty-one, was bound to Reynolds, the engraver, and practised the art which he was resolved to pursue, secretly, in his own room, and in hours stolen from sleep and needful exercise, and minutes from necessary food. Last July he became his own master, and since then he has regularly painted.

Everybody almost that sees his pictures desires to sit, and he is already torn to pieces with business. In short, I expect great things of him. But what I especially like is his character. I have seen nothing in all my life more extraordinary than his union of patience and temper and rationality, with a high and ardent enthusiasm. Moreover, my good friend, he puts me exceedingly in mind of you. He has your "Yeses," and "Noes," and your *piano* manner exactly; and, as far as a young man of one-and-twenty and very thin, can resemble a not thin gentleman a few years older, he is like you in countenance. I want you to meet astonishingly. You will understand that he will be very clever —very. His quickness of observation and nicety of tact surpass all that I have met with. At present he has of course to struggle against an imperfect education; a mind engrossed by his art; and a delicate sensitiveness which keeps him back for the moment, but which will blend finely with a firm and manly character hereafter. I believe it is having seen so much of Mr. H——'s violence that leads me so greatly to value the patient ardour (if I may be allowed such a phrase) of this most amiable young man, of whom (in the close intimacy which must exist between the inmates of the same house, in the country, and in winter) I have seen and known so much, and all so good. It is a woman's delicacy and kindness with a man's spirit and bravery. He sings exquisitely simple ballads, without accompaniment, and with a voice and taste and pathos that make them equal to the finest recitation—(I wonder what a musical professor would say to such praise—but you know what I mean)—a dangerous talent for most young men; but I think he may be trusted, for he has a constitutional temperance that will preserve him from coarse temptations." *

[*The rest is wanting.*]

To B. R. HAYDON, Esq.

[*A Fragment.*]

Three Mile Cross. No date.

History never will sell so well as more familiar and smaller subjects. I want you to try large, merry, rustic groups. I could make twenty pictures (only that I can neither paint nor draw), full of fun and incident and character, and with infinitely more of colour and beauty, as well as of grace and richness in the accessories, than any town scene can have ; a fair, with all its sights and shows; the same at night, lighted up ; a statute or hiring fair, with its pretty lasses and awkward bumpkins ; a Revel — a Maying — Hop-picking — Harvest Home. These are subjects, in which even daubers please ; they are so genial and so English! Only think what *you* would make of them !

To DR. MITFORD, *Old Betty's Coffee House, behind the new church, Strand.*

Three Mile Cross, Thursday, Feb. 15, 1828.

Nothing, my own dearest, was ever more comfortable and satisfactory than the manner in which you have managed this affair. Pray write to George Whittaker directly. Of course we must not take a farthing less than one hundred and fifty pounds, when we are sure of it from such a respectable quarter as Longman's. I never had the slightest hesitation in my liking for that

* Some additional particulars concerning Mr. Lucas will be found in a letter dated Oct. 27, 1842.

house, except their name for *closeness* ; but certainly this
offer is very liberal.   You have done the business most
excellently—just as I thought you would.   God grant
you an equal success with the dramatic affair!   I am
not the least afraid of your management there.   I'll
never write a play again, for I dare say Longman's
people would give a good price for a novel.

If you can without inconvenience, will you bring me
a bottle of eau de Cologne ; this is a piece of extravagance upon the strength of the fifty pounds ; but don't
buy anything else.   And pray, my darling, get quit of
the dogs.   I have had a most delightful letter from
Miss North—no letter for you.   I suppose the ' Belvi-
dera ' on Monday night at Covent Garden made no hit,
or we should have heard of it—or rather, with a great
actress, they would not hesitate an hour about ' Inez.'
We are pretty well ; and the gown gets on famously
and will be beautiful.

Ever your own,

M. R. M.

[The volume referred to in the next letter was the
third volume of ' Our Village.'   A note in the pocket-
book of Mrs. Mitford says: "The third volume, taken
by Whittaker at one hundred and thirty pounds, which
Mr. Orme, with unheard-of generosity makes up to one
hundred and fifty pounds—one hundred in the course
of this month and fifty within two months."]

From G. B. WHITTAKER *to* DR. MITFORD, *Old Betty's Coffee House,
Strand.*

Manchester, Feb. 22.

MY DEAR SIR,

You will perceive by a letter annexed for Miss. M.
that although distant I was not forgetful.   That was
written with an intention on Tuesday next to forward it

with other letters to London in a parcel ; and, on my
arrival here this afternoon, I lose no time in sending it
by a parcel in hopes of saving Saturday night's London
mail, as none from here could reach you until Tuesday.

I am willing to do what is correct, and shall not,
from correctness of principle, let the next volume slip
through my hands. My only motive for not saying
Yes, to your offer, is that, owing to my present circumstances, I wish to make a calculation, and also to make
an arrangement with some friend to carry the thing
into effect, and which I shall have no difficulty in doing.
I have now clearer prospects before me than when I
last saw you.

Believe me yours, very truly,
G. B. WHITTAKER.

P.S. Be easy on the subject.

N.B. If they had told you Liverpool instead of Manchester, an answer would have been sent by return of
post.

To the REV. WILLIAM HARNESS, *Heathcote Street.*

Three Mile Cross, Monday,
March 31, 1828.

They say in the papers that there is a Miss B——
learning to be an actress at the manager's expense.
I confess that it seems to me a sad blow on the respectability of that profession of which Mrs. Siddons
was once the ornament. If actresses are bad, no
manager can help it ; but to take pains to turn a bad
woman into an actress is another matter. I hope this
announcement is a mere newspaper report. They say
that she was brought up to be a rich man's mistress,
upon sale, unhappy wretch ! like a Georgian woman—
and did live with somebody or other. Now *can* such a

person as that think and feel as a high tragic actress ought to do? Honour, virtue, fidelity, love must be worse than words to her; she must have been used to consider them as things to spurn and laugh at. Besides, they say that she's as impudent in look and air as her sister.

Adieu, my very dear friend. Kindest regards from my father and mother to yourself, and dear Mary.

Ever most faithfully yours,

M. R. Mitford.

To Dr. Mitford, *Old Betty's Coffee House, Strand.*

Wednesday, April 17, 1828.

My dear Father,

I cannot bear this suspense. I have written to Mr. Kemble to say that I shall be in town to-morrow at half-past twelve, and will drive immediately to Soho Square—where, if he cannot see me then, I have requested him to leave word when and where he will see me. I only wish I had done this last Thursday.

Mamma is still mending. No news whatever. God bless you, my dearest!

Ever your own,

M. R. Mitford.

I shall come by the seven o'clock coach. Of course you will meet me in Piccadilly.

To B. R. Haydon, Esq., 4, *Burwood Place, Edgware Road.*

Three Mile Cross, Tuesday,

April 22, 1828.

A thousand and a thousand congratulations, my dear friend, to you and your loveliest and sweetest wife! I always liked the King, God bless him! He is a gentleman—and now my loyalty will be warmer than ever.

What has he given for the picture?* Where is it to
be? This is fortune—fame you did not want—but this
is fashion and fortune. Nothing in this world could
please me more—not even the production of my own
'Rienzi.' To see you in your place in Art, and Talfourd in his in Parliament, are the wishes next my
heart, and I verily believe that I shall live to see both.
Are you likely to know the King personally? If you
are, I'm sure you'll take his fancy. How should you
like to be " Sir Benjamin?" *She* would become the
" Lady," would she not?

God bless you, my dear friends! And God save the
King!

M. R. MITFORD.

My father and mother are as happy and as loyal as I
am. Once again, Long live the King! Thank you so
much for letting me know.

To SIR WILLIAM ELFORD, *Washbourne House, Totnes.*

Three Mile Cross, Sept. 23, 1828.

MY DEAR FRIEND,

My tragedy of ' Rienzi' is to be produced at Drury
Lane Theatre on Saturday, the 11th of October; that is
to say, next Saturday fortnight. Mr. Young plays the
hero, and has been studying the part during the whole
vacation; and a new actress makes her first appearance
in the part of the heroine. This is a very bold and ha-
zardous experiment, no new actress having come out
in a new play within the memory of man; but she is
young, pretty, unaffected, pleasant-voiced, with great
sensibility, and a singularly pure intonation—a qualification which no actress has possessed since Mrs. Sid-

---

* ' The Mock Election.'

dons. Stanfield* is painting the new scenes, one of which is an accurate representation of Rienzi's house. This building still exists in Rome, and is shown there as a curious relique of the domestic architecture of the Middle Ages. They have got a sketch which they sent for on purpose, and they are hunting up costumes with equal care; so that it will be very splendidly brought out, and I shall have little to fear, except from the emptiness of London so early in the season. If you know any one likely to be in that great desert so early in the year, I know that you will be so good as to mention me and my tragedy. I do not yet know where I shall be. I think of going to town in about a fortnight, and, if the play succeeds, shall remain there about the same time.

Adieu! Ever very affectionately yours,

M. R. MITFORD.

To SIR WILLIAM ELFORD, *Washbourne House, Totnes.*

London, Oct. 5, 1828.
5 Great Queen Street, Lincoln's Inn.

MY DEAR FRIEND,

Our success last night was very splendid,† and we have every hope (in the theatrical world there is no such word as "certainty") of making a great hit. As far as things have hitherto gone, nothing can be better —nothing. Our new actress‡ is charming. We shall not keep her long, for she'll be in the peerage before two years are over, and is just fit for such a destiny both in mind and manner. Mr. Young is also admirable; and, in short, it is a magnificent performance

---

* He first came into notice as a scene painter.
† The first performance of 'Rienzi.'
‡ Miss Phillips.

throughout. God grant that its prosperity may continue! and these are not words of course, but a prayer from my inmost soul, for on that hangs the comfort of those far dearer to me than myself.

Your last letter was delightful to me in every way—quite delightful—full of heart and head and youthfulness. I am proud of your good opinion, my dear Sir William, but prouder still of the kind mistake by which you are led to overrate me.

Make my very best and kindest love to both your daughters, and forgive my mistakes and blunders. I have twenty people in the room at this moment, all talking, not to each other, but to me. God bless you all!

Ever most faithfully yours,
M. R. MITFORD.

To the REV. WILLIAM HARNESS, *Heathcote St., Mecklenburgh Square.*

5 Great Queen Street, Lincoln's Inn,
Oct. 13, 1828.

MY DEAR FRIEND,

After consulting Mr. Talfourd and (between ourselves) Mr. Young, I have finally *determined* not to let 'Inez' be done at Covent Garden at present, and accordingly I have despatched a note, of which the following is a copy, to Charles Kemble:—

"MY DEAR SIR,

"Having heard from our mutual friend Mr. Harness that you some days ago expressed to him a wish to produce 'Inez de Castro' at Covent Garden, I think it right to tell you frankly and at once that, with reference to my own future prospects and the state of both theatres, it is my desire that that play should not be performed at present at either—that it should, in short, lie by for a while."

Now I hope I have not committed a breach of confidence in this. If I have, forgive me.

Miss Phillips *is* only sixteen—was born in 1812; and really, when one remembers that, she is very wonderful, and of very great promise indeed.

Kindest love to all of you.

Ever most faithfully yours,

M. R. Mitford.

To Sir William Elford, *Washbourne House, Totnes.*

Three Mile Cross, Monday,
Oct. 20, 1828.

My dear Friend,

I seize the very first moment after my return home to thank you for your most kind and gratifying letter. "Kind" is too cold a phrase; both yours and your daughter's had a glow of affection in them which went to my very heart. Tell her how sincerely I thank and bless you both.

Hitherto the triumph has been most complete and decisive—the houses crowded—and the attention such as has not been known since Mrs. Siddons. You might hear a pin drop in the house. How long the run may continue I cannot say, for London is absolutely empty; but even if the play were to stop to-night, I should be extremely thankful—more thankful than I have words to tell; the impression has been so deep and so general. You should have been in London, or seen the newspapers as a whole, to judge of the exceedingly strong sensation that has been produced by the tragedy.

I breakfasted one day with your friend Mr. Jones, who spoke of you with warm regard. He is painting a

very fine naval battle—that incident of the battle of
St. Vincent where Lord Nelson boarded one ship over
the deck of another. It will be very splendid; but I
prefer his 'Esther'—which is full of expression and
beauty and mind, as well as colour—to anything that I
have ever seen of his. He is a very elegant and delightful person.

Adieu, my very dear friend. My father and mother
join in all that is truest and kindest, and I am always
and unalterably

Your affectionate friend,
M. R. MITFORD.

To the REV. WILLIAM HARNESS, *Heathcote Street, London.*

Wednesday, Oct. 22, 1828.

MY DEAR FRIEND,

All that you say of 'Rienzi' is deeply gratifying
to me. Mr. Dyce's approbation is a very high honour;
and I had sooner be praised by you than by anybody
under the sun—my oldest friend, and the person with
whose taste mine has always had all the accordance
that is compatible with frankness, independence, and
individuality. I had rather you liked my play than
anybody. It is selling immensely, the first very large
edition having gone in three days.

I am very glad that Mrs. D—— and Dora have
called on dear Mary; love her they must, and she will
love them—they are so good, so true, such gentle
women, and have always been so very kind to me.
Besides, they speak good English, which Mary says is
a rarity in your quarter. Kindest love to you all. How
very quick and clever Henry is! Love from all to all.

Ever most affectionately yours,
M. R. MITFORD.

To the Rev. Alexander Dyce, *Welbeck Street, Cavendish Square.*

Three Mile Cross, near Reading,
Oct. 27, 1828.

My dear Sir,

Accept my very sincere thanks for your kind letter and your delightful books, which would have been most valuable to me even if I had not the additional gratification of receiving them from the editor, and of reckoning him amongst my acquaintance—may I say, amongst my friends? I am sure his kindness gives me cause to think him such.

Of Peele I have only yet read 'The Old Wives' Tale,' a most striking and imaginative drama, and doubly interesting when one considers the impression that it must have made on Milton. Was his imitation of that play, and of 'The Faithful Shepherdess,' conscious or not? "That is the question," and a very curious question it is. A critic would answer "Yes!" at once; a poet, who knows how strongly memory and invention are intertwined and interwoven, would hesitate. Any way, all lovers of high poetry are much indebted to you for the reprint. I must just say that it is the only edition of old plays that I have ever seen in which the notes are a positive good; generally they are a positive evil.

The authoress book is quite delightful ;* not only for the various specimens preserved from scarce works, but for the taste and candour of the latest selections, and of the characters of the writers. For instance, you are the only man I ever met with who did full justice to Charlotte Smith's fine and close observation of nature. Both her prose and her verse are full of nice and delicate touches of landscape painting; and, as far as trees

* 'Selections from the Female Poets,' by the Rev. A. Dyce.

and flowers are concerned, she has a mastery of the
subject, and a truth and vividness of expression, second
only to Cowper.

May I trouble you to let Mr. Harness have the enclosed letter? There is no hurry about it at all. I
take it for granted that two persons so well suited to
each other meet frequently. And it is only to thank
him for a fresh demonstration of the kindness which he
has been showing me all his life long. But you know
William Harness!

If ever you pass near us I trust that you will honour
our poor cottage by a call.

Ever, my dear sir,
Very sincerely yours,
M. R. Mitford.

To B. R. Haydon, Esq., *Buckwood Place, Edgware Road.*

My dear Friend, Sunday, Nov. 3, 1828.

I am now going to tell you something which I
earnestly hope will neither vex nor displease you; if it
do, I shall grieve most heartily—but I do not think
that it will. The patron of a young artist of great
merit (Mr. Lucas) has made a most earnest request
that I will sit to him. The picture is for a friend who
wants one. He comes here to paint it—and there is a
double view; first to get two or three people hereabout
to sit to him; next to do him good in London, by
having in the Exhibition the portrait of a person whose
name will probably induce people to look at it, and
bring the painting into notice. The manner in which
this was pressed upon me by a friend to whom I owe
great gratitude was such as I really could not refuse—
especially as it can by no accident be injurious to your
splendid reputation, that an ugly face which you happen

to have taken, should be copied by another. There is a project of having the portrait engraved, which would increase the benefit that they anticipate to Mr. Lucas, and would be so far satisfactory to us as it would supersede a villanous print out of some magazine, from a drawing of Miss Drummond's, which is now selling in the shops.

I have not yet been in Reading, but I hope to see the boys soon. I wish Simon were at sea, for school is a sad expensive place. The carelessness you speak of is quite characteristic of a sailor. God bless you all, my very dear friends!

Ever most sincerely yours,

M. R. M.

To the REV. WILLIAM HARNESS, *Heathcote Street.*

Three Mile Cross, Saturday,
Nov. 17, 1828.

MY DEAR FRIEND,

I am going to write another play, on a German story —a man under the ban of the Empire and succoured by his daughter. I took the notion from a faint recollection of a play called 'Otto of Wittelsbach.' According to my recollection, there is no daughter in the German play, and I believe that my piece will be altogether different—though I should like to see the old 'Otto.'

Marianne Skerritt once thought of writing a tragedy on the subject, and her programme, which she sent me, is quite unlike both, and would take, I should think, a week in acting. Her first act had ten long scenes! There's an old German story-book, called 'The Emperor Philip and his Daughters,' which also tells the same history, with variations; for there Otto is represented as a very young man. But that I have not seen either. I suppose it will end in my working up the story as well as I can in my own way. William Farren is to have a principal part at Mr. Young's especial desire, and I believe at his own.

Adieu, my very dear friend. My father and mother join in all that is kindest to you and Mary—and I am always,

Most gratefully yours,

M. R. MITFORD.

To SIR WILLIAM ELFORD, *Washbourne, Totnes.*
Three Mile Cross, Dec. 16, 1828.
(My birthday.)

Thinking over those whom I love and those who have been kind to me, as one does on these annual occasions, it occurred to me, my dear friend, that I had most unkindly checked your warmhearted interest in my doings. I was very busy—not quite well—and overwhelmed, beyond anything that can be conceived, by letters and visits of congratulation. I am now quite well again; and though still with much to do—much that I ought to have done to make up—yet, having fairly stemmed the tide of formal compliments, I steal a moment to tell you and your dear circle that 'Rienzi' continues prosperous. It has passed the twentieth night, which, you know, insures the payment of four hundred pounds from the theatre (the largest price that any play can gain); and the sale of the tragedy has been so extraordinary, that I am told the fourth edition is nearly exhausted—which, as the publisher told me each edition would consist of at least two thousand, makes a circulation of eight thousand copies in two months. You may imagine that I am heartily thankful for this success.

Did you ever see or hear of Mr. Haydon's portrait of me? It was so exaggerated, both in size and colour, that none of my friends could endure it. My father declared he would not have it home, and I believe it is now quite demolished. We are not the less good friends, for certainly he did not mean to produce a caricature; but such I believe it was. This gave me an aversion to the idea of sitting for a portrait; but we have been prevailed upon to suffer a young artist of high talent (a Mr. Lucas) to paint me. He was to have taken me a month ago; but I was so poorly at that time that I could not sit. So we introduced him to some friends of ours, who sate to him; and his pictures of them are so fine, and sitting for one's portrait is so catching, that I am quite sure he may, if he pleases, paint half Berkshire.

Have you read Mr. Smith, of the Museum's, 'Life and Times of Nollekens' the sculptor? It is a strange slip-slop style; but the matter is entertaining, and would be interesting to you who have lived so much amongst artists.

God bless you, my very dear friend! All good wishes, of this season and of every season, to you all. Kindest regards from my father and mother.

Ever most affectionately yours,

M. R. MITFORD.

To SIR WILLIAM ELFORD, *Washbourne House, Totnes.*

Three Mile Cross, Dec. 26, 1828.

The payment of which you speak * has been done away with these thirty years; and the sum that I have received is probably the largest given to any tragic author during the present century. I have no reason to complain. The play has been most eminently successful, and will undoubtedly be a stock piece. Heaven

* The old mode of paying dramatic authors in the last century, which was, the entire receipt of the house for the third, sixth, and ninth nights.

grant I may ever do as well again! I shall have hard
work to write up to my own reputation, for certainly
I am at present greatly overrated.

Now for my young artist. I should greatly have
wondered, my dear Sir William, if you had heard of
him, for he has only just sprung to light. He is not a
Berkshire man. He became known to me through a
mutual friend—Mr. Milton, of the War Office—author
of a very clever work on the pictures in the Louvre,
and one of the best judges of art in England. He fell
in with young Lucas, employed him to paint two of his
own children (twins), and was so enchanted with the
portrait, that he immediately determined to make me
sit to him, by way of bringing him into notice. Mr.
Milton is a lively, agreeable, enthusiastic person, who
always carries things his own way; and, being sure that
he would not propose an inadequate artist, I consented.
Accordingly, Mr. Lucas arrived to paint me. On that
very morning, however, I was taken ill; and, instead of
bringing him here, my father (who had gone to Reading
to meet him) conveyed him to the house of a friend in
the neighbourhood, who wished for portraits of some of
his family, hoping that by the time they were done I
might be well enough to sit. Whilst there he painted
two portraits—one of a venerable clergyman of seventy-
six, the other of a lovely woman of twenty-eight; and
then, I being still too unwell to sit, he was obliged to
return to town to fulfil some other engagements. Last
Monday he returned here; and in that time, such was
the sensation caused by his previous pictures, that almost every one who had seen them wished to be por-
trayed by the same hand. At present, however, he
only means to do my friend, the wife of the old clergyman, and myself. He will return in the summer to

take Mr. Walter's (of the 'Times') children; and, I
hope and believe, *our* friend, Lady Madalina, and one
or two other people of connexion and consequence.
But you may depend upon it that he is not likely to
prove a provincial painter. London is his place, and
that you will find. Several judges have seen these
pictures—amongst them Mr. Barnes, the editor of the
'Times;' and everybody feels assured that this young
man (he is only one-and-twenty) will be eminent in his
art. There is nothing wild, or odd, or eccentric, or
over-ambitious about his paintings. They are carefully
finished, firmly painted, charmingly coloured, and the
strongest and pleasantest likenesses that I ever beheld.
There is an ease about them—" a masterly *handling* "
(I think that is the painter's phrase)—that is equiva-
lent to great fluency of style and felicity of phrase in
writing. When you look at them they seem so natural,
so alive, that it is more like looking at a face in a
looking-glass than one in a picture. My portrait, on
which he is depending so very much, will be a great
contrast with the cook-maid thing of poor dear Mr.
Haydon. I have given him three very long sittings;
and I think you will like it, though even the head is
not finished yet. I am sure that you will like the style
of the picture, which is exceedingly graceful and lady-
like. It is of the kit-kat size, dressed in a high black
gown and Vandyke collar, and a black velvet hat with
white feathers—younger and fairer than I am, certainly,
but, they say, very like. My father says so; and I am
sure that to his fondness no flattery would compensate
for the absence of likeness.

I earnestly hope we may meet in the spring.

Most affectionately yours,

M. R. MITFORD.

CHAPTER XII.

LETTERS FOR 1829.

To SIR WILLIAM ELFORD, *Washbourne, Totnes.*

Three Mile Cross, Jan. 7, 1829.

A THOUSAND and a thousand thanks, my dear friend, for your most kind and cordial letter. I have told Mr. Lucas your kind order for a proof of the print,* which he will transmit to Mr. Cousins. The portrait, now just finished, is said by everybody to be a very splendid work of art. It is certainly a most graceful and elegant picture—a very fine piece of colour, and, they say, a very strong likeness. It was difficult, in painting me, to steer between the Scylla and Charybdis of making me dowdy, like one of my own rustic heroines, or dressed out like a tragedy queen. He has managed the matter with infinite taste, and given to the whole figure the look of a quiet gentlewoman. I never saw a more lady-like picture. The dress is a black velvet hat, with a long, drooping black feather; a claret-coloured high gown; and a superb open cloak of gentianella blue, the silvery fur and white satin lining of which are most exquisitely painted, and form one of the most beautiful pieces of drapery that can be conceived. The face is thoughtful and placid, with the eyes looking away—a peculiarity which, they say, belongs to my expression.

He will be exceedingly clever generally, as well as in

* The print of Miss Mitford, from Lucas's portrait.

his art. I caution him (am I not right?) against two perils, matrimony and historical painting. He must neither fall in love nor paint history until he has made money enough by portraits to afford the indulgence. He is at present full of employment, and has a copy to make of my portrait for a female friend, in addition to his other commissions.

Adieu, my very dear friend. All the good wishes of this season, and of every season, to you and yours.

Ever your faithful and affectionate friend,

M. R. MITFORD.

To the REV. WILLIAM HARNESS.

Three Mile Cross, 3 o'clock Sunday
morning, Jan. 19, 1829.

MY DEAR FRIEND,

Three hours ago I received your book, my father, who dined at Coley, having brought it from Mr. Milman; and I have since read it through—the second part twice through. That second sermon would have done honour to Shakespeare, and I half expected to find you quoting him. There would be a tacit hypocrisy, a moral cowardice, if I were to stop here, and not to confess, what I think you must suspect. although by no chance do I ever talk about it—that I do not, or rather cannot, believe all that the Church requires. I humbly hope that it is not necessary to do so, and that a devout sense of the mercy of God, and an endeavour, however imperfectly and feebly, to obey the great precepts of justice and kindness, may be accepted in lieu of that entire faith which, in me, *will not* be commanded. You will not suspect me of thoughtlessness in this matter; neither, I trust, does it spring from intellectual pride. Few persons have a deeper sense of their own weakness; few, indeed, can have so much weakness of character to deplore and to strive against.

Do not answer this part of my letter. It has cost me a strong effort to say this to you; but it would have been a concealment amounting to a falsity if I had not, and falsehood must be wrong. Do not notice it; a correspondence of controversy could only end in alienation, and I could not afford to lose my oldest and kindest friend—to break up the close intimacy in which I am so happy and of which I am so proud. Do not notice what I have said, and yet write soon. There is no cause why you should not. I occasion no scandal either by opinions or by conduct. The clergyman of our parish and his family are my most intimate friends. They render me their kindest services, their truest sympathy, and—which is more, far more—they ask for my poor service and my honest sympathy when they are in difficulty or in affliction. Write very soon—of anything or everything—of the bar, of the empire, of my picture, or of my young friend, Mr. Lucas. By-the-way, the picture will be with him all next week.

I have been interrupted, and the postman is at the door.

Ever yours,

M. R. MITFORD.

To Sir William Elford, Washbourne House, Totnes.

Tuesday, March 2, 1829.

MY DEAR FRIEND,

You must forgive a short note in answer to your very kind and very delightful letter. I fear that, unless at Somerset House, where I hope it will find a place, my picture cannot be visible this year. Mr. Lucas made me promise not to ask admission to Mr. Cousins's, even for myself. The reason is, that Sir Thomas Lawrence makes a great mystery of those pictures of his, which Mr. Cousins is engraving; does not like the prints in hand to be known or talked about until they come out; and therefore, for fear of offending him, Mr. Lucas particularly wishes no application to be made for entrance to Mr. Cousins's engraving room. He says that Sir Thomas is at once so particular about this concealment, and yet so unwilling for people to know of this secrecy, which he insists upon, that an engraver who works for him has the most difficult course to steer that is possible. Of course I must beg you not to mention this to him or to any one. It is a hundred to one but, if in town, you will be there at the time of the Exhibition, and then you would, of course, see the picture at the Royal Academy—in company, I hope, with the landscape, which I rejoice to hear you are painting.

I do not myself think that I shall be in town this year, having finally decided that I cannot, without undue haste, complete my tragedy for this season. . . . I am delighted at this affair * of the Catholics; it will be a means of pacification in Ireland, and everywhere, when once the question is settled.

Kindest regards to all from all here.

Ever my dear friend,

Most affectionately yours,

M. R. MITFORD.

To the REV. WILLIAM HARNESS, *Heathcote Street, London.*

Three Mile Cross, Tuesday,
May 20, 1829.

Once again, my dear friend, a thousand thanks for your great and constant kindness. Pray come and see

* Emancipation.

us as soon as you can, and stay as long. Come on
Monday morning, and stay till Saturday afternoon, as
you do at Deepdene ; and be sure and come *soon*, or *they*
will be in the country, and we shall have no chance. I
really think that you would not dislike our poor cottage ;
or, rather, I am sure that you would like my garden,
where we live now all day, having got the great comfort
of a long, cool, dark shed on one side—a sort of rustic
arcade—and a light, sunny, cheerful room, which serves
for a winter greenhouse and a summer parlour on the
other. And there is a clean, airy room at the little
inn opposite, at which my little artist felt himself very
comfortable, and with which Miss James herself was
satisfied.

I have been exceedingly worried by Mr. Haydon,
who has taken some affront at I know not what, and
sent me a message a month ago to say that a print from
his portrait of me would be out in a day or two. This,
if it had been so, would have been most shameful, inasmuch as he knew, before my sitting to Mr. Lucas, that
I meant to do so for the purpose of an engraving. I
told him myself, and hoped he would not be offended,
and he said not at all, and that he should be glad to be
of use to Mr. Lucas, or of any service to the print—for
which civility I duly thanked him ; so that his message
appears incredible. I wrote to tell him so, begging
him, at the same time, to let me know ; and at the end
of a few days wrote again to the same effect. He has
not thought proper to answer either letter. But, as I
hear no announcement of such a print, and as the principal printsellers know nothing of it, I begin to think
that it is merely a coarse and ill-natured joke. If he
had had the picture engraved, it would have worried
me much, not merely because it is unpleasant to have a

disagreeable portrait multiplied and perpetuated, but on account of our very amiable young friend, who has taken so much pains with *his* picture, and to whom I hope the sale of the print will be of some advantage. I could not help telling you this grievance, but pray don't mention it, for that might make Mr. Haydon do the thing.

Pray don't forget to come to us. It will be such a treat! I'll try if Mr. Milman will meet you here some day at dinner; I should think he would not refuse. And you must let us know the day and the hour when you come, that my father may meet you in Reading— for we have an old gig and an old horse, and can take you about. You don't know how often I have longed to press you to come to us, but have always been afraid; you are used to things so much better, and I thought you would find it dull; but now I really think that the calm and the country will pass us off—and it will be so great a treat, so great a comfort!

Kind regards from my father and mother to you and to dear Mary.

Ever yours,

M. R. MITFORD.

To SIR WILLIAM ELFORD, *Washbourne House, Totnes, Devonshire.*

Three Mile Cross, May 29, 1829.

MY DEAR FRIEND,

Your last delightful letter was just as convincing a proof to me as your picture was to Mrs. Jones, that age only mellows the strong rich wine of your fancy. You are *young*, my dear Sir William, in spite of the register, and long may you continue so!

You will be glad to hear that 'Rienzi' has been received rapturously all over America. No play, I am

told, has ever produced such an effect there. I gain
nothing by this; but one likes that sort of rebound of
reputation—that travelling along with the language. I
suppose the republican sentiments had something to do
with it . . . I hope soon to be able to resume my
labours, which have necessarily been suspended; but I
am still very nervous and languid, and quite unfit for
the work which I must do. It is very strange that,
ever since my great success, I have been more than ever
low-spirited. But this I *must* conquer, and I will try
to do so, and hope to succeed.

Adieu, my very dear and kind friend.

Most faithfully yours,

M. R. MITFORD.

To the REV. WILLIAM HARNESS, *Heathcote Street, London.*

Three Mile Cross, June 20, 1829.

MY DEAR FRIEND,

There is nothing I would not do to assist Mr. Cathcart* in his difficulties. He is a man of genius, and
worthy in every respect. If he thinks, and you think,
that I can be of service to him, I will go to London,
see Mr. Price, and do all that I can to forward his
wishes. But—to you—I confess that this measure
would be attended with great personal difficulty. My
father—very kind to me in many respects, very attentive if I'm ill, very solicitous that my garden should be
nicely kept, that I should go out with him, and be
amused—is yet, so far as art, literature, and the drama
are concerned, of a temper infinitely difficult to deal
with. He hates and despises them, and all their professors—looks on them with hatred and scorn; and is
constantly taunting me with my "friends" and my

* An actor of whom Miss Mitford entertained a high opinion.

"people" (as he calls them), reproaching me if I hold the slightest intercourse with author, editor, artist, or actor, and treating with frank contempt every one not of a certain station in the county. I am entirely convinced that he would consider Sir Thomas Lawrence, Sir Walter Scott, and Mrs Siddons as his inferiors. Always this is very painful—strangely painful; but sometimes, in the case of the sweet young boy Lucas, for instance, and in this of Mr. Cathcart, it becomes really hard to bear.

Since I have known Mr. C. I can say with truth that he has never spoken to me or looked at me without ill-humour; sometimes taunting and scornful—sometimes more harsh than you could fancy. Now, he ought to remember that it is not for my own pleasure, but from a sense of duty, that I have been thrown in the way of these persons; and he should allow for the natural sympathy of similar pursuits and the natural wish to do the little that one so poor and powerless can do to bring merit (and that of a very high order) into notice. It is one of the few alleviations of a destiny that is wearing down my health and mind and spirits and strength—a life spent in efforts above my powers, and which will end in the workhouse or in a Bedlam, as the body or the mind shall sink first. He ought to feel this; but he does not.

I beg your pardon for vexing you with this detail. I do not often indulge in such repining. But I meant to say that it will be a scene and an effort to get to town for this purpose. Nevertheless, *if you think I could do good I would most assuredly go.* God bless you!

Ever yours,

M. R. M.

To the REV. WILLIAM HARNESS.

Three Mile Cross, Thursday,
Sept. 1829.

MY DEAR FRIEND,

I need not, I hope, tell you how delighted we shall
be to see you at the time proposed, or at any time, and
for as long as your own convenience or your own incli-
nation may induce you to give us the pleasure of your
company. My mother, whom few things touch now, is
particularly pleased. I lament only that my garden
will have lost its bloom and the days their length. But
you must try us now at our worst; and then, if you
like us, come next summer, when the roses and the sun
may make us more tempting. You cannot think how
deeply I feel your kindness in coming at all.

I have got the 'Bann of the Empire'—the real words
in German and English; and, after the great chain of
literary connexion that has been set in motion on this
question, the libraries that have been ransacked, the
German historians and law professors that have been
written to, the document has been discovered and sent
to me by a Westminster schoolboy! Perhaps you know
his mother, and I am indebted after all for it to you.
She is a Mrs. Hutchinson Simpson, living at Frognal,
Hampstead, and the youth, my friend, is her only child
by a former husband, a boy of the name of Cotton.*
Do you know them? The letters both of mother and
son (of whom I never heard before) are very interesting;
hers, especially, remind me much of Mrs. Hemans. The
lad heard that I wanted the document from "a friend,"
and sent me first the Ecclesiastical Bann which he
found in a French book. When I told him, with many

* George Edward Lynch Cotton; he became Bishop of Calcutta, and
was recently drowned in the Ganges.

thanks, that that was not the thing wanted, he set about learning German, and, by the help of a Saxon friend, who was recently drowned in the Ganges, has actually sent me the undiscoverable prize, as I have told you. We shall hear of that youth himself in literature some day or other. In the meanwhile I am more touched and pleased by the interest which he has evinced in the matter than I have ever been by any compliment in my life. Is it not striking and interesting?

After I have finished this detestable play (which is as yet sadly little advanced, I feeling within myself the certainty—though I must not say so—that Young can't act it)—when I have done this job I have another affair in contemplation that I must have some talk with you about. Do you know Mr. Jephson's plays? They are now so scarce that even his grandniece, Emily Jephson, has only seen three of them. She is a very particular friend of mine, and has been staying for some weeks about twelve miles off with Lady Sunderland and Miss Malone, the sister-in-law and sister of Edmund Malone, your brother editor of Shakespeare. We have ferreted out an immense number of Mr. Jephson's letters amongst Mr. Malone's papers, and find that there is a MS. play—a translation of Metastatio's 'Vitellia,' with a new last act—which we have no doubt of finding amongst Mr. Jephson's own papers, as well as other letters and *jeux d'esprit* (he being a man of great wit and living amongst the highest people, English and Irish), and Emily wants me to get up an edition of his dramatic works and some of the letters, and a critical and biographical preface, and so forth. Certainly I should like any fair opportunity of putting forth my own notions on the drama; the object which has employed my thoughts during my whole lifetime, and which I have never yet seen treated to my satisfaction.

Among the letters there is a most diverting quarrel between Jephson and Horace Walpole about the placing a statue on the stage in the representation of the 'Count de Narbonne.' The author, being in Dublin, had unluckily left to Mr. Walpole the charge of bringing out the play. Horace, with his antiquarianism, had laid the statue sprawling on its back on a tomb, instead of having it standing upright in the middle of the scene, to the utter ruin of the poor dramatist's *effect* and the great benefit of his correspondence; for I think the three or four letters about that subject are the most natural, characteristic, and comical that I ever read in my life. You must remember Mr. Jephson. He was a furious Anti-Jacobin, wrote a fine poem called 'Roman Portraits,' and a book called 'The Confessions of Jean Baptiste Couteau,' in ridicule of the French Republicans. Our plan is as yet only in embryo, but I thought you would like to hear of it.

Ever most gratefully and affectionately yours,

M. R. MITFORD.

To the REV. WILLIAM HARNESS, *Heathcote Street, London.*

Three Mile Cross, Sept. 9, 1829.

MY DEAR FRIEND,

We have had a sad check in the Jephson correspondence. Emily's chief reliance for materials was on a Mr. Baker (his nephew), whose address she had lost, but whom she was sure of getting at through their mutual friend Mr. Luttrell. Mr. Luttrell, in answer to her letter, says that, six weeks ago, Mr. Baker died suddenly of apoplexy, and that he cannot point out any one likely to give us the information we require. This is very shocking. Perhaps I like Mr. Jephson's poetry the better from being so very fond of his grand-niece, who is one of the most cultivated women that I have ever known, with a sweetness and simplicity of character, a charm of mind and manner which really makes one forget how very clever she is. She is pretty, too, about seven-and-twenty, well born, well connected, quite independent, and with four hundred a year; in short, after all my disclamations of match-making, I very sincerely wish that Emily Jephson were your wife. This wish (although a great compliment to your reverence) is the more absurd, as she was going out of the neighbourhood before you were expected in it, and lives generally between Bath and Ireland ; so that you are not at all likely to meet anywhere but in my imagination.

I think more highly of Mr. Jephson's plays than you do, perhaps because I prefer *eloquence* in the drama to poetry, and because I set a higher value on situation and effect. Just look at the effects of Shakespeare, the great master of dramatic situation, and tell me if they be not the finest parts of the plays in which they occur ; the play scene in ' Hamlet '—the banquet scene in ' Macbeth ' —the quarrel in ' Julius Cæsar '—the trial in the ' Merchant of Venice ;'—what are these but effects ? And in what do they depart from Nature and from pathos ? It is all very well for those who cannot write acting tragedies to declaim against situation ; but rely upon it that the thing is an essential part of the drama in its very highest sense. The Greek tragedies are full of situation ; so is Alfieri—so is Schiller—so is Corneille—so are all the greatest tragic writers of all nations.

Of course I don't mean processions and pageants—the trash of Reynolds or the bombast of Morton ; but such effects as arise from story and construction, skilful surprises and unexpectedness of fortune. One might as well exclude contrast from painting as effect from the drama.

There is no little cant in the contempt for situation which infests the criticism of the day, and I think that you are in some measure caught by it. Tell me more of young Cotton. How old is he? And ask, if you see him, in what book he found the 'Bann.' God bless you, my dear friend!

Ever yours,
M. R. MITFORD.

To MISS JEPHSON, *Binfield Park.*

Three Mile Cross.
Friday night, Oct. 3, 1829.

MY OWN DEAR EMILY,

A thousand thanks for the nativity. You shall have it safe back. I think that I should like a copy of Lord Inchiquin's letter. Harriet Palmer and I (both a sort of believers, she almost quite, I a *demi-semi* kind of convert) are going to copy the horoscope; and I (don't tell) have prevailed on Clarke—as great an adept in judicial astrology as John Dryden himself—to cast my nativity, and am going to send to our friend, the fat woman of Seven Dials, to get me an ephemeris (White's London Almanack) for the year 1788, on the 16th of December, in which year, at a quarter before ten at night, I had the honour to be born. You shall hear the result. Harriet wanted hers to be done, but Clarke refused point blank, and is only tempted into doing mine by the knowledge that my life has been one of vicissitudes, and will bring his science to the test.

Would Lady Sunderland, do you think, like a plant of the variegated jessamine, and some seed (if I can get any this wet season) of the new snapdragon? If so, I will get her certainly the one, and if possible the other. And will you come and fetch them?

Dash has nearly been killed to-day, poor fellow! He got into a rabbit burrow so far that he could neither move backward nor forward; and my father, two men and a boy, were all busy digging for upwards of two hours, in a heavy rain, to get him out. They had to penetrate through a high bank, with nothing to guide them but the poor dog's moans. You never saw any one so full of gratitude, or so sensible of what his master has done for him as he is. He is quite recovered, and has been sitting all the evening with his head leaning against my father's knee, looking up in his face with eyes full of such expression! My father was wet to the skin; but I am sure he would have dug till this time rather than any living creature, much less his own favourite dog, should have perished so miserably. I really wish you could have seen Dash's manner of expressing his gratitude. He is an animal of great sagacity at all times, and also of great sensibility.

Adieu, my own very dear friend. Pray come and see us again.

Ever your affectionate,

M. R. MITFORD.

To Miss JEPHSON, *Binfield Park.*

Three Mile Cross, Oct. 16, 1829.

Ten minutes after you were gone, I recollected, dearest, that it was Peele's poems you were to take home, for the sake of the 'Old Wife's Tale'—the original of 'Comus.' I'll bring them on Tuesday with another book edited by the same friend, Mr. Dyce, and which contains a poem that I wish you to see, by a Lady Winchilsea of a hundred years ago. I hope I shan't forget this.

I have been dining to-day at Calcot Park, where I

met Dr. Routh, the President of Maudlin. He has a spaniel of King Charles's breed, who, losing his mamma by accident when a pup, was brought up by a cat. (N.B. The identical cat belongs to the park and was present at the dinner to-day, *assisting* at the ceremony, according to both idioms, French and English.) Well; he and his brother (for there were two pups, orphans of three days old, and they are called Romulus and Remus) were nursed by this cat; and Romulus belongs to the Doctor, who has no children, and makes a great pet of it. But what I mentioned him to you for, is, to tell you the curious account which the Doctor (a man of perfect veracity) gives of his habits. He is as afraid of rain as his foster-mother; will never, if possible to avoid it, set his paw in a wet place; licks his feet two or three times a day, for the purpose of washing his face, which operation he performs in the true cattish position, sitting up on his tail; will watch a mouse-hole for hours together; and has, in short, all the ways, manners, habits, and disposition of his wet-nurse the cat.

Is not this very singular? Put it into more connected English, and tell it to Lady Sunderland. I thought it would amuse her when I heard it. But it's puzzling as well as amusing, and opens a new and strange view into that very mysterious subject, the instincts of animals. Mrs. Routh and Mrs. Blagrove (the mistress of the cat) confirmed all the facts of the case. They say that one can hardly imagine how like a cat Romulus is, unless one lived with him. Dr. Routh, by far the finest old clergyman I ever saw, knew Mr. Malone, and spoke of him very highly.

Ever most faithfully and affectionately yours,

M. R. MITFORD.

To Miss Jephson, *Hatfield, Herts.*

Three Mile Cross. Friday.
Oct. 30, 1829.

Did I tell you that it is the scarlet potentilla, which sells at fifteen shillings, being manufactured (I don't know how) out of the *Potentilla Formosa* and running from the colour when propagated by seed. *Our* plant, which is quite as pretty — prettier, I think — hardy and generous both in seed and root—will be an established garden flower, like pinks and roses, and always a pet with me for your sake, dearest, and for Mr. Wordsworth's. Don't let us forget to send you some seed from the Rydal Mount plant next season.

I have had a magnificent present of greenhouse plants, chiefly geraniums—a whole cartload—and am at present labouring under *l'embarras des richesses*, not being sure whether even the genius of Clarke will make the greenhouse hold them. *A propos* to that astrologer, I have got the ephemeris. Marianne finding even Mrs. Scott fail, took heart at last and applied to Captain Kater; who, being himself a demi-semi believer, has lent us the identical thing for our purpose, in the shape of an almanac published by order of the Board of Longitude. Between ourselves, I believe it's the identical Board of Longitude copy, from which, he says, a horoscope can be framed with the most perfect nicety and exactness. I have not seen Clarke since I obtained this treasure, but am expecting him every day.

Now, my dearest, I am going to tell you of an exploit of mine which I longed for you extremely to share. Last Saturday I dined out, and was reproached by a young fox-hunter with never having seen the hounds throw off. I said I should like the sight. The lady of the house said she would drive me some day. The conversation dropped, and I never expected to hear more of it. The next day, however, Sir John Cope (the master of the hounds) calling on my friend, the thing was mentioned and settled; and the young man who originally suggested the matter rode over to let me know that at half-past nine the next day our friend would call for me. At half-past nine, accordingly, she came in a little limber pony-carriage drawn by a high-blooded little mare, whom she herself (the daughter and sister of a whole race of fox-hunters) had been accustomed to hunt in Wiltshire, and attended by her husband's hunting-groom excellently mounted.

The day was splendid and off we set. It was the first day of the season. The hounds were to meet in Bramshill Park, Sir John Cope's old place; and it was expected to be the greatest field and most remarkable day of many seasons; Mr. Warde, the celebrated fox-hunter— the very Nestor of the field, who, after keeping fox-hounds for fifty-seven years, has just, at seventy-nine, found himself growing old and given them up—was on a visit at the house, and all the hunt were likely to assemble to see this delightful person; certainly the pleasantest old man that it ever has been my fortune to foregather with—more beautiful than my father, and in the same style.

Well, off we set—got to Bramshill just as breakfast was over—saw the hounds brought out in front of the house—drove to cover—saw the fox found, and the first grand burst at his going off—followed him to another covert, and the scent being bad and the field so numerous, that he was constantly headed back, both he, who finally ran to earth, and another fox found subsequently, kept dodging about from wood to wood in that magnificent demesne — the very perfection of park scenery, hill and dale, and wood and water—and for about four hours, we with our spirited pony, kept up with the chase, driving about over road and no road, across ditches and through gaps, often run away with, sometimes almost tossed out, but with a degree of delight and enjoyment such as I never felt before, and never, I verily believe, shall feel again. The field (above a hundred horsemen, most of them the friends of my fair companion) were delighted with our sportsmanship, which in me was unexpected; they showed us the kindest attention—brought me the brush—and when, at three o'clock, we and Mr. Warde and one or two others went into luncheon, whilst the hounds went on to Eversley, I really do not believe that there was a gentleman present ungratified by our gratification. Unless you have seen such a scene you can hardly imagine its animation or its beauty. The horses are most beautiful, and the dogs, although not pretty separately, are so when collected and in their own scenery; which is also exactly the case with the fox hunters' scarlet coats.

I had seen nothing of the park before, beyond the cricket-ground, and never could have had such a guide to its inmost recesses—the very heart of its sylvan solitudes—as the fox. The house—a superb structure of Elizabeth's day, in proud repair—is placed on so commanding an eminence that it seemed meeting us in every direction, and harmonized completely with the old English feeling of the park and the sport. You must see Bramshill. It is like nothing hereabouts, but reminds me of the grand Gothic castles in the north of England — Chillingham, Alnwick, &c. It was the residence of Prince Henry, James the First's eldest son, and is worthy his memory. It has a haunted room, shut up and full of armour; a chest where they say a bride hid herself on her wedding-day, and the spring-

lock closing, was lost and perished, and never found
until years and years had passed (this story, by-the-
way, is common to old houses; it was told me of the
great house at Malsanger); swarms with family pictures; has a hall with the dais; much fine tapestry;
and, in short, is wanting in no point of antique dignity.
The Duke of Wellington went to look at it as adjoining
his own estate and suiting his station; but he unwilling, I believe, to lose the interest of so much capital,
made the characteristic reply that Strathfieldsaye was
good enough for the duchess, and that he saw nothing
to admire at Bramshill except Sir John's pretty housekeeper. I am sure Sir John is much fitter for the
master of Bramshill, with his love of cricket, his hospitality, and his fox-hounds, than the Duke with all his
fame.

God bless you! Tell me when you come, and how
long you stay.

Ever yours, in galloping fox-hunter's haste,

M. R. M.

To Miss Jephson, *Binfield Park.*

Three Mile Cross, Dec. 11, 1829.

My dearest Emily,

My horoscope turns out singularly true—one part
curiously true. I have been very much entertained
and interested by it, and so will you be, when our astrologer explains it to you in May in the greenhouse, for
it is not easy to tell in writing, or rather it would be
puzzled and long. The misfortune to my greenhouse
had not occurred when you were here : the snow got into
the tube or chimney, and generated a vapour intoler-
ably thick and nauseous. We have cured the evil by

a larger cap to the chimney, but the plants are greatly
injured, and that is vexatious, for, till that misadventure, they continued to look as well as when you saw
them. However, May will repair all evils, month of
delight as it is !

Many thanks for the charming story of Napoleon, so
charmingly told. I have heard a great many delightful
traits of him lately, a friend of ours having purchased
the château of Madame la Maréchale de le Febvre,
Duchesse de Dantzig, near Paris. She lived there
twenty-seven years, and is quite a chronicle of the imperial court and camp—talks of war as if she fought by
her husband's side in all his campaigns—and is a woman
of remarkable courage and vigour of mind and body.
Her late husband's room is fitted up as an armoury, full
of curious weapons, and contains an urn with the heart
of her son, who was killed in Russia.

By-the-way, my astrologer showed me the other day
a horoscope of the young Napoleon. He says there is
no promise of success as a warrior, but much triumphing
over ladies' hearts. The father, I believe, was a great
conqueror in both ways.

Did I ever show you some lines which I wrote on my
picture ? Probably not. They were printed in the
'Friendship's Offering' (one of the annuals for this
year), and have been transcribed into half the newspapers in the kingdom, and will, I hope, be as I intended, of service to the young artist ; but why I mention
them is because I should like you—whose praise of me
always pleases, to see what is said of them in 'Blackwood's Magazine' for this month. It is in an article
called 'Monologue on the Annuals.' In general, I care
very little for praise ; but this pleased me and touched
me, and so it will you. The lines were written under

very genuine feelings of their truth, and were occasioned by Mr. Lucas having asked a mutual friend for a scrap of my writing, which I gave him in that form. There are two or three mistakes in ' Blackwood's ' copy, which looks as if it were transcribed from memory. The date also is wrong, and they have said the 'Forget-me-not,' instead of the ' Friendship's Offering.' But you'll forgive the mistakes, and also my vanity in directing you to it, when you read the article.

Ever affectionately yours,

M. R. M.

To B. R. HAYDON, ESQ., *Burwood Place.*

Three Mile Cross, Friday,
Dec. 12, 1829.

MY DEAR FRIEND,

Your very kind letter has given me much pleasure and some pain—pleasure, the greatest and the sincerest, to hear that you are going on so prosperously. What an exhibition it will be! how varied in talent, and how high in either scale!—the ' Eucles ' and the 'Punch' —Rubens and Hogarth! Be quite assured that my sympathy with you and with art is as strong as ever, albeit the demonstration have lost its youthfulness and its enthusiasm, just as I myself have done. The fact is that I am much changed, much saddened—am older in mind than in years—have entirely lost that greatest gift of nature, animal spirits, and am become as nervous and good-for-nothing a person as you can imagine. Conversation excites me sometimes, but only, I think, to fall back with a deader weight. Whether there be any physical cause for this, I cannot tell. I hope so, for then perhaps it may pass away; but I rather fear that it is the overburthen, the sense that more is expected of me than I can perform, which weighs me down and prevents my doing anything. I am ashamed to say that a play bespoken last year at Drury Lane, and wanted by them beyond measure, is not yet nearly finished. I do not even know whether it will be completed in time to be produced this season. I try to write it, and cry over my lamentable inability, but I do not get on. Women were not meant to earn the bread of a family—I am sure of that—there is a want of strength. I shall, however, have a volume of 'Country Stories' out in the spring, and I trust to get on with my tragedy, and bring it out still before Easter.

God bless you and yours! My best love to them all. God bless you, and farewell! Do not judge of the sincerity of an old friendship, or the warmth of an old friend, by the unfrequency or dulness of her letters. When I have anything pleasant to tell, you shall be the first to hear.

Ever yours,

M. R. Mitford.

To Douglas Jerrold, Esq., 4, *Augustus Square, Regent's Park.*

Three Mile Cross, near Reading,
Dec. 14, 1829. Saturday evening.

My dear Sir,

I have just received from Mr. Willey your very kind and gratifying note. The plays which you have been so good as to send me* are not yet arrived; but, fearing from Mr. Willey's letter that it may be some days before I receive them, I do not delay writing to acknowledge your polite attention. I have as yet read neither of them, but I *know* them, and shall be greatly

* 'Black-eyed Susan' and 'Thomas à Becket.'

delighted by the merits which I shall find in both ; in the first, by that truth of the touch which has commanded a popularity quite unrivalled in our day ; in the second, by the higher and prouder qualities of the tragic poet. The subject of 'Thomas à Becket' interests me particularly, as I had at one time a design to write a tragedy called ' Henry the Second,' in which his saintship would have played a principal part. My scheme was full of license and anachronism, embracing the apochryphal story of Rosamond and Eleanor, the rebellious sons—not the hackneyed John and Richard, but the best and worst of the four, Henry and Geoffrey ; linking the scenes together as best I might, and ending with the really dramatic catastrophe of Prince Henry. I do not at all know how the public would have tolerated a play so full of faults, and it is well replaced by your more classical and regular drama. I was greatly interested by the account of the enthusiastic reception given by the audiences of ' Black-eyed Susan ' to a successor rather above their sphere. It was hearty, genial, English—much like the cheering which an election mob might have bestowed on some speech of Pitt, or Burke, or Sheridan, which they were sure was fine, although they hardly understood it.

If I had a single copy of 'Rienzi' at hand this should not go unaccompanied. I have written to ask Mr. Willey to procure me some, and I hope soon to have the pleasure of requesting your acceptance of one. In the mean time I pray you to pardon this interlined and blotted note, so very untidy and unladylike, but which I never can help, and to excuse the wafer.

Very sincerely yours,

M. R. MITFORD.

CHAPTER XIII.

LETTERS FOR 1830.

To the REV. WILLIAM HARNESS, *Heathcote Street, London.*

MY DEAR FRIEND,   Friday, Jan 2, 1830.

You will have heard from Mr. Talfourd, whom I begged to inform you of it, of my blessed mother's seizure on Saturday morning. Her exemplary life is now at an end; she passed away easily and quietly at nine this morning. It is a consolation that she revived for a few hours on Sunday, knew us, and blessed us; but the great comfort is in the recollection of her virtues, and the certainty of her present happiness. You knew her, and you know that never lived a more admirable woman. God grant that I might tread in her steps!

We are as well as can be expected under this great affliction; and surrounded by kindness and sympathy. But what a beginning of the new year! God bless you my dear Mary!

Ever yours,

M. R. MITFORD.

*My blessed Mother's last illness.**
(Written Jan 10, 1830.)

On Christmas Day, 1829, the dear creature was quite well and cheerful—particularly so—ate a hearty dinner of roast beef. She had eaten a mince-pie for luncheon,

---

* We print this paper *in extenso*, as there is a homely particularity and perfect truthfulness in its details, which to us appears very affecting.

and drank our healths and Mr. Talfourd's in a glass of
port wine. She read a sermon (one of the fifth volume
of Blair's) in the evening, and went to bed quite well
and comfortable. The next morning she was quite
well and cheerful whilst she and my father were getting
up. He went down, and she said she would soon follow.
She did not, and, on going to see for her, she was found
lying across the steps between her own inner and outer
room in our little cottage at Three Mile Cross. She
spoke with her usual sweetness and patience, but with
an altered voice—deeper, hoarser, more inward—said
that she felt giddy, but in no pain. She was carried to
bed, dressed, as she had got up, in her grey cloth gown
and a cap lined with blue. When there, she ate a hearty
breakfast, drank two cups of tea and ate six slices of
bread and butter, and said she was quite easy and comfortable. When I returned to her she was getting her
dear right hand rubbed by Anne, whom she presently
sent down to breakfast, saying 'she had nothing to do,
and would rub her hand herself—it would employ her'
—quite vivacious, dear angel, though her left hand and
all her left side were paralysed. My father went into
Reading for medical advice. We continued with her,
and the dear saint continued talking and cheerful. I
told her of a letter I had received from Mr. Willey,
with an American playbill of 'Rienzi,' which I took to
her. I then remarked that she did not open her eyes;
her mouth was drawn a little towards the right side;
but she smiled, and spoke quite cheerfully. I read
her a note from Lady Madalina Palmer, which she was
much pleased with, and reverted to ten minutes or a
quarter of an hour after, saying, 'So Madalina says all
her ideas are frozen, and everything but her regard for
her friends!' (the identical words of the note). Also

she said, when I told her the commotion Molly* had
made in the bed by getting out at the bottom, 'Poor
thing! so she must have made a great fuss;' and
seemed amused. She planned to have some minced
beef for her own dinner, inquiring 'whether there was
any of the beef left to make it—not the roast, which
had been dressed the day before—but some boiled,
which we had had earlier in the week' (this was Saturday); and on my telling her that my father meant to
get some chickens for chicken broth, she said 'that
would do nicely, for it would warm up two or three
times,' and seemed to like the notion of having some
gingerbread cakes of Perry's for luncheon. Her dear
right hand was kept rubbed by us: it twitched con-
vulsively, but had some power of voluntary motion.
Her left hand, which was under the clothes, was terribly
bruised, but that she did not know or feel. The right
hand was held up out of bed. Mr. Harris came, and
the dear saint answered his questions. He asked if
she felt any pain in her head; she answered 'No, she
was quite easy—quite comfortable.' Whilst I went
down with Mr. Harris, and whilst he was telling me
that it was an attack of serous apoplexy, and that
nothing could be done, she had another attack, and
Harriet came for us. She was then sick, her dear eyes
were closed, and she was speechless. Anne Brent† had
come before Mr. Harris. She did not notice my father
when he returned. We gave her some water and sal
volatile, which she swallowed, and then, some time after,
some chicken broth, which she took well, and swallowed
as well as she could for the phlegm, which sadly tormented her, and constantly wiped her mouth with her

* Miss Mitford's spaniel.
† A woman of the village, engaged as nurse.

dear right hand, the only thing which had any power, and which she was constantly moving. She pushed off her cap from her forehead, so we took it off and replaced it by her nightcap, and the next morning she was undressed and put into bed altogether. The weather was bitterly cold, with snow on the ground all the time, but there was a good fire in the room constantly, and we were able to keep her warm. She untied her nightcap and strings so constantly that we were sometimes obliged to hold her dear hand to prevent her letting in the cold. She certainly knew my hand and my father's, for she would hold them herself, and sometimes press them; and once, when I had been kissing her dear hand, she suddenly brought mine to her dear lips. God bless her, sweet angel! Oh! what a grief it is to have no longer that dear feeling of my mother's warm hand! the only way she had left to show her affection! She evidently knew her silk handkerchief from the sheets and bed-clothes by the feel, and a dry and clean from a stiff and wet one; and she knew my father's voice when he spoke to her, and mine. No one else gave her anything except my father and myself, and we very seldom left her. He and Harriet went to bed for a few hours in the first part of the night, and at four, five, or six o'clock Anne Brent and I, who sate up, woke them; then, whilst they watched, we went to bed for a few hours.

On Sunday we sent Ned after Mr. Sherwood, at Aldermaston, who would not come. Ned having stayed till past dark (having gone to see his own friends at Bucklebury), the delay, and then the refusal, were hard to bear in our great grief. When my father and I were kneeling alone by her bedside, whilst they were at tea (Sunday evening, the night after her attack), she tried to speak to us. She said, I think, in answer to his fond calls upon her, "dear husband;" and "dear child" in answer to mine. Then I begged her blessing, and as well as she could she gave it: "Bless you, my own dear child." Then my father begged her blessing, and she blessed "her own dear husband," wiping her eyes with her dear right hand, and crying as we did. Then I begged her to pardon my many faults against her. She said, "Yes, my dear," and pressed my hand and my father's, and at last went to sleep with her hand in his.

After he was gone to bed that same night, as I was giving her some broth I thought she again seemed sensible, and asked her if she liked it: "Is it nice, dear mamma?" "Very good," she replied, quite articulately. "Do you like it, dear mamma?" "Very much," she said, as plainly as I could speak. I went on: "You are better, dear mamma?" "Yes," the dear saint said; "I have had a good sleep." Then she seemed to drop asleep again. A little while after, as Harriet and I were at the bottom of the bed, she said, "I want some caudle." At first I thought it was her pocket handkerchief, and gave her that; but that was not it: she said, "No, no." Then Harriet thought it was coffee, but she repeated quite distinctly, "I want some caudle," and I said, "Caudle with nutmeg and wine?" She said, "Yes," and I said it should be made directly; and then she spoke inarticulately something we could not make out, and those were the dear saint's last words. She never complained or struggled, or did anything but what was sweet, and gentle, and patient, and feminine; and the motions of her dear right hand were most affecting. After her last words her dear mind seemed wandering, for she put her fingers up my sleeve and tried to feel my pulse, and this I believe she did to my father afterwards; but many times I think she knew us when we spoke to her, and pressed our hands when we put them in hers. Once she did this (on Tuesday morning, I think) in presence of Mr. Harris.

On Monday morning my father went into Reading for further advice : he met Dr. Smith, who returned with him. Dr. Smith advised leeches and a blister. In the evening we put on the leeches on her left temple, but no amendment took place. We now gave her caudle, with a glass of wine and nutmeg and sugar in it, and she seemed to like and relish it. We also gave her currant-jelly water to prevent the poor tongue and throat getting dry, when she breathed (as she often did) through her throat with the mouth open.

Next day (Tuesday) Dr. Smith called, and gave but little hope, if any. Mr. Harris came afterwards and gave none, advising us to use no remedies, saying they would only torment her. Accordingly, we did *not* put on the blister, but gave her nourishment—as much as she would take—amounting to nearly two basins of gruel that day.

Next day (Wednesday) Dr. Smith came again and advised leeches, though without giving hope. We did not put them on, she being in a great perspiration, and then falling asleep. Mr. Harris, who came the next day, found her much weaker, and said that if we had put on the leeches she would have died under them. Dr. Smith said that it was only to prevent suffering—that there was no chance of life—and advised support. We gave her wine with her gruel, but she got weaker and weaker— breathed fast and loud ; her dear hand trembled as she lifted the handkerchief; then she could not lift it at all, she was so weak.

This was Thursday night. She grew cold, and we thought she was going, but the warmth came again, and then about twelve o'clock we heard the rattle in the throat. Before this she had great difficulty in swallowing, then we wetted her dear lips and tongue with a feather; then she took, with great difficulty, a little more gruel; then the perspiration came again, and the fast, difficult breathing; then the pulse and the breathing sank, and about nine o'clock on the morning of Friday (New Year's Day, 1830) the dear angel, after gradually sinking and catching an interrupted breath, expired without a sigh: there was a slight foam on her lips, and she was gone. I had kissed her dear hand and her dear face just before. She looked sweet, and calm, and peaceful: there was even a smile on her dear face. I thought my heart would have broken, and my dear father's too.

On Saturday I did not see her; I tried, but on opening the door I found her covered by a sheet, and had not courage to take it down. On Sunday I saw her both out of her coffin and in it; still sweet, and calm, and placid, looking like one happy. On Thursday I saw her for the last time, in the coffin, with her dear face covered, and gathered for her all the flowers I could get—chrysanthemums (now a hallowed flower), white, yellow, and purple—laurustinus, one early common primrose, a white Chinese primrose, bay and myrtle from a tree she liked. verbena, and lemon grass also. I put some of these in the coffin with rosemary, and my dear father put some.

We kissed her cold hand, and then we followed her to her grave in Shenfield Church, near the door, very deep and in a fine soil, with room above it for her own dear husband and her own dear child. God grant we may tread in her steps! Mr. Feilde performed the service, and many persons were there, all silent and respectful—the Feildes, Mrs. T——, Harriet Palmer, and Ellen Gorton. All had been very kind, especially Harriet. So had the Walters, Moncks, Hodgkinsons— in short, everybody; the respect felt for her was universal. She was in the eightieth year of her age: a small, delicately-framed woman, with a sensible countenance, a very fine head and forehead, a very beautiful and delicate hand and arm, still very upright and active, and her voice pleasant and articulate. Of her mental qualities I shall speak hereafter, and of her angelic perfection of character. No human being was ever so devoted to her duties—so just, so pious, so charitable, so true, so feminine, so industrious, so generous, so disinterested, so ladylike—never thinking of herself, always of others—the best mother, the most devoted wife, and the most faithful friend. Heaven bless her, for she is there! Her coffin (a handsome one) was made by Wheatley. The bearers were Farmer Smith, Farmer Bridgewater, Farmer Love, Bromley, Brown, and Wheatley—all persons she liked—and Hetherington was the undertaker. We had a hearse and a mourning coach, none going except ourselves. Anne Brent laid her out, as she had desired. The servants in the house at the time were Harriet and little Anne, both very attentive, and old Hathaway.

During the dear angel's illness her breath, on three different days while sleeping, seemed to speak words—to continue, as it were, in one chime. On the first day (Tuesday, I think, or perhaps Monday) it seemed to say, " Why that knell? why that knell?" and so on for many minutes. It struck on me like *words*. On Wednesday night, when not thinking of it, it again seemed to say, " Where are you going? where are you going? where are you going?" On Thursday (whilst still not thinking of it) again it struck me even more vividly: " It is home! it is home! it is home!"

And so it was—to heaven, her real home. On the Tuesday or Wednesday night preceding her death there was a large winding-sheet in the candle pointing to her bed—the candle that stood on the washing-stand near the chimney. We all saw it, but none of us cared to mention it, until at last my father took it off, that I might not see it. There was one in the maid's room, which Anne Brent saw, the same evening. Nothing could equal the dear angel's patience and gentleness. We hope she did not suffer much; but certainly she was conscious at times, from the constant attention she paid to keep her dear face nice—(there never was the slightest drivelling, or anything unpleasant, from her opening her mouth to take in the spoon. No one ever gave her anything except my father and myself); and from her seeming conscious of our voices and pressing our hands. Oh, that I could but again feel the living touch of that dear hand! God forgive me my many faults to her, blessed angel, and grant that I may humbly follow in her track! Nothing could be so affecting as the motion of that dear hand from the time when its pressure was warm and comparatively strong until it became faint, and damp, and feeble.

God bless her, sainted angel! Oh, that I might live like her! She was fond of Molly. She used to say "she liked poor Molly, because she was old and faithful;" and of Dash, whom she called "her dog;" and *we* like them the better for her dear sake. God bless her! She is a saint in heaven! She told Harriet Palmer (of whom she was fond) that she meant to get a guinea, and have her father's old Bible—the little black·Bible which she read every day—beautifully bound, with her initials on it, and give it to me. She told me, when 'Otto' should be performed, she wanted a guinea—but not why—and would not take it before. It shall be done, blessed saint!

To *the* Rev. WILLIAM HARNESS, *Heathcote Street.*

Three Mile Cross, Friday,
Jan. 9, 1830.

MY DEAR FRIEND,

You know how much I always feel your kindness,
and may imagine that on this occasion your sympathy
was most grateful to my feelings. You knew my blessed
mother; knew how full she was of the highest virtues—
pious, generous, disinterested, true, and just; how
devoted in her attachments; what a wife, what a mother,
what a friend; how feminine and ladylike in every act
and thought; and, knowing all this, you may imagine
how much we must grieve. These virtues are, however, at the same time a consolation—the greatest that
we can ever experience. For my own part I never
deserved her; but I trust to follow her example better
than I have done, and to make up, as well as I can, to
my dear father (the only natural tie that I have left in
the world) for this grievous deprivation. He was a
most excellent husband, and is a most sincere mourner.
We followed her dear remains to the grave yesterday;
and, I think, he is better to-day.

We have every comfort from the kindness and sympathy of our friends and neighbours, the respect held
for her being universal, and this is an alleviation of our
sorrow. I shall try to get my father out as soon as I
can—to the sessions next week, if possible—for I am
sure that nothing will do him so much good as resuming
his accustomed habits and avocations. For my own part
I have plenty that must be done; much connected painfully with my terrible grief; much that is calculated to
force me into exertion, by the necessity of getting money
to meet the inevitable expenses. Whether it were
inability or inertness I cannot tell, but 'Otto' is still

but little advanced. I lament this of all things *now ;* I grieve over it as a fault as well as a misfortune.

The funeral was, of course, quite private — only ourselves, in a mourning coach—but handsome and respectful. She lies in the best part of the church, with room for us in the same grave; and, besides the stone that covers her, I wish to have a tablet. I know that you will enter into these feelings, and forgive the trouble that I cause you.

Ever, my dear friend,

Most sincerely yours,

M. R. MITFORD.

To the REV. W. HARNESS, *Heathcote Street.*

Three Mile Cross, Jan 24, 1830.

MY DEAR FRIEND,

My father thought that, as Whittaker had published the previous volumes, this should be offered to him, and he has agreed to give a hundred and fifty pounds for it, which I think a fair price, and, as he has now two moneyed partners, I suppose the cash is safe. With regard to the American affair, the man (a deaf, and most disagreeable scarecrow) has been here. He makes a great point of secrecy. So I tell you *in strict confidence* what our agreement is. He is to give me in the notes of his publisher (whom he expects to be Colburn) two hundred pounds for two selections from the lighter American literature ; I mean, he is to give me that sum for my putting in the title-page, "selected and edited by Mary Russell Mitford" (the first title-page is to run thus :—"Stories of American Life by American writers ; selected and edited," &c. &c.), and for two short prefaces which I am to write. They have been, of course, really selected by me from an immense mass of material; and the first work, especially, will be really very good—characteristic, national, various, and healthy —as different from the ' Sketch Book' (which, in my mind, is a pack of maudlin trash) as anything you can imagine. Mr. Talfourd earnestly advised my doing this. He says that the thing will not in the slightest degree interfere with my own works, and that it was an easy way of getting money, though I never worked harder in my life than in wading through the mass of MSS. and letter-press to make the selection.

My dear father is much better in spirits. I am tired to death with bawling to this man and reading so much MS., but greatly relieved at the prospect of getting the money. As to myself, my irreparable loss, the moment I am alone, comes over me more and more. Kindest love to dear Mary.

Ever, my kind friend,
Most faithfully yours,
M. R. MITFORD.

To MISS JEPHSON, *Bath.*

Three Mile Cross, Thursday.
Feb. 1830.

MY DEAR LOVE,

My continued silence has been occasioned by excessive occupation, and also by indisposition, having had, and still having, a cough, which nothing silences but opium—a remedy which, whilst it pacifies the nights, stupefies the days. I am still terribly busy with my own volume. I had overrated the quantity of material ready, and tied myself to time, so that I am worked to death to get the original matter by the period fixed. Moreover, I am greatly worried by the American affair, the man who employed me having quarrelled with his

publisher, and the whole affair is afloat. We do not
know who will purchase the works, or when; and instead
of a large sum of money—a certainty—I find myself,
after an immense deal of most irksome labour, in the
midst of risks and chances and anxiety—my constant
destiny, and one which no constitution can stand long.

[*The remainder is wanting.*]

To Miss Jephson, *Bath.*

Three Mile Cross, Thursday,
Feb. 25, 1830.

My very Dear,

In the first place my cough is much better; I am
sure you will be glad to hear that. These three fine
days have done it incalculable good. In the next place,
I am getting on rapidly with my new volume, and,
altogether, am in far better heart than when I wrote
last, at which time I had really a feeling of depression
which no words could describe. I have still plenty to
worry and torment me.

All your Italian news is very interesting, and quite
new to me. Goldoni is the most insipid writer I ever
read; Alfieri is a very fine one, but unactable. A
friend of mine (the Rev. Maurice James) translated his
' Filippo,' and Charles Kemble used to want me to work
on that, and make a new ' Don Carlos ' out of Schiller's
and Alfieri's tragedies. To these I should have added
the two scenes from the ' Hippolitus ' of Euripides,
which Racine took for the famous scene in the ' Phèdre '
the *c'est toi qui l'as nommé* scene, which is very inferior
to the original Greek. All this, perhaps, I may do some
day or other, for certainly it would make a fine play.
' Werner ' is Lord Byron's most dramatic tragedy, and

undramatic enough too. Miss Lee made a play on the subject, which was played three or four nights at Covent Garden, under the name of 'The Three Strangers.' But by far the most striking drama on that striking story was one which I found above twenty years ago in a table-drawer at Kirkley Hall, in Northumberland, a seat belonging to the late Nathaniel Ogle, the eldest brother of Mrs. Sheridan. I was staying there with my father, and looking for some cards in a Pembroke table in the drawing-room found the manuscript. Mr. Ogle said that Sheridan had been staying there the year before, and he supposed that he had brought it to read, and had left it in his careless way. He wrote to his sister, but she knew nothing of it, and said that her husband denied all knowledge of the subject. So then Mr. Ogle gave it to me. Lady Charles Aynesley, a cousin of my father's, to whom I went afterwards, begged me to lend it to her, and I never got it back again, and never knew who wrote it. It was a most striking and interesting play, written in powerful prose, and could not have failed of eminent success. What a new combination of incidents that story contains! And how very rare a *new* story is!

How ignorant people are about their own places! Sir John Cope does not know whether Inigo Jones built his house of Bramshill, and I am obliged to send to the Duke of Bedford's and Lord Spencer's libraries for Birch's 'Life of the Prince of Wales,' to ascertain the fact.

God bless you, my dearest! Your letters are always grateful to me.

Ever most affectionately yours,

M. R. M.

May 22, 1830.

My dear Friend,

I have just received your very welcome letter, and I hasten to tell you that, though not likely, I fear, to see *you* at present (I have just refused a pressing invitation into Devonshire to myself and my father from Mr. Heathcote, the member for Tiverton), yet I shall see that which you will agree is next best to yourself, namely, your picture. I am going to town to witness the representation of ' Ion,' and after a triumphal course of parties (dinners, of course, for I never go to odious blue-stocking *soirées*) I shall, if possible, return in about a week. N.B. I have already engagements for more than double that time, but I must break off at some point, or I might stay the whole season ; and I have my father, my garden, and my yet hardly half-finished novel to draw me homeward.

I go to Mr. Sergeant Talfourd's house, 56, Russell Square, so that I shall be in the midst of his " agony of glory," and sharing it with the fullest sympathy ; and between him and Wordsworth (who is in town just now, and half living at my friend's) and my own acquaintance, I shall see all the high literary people of London in the pleasantest manner possible ; that is to say, the most undressed and familiar. I shall also see most of the eminent Whigs in the Lords and Commons in the same way ; but I don't expect to be much thrown amongst the Tories, although Sir Robert Peel is, of course, a man of too much general taste to confine himself to one party in the intercourse of society. I know that he applied to the author for a copy of ' Ion,' and I presume that they are acquainted.

It seems great presumption in me to talk in this way ;

but such is the passion for persons of literary reputation now-a-days that, if combined with respectability of character, it evens the professor with princes and ministers; and I myself am so seldom in London, and have always kept so aloof from the common race of blue-stocking people, that I pass for far more than I am, and am made a fuss about, such as would really seem incredible to those who are not aware of the London passion for novelty in everything. It pleases my dear father however; and certainly I can only be gratified by the attention and kindness of so many cultivated persons. Moreover, it gives an *entrée* to pictures, &c., which is exceedingly pleasant; and for the short time that I can stand the fatigue and the expense (for the dress is ruinous) nothing can be more agreeable. I love the beautiful city, if it were nothing else; most assuredly there's no such picturesque assemblage of buildings in the world.

My Dash I really believe understood your message, and looked up with his beautiful eyes, and made the pretty gentle sound which we all understand, and by which (by-the-way) he conveys distinctly "Yes" and "No," and three or four other phrases, and shook his head as he listened. The inside of his ear is injured; the outside is not at all disfigured, but in the interior there is a succession of gatherings which I fear will continue. He goes coursing, nevertheless, and likes it as well as ever. About three weeks ago, when a terrible operation had been performed on him in Reading, I, not knowing it was to happen, had gone to a copse primrosing, and was not returned when he came home. Poor Dash not finding me to comfort him, slipped out after my father, who followed me with the phaeton, and came up to me, in the middle of the coppice, covered with blood, and with half the inside of his ear just cut away. I sat

down to pet him, and then made my way out of the
bushes as fast as I could to get my poor dog home, when
a hare crossed us, and Dash followed it, questing all
through the copse, across half a dozen fields, along a
dozen thick hedgerows, then back to the coppice, every
inch of which he beat, although it has not been cut for six
years, and is (except in the paths) the thickest covert in
the neighbourhood. It was a full hour before we could
get him back to put him into the phaeton to carry him
home. He never seemed to think of his poor ear,
although there was a fresh wound, as big as the palm of
my hand, cut away that very morning, and which must
have been scratched by the bushes every instant. My
father says that it was the greatest triumph of high
blood and spirit that he ever saw or heard of. But he
is a most extraordinary dog.

Yours most affectionately,

M. R. M.

To Miss Jephson, *Bath.*

Tuesday, July 26, 1830.

I seize the opportunity of writing to you, my dear
love, before the extinction of franks, which I presume
to be approaching. I hope and trust that your friend
is better.

I am dreading the spread of liberal opinions. The
French Revolution is most happily over; never was
anything French so reasonably conducted. *Our* king
is ultra-popular. Have you heard Lord Alvanley's *bon
mot* respecting him? He was standing at the window
at White's, when the king, with a thousand of his loving
subjects at his heels, was walking up St. James's Street.
A friend said to him, "What are you staring at,
Alvanley?" "I'm waiting to see his Majesty's pocket

picked," was the reply. And, really, one wonders that the accident has not happened.

Did I tell you that I had had a great fright about a fortnight ago? My father was thrown out of the gig, returning from a dinner-party, and the horse and chaise came home empty. Of course we all set off, and found him stunned by the side of the road, just on this side of the vicarage—a full mile off. Only think what an agony of suspense it was! Thank Heaven, however, he escaped uninjured, except being stiff from the jar; and I am recovering my nervousness better than I could have expected. I find that my book is selling so well that they talk of reprinting the whole set in two pocket volumes, with vignette title-pages, like the Waverley Novels. This is a great practical compliment, for unless they sell five thousand copies they will lose by the edition; but I suppose they may be trusted to know what they are about. I don't imagine it will come out just yet. It is really a great circulation, for I believe that not less than eight editions of the first volume have been printed already, and the others in proportion.

I have read Sir Walter's plays. What a shocking conclusion that tragedy has! The other is very pretty in an odd way; but both are essentially undramatic. God bless you, my own dear Emily!

Ever most faithfully, and affectionately yours,

M. R. MITFORD.

To Miss Sedgwick [*the American authoress*].

Three Mile Cross, Reading, Berks,
Sept. 6, 1830.

MY DEAR MISS SEDGWICK,

Few things can be more gratifying to the feelings of an author than to hear of the diffusion and approval of

her works in such a country as America, and from such
a person as you. I should have written instantly to
thank you for your most kind and flattering letter, had
I not waited for 'Clarence,' the valuable present which
you announced to me. It has not yet arrived, but I
will no longer delay expressing my strong feelings of
obligation to the writer, since having read 'Redwood'
and the 'New England Tale,' I know how much of
pleasure I shall derive from the later production, which
is no doubt waiting at some London bookseller's till
they shall send a parcel to Reading. I have even seen
the highest possible character of it in one of the best of
our own magazines, the 'Monthly Review.' I rejoice to
find that it is not merely reprinted but published in
England, and will contribute, together with the splendid
novels of Mr. Cooper, to make the literature and
manners of a country so nearly connected with us in
language and ways of thinking, known and valued here.

I think that every day contributes to that great end.
Cooper is certainly, next to Scott, the most popular
novel writer of the age. Washington Irving enjoys a
high and fast reputation ; the eloquence of Dr. Channing, if less widely, is perhaps more deeply felt ; and a
lady, whom I need not name, takes her place amongst
these great men, as Miss Edgeworth does among our
Scotts and Chalmerses. I have contributed, or, rather,
am about to contribute, my mite to this most desirable
interchange of mind with mind, having selected and
edited three volumes of tales, taken from the great
mass of your periodical literature, and called 'Stories
of American Life by American Authors.' They are not
yet published, but have been printed some time ; and I
shall desire Mr. Colburn to send you a copy, to which,
indeed, you have every way a right, since I owe to you

some of the best stories in the collection. It was a Mr. Jones who put the annuals and magazines from which I have made this selection into my hands. He is himself an able writer and an intelligent man, and I owe to him, probably, the great pleasure of being known to you.

The indices of my private story in the books, which have been so kindly received by the public, are for the most part strictly true. I am a woman of now past forty, and was born and reared in affluence, being the only child of very rich parents. About fifteen years ago a most expensive chancery suit and other misfortunes too long to detail, reduced my dear father from opulence to poverty; and we are now living in the small cottage, which you will find described, in the same village with the mansion which once belonged to us. There was, however, no loss of character amongst our other losses; and it is to the credit of human nature to say, that our change of circumstances has been attended with no other change amongst our neighbours and friends than that of increased attention and kindness. Indeed, I can never be sufficiently thankful for the very great goodness which I have experienced all through life, from almost every one with whom I have been connected. My dear mother I had the misfortune to lose last winter. She died in a good old age, universally beloved and respected. My dear father still lives, under similar advantages, a beautiful and cheerful old man, whom I should of all things like you to know; and if ever you do come to our little Englar.d, you must come and see us. We should never forgive you if you did not.

I have given you this outline of my story because you expressed so kind an interest in my concerns, that

I thought you would like to know all about me. Our family losses made me an authoress; for although I had, when a very young girl, published two or three very rapidly written volumes of poetry, which had much more success than they deserved, and some of which ('Poems on the Female Character,' 'Blanch,' and the 'Rival Sisters') had the honour of being reprinted in America; yet I am confident that, having repented those sins of my youth, I should have abstained from all literary offences for the future, had not poverty driven me against my will to writing tragic verse and comic prose; thrice happy to have been able, by so doing, to be of some use to my dear family.

Once again, my dear Miss Sedgwick, accept my truest thanks for your kindness, and my sincerest good wishes for your health and happiness, and that of all belonging to you. Your dear little niece must have a postscript to herself; I am charmed with her delightfully natural letter.

I remain, dearest madam,
Your obliged friend and servant,
M. R. MITFORD.

To MISS C. M. SEDGWICK, JUN.

MY DEAR YOUNG FRIEND,

I am very much obliged to you for your kind inquiries respecting the people in my book. It is much to be asked about by a little lady on the other side of the Atlantic, and we are very proud of it accordingly. 'May' was a real greyhound, and everything told of her was literally true; but, alas! she is no more; she died in the hard frost of last winter. 'Lizzy' was also true, and is also dead. 'Harriet' and 'Joel' are not married yet; you shall have the very latest intelligence of her: I am expecting two or three friends to dinner, and she is making an apple tart and custards—which I wish, with all my heart, that you and your dear aunt were coming to partake of. The rest of the people are doing well in their several ways, and I am always, my dear little girl,

Most sincerely yours,
M. R. MITFORD.

To MISS JEPHSON, *Bath.*

Three Mile Cross, Friday,
Dec. 19, 1830.

Never imagine for an instant that I shall put your purse or my own in jeopardy by our book. The letters transcribed by your dear father and the later ones of Horace Walpole, combined with those of Mr. Jephson about the statue, form a most entertaining portrait of his frank, wayward, imprudent, but most delightful character. Horace Walpole also is excellently shown in his own last letter, with his gout, and his self-importance, and his courtly way of showing his anger. But I fear we still want more material.

I have the sweet-scented cyclamen and the Italian narcissus (the double Italian narcissus, sweeter far than the double jonquil) blooming in pots and glasses in the parlour window, whilst my autumn flowers, chrysanthemums, roses, Michaelmas daisies (the large new late one), and salvias, blue and red, are still in full bloom. I like this junction of the seasons, this forestalling of spring and prolonging of autumn—don't you? The parlour window would be the best place for the white evening primrose. Warmth will do it no harm, so that it has light and plenty of water, and a little air on mild days.

Did I tell you that I have six volumes of American children's books in the press? three for under, and three for over, ten years of age. The little ones are plain, practical, religious, and moral—I like them; the others varied and amusing. 'A Journey through the United States to Canada' forms the chief part of one volume—children, of course, being the principal travellers; 'A Sea Voyage to England' of the second; and 'Evenings in a Merchant's Family at Boston,' the third. This is new, at all events, and to me seems likely to take. The booksellers (Messrs. Whittaker & Co.) think so also, I imagine, for they are printing 3500 copies.

My play is, I find, coming out with the following cast, the best, I think, that they can make in that theatre :— Pedro, C. Kemble ; Alphonso, Warde ; Manuel, Bennett; Inez, Miss Fanny, and Constance, either Miss Ellen Tree* or Mrs. Chatterley. Mr. Talfourd, who brought me this news, and has been spending the day here, says that Fanny Kemble's Callista (odious as the part is) displays far higher talent than anything she has hitherto done, and that, at a distance from the stage, he could almost have imagined her a smaller and younger Mrs. Siddons. This is very comfortable. He told Mr. Kemble how much he was pleased with her in that part; and Kemble said that he liked her in it best himself, and had put her into it to accustom the town to seeing her in a higher range of characters, wishing her to occupy the place of Mrs. Siddons. I have never seen Fanny Kemble act ; but I am well acquainted with her off the stage, and know her to be a girl of great ability. The difference of age makes it singular, that she in Paris and I in London,

* Afterwards Mrs. Kean.

should have been educated by the same lady. What I hear of her acting pleases me, and I hope that my play and she will do well together. Of course I always know that *no* play is absolutely safe, and hope fearingly; but the female character is splendid, and the tragedy itself, though less powerful, far more interesting than 'Rienzi.'* God bless you!

Ever affectionately yours,

M. R. MITFORD.

To Miss Jephson, *Bath.*

Three Mile Cross,
Thursday night, Dec., 1830.

Oh, that you could see my chrysanthemums! I have one out now unlike any I ever saw. It is the shape and size of a large honeysuckle,[1] and the inside filled up with tubes. Each of the petals or florets (which are they?) is, on the outside, of a deep violet colour, getting, however, paler as it approaches the end, and the inside shows itself much like the inside of a honeysuckle tube, of a shining silver white, just, in some particular lights, tinged with purple. I never saw so elegant a flower of any sort; and my jar of four kinds, golden, lemon, yellow, purple, lilac, crimson, and pink, exceeds in brilliancy any display that I ever witnessed. The brightest pot of dahlias is nothing to it. My father, who has been twice in London lately (about my American 'Children's Books'

---

[1] *Note by M. R. M.*—This, by-the-way, is the shape and size of the tassel white, only that that flower is still more curved and curled, and all of one colour.

---

* Which, after its success at Drury Lane, was acted for several weeks in succession at the Pavilion Theatre, at this time, under the name of 'The Last of the Romans,' to evade prosecution by the great theatres.

and your friend 'Inez'), says that they have nothing
approaching it in splendour in the new conservatories
at Covent Garden. I am prodigiously vain of my
chrysanthemums, and so is Clarke.

Mr. Macready once told me that he sat up all night
in a room opposite the Old Bailey (I think) to witness
the execution of Thistlewood, &c., by way, I suppose,
of taking hints from their deaths. He said that there
he was disappointed; that even the masked headman
and the holding of the head of a traitor, was, in
theatrical phrase, ineffective; but that the most tremendous thing he ever saw was the congregation of
human faces, especially of human eyes, in that dense
and extensive crowd, all pointed to the same object
with an intensity so fixed and so absorbing. He never
before, he said, knew the power of that mighty thing,
the gaze of a multitude.

I never saw Mr. Denman; only he has the goodness
to take a very strong and partial interest in my books
and plays, and to let me know that he does so. Neither
did I ever see Mr. Brougham out of a court of justice;
but I know a great many of his friends and a great
deal about *him*, and admire him more than I can tell.
Oh, how could he stoop to be a lord! He sleeps nine,
ten, eleven hours, except, of course, on great debate
nights; spends some time at table; and allows himself
far more relaxation in society than most lawyers; and
what enables him to do this, whilst performing the
work of ten busy men, is the wonderful power which he
has over his attention. He says himself (talking con-
fidentially to a clever man, his intimate friend) that he
owes all his success to the habit of concentrating his
mind on the particular subject needful, whatever it be;
and then, the moment that is over, directing his powers

to another object and never thinking of the first again, unless the course of his business leads him to it. Concentration and instantaneous transition—these are the spells by which he works. Something of this power he owes, of course, to his legal habits; but no lawyer possesses it as he does, and very few have ever embraced such a variety of objects. The same versatility belongs in part to his character. He enters with the warmest sympathy into the feelings of those with whom he converses; but though at the moment the interest be most unfeigned and genuine, there is great danger that it shall vanish with the object. He is a delightful companion, gay, simple, and frank, and so good-natured that the humblest barrister might ask Mr. Brougham for a cast in his carriage, and the lowest clerk in the House of Commons make sure of a frank. I suppose the old title tempted him to be lorded; an old title in a family *is* a temptation.

I have been reading Head's ' Bruce,' which pleases me much less, because I am an adorer of Bruce's own book at full length, and hate abridgments of a favourite author; besides, I don't think it well done, though it is so odd, that it makes one laugh against one's will. (Before I forget, Mr. Brougham has a remarkable trick, or rather peculiarity of countenance; when he is beginning to be in a passion his nostrils and his whole nose twitch in the most extraordinary manner. They say that in debate his antagonists while speaking know the dressing they are going to have when they finish, by observing this indication. I have seen it myself in the Court of King's Bench, when the judge was charging against him.)

Ever most faithfully and affectionately yours,

M. R. MITFORD.

CHAPTER XIV.

LETTERS FOR 1831.

To MISS JEPHSON, *Bath.*

> Three Mile Cross, Thursday,
> Jan. 14, 1831.

YOU like to hear about Lord Brougham. Inquiring as to his daughter from an intimate friend of his the other day, I heard that she was a *blue* child—that children of that complexion never live past twelve or fourteen (I have heard this before)—but that he dotes upon her and educates her himself. It is singular that some years ago, when not seven years old, she prophesied that her father would be Lord Chancellor: "Papa will be Chancellor—you'll see that!" "Will he?" was the reply; "and what will your friend, Mr. Denman, be?" "Oh! Master of the Rolls, perhaps— I'm not sure about him—but you'll see that papa will be Lord Chancellor." He tells this with great glee; and I should not wonder if it had influenced him in accepting the situation. It certainly shows a wonderful *professional* knowledge in so young a girl. What a man he is! All last summer he was up at six every morning studying chemistry; and only yesterday I received a letter from my friend Archdeacon Wrangham (a man celebrated for his scholarship at Cambridge), saying that he had just received a letter from the Chancellor, whom he calls "a miracle of a man," on the sub-

ject of the Greek metres, showing a degree of learning
that would do honour to any scholar of the age.   This
is perhaps the most astonishing thing that I have heard,
even of that astonishing person.

I have not myself seen the second volume of the
'Life of Byron,' but doubtless the letters are to William
Harness.   There are several addressed to him in the
first volume ; and it is an honourable distinction, that
of all Lord Byron's intimate friends William seems to
be the only one whom he respected to the point of never
addressing to him one line that might not have been
sent to a delicate woman.   He intended, if you remember, to have dedicated to him his 'Childe Harold,'
and refrained only lest it should injure him in the
church.   William still speaks of him with much affection.

My father joins in most affectionate love, and

I am ever,

Most faithfully yours,

M. R. M.

To the DUKE OF DEVONSHIRE, *Devonshire House, London.*

Three Mile Cross, near Reading,
March 15, 1831.

MY LORD DUKE,

The spirit of liberality and justice to dramatic
authors by which your Grace's exercise of the functions
of Lord High Chamberlain has been distinguished,
forms the only excuse for the liberty taken in sending
my tragedy of 'Charles the First' direct to yourself,
instead of transmitting it, in the usual mode, from the
theatre to Mr. Colman.   To send it to that gentleman,
indeed, would be worse than useless; the play having

been written at the time of the Duke of Montrose, and
a license having been refused to it on account of the
title and the subject, which Mr. Colman declared to be
inadmissible on the stage. That this is not the general
opinion may be inferred from the subject's having been
repeatedly pointed out by different critics as one of the
most dramatic points of English history, and especially
recommended to me both by managers and actors. That
such could not always have been the feeling of those in
power is proved by the fact, that there is actually a
tragedy, on the very same subject and bearing the very
same title, written some sixty or seventy years since by
Havard the player, in which John Kemble, at one time,
performed the principal character, and which might be
represented any night, at any other theatre, without
the necessity of a license or the possibility of an objection. It is the existence of this piece which makes
the prohibition of mine seem doubly hard, and em-
boldens me to appeal to your Grace's kindness against
the rigorous decree of your predecessor.

Of my own play it hardly becomes me to speak. It
is an attempt to embody and present great historical
events and remarkable historical characters with as
much vividness and fidelity as my poor abilities will
permit. The manuscript has been seen by many eminent literary persons, who have considered it as the
least imperfect of my dramatic efforts, and have uni-
formly declared that it appeared to them quite unex-
ceptionable as an acting play. From anything like
political allusion it is undoubtedly free. I am not
aware that there is in the whole piece one line which
could be construed into bearing the remotest analogy
to present circumstances; or that could cause scandal
or offence to the most loyal. If I had been foolish or

wicked enough to have written such things, the reign
of William the Fourth and the administration of Earl
Grey would hardly be the time to produce them.

I have the honour to be, my Lord Duke,
Your Grace's most obedient servant,
MARY RUSSELL MITFORD.

To Miss JEPHSON, *Binfield Park.*

[*A Fragment.*]

Three Mile Cross, March, 1831.

You will see that literature and everybody, above all
his friends, have had a great loss in Thomas Hope. He
had been very ill, and was getting better, but went out in
an open carriage in one of these fogs, caught cold, and
sank under the remedies which an inflammation on the
chest rendered necessary. Of all the persons I ever
knew I think he was the most delightful. There was
a quick glancing delicate wit in his conversation such
as I never heard before—it came sparkling in, chequer-
ing his graver sense like the sunbeam in a forest; he
had also (what all people of any value have) great truth
and exactness of observation, and said the wisest things
in the simplest manner; above all, there was about him
a little tinge of shyness—a modesty, a real and genuine
diffidence, most singular and most charming in a man of
his station, his fortune, and his fame. Everybody
knows the noble things he used to do, but he was as
careful not to give pain as he was earnest to confer
happiness, and perhaps this humble and easier virtue
is the rarer of the two.

People called him proud, and a detestable French artist
painted him and his wife, as I dare say you have heard,
as ' *La Belle et la Bête.*' To me he seemed almost

handsome; he was very much underhung, which gave a lion-like look to the lower part of his face, but he had a grand Shakespearian pile of forehead, an expression of benevolence and intellect, and the air and bearing of a man of the highest distinction. He was not, I find, so rich as has been thought, in spite of his magnificent house in Duchess Street—the very temple of art, where Mrs. Hope's parties united all that was distinguished in rank, talent, and literature—and of his still more beautiful villa of Deepdene, where princes of all nations used to take their abode for weeks together, all was accomplished by the most admirable system of order, a large and liberal economy. He knew to a fraction the expense of every day, and even the amount of meat consumed. Nothing ever approached the exactness of his establishment; perhaps the Dutch blood may have had some influence.

To the Rev. William Harness, *Heathcote Street.*

Three Mile Cross, March 31, 1831.

My dear Friend,

You will probably have heard by this time, from your friend Mr. Collier, that the Duke of Devonshire could not—consistently with his established rule not to reverse the decisions of the Duke of Montrose—license the 'Charles.' Nothing could exceed the kindness and gentlemanlike feeling of his letter (for he wrote himself), and I beg you to convey my best thanks to Mr. Collier for his goodness in the affair. Never was a refusal so amiable as the Duke of Devonshire's.

I send, for your acceptance, my American Tales, and a smaller set for a smaller—but, my father says, very delightful little—personage, your niece. The children's

stories are very plain and homely, but I have been much
gratified by the approbation of several sensible mothers,
who say that their children are very fond of them, and
that they consider them sound and practical. There
was a good deal of cant in them, which I swept away,
leaving, I think, as much religious feeling as children
of that age can enter into. I wish you would run over
half a volume, and give me your opinion on this point.
If I utterly fail in the drama, and should also fail in a
novel, why then children's books would be something to
fall back upon. Mine would not be at all like these;
but I think that I could write English stories which
children would like, and which would do them no harm
at least, if not much good.

So you are against the Reform Bill! Well, I should
not care much for it myself, if I were not persuaded
that it is the only preservative against a much worse
state of things. If we have not reform we shall have
revolution, and I cannot help thinking but a House of
Commons, chosen according to the new plan, will be a
much better thing than the mob.

I hope you will contrive to come to see us this summer. Mr. Talfourd will tell you that my greenhouse is
a pleasant room to live in, and that some of our Berkshire friends are nice people. We should be so proud
of making you known to them. Pray do come. Mrs.
W—— said the other day—what worried me at the
moment, for fear you should believe it—that M——
had told you that I had looked you out a wife. Now
M——, with a thousand fine qualities—good-nature,
generosity, absence of selfishness, and an overflowing
and faithful attachment to her friends—has one peculiarity, which has a thousand times threatened to alienate
me from her, kind as she is to me. It is one which

I dislike so much, and which comes so directly in opposition to my own peculiarities—I mean her habit of considering and talking of every man and every woman as if he and she were born for no other purpose than that of marrying and falling in love. She even used to joke *me*, at my age, with my person, and with my resolute oldmaidishness and hatred of the subject, about every man that came near me. I think it is not possible to give a stronger instance of her determination to pursue the subject than her choosing to consider the marriage of such a one as I to come within the verge of *possibility*. It happens, however, that I hate match-making in the first place; that I should never dream of taking such a liberty as to lay schemes for you in the second; and, in the third, that the young lady whom I believe her to mean is, although a good and clever girl, one entirely unworthy of you in person, family, fortune, connections, and manners—things that, in my mind, come next to goodness, and before talents. You may come here in perfect safety. Adieu, my dear friend.

Ever most gratefully and affectionately yours,

M. R. MITFORD.

To Miss Jephson, *Binfield Park.*

May 20, 1831.

COPY OF SOME VERSES ADDRESSED TO MY FRIEND MISS JAMES, WRITTEN DURING HER STAY AT THE SWAN INN, THREE MILE CROSS, JANUARY, 1829.

The village inn ! The woodfire burning bright !
The solitary taper's flickering light !
The lowly couch ! the casement swinging free !
My noblest friend, was this a place for thee ?
Yet in that humble room, from all apart,
We poured forth mind for mind and heart for heart ;
Ranging from idlest words and tales of mirth
To the deep mysteries of heaven and earth ;

Yet there thine own sweet voice in accents low
First breath'd Iphigenia's tale of woe,*—
The glorious tale, by Goethe fitly told,
And cast as finely in an English mould
By Taylor's kindred spirit, high and bold.
'Twas no fit place for thee! yet that blest hour
Fell on my soul like dewdrops on a flower,—
Freshening and nourishing and making bright
The plant decaying less from time than blight,—
Flinging Hope's sunshine o'er each feeble aim,
Thy praise my motive, thine applause my fame.
No fitting place! yet (inconsistent strain
And selfish!) come, I prythee! come again!

Are not these lines (except the wood fire and the 'Iphigenia') very *à propos*—quite "germane to the matter?" especially the last words, the "come again, come again," which I can but reiterate with heart and soul. You cannot imagine how delighted I was to hear of the Kingfisher (for it was the first word Anne told me when she came to me), and how pleased I was to see it. You must come again, although it be no fitting place, and I do really think that you will. The little girls there are honest, for they have found and have brought me your signet ring, which I keep for you safely.

I have been but indifferent for a long while until now. Mr. Merry has been with me for two hours to-day, lamenting over his own bad singing, and hoping to see you again that he might do better. I told him I hoped he would see you again, but that *we* were quite satisfied with his doings.

* *Note by M. R. M.*—Mr. Taylor's translation of Goethe's 'Iphigenia in Taurus,' which is in some parts only a free imitation of Euripides—one of the finest translations in our language, and now out of print long since. Did Emily ever see it? I have a copy, but have lent it at present to Mr. Milman, who is in London.

I have just had a visit from Mrs. Dickenson. She was one of the poor Duchess of Wellington's most intimate friends; and she says it is certainly true that the Duke is a changed man since her death—has scarcely left his room, or had courage to ring for a servant. I have been driving to Arborfield, and have heard terrible news of everybody's gardens and greenhouses; all the dahlias and geraniums of the county seem to have been killed, and Mrs. Blagrove, on the other side, has lost a great part of her matchless collection. I am so sorry for her, she loved them so. God bless you, my dear love!

Ever yours,
M. R. M.

To Miss Jephson, *Bath.*

Tuesday night, Oct. 20, 1831.

Last night I was at a phrenological lecture given by a Mr. Dowton, a travelling lecturer, in Reading, and very much pleased and interested I was. I am a sort of a demi-semi believer (are you?), and have heard Dr. Spurzheim and Mr. Deville frequently, but I prefer Mr. Dowton. Amongst the novelties, the most striking was a cast of the skull of Raphael—the veritable skull dug up at Rome. There is no doubt of the authenticity, and it displays more intellect and finer imagination (ideality is the technical word) than any skull ever before met with; finer even than Edmund Burke's. You would have liked the whole lecture. I wished for you. The worst objection to the science is, that it approaches too closely to the doctrine of election.

You will like to hear what he says of my head, which he examined so far as regards the intellectual qualities, not the moral propensities, in which I have less faith, and which it is awkward enough to have doled out to one. First of all, he was most urgent with me to have it cast, meaning, I believe, to do it himself. He said that it was, in the size of the cranium, the greatest illustration he had ever met with of the science. Generally speaking, the female head is much smaller than the male—almost always—and mine, he says, is larger than the average male head; and all power, all force, all reality of intellect depends upon the actual, not the relative size of the organs.

Now I half wish I had undergone the operation, for I believe they take four casts, giving you three, and you would like to have had one, for it is more a real part of oneself than a print, or even a painting—more completely the true face and head. He remarked on the indentation of the middle of the forehead as indicating a want of the power of remembering small things, such as names of streets and numbers of houses, and names of dates generally. Now, this is so true! And he enlarged much on the extraordinary development of imitation, the principal organ of Scott, and the one which produces dramatic, or rather creative power. It is situated on each side of benevolence (which rather, I believe, means kindness), and when they are both large, as he says they are in me, give the peculiar roundness to the top of the head ⌒ which, with the great development of the other reflective and perceptive organs, gives the remarkable shape to the forehead which all painters have observed in mine. He says that both ideality and constructiveness are large, but that it is the striking development of imitation (by which phrenologists mean imitation of nature) which gives the power of conceiving and executing dramatic situation and character; that it was the principal characteristic of Sheridan's head and of Shakespeare's, as it appears in the monument which Ben Jonson called so like him.

This is curious, and I tell it you, in spite of the apparent vanity, because it will be sure to interest you. He certainly did not do it to flatter me, for at first I did not like the word imitation. It seemed to me fitter for an actor than a dramatic writer, and I dwelt on the constructiveness and ideality which painters had told me I had so large; but he stuck to his text, and convinced me, by his own head, how much larger, proportionately, my imitation was than his, though his is large. He says that Mr. Cathcart's head, though that shy and sensitive person would not let him touch it, is magnificent. And he felt Dash, and made a great hit, for he said that he was the only spaniel in whom he had ever found so large a combativeness; and he fights every dog he comes near, and is king of the street, having conquered, after twenty pitched battles, two bull-dogs, a Dane, and a Newfoundland, his neighbours. He said the distance between the eyes showed an immense portion of good-humour, and the space and roundness of the top of the skull great sagacity.

Is the top of Miss Edgeworth's forehead round? and is her head large? Mr. Dowton asked me these questions, and I could not answer him. Pray are you a great educator of the poor? I am not, and I am going to give you a case against it. I took, about three days ago, a girl from a school at Reading as an under-maid. Well, I left a proof-sheet in my desk, corrected and folded, and ready for the post. I took a ride out, and on my return found that the young lady had ransacked my desk, and opened my proof. Not being able to refold it *secundum artem,* she was obliged to leave it open, and so was found out. This is a fine specimen of the march of intellect. Of course she is going. These things are exceedingly vexatious, especially to one who hates strange faces.

Have you met with the 'Book of the Seasons,' by William and Mary Howitt? It is very pretty indeed. Let me hear soon and often. I am quite glad you are with Mr. Smith, for whom, on your report, I have great respect, esteem, and liking.

Ever, my dearest Emily,

Your faithful and affectionate,

M. R. MITFORD.

To MISS JEPHSON, *Castle Martyr, Ireland.*

Three Mile Cross, Nov. 11, 1831.

MARY QUEEN OF SCOTS' FAREWELL TO FRANCE.

" Oh ! pleasant land of France, farewell !
　　My country dear,
　　　Where many a year
In peace and bliss I hoped to dwell.
Oh ! pleasant land of France, farewell !"
So sang the Scottish queen what time she stood
On her proud galley's prow, and saw the shores
Of France receding—the beloved shores
That she should never see again. Big tears
Dropt from her eyes, and from her lips the words
Broke in fond repetition—" Pleasant land,
Farewell ! farewell !" Then silently she stood,
The lovely one, silent and motionless,
Amidst the weeping train ; her lofty head
Thrown back, her fair cheek colourless, her eyes
Fixed on the cloudy heaven. There was a passion
Of grief in that fine form might have beseemed
Andromache, a captive—or the Maid
Of Thebes, Antigone, when doomed to die.

But this was a young queen—the fairest queen—
The fairest lady of the earth—whose name
Was as a spell for men to work by—Mary,
The peerless Queen of Scots, returning home
To reign.   Yet there she stood all motionless,
Striving with fondest thoughts and deepest fears —
Thoughts true and tender of her tender youth,
And fears that took a tone of prophecy :
There stood she silent, till again the words
Burst from her lips :

      "Oh ! pleasant land, farewell !
Farewell to pageants glittering bright,
The joust by day, the dance by night.
   Proud realm of chivalry, farewell !
Farewell ! in this sad hour more dear
To loving friends and kinsmen near—
   Oh ! land of loyal hearts, farewell !
From thy fair hills and orange bowers,
I go where dreary winter lours ;
From courteous knights, quick, ardent, bold,
I go to bigots stern and cold ;
From Hope's gay dream for ever hurled,
I go to breast the stormy world ;
   Oh ! pleasant land of France, farewell !
Thy sunny shores no more I see,
Yet still my heart abides with thee.
Home of my happy infancy,
A long, a last farewell !"

I begin with this, dearest, although perhaps I may
have shown it to you before, because from these few
lines I derive my hope of that enduring fame which
poets call immortality—not from their own merit, but
from their being "married to immortal" music. About
three years ago Charles Parker asked me for a *scena* in
English verse—something composed of recitative, air
and chorus, analogous to the Italian *scena*. I happened
to have begun this subject for one of the annuals, and
finding, on mentioning it to him, that it was exactly

what he wanted, he has just completed the composition, and it is said by some of the best judges in town to be as fine as anything in English music. It is not published yet, but all the great people have heard it. I invited Mr. Merry and Emma Vines (another exquisite musician) to hear him sing it here. They were charmed with it; and yet we heard it to a disadvantage, for it makes fifty pages of music, and requires the united bands of Drury Lane and the Royal Musical Academy and above fifty chorus women. The first five lines (an almost literal translation of Mary's own verses,

" Adieu! plaisant pays de France!")

are the air—then the blank verse in exquisite recitative —then a magnificent chorus—then the song again—and then a chorus fading into the distance. No woman in England except Mrs. Wood (Miss Paton) can sing it; so that whether it will be performed in public at present is doubtful; but it is something to have furnished the thread on which such pearls are strung. Charles Parker is a musical wonder, like Mozart—a native of Reading, who *was* a pupil, and *is* a master of the Royal Musical Academy in London—not yet twenty-one. He is a most sweet and charming lad in mind and temper, and making a friend of every one who sees him.

It is not because Mr. Talfourd is eminent at the bar that he beats Mr. Merry in conversation. Eloquence in conversation is quite a different thing from forensic talent. Barristers are seldom pleasant. They are coarse and loud and noisy; and pun and vent jokes. I have known almost all the most eminent; and, except Romilly and Lord Erskine, can hardly name one to whom this character does not apply. I believe that your Irish barristers are better. Of them I only knew Mr. Curran; and he, in his latter days when I used to see him, was certainly very coarse and disagreeable.

Are not these fires frightful? They began hereabouts; but I hope that the example of Bristol will frighten ministers into some discretion, and force them to discourage political meetings of all sorts. The cholera will certainly do great good in enforcing cleanliness where it never otherwise would have found its way; and, if it do take hold of some of our overcrowded cities, it will be a blessed dispensation. I am sick of the wickedness of this dense population. God bless you, my dear love! I wish you could see my chrysanthemums. My father's best love.

Ever most faithfully yours,

M. R. M.

To Miss Jephson, *Castle Martyr, Ireland.*

No date. Middle of November, 1831?

I write to acknowledge your dear letter just received. There is another letter of mine on the road to you—or rather probably received by you before now—but I send this chiefly to enclose some anemone seed, which we are sowing to-day. I have a great love of those gay winter flowers, which give colours so like the lost colours in old stained glass; and I shall like you to sow some of my seed in your garden. How curiously the seed expands, opening and turning back like a frieze jacket: franks are nice conveyers of seed. Have you the great white Œnothera—almost as big as a saucer—which opens at night and is so like a cup of alabaster? If you have not, I must send you seed of that when it ripens, for it is one of my pet flowers. I'll also send

some seed of a certain blue pea (Lord Anson's pea)
which is just the colour of Aqua Marina—the most
beautiful blue of any flower; have you that? It has a
small pink mark in the centre, which adds to the beauty
greatly. It is small and scentless and very rare—and
very rare it always will be, because it is very shy of
seed. I enclose one of the petals. No—we don't use
salt. Of course our geraniums won the prizes; and
one seedling especially (which I have called the 'Ion,'
after Mr. Sergeant Talfourd's play) is said to be the
finest that has been produced for many years. I enclose the leaves of one flower of that also. We have at
present twelve seedlings, each of which would win a
prize anywhere, and one hundred and fifty more to
blow. One effect of raising seedlings is, that one ceases
to care for other plants—a very vain and dangerous
feeling. My friend, Mr. Foster, has it to such a degree
that he does not suffer any plant not raised by himself
or his brother in his greenhouse; but even he con-
descended to ask for a cutting of 'Ion,' and I shall (if
possible) rear one for you. By "if possible" I mean,
if I can rear three—one for Mr. Sergeant Talfourd, one
for Mr. Forster, and the third for your dear self.

Did I tell you, when talking of the Gores, that they
are friends of Colonel Wildman, who lent them Newstead Abbey for their honeymoon abode, and that there
they spent the first four or five months after marriage,
about a dozen years ago? They confirm the legend of
the White Lady, and all the facts both of Washington
Irving's book and the still more interesting accounts
both of Newstead and of Annesley, published last year
in the 'Athenæum,' and written by my friend William
Howitt. My father thank Heaven! is well. So is Dash.
Is it not strange—just before the coursing season began,

he began to dream of going out and *quested* in his
sleep? So he did last year. Is not this very remarkable? By what indications could he know that the
time of year was coming? He knows Saturday, when
he accompanies his master to the Bench, as well as I
do, and, on that day only, refrains from coming up to
my room the moment I am awake, lest he should be
left behind. When my father did go out two days ago,
he was so enchanted with the strong boots and the
gaiters that he kissed them both. He only kisses *me*
when he has been ill and I have nursed him; or when
I am very ill or very low-spirited; then he looks at me
with such a look! and licks my hand, and lays his head
against me. Can anybody wonder that one loves that
dog? Have you a pet dog now? They are a great
source of happiness, in my mind.

Yours ever affectionately,

M. R. M.

To Miss Jephson, *Castle Martyr, Ireland.*

Three Mile Cross, Dec. 14, 1831.

Your account of Miss Edgeworth is charming. High
animal spirits are amongst the best of God's gifts. I
had them once; but anxiety and loneliness have tamed
them down. The highest I have ever known are Lady
Croft's. They have borne her through all sorts of
calamities—her husband's sad death—the death of her
favourite son—comparative poverty—the marriage of
her only daughter to a Frenchman living in France—
every sort of trial; and still she is the gayest and most
charming old lady in the world—as active in mind and
body at nearly eighty as most girls of eighteen. It is
always bad criticism to say there is no more to be

done. Beside Sir Walter's novels, the American are a new class (I mean Cooper's and Bird's—especially the Mexican stories of Dr. Bird), and so are the naval novels, for 'Roderick Random' can hardly be said to have done more than opened the vein. Oh! it is false philosophy to limit the faculties and the productions of man! As well prophecy that there should be no new flowers! If T——'s money were coming to me, I should have avaricious views of accumulating geraniums, although I have already more than I can keep; and piling chrysanthemum upon chrysanthemum, although as it is I have beaten the whole county. Don't you love that delicious flower which prolongs the season of bloom until the Roman narcissus blows, and keeps the world blossoming all the year round? My salvias have been superb this year. I planted them in the ground about the middle or towards the end of July, and took them up in October—so that we got all the growth of common ground and open air, and brought them full of bud to blow in the greenhouse. Two of them nearly reached the top of the house.

At present I am altogether immersed in music. I am writing an opera for and with Charles Parker; and you would really be diverted to find how learned I am become on the subject of choruses and double choruses and trios and septets. Very fine music carries me away more than anything—but then it must be *very* fine. Our opera will be most splendid—a real opera—all singing and recitative—blank verse of course, and rhyme for the airs, with plenty of magic—an eastern fairy tale.

God bless you, my dearest love! My father joins in most affectionate remembrances, and I am

Ever most faithfully yours,

M. R. MITFORD.

CHAPTER XV.

To MISS JEPHSON, *Castle Martyr.*

Three Mile Cross, Feb. 22, 1832.

I THINK you like Mr. Bennett's things that I have sent you; and in that case you will be glad to hear that an American visitor of mine is reprinting them in Boston. It is quite wonderful how, when our brethren across the water like an English writer, they buy editions of his works by the score. You will pardon the apparent vanity of my telling you, according to the information of the same friend, that my poor doings, prose and tragedies, have been printed and reprinted in almost every town in the Union. He sent me himself a very beautiful edition printed last year at Philadelphia; but it is the cheaper and commoner ones which are the real compliment. I am going to-morrow to hear Elihu Burritt, the American blacksmith. He is to give a lecture on Peace and Progress at our news rooms. One of his plans is to establish a penny postage between England and America.

I have a fifth and last series of ' Our Village ' in the press, and having sent up too little copy, as it is technically called, I am now literally running a race with the printer. You cannot conceive the miserable drudgery it is, to pass one's day in writing gay prose whilst in such bad spirits! You must therefore pardon this wretched scrawl. As to public affairs, they seem to me in a most deplorable way. But I never read newspapers and know little about them.

Ever most affectionately yours,

M. R. MITFORD.

To DR. MITFORD, *Sussex Hotel, Bouverie Street, Fleet Street.*

Three Mile Cross, Tuesday,
Sept. 26, 1832.

I am rather in a taking about this notice of objection to your vote, not on account of the vote, but for fear it should bring on that abominable question of the qualification for the magistracy. Ask our dear Mr. Talfourd whether the two fields, forty shilling freehold, will be enough, without bringing out the other affair. In short, it worries me exceedingly ; and if there were any danger in it one way or other it would be best to keep out of the way and lose the vote, rather than do anything that could implicate the other and far more important matter.

I send up to-day the rest of the ' Tambourine ' article, the best I ever wrote in my life. Pray call there and get the money—I mean in Lancaster Place. Shall we be able to go on, if the opera is delayed till February ? This makes eighteen guineas there ; and I have two more articles on the stocks, which will be ready by Friday, making twelve guineas more ; and ten from Alaric Watts—and ten from Elder and Smith —and five from Ackermann : that will be all, except the money, which I fear you will not get, from Westley (try for it, though). Will this and the dividend last us past Christmas, if the opera do not come out ? If not, you had better get an advance from George Robins.

To-day is so beautiful, that, as the boys have had the strawberry mare up for the hay, I shall get Ben to put her into the chaise and drive up to the Merrys and round by the Fieldes. My mare is pretty well; but I shall not take her out to-day. Poor Dash is stiff, but better than I expected, and the jay quite well.

God bless you, my own dear darling! I long to see you.

Ever your own,
M. R. Mitford.

To the Rev. William Harness, *Heathcote Street.*

Three Mile Cross, Oct. 17, 1832.

My dear Friend,

This last volume,* only published a month ago, is now at press for the third time—the first edition was sold the second day.

At present I am exceedingly unwell. My complaint is one which is brought on by anxiety, or fatigue, or worry, or anything. Mr. Brodie has cured a friend of mine of the same disorder, and perhaps (though I doubt it) may cure me. But as I have promised Mr. Laporte a tragedy in January I must finish it; and as I well know that the first prescription of Mr. Brodie would be not to write, it is of no use putting myself under his care till I can follow his orders implicitly.

I must complete the work if I can; and then try and obtain some relief for this very painful and harassing complaint, the depressing effect of which upon the spirits no one that has not experienced it can imagine. It has been coming on for some years. I should be better if I were less worried by invitations—of which,

---

* The fifth of 'Our Village.'

at my gayest, I never accepted one in twenty, and which I now decline altogether—and by visitors. Every idle person who comes within twenty miles gets a letter of introduction, or an introduction in the shape of an acquaintance, and comes to see my geraniums or myself—Heaven knows which! I have had seven carriages at once at the door of our little cottage; and this sort of levée—bad enough in health—is terrible when one is not well. Mr. Milman, who has establsihed for himself a character for inaccessibility, is a wise person. I wish I could do the same; and I would have done so had I ever thought it possible that the mere fact of being a writer of books would have brought such a torment in its train.

This country is thickly inhabited, with few established rides or show-houses or lounges of any sort; and the local connection of the place and myself must, I suppose, be the cause of this kind of popularity—if popularity it be. I should certainly go to London to be *quiet;* if it were not that we have many valuable friends in the neighbourhood, and that my father would lose much of happiness in relinquishing his country habits; and he must always be my first object. And, if I can but get well again so as to be able to write with less effort, we shall get on very comfortably. I have much to be thankful for—above all, for friends.

God bless you, my dear friend! I began this letter in such bad spirits that I may perhaps have unintentionally conveyed to you a notion of my health being worse than it is. The attacks are only occasional, and my father says not dangerous. Kindest love to dear Mary.

Ever yours,
M. R. MITFORD.

To the REV. WILLIAM HARNESS, *Heathcote Street.*

Three Mile Cross, Monday,
Oct. 21, 1832.

MY DEAR FRIEND,

I write by the earliest post to prevent Mr. Dyce's taking any more trouble about the book which you were so kind as to mention to him, having been so lucky as to procure it unexpectedly in Reading—I mean the translation of the 'Alf Von Dealman,' for such, I find, is the gentleman's English name.

How pleased I was with the story you told me so kindly and so prettily—and how more than pleased was my father.* Another instance, nearly similar, came to my knowledge from the patient herself, a Miss Russell. She, when sinking under hypochondriasis, met with the book accidentally, and wrote to me that she believed the turn so given to her thoughts saved her intellect, if not her life. She still writes to me occasionally, and appears to be a woman of a fine and ardent mind, but over-stimulated—over-educated—as your rich heiresses so frequently are now-a-days. She is since married to a Mr. Price. After all, this is *your* cure. Any healthy and cheerful book would have answered the purpose; but it is very pleasant to be the writer prescribed by such a physician; and it has done *me* good as well as your other patient.

Did I tell you that I had received a pressing offer from our good old relation, Mrs. Raggett,† to give up authorship altogether and live with her and her husband—who, nearly blind, requires some one to read

---

* The story was of a young man in a nervous fever, whose mind had been calmed and soothed by having the tales of Miss Mitford read to him.

† Mrs. Raggett was a cousin of Miss Mitford. They were people of considerable property.

the paper to him and write his letters; and still more, to serve as a friend and companion in their old age? The offer had great temptation, since she said with perfect sincerity that what she wanted in me was not a dependent but a daughter; and I have no doubt but we should have been happy together. It was, however, clear that my father's comfort would have been destroyed by such an arrangement. To have left him *here* would have been impossible; and if Mr. Raggett had (as I believe he would have done) given him a home at Odiam; the sacrifice of his old habits—his old friends—the blameless self-importance which results from his station as Chairman of the Reading Bench— and his really influential position in this county, where we are much respected in spite of our poverty, would have been far too much to ask or to permit. Besides, *he* would have felt himself dependent though I should not. I refused it therefore at once; and, as they will certainly engage some one of the many persons who are applying for the situation of companion, I have no expectation of any pecuniary result from their kindness. If I had gone to reside with them, of course some moderate provision would have been made by will; but as it is I have no claim, and can only think of it very thankfully with reference to the affectionate feelings and the great delicacy with which the proposal was made. They are a very fine old couple—still clear of intellect and vigorous in body, and with minds and tempers softened and mellowed by age. Kindest love to Mary.

Ever most faithfully and affectionately yours,

M. R. M.

To Sir William Elford, *The Priory, Totnes.*

Three Mile Cross, Nov. 4, 1832.

The most delightful part of Miss Elford's delightful letter was her account of you, to which your own brilliant postscript bears ample testimony.* I can give an equally good report of my father, who sends his very kindest regards to his old friend; and my father's daughter, though still as poor and as busy as ever, is, you will be glad to hear, better in health and much better in spirits than when she wrote last. I have been talking to Miss Elford of the cholera. Have you happened to observe that the swallows desert the places where it appears? thus corroborating Shakespeare's observation (in the beautiful dialogue in 'Macbeth,' on which Sir Joshua Reynolds wrote so tasteful a note) that "where they breed the air is delicate."

Are you not grieved for Scott? And is it not most grievous that these national testimonials, which are so proper, should not have been bestowed when they might have relieved and saved him? Have you met with, or heard of, Miss Martineau's 'Illustrations of Political Economy?' I am told that she has made above one thousand pounds by those little eighteen-penny books. I like the first, 'Life in the Wilds,' best: it is very interesting and Robinson Crusoe-ish; but I am afraid that they are rather too wise for me. I have an old aversion to do-me-good books in general, and to political economy in particular—perhaps because I don't understand it.

God bless you, my dear friend! Believe me ever most faithfully and affectionately yours,

M. R. Mitford.

* Sir W. Elford was at this time nearly ninety.

What a pleasant, gossiping book Moore's 'Life of Byron' is! so totally free from the finery and gaudiness of the 'Life of Sheridan'—leaving the hero so comfortably where it found him, except in the article of personal vanity, which seems to have been more excessive than anything ever heard of before, *even in a man;* for you'll grant, I suppose, my good friend, that men, when they are vain, beat the women hollow in that good gift, as in others—and never tempting one to skip anything but the criticism!

To Dr. Mitford, Post Office, Wantage.

Three Mile Cross, —— night—no,
Thursday — Nov. 15, 1832, my
own dear darling's birthday.

Many and many happy returns of the day to you, my own dear father! I have been longing to *say* so to you, and to kiss you, and wish you joy in person, and I have drunk the toast in wine. I hope you told our dear friends of the anniversary, that they might do the same. How very good it was of you, since you could not be here, to write to me. I hope I shall get another letter to-morrow morning, for I miss you sadly. Never since the world began were people happier than ours have been this evening, especially Ben. You might almost have heard him laughing at Ilsley; and he has been singing, without music, and dancing to John's fiddle, and talking incessantly—poor urchin! The first thing he said to me was, "I wonder how we shall get on to-night," and I should imagine the question has been most satisfactorily answered. I bestowed about twenty brandy cherries upon them (the fruit, not the liquor) in addition to their beer, and you never saw people so enchanted! Also all the pets—Dashy, Selina, the fishes, the jay, the dogs, and the horses—have been taken especial care of. I fed Selina myself.

God bless you, my dear darling!

Ever most fondly your own,

M. R. MITFORD.

To SIR WILLIAM ELFORD, *The Priory, Totnes.*

Three Mile Cross, Sunday, Dec. 8, 1832.

MY DEAR FRIEND,

I send the enclosed as you seem to wish, and earnestly hope you will succeed in your undertaking.*

I must be obliged to get out another book this spring, although how I shall be able to write it God only knows. I am glad you like my last volume; I myself hate all my own doings, and consider the being forced to this drudgery as the greatest misery that life can afford. But it is my wretched fate, and must be undergone—so long, at least, as my father is spared to me. If I should have the misfortune to lose him, I shall go quietly to the workhouse, and never write another line—a far preferable destiny.

God bless you, my very dear friend! Say all that is kindest to your family.

Ever most faithfully yours,

M. R. MITFORD.

[*Enclosure to the foregoing.*]

Three Mile Cross, Dec. 8, 1832.

MY DEAR FRIEND,

I write in great haste just to say that I heartily approve of your plan for a cheap and general subscription for the purchase of Abbotsford; a feeling in which

---

* A subscription for the purchase of Abbotsford.

1 should hope that every admirer of the great writer, whom we have unhappily lost, will most cordially join. Be so good as to advance the small sum necessary for me.

Ever most affectionately yours,
M. R. MITFORD.

To Sir W. Elford, Bart.

END OF THE SECOND VOLUME.

LONDON : PRINTED BY WILLIAM CLOWES AND SONS, STAMFORD STREET AND CHARING CROSS.

www.ingramcontent.com/pod-product-compliance
Lightning Source LLC
Chambersburg PA
CBHW021802110726
47902CB00006B/1615